I0824650

The MAY HOUSE

ALSO BY JILLIAN CANTOR

The Greatest Lie of All
The Fiction Writer
Beautiful Little Fools
Half Life
The Code for Love and Heartbreak
In Another Time
The Lost Letter
The Hours Count
Searching for Sky
Margot
The Transformation of Things
The Life of Glass
The September Sisters

The MAY HOUSE

A Novel

JILLIAN CANTOR

ATRIA BOOKS

New York Amsterdam/Antwerp London
Toronto Sydney/Melbourne New Delhi

ATRIA
BOOKS

An Imprint of Simon & Schuster, LLC
1230 Avenue of the Americas
New York, NY 10020

This book is a work of fiction. Any references to historical events, real people, or real places are used fictitiously. Other names, characters, places, and events are products of the author's imagination, and any resemblance to actual events or places or persons, living or dead, is entirely coincidental.

First Atria Books hardcover edition May 2026

ATRIA BOOKS and colophon are registered trademarks of Simon & Schuster, LLC

Interior design by Davina Mock-Maniscalco

Manufactured in the United States of America

1 3 5 7 9 10 8 6 4 2

Library of Congress Control Number: 9781668091159

ISBN 978-1-6680-9115-9
ISBN 978-1-6680-9117-3 (ebook)

For my one and only wonderful sister
And all the birds that watch over us

"Sisters make the best friends in the world."
—Marilyn Monroe

"If I ever go looking for my heart's desire again,
I won't look any further than my own backyard.
Because if it isn't there, I never really lost it to begin with."
—L. Frank Baum, *The Wizard of Oz*

PROLOGUE

1985

"ONCE UPON A TIME," Grandma Vera said. "There were three sisters . . ."

Julia, Emily, and Nora May sat perched on the edge of a lounge chair, huddled up close, listening with rapt attention to their grandmother, who was fresh off performing in a run of *Lilies of the Field* at the Coronado Playhouse and had a flair for telling dramatic stories, making even her small California backyard feel like a stage.

The evening fog descended from the ocean as Grandma Vera told her story, blanketing Coronado Island, and despite the glow of the firepit in front of them, and the warmth of Grandma Vera's voice so close, the three sisters still let out a collective shiver.

Grandma Vera picked up a big wool blanket and gently threw it across their laps, tucking it around their legs. Then she picked up three sticks, each with a marshmallow on the end, and handed one to each girl to roast over the fire, before continuing her story.

"You, my tiny songbird," she said to the youngest sister, Nora, as she began to assemble their treats, "are like these graham crackers. You squish us all together with the best and biggest hugs."

Six-year-old Nora giggled and handed over her stick with the browned marshmallow so Grandma Vera could finish assembling her s'more.

"And you, my beautiful cynic," she said to the middle sister, Emily, "are both deliciously bitter and sweet like this glorious dark chocolate."

Nine-year-old Emily wasn't exactly sure if that was a compliment, but chocolate was her favorite food group, and anyway, being the chocolate seemed altogether better and more special than either graham crackers or marshmallows.

"And you, my darling, responsible Julia," she said to the oldest sister, "are like these marshmallows. You're the glue that holds everything together."

Twelve-year-old Julia shook her head, uncertain, as she took the assembled s'more from Grandma Vera. As a rule, she wasn't a fan of anything gooey, sticky, or messy, but Grandma Vera had promised them that a s'more roasted over her backyard firepit would be the very best thing they'd ever tasted. And also, as a rule, Julia trusted Grandma Vera more than any other adult in her life, aside from Dad.

"And what are you, Gramma?" Nora asked, giggling as the warm chocolate leaked out onto her finger. She licked it off and looked up expectantly at Grandma Vera.

"I'm the one who gets to savor the magic of all three of you now that I've gotten your father to agree to let me have you this one week a year." She smiled, picking up her own s'more to take a bite. "So I want you all to promise me something," Grandma Vera added. "That no matter how old you get or how many important things you're off doing, that the three of you will always come back here to visit me, together, just like this. You can't have a s'more without the graham crackers, or the chocolate, or the marshmallows. You need all three."

"I promise," the May sisters said in unison.

They were sticky, and chilled, and warm, and happy all at once, when Grandma Vera wrapped her arms around them, smooshing them into a giant hug.

"Good," Grandma Vera said. "A promise is a promise. And I'm going to hold you to it."

CHAPTER 1

2019

AS IT TURNED OUT, Julia hadn't gone to work for three whole weeks before anyone noticed she was missing.

But Emily and Nora wouldn't know this yet when they first stepped foot inside the Ocean Boulevard house, that place all three of them thought of as the keeper of memories in their lives, both good and bad. They just knew that the Pacific Ocean air smelled so familiar, and the house itself felt strangely like home, even though they hadn't spent more than one week a year here their entire lives.

It was a Sunday in May when Emily and Nora arrived in Coronado. (It was always a Sunday in May when they arrived these last thirty-some years.) And by coincidence (not coordination) their flights had arrived at the San Diego airport at similar times, and Emily and Nora had shared an Uber to the house. Emily had flown in from Florida, Nora from New York City. Their conversation on the twenty-minute car ride, through downtown and across the bridge, had been the habitual small talk of two women in their early forties with little in common. Had the Uber driver paid any attention, he might've been shocked to realize they were sisters. They didn't really even look alike: tall Emily with her cropped white-blonde hair and hazel eyes; tiny Nora with her long, dark brown curls and green eyes. Except for the fact that they had the same exact chin and same exact left cheek dimple—all three of them did: Nora, Emily, and Julia. It was, in addition to the house on Ocean Boulevard, what they had inherited from Grandma Vera.

"Where's Julia?" Nora asked, after they stepped inside and set their suitcases down in the living room.

The house was dark still, and Emily flipped on some lights. It felt like an exceedingly warm day for May, in a town known for the chill of "the May gray." And she walked across the room to fiddle with the window air conditioner Nate had installed for them a few summers ago.

Nora ran upstairs to see if Julia was in her room. But it was dark up there too, her room looked untouched, and Julia's suitcase was nowhere to be found. Julia wasn't here yet. Nora ran back downstairs and reported this strange fact to Emily.

"Hmmm," Emily said, as she let the air blast her neck. "I guess . . . she's running late?" She noticed Nora seemed undaunted by the heat. Even having just run up and down the stairs, she didn't appear sweaty at all. And Emily briefly wondered if, at forty-three, she was too young to be having a hot flash? Or was it that Nora was just used to being constantly overheated, performing under all those lights onstage?

"I'll text her," Nora said, pulling her phone from her designer bag. Which designer, Emily wasn't all too sure, but she felt certain her younger sister's purse was something trendy and definitely too expensive.

Julia, the oldest of the three of them, lived in Maryland, but she almost always managed to arrive first at the Ocean Boulevard house for their sisters' week each May. Julia was also the planner. Usually, by the time Emily and Nora would walk in the door, Julia would have a spreadsheet of activities and dinners for the week ready to hand out. Emily, the middle sister, was the perpetual screwup. Nora, the youngest, was the flighty star. But, Julia, the oldest, held everything together. She somehow knew how to fill in the awkward spaces Emily and Nora never could on their own. They both already felt it was strange to be in this house without her.

Em and I are here, Nora texted. What time are you coming?

"Well?" Emily peered over Nora's shoulder, and they both stared at the blank space on Nora's screen, waiting for a response that didn't immediately come.

"Maybe her flight got delayed and she's in the air?" Nora scrolled up as if searching for some mysterious lost communication from her sister, and she could see the last text Julia had sent just to her. May 2018. This same week, last year.

What were you thinking?

Nora felt her cheeks reddening as she remembered what had happened right before that. She quickly moved her phone away, hoping Emily hadn't seen it.

If she had, she wasn't saying anything. Emily was fanning herself with her hand. "Global fucking warming, I swear. It never used to be this hot here in May."

"Isn't it hotter in Florida?" Nora asked, switching over to their sisters' chat on her phone, scanning through the most recent messages. Now she noticed both she and Emily had sent their flight information a few weeks ago, but Julia hadn't responded. The last text in their group chat from Julia was in January. She'd sent a picture of their niece, Veronica, standing in her dorm room after finally moving in. She'd gotten accepted off the waitlist last May, to her first-choice college, Adley, a small liberal arts school in Connecticut, but as a spring-semester start, which meant Julia had gotten to keep her at home a few months more than she'd originally expected: My baby at college, Julia wrote, in January, underneath the photo, with a crying emoji. Emily had loved the photo. Nora realized now she'd never responded. She had seen the photo when she was about to go onstage and then forgotten about it after the show. God, she was a terrible aunt.

"I don't think the AC is working." Emily stopped fanning herself to hold her hands in front of the unit. "It's blowing warm air. I'll go see if Nate is home and can come over here to fix it."

Nora nodded, but the last thing she wanted to do was see Nate.

"Julia will probably be here by the time I get back," Emily added hopefully.

"Probably," Nora agreed. But something uneasy was already settling in her stomach, a creeping sense of uncertainty. And she realized it was the same feeling that had been hanging over her, vaguely, since she had left here last May. As if she, alone, had ruined everything.

The truth was, Emily was feeling uneasy too. Worry had been pushing up inside her ever since she'd left for the airport earlier, and now it was swimming to the surface, cresting in her chest like one of the waves that were just steps away at the beach.

But Julia would be here soon. She had to be.

They came every year. No matter what. It was a sisterly pact. And more important, a promise they had made to Grandma Vera that none of the three sisters had ever been willing to break, no matter what.

CHAPTER 2

1990

JULIA HAD JUST NOTICED a bit of chocolate on her lip from their first-night s'mores and was leaning over the bureau, using the mirror to wipe it off with her thumb, when a paper airplane whizzed in through the open window and hit her on the shoulder.

It sent a small jolt down her arm, through her body, and she quickly wiped away the chocolate, grabbed her Lip Smacker from her pocket, and ran it across her lips, before picking up the airplane and seeing the message written inside.

Meet me on the beach?

Nate's handwriting was so distinct, a little bit messy and oddly charming, just like he was. Nate and his mom had lived next door to Grandma Vera on Ocean Boulevard since Nate was a baby. He was a year older than Julia, and he'd hung out with the May sisters, building castles on the beach and threatening to teach them to surf, for as long as they had been coming out here to visit.

Holding the paper in her hand now, thinking about how close he was, made her heartbeat quicken. She pulled a purple pen from her small backpack purse that was hanging over the bedpost and wrote her reply, in her own neat and perfectly measured cursive:

I'll be there in five minutes!

She refolded the airplane, threw it out her window, and watched it soar the short distance into his—an art she had perfected over the last five years, since thirteen-year-old Nate had realized their windows were close enough for paper airplane messages. Even though it might sound silly, if she were to describe it to her friends back home in Chicago, the truth was, Julia looked forward to these paper airplanes almost more than she looked forward to their first-night s'mores.

She ran her Lip Smacker across her lips one more time for good measure and then ran downstairs.

"Where are you going?" Nora called from her place on the couch, tucked under a blanket and snuggled up with Grandma Vera, where they were watching *Some Like It Hot.*

"Honey, where's the VCR remote?" Grandma Vera said to Nora. "Pause it."

Nora shuffled to find the remote, hit pause, and then they both turned and stared at Julia, expectantly. Fourteen-year-old Emily, who had become obsessed with both poetry and the subject of death that spring, sat alone on the love seat reading Emily Dickinson, and she didn't even look up or register Julia's presence.

"I'm just going to take a walk with Nate," Julia said, trying to keep her voice even, nonchalant, like it was no big deal. It *was* no big deal. She'd walked with Nate many times by this point in her life. But something about this May already felt different. Before now, she and Nate had been friends only the one week in May when she and her sisters came to visit Grandma Vera. But this past year, Julia's dad and Grandma Vera had both installed dial-up internet and had given each of the girls CompuServe email so that they could communicate with Grandma Vera all year long without racking up enormous long-distance phone bills. Nate also had gotten email, and he and Julia had been emailing each other almost every day for the last six months. The anticipation now to run down to the beach, to actually *see* him, welled up inside her, hot and heady, making her face flush.

Eleven-year-old Nora was already bored with the conversation and fiddled with the remote, while Grandma Vera smiled and nodded. "It's a beautiful night for a walk," she finally said, knowingly, a small smile escaping across her lips.

———

Julia took off her flip-flops, stood on the sand at the top of the beach, and listened to the roar of the Pacific Ocean. It was high tide, and breezy enough that she could practically taste the salty water on her tongue. This was her favorite moment of the whole year, that first time she found the beach again after an entire year away.

"Hey, Jules!" Nate's gravelly voice.

No. *This* was her favorite moment of the whole year.

She turned, and he was jogging toward her from his house. The yellow light from the streetlamp on Ocean Boulevard slanted across his face, and he was smiling so wide it engulfed his boyish cheeks. The last thing he'd sent to her over email—which she had printed out, folded up, and locked inside her diary at home—was a poem that he'd written just for her:

Jules, light and order.
Like a star you walk
on water. No, please—
walk through water instead
with me.

She'd read it a thousand times, vacillating over whether it meant something. *With me.* Was he asking her out? Or did he just like writing poetry?

"Oh my God, Jules, you're finally here!" He'd reached her on the beach, his arms around her, hugging her so quickly she could barely register what was happening as her cheek hit his chest and she inhaled the sudden sandalwood scent of him.

She clung to him for a few moments, and then forced herself

to take a step back. He put his hand on her cheek, traced her cheekbone with his thumb as if trying to memorize her face. Or recognize it again after all this time apart. And then Julia, always wanting to know exactly what was what, blurted out the stupidest thing possible: "Are we dating now?"

He laughed but didn't move his thumb from her cheek. And maybe that was a yes?

Then he leaned down, and his lips were on hers, softly, gently. It was exactly the way Julia had always imagined a kiss should feel. Nate's lips were perfect and warm and intoxicating. She suddenly felt light, untethered, like she could just float away. This was definitely a yes?

"You taste like cotton candy," Nate murmured.

"Lip gloss," she said.

"I like it." He kissed her again quickly, and then he said, "For the record, I thought we've been dating for three months. Didn't we email in February about how much we missed each other and wanted to be together?"

"But can two people really date on email?" Julia asked.

"Why not?" Nate said.

And she realized that was exactly what she liked about him. If Julia saw the world as straight lines and ordered shapes, Nate saw it in blurs of bright and exciting colors.

He reached for her hand, held on to it. "Let's go for a walk," he said.

The last few years, it had become a tradition for Julia and Nate to walk the sidewalk on Ocean Boulevard all the way down to the Hotel del Coronado and back. In the one mile, amidst the sweet smell of fresh-bloomed honeysuckle, the soothing sound of the ocean just next to them, they usually had all the time they needed to catch each other up on everything that had happened the year before.

But this time, thanks to email, they were already all caught up, and now they just walked, side by side, holding hands, not feeling like they had to say anything at all.

The next morning, Nora woke Julia by jumping on the end of her bed. "Let's gooo to the beee-ach!" she exclaimed, arms in the air, bouncing up and down on the mattress.

"Okay, Oprah Winfrey," Emily said, wandering in from across the hall, rubbing sleep from her eyes. Julia laughed. Nora recorded *The Oprah Winfrey Show* each day and diligently watched it every night after dinner. Julia and Emily usually sat with her, doing their homework while it was on.

"Come on," Nora said, jumping down from Julia's bed. "For real. The sun's out!"

May was often cloudy when they visited—something Grandma Vera told them was called *the May Gray*, and, she said, the only thing worse was *the June Gloom*. The rare days when the sun was actually shining on their visits were always beach days.

And so, the three of them put on bathing suits and shorts and wandered down the beach to the edge of the water, before even eating breakfast. On days like this, Grandma Vera would bring them waffles and bacon midmorning, and they'd have a beach picnic brunch.

They all stood with their feet in the chilly surf, watching as Nate was just walking out of the water, surfboard under his arm. He waved with his free hand, then put his board down on the sand and unzipped his wet suit before walking over toward them. He caught Julia's eye and smiled. She stared at his lips for a moment, remembering what they'd felt like on hers last night. But suddenly Nora let out a bloodcurdling scream, interrupting her thoughts.

"Nora, what's wrong?" Julia looked away from Nate toward her youngest sister, who was hopping on one foot.

Then, Emily let out a bloodcurdling scream of her own.

And before Julia could ask her what was wrong, suddenly something brushed against her foot and a sharp, stinging pain shot through her toes, up her leg, and she let out a scream.

"Jesus," Nate said. "Did all three of you manage to get stung by the same stingray?"

"Come on, let's go up to Vera's house," Nate continued. "You need to soak your feet in warm water."

Julia started to hobble up the beach, but then she heard Nora scream again. "I can't walk! It hurts too much!"

She stopped hobbling and turned, but Nate had already reached Nora and was scooping her up off the sand, lifting her in a fireman's carry. "Em, Jules, you okay to walk?" he called out. Emily nodded and so did Julia, and they hobbled alongside him, back up the beach.

"My goodness, what's with all the screaming?" Grandma Vera stood on her porch in her long floral nightgown, her gray hair still in pink rollers.

"The Trouble Trio over here all got stung by a stingray," Nate told her, as he gently placed Nora down on the porch steps.

"I'm dying!" Nora exclaimed through sobs.

"Trouble Trio sounds about right." Grandma Vera laughed at Nate's nickname for them. "And no one is dying on my watch, my tiny songbird, I promise you. A stingray hurts like the dickens but it isn't going to kill you."

Nate turned to Julia, put his hand gently on her shoulder. "Are you okay?" he said softly. Her foot was really throbbing, but she smiled at him. He brushed her cheek lightly with his thumb. "I'm gonna go change out of my wet suit, but then I'll be back to check on you."

"You like Nate, don't you?" Grandma Vera said to Julia later that evening after dinner, as Julia helped her dry the dishes.

"Shhh!" Julia's face reddened.

"Oh honey, they're not listening." Nora's foot had swelled so much after the sting that Grandma Vera had taken her to the ER, where they'd dosed her with so much Benadryl that it had knocked her out. She was fast asleep. Julia and Emily had milder stings, and were feeling mostly better by that evening, after long hot-water soaks. But Emily was sitting out back by the firepit, drinking a cup of hot chocolate Vera had just made for her and listening to her Walkman. "And besides"—Grandma Vera was still talking—"there's nothing to be ashamed of."

Julia nodded, unsure why she felt embarrassed at the thought of her sisters knowing she liked Nate. She was seventeen for goodness' sake, and all she and Nate had done was kiss. Her friend Tina, back at home, had already had sex with her date after the junior prom. But maybe it was that Nate had always been such a part of their time in Coronado, that something about him almost felt sacred. What had he called them earlier? *The Trouble Trio*—they were a unit, and Nate was their sidekick. She had this weird sense her sisters might be annoyed with her if they knew she'd suddenly claimed Nate as her own.

"But you do like him," Vera said. "And I don't know what your father tells you, and your mother is gone, so that puts the birds and the bees squarely in my court."

Julia's cheeks flamed even further. "Gram, we have health class at school!" They had in fact practiced putting a condom on a banana, three years ago, in Emily's grade. So even Emily already knew this stuff. "And Nate and I are not doing anything like that." Though even as she said it, she realized that maybe she wanted to. "Yet."

Grandma Vera nodded. "I bet I can get you in with my gynecologist this week, while you're here."

In Chicago, where their single father had tried very hard to be everything three girls with a dead mother could ever need—the man had learned how to French braid hair when Nora had started taking dance for heaven's sake—no one had ever once mentioned the word *gynecologist*.

"We should get you on the pill. Just in case," Grandma Vera added.

Julia laughed. "Just in case what? I can't get pregnant over email." After this week she probably wouldn't see Nate in person again for a whole year.

Grandma Vera shrugged. "Well, maybe there will be another boy in Chicago. And this is my one week a year when I get you. Let's make sure you're protected, and you have everything you need to be a woman out in the world."

It hit Julia, in that moment, the way it often did these weeks in May, how unlucky they had been to have their mother die after giving birth to Nora. But also, just how lucky they were to have her mother, Grandma Vera, in their lives. This was the first time it had ever occurred to her to say this very thought out loud to Grandma Vera.

"Oh honey," she said in response, putting the plate she'd been washing back in the sink, then drying her hands on a towel. She wrapped Julia in a big hug, and even though Grandma Vera was shorter than all of them except for Nora now, somehow, she felt like a giant when she was hugging them. "I'm the lucky one to have you three wonderful girls in my life. And your mother . . ."

Grandma Vera's tidbits about their mother were few and far between, and so Julia was suddenly listening with rapt attention. But Grandma Vera didn't finish her thought.

"My mother what?" Julia asked.

"Your mother sure missed a lot," Grandma Vera finally said, and Julia felt a wave of disappointment ripple through her. "Now, do me a favor and go to the armoire in the dining room. My doctor's card is in there. Can you get it for me? I'll give her a call first thing in the morning." She paused for a second, and then she said, "Top drawer on the left."

She released Julia from the hug, and Julia walked slowly, favoring her non-stung foot, into the dining room and did what Grandma Vera asked. The armoire was a beautiful, stately chestnut structure that lined almost an entire wall with drawers of all shapes and sizes. Grandma Vera's second husband, Grey, had built it for her, the summer before he'd died. And now it was lined with framed family photos on the top, the drawers filled with what Grandma Vera always called *the miscellany of life*.

Julia opened the top drawer on the left, her eyes glancing over the contents for a business card, but what she saw instead was something else. A letter-sized envelope. Her eyes grazed over the handwritten return address, and she blinked, sure she was seeing it wrong. She shut the drawer quickly.

In the kitchen now, Grandma Vera was singing "The Sound of Music."

"I don't see a card," Julia called out, her voice wavering. "Top . . . left?"

The singing suddenly stopped. "Sorry! Did I say top *left*?" Grandma Vera called out, in what Nora always described as her *stage voice*. Loud, overly effusive, and dramatic. "I meant to say top *right*."

Julia's hands were still shaking as she opened the top-right drawer and saw the business card sitting there, right on top.

CHAPTER 3

1993

ON THE FIRST MORNING in Coronado, Emily set her alarm for 5:45 a.m.

Nate had been trying to talk all three May sisters into letting him teach them to surf for as long as they all had been coming to Coronado, but this was the first time any of them had agreed to go with him.

It wasn't that Emily wanted to learn to surf, really. It was more that Nate had looked so forlorn as he'd sat out on Grandma Vera's porch with the three of them last night, as he'd told them the devastating news about his mom. Emily didn't know much about cancer. But she knew stage four was really bad. And she knew that Nate was likely about to become what she and Nora and Julia had been almost their whole lives: motherless. Nate didn't have any siblings, his father had always been out of the picture, and as far as she knew, Nate didn't have a grandmother like Vera either. Nate would become both motherless and all alone.

Nora had sat on the porch swing, silently crying. Julia had tried to put her hand on Nate's shoulder to comfort him, but he'd brushed her off. And Emily had found herself suddenly standing up and saying the only thing that came into her head, which was, strangely: "Teach me to surf this week."

Julia had raised her eyebrows. Nora had paused crying for a

moment to ask Emily if she was joking, and Nate had only said, "Okay, meet me on the beach at six a.m. tomorrow."

Emily slipped out of the house now and shivered as she stepped into the gray extremely early morning. Growing up, she had always been fascinated with the fine line between life and death. She sometimes contemplated things such as whether or not van Gogh had shot himself in a wheat field or why Sylvia Plath put her head inside that oven. She had convinced herself that somehow death could be understood this way, by studying artists who had made a choice. Unlike what had happened to her mother, who'd died unexpectedly and in the least poetic way possible. And unlike what was happening to Nate's mother now.

But no matter how many poems she read or how many tragedies she explored, she could never quite understand the unfairness of a mother dying too young. And she knew she had no real answers for Nate, no way to comfort him at all, other than spending time with him while he did something he loved.

Still, as she was walking down the beach that morning, she found herself wishing she'd just given Nate her copy of *The Bell Jar* rather than volunteering for this ridiculous endeavor. Surfing?! What the hell had she gotten herself into?

"Hey, Em." Nate was standing by the edge of the water, and he paused from pulling on his wet suit to wave to her. "This is so cool that you're finally going surfing with me. I'm so pumped. Are you pumped?" He looked and sounded more like himself this morning than he had last night, when he'd been fighting back tears on Grandma Vera's porch.

Emily nodded and bit her lip. If she opened her mouth, she would a hundred percent be backing out. And Nate would be back to wallowing alone in the ocean over the shitty hand he'd just been dealt. Nate wasn't quite her brother, but he wasn't quite *not* her brother either. She felt this strange, sudden urge to make sure he was okay. So she swallowed back her doubts and echoed his word: "Pumped."

Nate finished zipping himself into his wet suit, then picked up another one from where it was resting on top of his board and handed it to her.

She eyed it skeptically. It looked small, like something tiny Nora would fit into. Emily's dad referred to her as big-boned, which truly wasn't a euphemism. She wasn't overweight, just not at all petite like both her sisters. "I don't know if that will fit me," she said.

"Sure it will. You just kind of have to squeeze yourself into it."

Well, this sounded like a delightful activity. "Great," Emily said, as she forced one leg through the tight opening, jumping to try to get it up her body. Though she knew they were still asleep, she irrationally felt Nora and Julia watching from the porch and laughing at her right now.

She finally squeezed herself all the way into the wet suit, Nate zipped her up, and then she could barely breathe. "Is it supposed to feel this tight?" she asked.

"Come on." Nate ignored her question and gestured for her to follow him into the surf. The water felt like ice as it shocked the soles of her feet, but then the suit numbed it as she waded in. She walked in a little farther, but she couldn't keep up with Nate. The wet suit made it hard to walk; it was more like moving through mud than water.

Waist-deep, she felt like she was a thousand pounds, trudging through quicksand. "Nate!" she screamed. "I can't do this!"

He registered what she said and turned to wade back toward her.

"Do you know what I like about surfing?" he said when he reached her. "I have to focus only on my body, one moment at a time. Staying upright on the board. Keeping my center of gravity. There's nothing else. There can't be anything else."

She nodded. But the wet suit felt so constricting, her body felt so heavy, all she wanted to do was get out, of the water, of the wet suit. Get out of this ridiculous idea that she was somehow helping Nate by being here. The truth was, his mom was still going to die, he was still going to be devastated, whether she learned to surf or not.

"I know the Trouble Trio only gets one week a year by the water, but I was so happy when one of you wanted to finally learn why I love it so much." He grinned and pushed his surfboard gently toward her. "We can start slow, Em," he said. "Right here, where it's shallow and you're comfortable."

Emily wasn't in the least bit comfortable, but still she thought, *I should give him this. I should let him have this.*

"Okay," she finally said. "Show me how to get up on this thing."

An hour later, Emily was sore and feeling irritable when she trudged back up the beach, having finally managed to squeeze herself back out of the wet suit. She found Grandma Vera sitting out on the porch swing, still in her nightgown, her hair in curlers, sipping from her red Coronado Playhouse coffee mug.

"Looks like you had an adventure, *ma chérie*." Grandma Vera was newly prone to slipping into French, as she was rehearsing to audition for a role at the playhouse next month. Nora had giggled about it last night during s'mores, as chocolate had become *chocolat*. But now Emily barely noticed as she walked up the porch steps and plopped down next to Grandma Vera on the swing, exhausted. Trying to stand up on that surfboard was the most physically demanding thing she'd ever done, and she was pretty sure her shins would be black and blue for the entire summer after all the times she fell and smacked them. And then when Nate had said *Should we try again tomorrow?* before he'd paddled back out into the water, she hadn't had it in her to tell him no.

"I let Nate try and teach me to surf. I was very bad at it," Emily said.

Grandma Vera laughed, and she reached up and tousled Emily's damp, salty ponytail. "Well, I never took you for a surfer. A tortured artist, yes. But you're not really the hang-ten type."

"I was trying to cheer him up. His mom might die," Emily said softly.

Grandma Vera nodded. "It doesn't sound good."

"I was only three when Mom died," Emily said. "I can barely remember her. But . . . her death is still everywhere. All around me. All the time. I just feel . . . I feel . . . so bad for him."

Grandma Vera leaned over and kissed the top of her head. "You're a good egg, Emily May. You hide behind that hard exterior shell, but underneath it, you're the sweetest, kindest young woman. You just have to remember to try surfing more often."

Emily grimaced. "Ugh, no. Never again."

"Metaphorically speaking, of course," Grandma Vera chuckled. "You have a beautiful heart. Keep being bold and meeting others where they are, like you did this morning."

Beautiful heart her ass. She was stupid, that's what she was. Julia and Nora weren't out there this morning. They were both still soundly and comfortably asleep. And they would both probably figure out normal ways to console Nate this week.

Emily tried to stand and then she groaned as every single muscle in her body ached. "I'm so sore. I'm going to go take a long soak in a hot bath."

Grandma Vera reached for her hand, squeezed it, and then she smiled. "I have some pain patches that might help too. Grab some on your way in, why don't you, honey?" She paused for a moment, gave Emily a long, hard look. Then she said, "Top-left drawer of the dining room armoire."

Emily limped inside the house to the dining room. Julia had played tennis all through high school and Nora, who had done dance since she was little, would be auditioning for the ninth-grade pom line when they returned to Chicago next week. But Emily had always been the unathletic sister. She'd seen her sisters with pain patches from time to time, but the concept of them, and any kind of athletically oriented pain in general, were foreign to her.

And so when she opened the top-left armoire drawer and saw

a stack of what looked like letters, she thought it was just weird packaging, at first. But then she picked the top letter up. She saw the recent postmark. The return address. *Santa Monica?*

"Oops. I meant bottom left!" Grandma Vera's voice floated in from the distance, but Emily barely registered what it was saying. Her hands shook, and she threw the letter back into the drawer, shutting it quickly. She took a step back, suddenly feeling like she was back in the water, in the tight wet suit, and the world was heavy and impossible. Mud.

Grandma Vera walked into the dining room, opened the bottom-left drawer herself, and pulled out a pain patch. Then held it out for Emily to take. "I'm always getting these dang drawers mixed up, *une gaffe. Mes excuses.*" The French rolled so easily off her tongue, as if she had been rehearsing this line, along with all her others.

Had she?

There were so many things Emily should've asked Grandma Vera right then. She should've flung back open the wrong drawer, demanded an explanation.

But instead, she took the pain patch, and all she heard herself saying, the word itself sounding like it was coming from underwater, was "Thanks."

Grandma Vera was wrong.

Emily was not a good egg.

After a hot bath, and the pain patches, she crawled into her bed. Whatever she had seen, whatever she had thought she'd seen, she decided she would never, ever allow herself to think about it again. And for sure, she could never tell her sisters. She would bury it so far underneath her hard exterior shell that no piece of her heart would ever be able to access it.

"Em." Nora wandered into her room later that afternoon. "Will you help me? Nate told Julia he just wants to be friends, and she is pretending to be okay. But she is so not okay. She's scrubbing down the lounge chairs in the backyard with Lysol because she told Gram the dirt hurt her eyes."

"Too bad. She should've gone surfing with him," Emily retorted, which was an entirely obnoxious thing to say, and she regretted it as soon as it came out of her mouth, but still, she didn't take it back.

Nora huffed loudly. "You're such a bitch sometimes."

Sometimes? Pretty much all the time. Grandma Vera was wrong about her being even remotely good.

Nora turned to stomp out. "Nora," Emily called after her, and Nora stopped for a moment. "Julia just needs to give him some space. He's going through a lot."

Nora put her hands on her hips and frowned. "Right. You should get out of bed and tell her that. She's a mess. And she listens to you more than she listens to me."

"I'm too sore," Emily said, which was by this point in the afternoon mostly a lie.

The truth was, Emily was afraid that if she got out of bed and huddled up with her sisters, she might tell them what she saw. And she could never tell them. Nora was beautiful and so talented. Julia was brilliant and probably on the path to becoming a Supreme Court justice one day. And Emily was just . . . Emily. She was already dark and cynical and expected life to always let her down. If any one of the three of them had to be tortured, ruined, it might as well be Emily.

Later that night, after everyone was asleep, Emily was restless. Her mind was going in circles, and she couldn't just lie here any longer. She hobbled out of bed and quietly went down the steps, out the front door, trying not to wake anyone. Once she was outside on Ocean Boulevard, walking, her muscles loosened up, and she took deep breaths, wishing for the sea air to soothe her. But the night was silent, still, and her mind wouldn't stop.

She headed toward Clayton's, the twenty-four-hour diner on Orange Avenue. She wasn't hungry, but she'd been here late at night with her sisters in years past, and she knew it was always crowded, filled with strangers. Emily suddenly craved the presence of anonymous people. A sea of humans who knew nothing about her.

She walked in through the large glass front door and was comforted by the clang of the brass bell, by the fact she'd been right, the place was, indeed, packed. She hobbled past the crowded red booths and took the last seat at the old-fashioned diner counter, before ordering a root beer float.

"You look like you had a rough day." A blonde-haired woman in a Cal sweatshirt sat next to her, picking at a piece of cherry pie with a fork.

I learned my entire life is a lie, she thought. "I learned to surf," she said.

"That's some bullshit. Surfing."

"I couldn't agree more," Emily said.

"I'm Monica, by the way," she said.

"Emily," Emily said.

"That's a pretty name, Emily." Emily shook her head. She had always thought her name to be weirdly average. Or maybe that was just her middle-sister syndrome. "And it sounds to me like you need something stronger than root beer right now," Monica added.

Emily laughed. Did Monica actually think she was old enough to drink? Taken out of context of her high school, her sisters, her family unit, sitting here at the Clayton's counter, just a girl with a pretty name, did Emily look more twenty-one than seventeen?

"For real," Monica was saying now. "I have some beer back at my hotel room, if you want to join me when we're finished here? It might be fun."

Emily looked at her for a moment. Monica had a pretty heart-shaped face, big blue eyes. She looked both innocent and kind. But Nora had gotten obsessed with a new TV show this year, *Dateline*, and Emily had caught enough episodes with her to know that this was definitely one of the ways you could be murdered.

Still, Monica didn't seem like a murderer. She seemed like a college student, in Coronado on vacation. And Emily was only one year away from being a college student herself. This really wasn't all that weird. She'd probably drink at college, and what was the big deal if she tried it now? It felt like a better option than going back to Grandma Vera's and being alone with her thoughts.

"Sure," Emily finally said, attempting to sound nonchalant, like she drank beer all the time. "That sounds great."

CHAPTER 4

1996

THIS IS THE LAST time I'm doing this, I swear to God," Emily announced, as the three of them tumbled out of the taxi on Ocean Boulevard. None of them were in the best mood after a long flight delay out of O'Hare and having not eaten most of the day. But Emily, as always, was taking it to the next level. "I mean, I just don't have the time to fly out this same week, every year. We're too old. I'm over it."

Nora closed her eyes for a moment, inhaled the familiar cool, salty air. "I'll never be too old to come here," she insisted. "And besides, we promised Grandma Vera when we were little that we'd always come back here to her. All three of us."

"That's easy for you to say, because you're still in high school." Emily frowned. "I had to beg my internship to let me start a week late because of this."

Julia nodded. She would be starting law school in the fall and Nora knew she was moving from her apartment in New Haven to DC the day she got back, where she had secured a summer job working for a congresswoman.

"Come on, you two old ladies," Nora joked, hoping her humor covered how much she still hated being the youngest. She always felt out of sync, left behind in every possible way. Starting the moment she was born, in the first and most awful way of all:

Emily and Julia both had memories of their mother, while Nora had none. "What a terrible life you lead, forced to spend one week on the most beautiful island in the world with our awesome grandma," Nora continued.

"That's not what I meant," Emily said. "I just don't know that anyone should really expect us to come the *same exact week* in May, all together, every year now that we're all starting to have lives and stuff."

"No offense, Nora," Julia said.

Nora rolled her eyes, pulled her pink duffel bag from the trunk of the yellow cab, and walked up the front walk to Grandma Vera's porch. The screen door suddenly swung open and Grandma Vera stepped out, her arms already outstretched for hugs. "It's my favorite day of the year," she called out. "May day!"

Nora chuckled. Emily and Julia might have thought they'd grown up, but Grandma Vera never changed. She announced this upon their arrival, every single year. The May sisters, arriving to visit her in May. *May day!*

Nora jumped into her arms, inhaling the comforting rose petal scent of her grandmother's familiar perfume. "May day is the best day," she said, happy at least Grandma Vera agreed with her on this.

"The very best," Grandma Vera agreed as she took a step back, squeezed Nora's forearms gently, and took a good look at her. "Even more beautiful than last year," she proclaimed. Then released her to run down the steps and offer a one-armed hug each to Emily and Julia.

"Okay, girls," she announced. "I got lobster tails for dinner, and s'mores out back for dessert. Go put your bags upstairs, and then we'll dig in."

After s'mores, Julia and Emily turned down Grandma Vera's invitation to watch *Some Like It Hot.* Julia said she had work to do to prepare for her summer job and went up to her room, and Emily said she had a college friend also in San Diego for the week who was going to meet her at Clayton's for pie.

"Suit yourselves." Grandma Vera waved them away with a flick of her wrist. Then she turned to Nora: "I can always count on you to watch with me, can't I, honey?"

Nora settled in on the old sagging couch under a blanket, while Grandma Vera popped the tape into the VCR. Then they watched the familiar movie curled up under the blanket together, the same way they had every May for as long as Nora remembered.

And as the ending credits rolled, Grandma Vera was already humming "I Wanna Be Loved by You" as she stood to eject the tape.

"The older I get, the sadder this movie makes me," Nora said. "Marilyn's life was utterly tragic. She struggled so much. She rose so high and then she fell so far. Do you think that's the price of fame, Gram?" Nora had been thinking about this kind of thing a lot lately, as she was about to apply to college in the fall. Her dad had talked her into pursuing a practical degree, maybe in science, something she could get a job in. *You can always act*, he told her. *You don't need a degree in that.*

Grandma Vera shook her head. "I think Marilyn had her own demons that probably would've gotten her, famous or not."

Nora told Grandma Vera what she and Dad had been discussing for college and then Vera frowned. "So Bobby doesn't think you should follow your dreams?"

Maybe she shouldn't have said anything. Her dad and Grandma Vera had a weird relationship. The older she got, the more Nora could sense a strange sort of tension that existed between them. Dad never once came with them out to Coronado, and Grandma Vera hadn't come out to visit them in Chicago in at least ten years. They occasionally spoke on the phone, but when Nora caught pieces of the conversation from one end or the other, it always sounded strained. But maybe that kind of thing was normal, considering Vera was Dad's dead wife's mother. Nora knew she couldn't possibly understand their relationship, given that it had mostly existed before she was born. "That's not exactly what he said," Nora backtracked. "He just wants me to get a degree in something more practical. Then maybe try acting later. After college."

"Hmmph." She put the tape into its case and then back in its place on the shelf. "Well, far be it from me to go against Bobby's advice, but sweetheart, you have to do what's going to make you happy. The heart wants what the heart wants."

"I am happy," she said quickly. She was happy right this very moment, in her favorite place in the world, with her favorite person in the world. But she knew that wasn't exactly what Grandma Vera meant.

"Your mother . . ." Grandma Vera began, but then her voice trailed off. Hardly anyone ever talked about her mother, and certainly not in a way that Nora could understand, never having actually met her.

"What about my mother?" Nora asked softly.

"Your mother always loved acting. Did I ever show you the picture of her when she was in *Guys and Dolls* in high school? She was your age then, and you look so much like her now."

Nora nodded. She had seen the picture. Or *a* picture of her mother as Sarah Brown, up onstage. Their mother's high school yearbook still sat on a bookcase in the den at home in Chicago, and Nora had taken it out and looked at it probably a thousand times. "Mom didn't become an actress though," Nora said pointedly. "She went to college as a biology major, then married Dad and had us."

Grandma Vera sighed. "Sometimes I wonder how things might've turned out if I'd encouraged her to follow her dreams when she was your age, and then—"

"And then she wouldn't have had me, and I couldn't have killed her," Nora burst out, tears welling up in her eyes, the way they always did when she thought about this particular truth. The first thing that she had ever done coming into this world was take their mother's life, just by the very act of being born.

"Oh, honey." Grandma Vera sighed and walked to the couch to give Nora a hug. "Is that really what you think?"

Nora nodded.

She kissed Nora's forehead. "That's simply not true. Nothing that happened is your fault, Nora. You have to understand that, right?"

"I don't know," Nora said. "Aren't you ever angry that the universe said me or her, and it took her away from you and gave you me instead?" Sure, Nora hadn't chosen to be conceived, or born, and hadn't actively had any control over the eclampsia that quickly and silently ravaged her mother's body. But, what if her mother had decided to stop at two kids? Julia and Emily would still have their mother. Grandma Vera would still have her daughter.

"No, no, my tiny songbird," Grandma Vera said emphatically. "I have never once been angry about that. I'm so grateful to have you. You know how much I love you." Vera gave her a tight squeeze and kissed the top of her head.

Nora nodded. She did know that much.

Grandma Vera rocked her in a hug for a moment and then she started singing softly in her best Marilyn voice, "*I wanna be loved by you . . .*"

She pulled Nora up off the couch, ran and grabbed a spatula from the kitchen, and then handed it over, encouraging Nora to sing with her in harmony, the way they always did.

After they finished the song with a flourish of Nora going up an octave, Grandma Vera smiled and gave her another squeeze. "Okay, sweetheart, I'm going up to bed. But go take a peek at that picture before you go up. Top-left drawer of the dining room armoire."

Nora sat back down on the couch for a minute after Grandma Vera went upstairs and felt a wave of sadness wash over her. She stood and was walking toward the dining room armoire when suddenly she heard a noise from outside that made her stop. A guy's voice yelling in the distance. *Nate?* And he was calling, *for her*?

She forgot all about the armoire, the picture of Mom, and walked outside to the front porch instead.

There was Nate, standing out on the beach side of the sidewalk, right across from the house, waving his arms in the air. "Nora!" he called her name again when he saw her on the porch.

Grandma Vera had told them at dinner that Nate had recently moved back next door as the new owner of his childhood home after his mom's death last year, and that she was worried he was struggling. *Be extra kind, girls! He could really use the May sisters to cheer him up this year.* Julia had looked down at her plate and ignored the request, which was fair, since things had been awkward with her and Nate, ever since he'd told her he just wanted to be friends right after his mom got sick three years earlier. Emily had commented that she would do whatever she could but drew the line at surfing again. And Nora had said, *Don't worry. I've got this!* Here was her chance.

She walked down the porch steps and then ran across the street. Once she got closer, she could see he wasn't just waving his arms in the air, he had something in his hands. "What are you doing out here?" she asked, breathless, as she reached him.

He held his hands out in front of him. "I got two last-minute tickets to *Cyrano de Bergerac* at the Lamb's Theatre for tomorrow night. A friend of mine from high school is doing tech for the show. And then I realized what week it was, and that you were here!"

Remarkably, for such a small island, Coronado had two playhouses. Lamb's Theatre was the one Grandma Vera did not regularly perform in, which had something to do with an old feud with Grey's ex from back before they were married, the details of which Nora was not totally clear on. And though Nora had been to the Coronado Playhouse a few times, and had once even seen Grandma Vera perform there, she had never gotten to go to Lamb's Theatre.

"Well?" Nate said. "What do you think? Should we make a date of it tomorrow night?"

A date? Her cheeks warmed. The truth was she would go anywhere Nate asked. And theater? Double yes. She nodded. "I've never seen *Cyrano de Bergerac*," she said. Though she did like Daryl Hannah and Steve Martin in *Roxanne.*

"Me neither," Nate said. "It's at seven tomorrow night. I'll meet you out here at six thirty?"

Nora agreed, and as she turned to walk back across the street, back up Grandma Vera's porch steps, she felt weirdly as if she were floating. She forgot all about her sisters, her dead mother, and the picture Grandma Vera had wanted her to see in the armoire.

As she walked back inside the house, she heard Grandma Vera call out that she'd told Nora the wrong drawer, that she'd meant *second from the left.*

"Okay!" Nora called back. But the picture of her mom would have to wait. She was too busy floating now to pay attention to some old silly picture.

In fact, she floated all the way upstairs to her room, burrowed under her covers in the darkness, and let out a muted cry of joy.

"Where are you going?" Julia asked Nora the next evening, as she walked down the stairs in her pink crop top and black overalls. Her curls were still damp from the shower, and she'd put on lipstick the same exact shade as her crop top.

Julia was curled up on the couch with a book, wearing a Yale T-shirt and sweats. Grandma Vera was at the other end, bright red readers on the bridge of her nose, working diligently on a cross-stitch—a brand-new hobby she had picked up that she was "terrible" at. Emily was sitting out back, sipping what she said was lemonade from a thermos, but even Nora knew she was sneaking something stronger.

"Nate got tickets to the Lamb's Players show," Nora said.

Grandma Vera made a face. She was never one to let go a grudge. And Julia raised her eyebrows. "You're going out, with Nate?"

Nora shrugged like it wasn't a big deal. "I'm cheering him up, just like Gram wanted us to. Plus, I can never turn down live theater. Sorry, Gram."

Grandma Vera laughed. "Don't be silly. Their *Cyrano* is brilliant. I saw it last week myself. Have fun, my tiny songbird."

The show was very well done, and afterward Nora and Nate both walked out of the theater, landing on Orange Avenue, smiling. "Should we get a drink?" Nate asked.

Nora bit her lip, not exactly wanting to remind him that she was only seventeen. But she was only seventeen. "Ice cream?" she said instead.

He nodded. "I have some Ben and Jerry's in my freezer."

"What flavor?" Nora asked, though she would eat any flavor if it meant hanging out with him more.

"Chocolate Chip Cookie Dough. Maybe Em and Jules would want some too?"

She frowned at the mention of her sisters. She felt greedy now, and she wanted more time with Nate, all by herself. She glanced at her watch. It was close to ten—Emily was probably buzzed and Julia was probably already in bed. She told Nate that, and he nodded. "Well, maybe another night this week then. I didn't realize it was so late. I guess I should get you home too."

"No way," Nora said firmly. "Now that you've promised me Chocolate Chip Cookie Dough, you can't just take that away."

Nate laughed and shook his head. "Okay, Noradora," he said. "One small bowl of ice cream for you coming up."

Though the May sisters had been coming to Coronado for most of Nora's life, and had seen Nate almost every visit, Nora could count on one hand the number of times she'd ever been inside Nate's house. It was dark when she followed him in now, and she waited in the entryway for him to flip on the lights. She blinked to adjust her vision, and the living room was mostly empty, save one Barcalounger. "It looks like Chandler and Joey's apartment in here."

"Who?" Nate asked.

"*Friends.* You don't watch?"

Nate shook his head. "I got rid of all my mom's furniture. I didn't want to sell the house. I love it here. But I didn't want it to feel like I was living in the past, or in some mausoleum either."

"It looks . . ."

"Empty," he said. "I know. I got accepted to medical school in Philadelphia for the fall. I'm still deciding if I want to go or if I want to furnish the house." He shrugged.

Medical school? Nora hadn't known about this, and selfishly, she hoped he'd choose to furnish the house, that he would stay next door to Grandma Vera forever.

"I'd offer you a seat," he said now. "But there's only that one. Feel free to take it."

"Or you can get the ice cream and we can go sit on the beach?"

"Good idea," he said. "Hold on a sec."

He vanished into the kitchen and then returned a moment later with a small pint of Ben & Jerry's and two spoons. They headed back out, across the street and down the beach to where the sand was hard enough to sit on. In front of them the Pacific roared and glowed from the lights of a helicopter running a military exercise not too far offshore.

Nate handed her a spoon and opened the ice cream. She dug in and took a big bite, and between that and the damp night air she shivered. Nate took off his sweatshirt and threw it casually over her shoulders, and suddenly she could hear the roar of her heart beating, louder than the ocean or the helicopter.

"Thanks for coming with me tonight, Nora," Nate said. "It was nice to get out of my head for a while."

"Thanks for taking me," she said. And then she was brave enough to speak something true: "I always love being with you."

"Aw." He half hugged her with one arm, squeezing her shoulder. "I always love being with you too."

"I know I'm only seventeen," she said softly. "But in a few years, if you come back here, after medical school, I'll be twenty and you'll be twenty-seven."

Nate laughed. "That is how math works."

She leaned into him and let her cheek drop on his shoulder for the briefest of moments. She inhaled the salty smell of the ocean, the sandalwood smell of his neck. "Someday everything could be different," she said, not looking at him.

"I sure hope so," Nate said, but the roar of the ocean and the helicopter above swallowed up his words. And later, Nora couldn't be sure if she'd heard him correctly at all.

CHAPTER 5

1999

JULIA WAS NOT PREPARED for the way the smell of the Pacific Ocean would make her cry. But as she stepped out of the taxi in front of Grandma Vera's house on Ocean Boulevard, it was exactly that smell, that dark, chilly, sea-salt scent rushing into her nose that suddenly made her let out an unexpected sob. This smell. This ocean. This house. It was her childhood. Her sisters. Her grandmother. And the realization, quite suddenly, that Grandma Vera was gone now forever. She had left Julia, Emily, and Nora this house, and Julia, as the oldest and frankly most equipped to deal with these sorts of things, had been the one tasked with flying out here, figuring out exactly what to do with it.

Grandma Vera had willed them the house under the condition that the three of them use it to spend time together. It was a nice thought, if not altogether impractical. Julia was halfway through her last semester of law school at Georgetown. Emily had just graduated from Smith and was spending the spring in France "studying art." And Nora was a sophomore at Northwestern. It wasn't like they were all about to stop what they were doing, pack up their belongings, move out here, and live together in Grandma Vera's old house. In their twenties, they all had their own separate lives, dreams, and goals, none of which involved them permanently relocating to this sleepy seaside island off the coast of San Diego.

Even their visits these last few years had been tough to schedule and manage. Unlike when they were kids, when a trip to Grandma Vera's had felt like an amazing adventure, last May Emily had spent most of the week buzzed, Nora had been reading romance novels on the porch while complaining she was bored, and Julia had helped Grandma Vera pick the ripe tomatoes from her garden, can them into sauce, and trudge over to the farmer's market to sell. That was not the kind of life Julia aspired to live once she graduated law school. She had no idea what the three of them were supposed to *do* with this house.

And now, actually standing on the porch, inhaling the scent of the ocean, she found herself furiously brushing tears off her cheeks, thinking about how empty it would be inside without Grandma Vera. She was what had made this house, this island, so special. And Julia couldn't even bring herself to unlock the front door and walk inside.

"Hey, Jules." The sound of Nate's voice interrupted her thoughts, and she put her bags down by the front door and turned. He stood on his own porch next door, held up his hand, and waved. He was wearing a half-zipped wet suit, his dark hair still dripping wet, slicked back, flattening his curls. He'd just gotten out of the ocean. A wave of memories rolled over her; every summer she came here to visit as a teenager, Nate, it seemed, had been perpetually getting out of the ocean in his wet suit. "Long time no see," he added.

She nodded. "How long has it been . . . ?" Her voice trailed off. The truth was, she remembered exactly the last time she had seen him. Almost three years earlier. And she blushed thinking about it now. The way he'd whispered into her hair, his lips brushing against her earlobe as he hugged her goodbye on this very porch. *Don't let law school make you forget how amazing you are.* They were no longer dating by then, but still, a hug from Nate always seemed to make her feel things.

"Too long," he said now, and he grinned for a moment, as if he was sharing the same memory. Maybe he was. Then his expression quickly turned serious again. "I'm really sorry about Vera."

"I know. Thanks for your condolences," she said, which felt like a stupid thing to say to Nate, but it popped out of her automatically nonetheless.

"She was the best," Nate added sincerely.

Grandma Vera *was* the best, and Julia knew she'd helped Nate out a lot when his own mom got sick, then died, when he was in college. When he'd moved back into his childhood home, for good, last year after dropping out of med school, Julia had felt assured knowing that Nate was right next door if Grandma Vera ever needed anything. She'd never told him that though, and she couldn't bring herself to say it out loud now either.

"Where's the rest of the Trouble Trio?" Nate asked.

Julia grinned at his use of his adolescent nickname for the three of them. For a moment, it took her back to that summer he'd kissed her for the first time. She cleared her throat and tried to push that memory away. "Em is in France for a few months and Nora has school this week," Julia said.

"So you're out here all alone?"

Julia nodded. "Yep, just me." She had flown out over her spring break, but scheduling aside, neither Emily nor Nora had offered to join her. Julia had told them she'd figure out the details and her sisters had gladly agreed. Grandma Vera had also left behind very specific wishes, no funeral—she wanted her ashes scattered in the Pacific, which all three of them had agreed they would do together at some later date, when Emily was back from France. But she didn't tell Nate any of that. Instead, she said, "I didn't realize how hard it would be to actually walk in her house, all by myself."

"Do you want me to get changed? Walk in with you?" Nate offered.

She shook her head. "No, I just . . . need a minute." She wasn't sure if that was actually true, but she supposed she would have to make it so. She couldn't spend the next week out here on the porch.

"Well, at least come over here for dinner tonight," Nate said.

She chewed on her bottom lip, understanding that dinner with Nate was probably the world's worst idea. "I don't want to bother you," she said.

He smiled and shook his head. "Jules, I haven't seen you in years. Vera just died and you're all alone. If I know you're eating next door by yourself, that's what will bother me."

When he put it like that, she suddenly felt like she was going to start crying again.

An hour later, she'd unpacked, thrown on clean jeans, a sweater, and a little lipstick, and she found herself knocking on Nate's front door. It took him a beat to answer and as she waited on his porch, she considered whether it was smarter to flee than to actually go inside. But then he flung the door open and he was right there, in front of her, showered and changed into jeans and a fitted T-shirt. Close enough for her to notice he still smelled like a mixture of the ocean and sandalwood aftershave.

"Come on in." He opened the door wider; she kicked off her flip-flops by the entryway and followed him inside. "I have some shrimp on the grill out back. Can I get you a beer?"

She desperately wanted a beer, but what popped out of her mouth instead was, "I have a boyfriend." She did not, however, elaborate on the details, that Ted was in her law school class, that they had been dating for nine months already, and that he was exceedingly handsome in a very classic, clean-cut sense of the word. Nothing at all like Nate, who had always been handsome in his natural messiness: hair that was a little too long, smile that was a little too lopsided, square jaw that was a little too unshaven.

Nate walked to the fridge and pulled out two cans of Bud Light, a beer no one in her circle of DC law school friends would be caught dead drinking. He opened both cans, handed her one, and shot her that crooked grin. "I'm seeing someone too," he said nonchalantly. Of course he was. Anything that had happened between them in summers past could be chalked up to teenage hormones. But now they were both bona fide adults, in real relationships.

She exhaled, releasing a breath of relief, and took a long swig of the beer, swallowing it too quickly, feeling it warm all the way down to her toes.

Nate put his beer down on the island. "I'm gonna check the shrimp." He walked toward the backyard. When he opened the door, the delicious barbecue smell wafted into the kitchen and suddenly she was starving. She'd eaten nothing all day, save a bag of pretzels on the flight.

He returned only a minute later with a plate of shrimp skewers he placed on the island. He pulled a green salad from the fridge and gestured for her to have a seat on one of the barstools, where he'd laid two place settings. He sat down next to her, close enough that she could smell his salty sandalwood scent, and she took another long sip of beer.

"So how was Vera's house?" he asked, as he put shrimp and salad on her plate. "It's been a while since I've been over there."

Grandma Vera had been vital and independent up until the end, not the kind of older woman who'd needed any help, not even from her generous and handsome next-door neighbor. She'd died in her sleep, at the age of eighty-two, of an apparent heart attack. The day before that, she had called Julia, Emily, and Nora separately and regaled each of them with a story about that morning's beach spin class, which, much to her delight, had featured all music by Madonna. When they had a three-way (very expensive) call two days later, connecting them in DC, Evanston, and Paris to cry over the news about Grandma Vera's passing, all three sisters could not stop talking about the spin class.

Madonna! Nora had exclaimed, her voice shaking with tears. *Who dies of a heart attack after biking to "Material Girl"?*

Spin class might make me want to kill myself, Emily had deadpanned from across the Atlantic.

While Julia had added: *At least Grandma Vera lived doing the things she wanted to do, right up till the very end.*

And then they'd all murmured in agreement to that.

Julia knew it wasn't the spin class that was so disconcerting, it was more that Grandma Vera had always seemed like a force of nature, like the kind of woman none of them, against all reason and logic, had ever been able to picture *dying*.

"Was the house in good shape?" Nate asked, interrupting her thoughts. *Right.* He'd been asking about the house.

She had realized, as she'd walked through earlier, that it was maybe the only thing in her life that had remained completely unchanged in the last fifteen years. The inside of the weathered Victorian had barely been updated in the forty years Vera had lived there: a 1950s kitchen with ancient appliances, the old chestnut armoire and furniture in the dining room, the worn velvet couches, the pale pink walls. From a sentimental perspective, the sight of it all had made her tear up again. From a real estate perspective, it probably wasn't great.

"It's exactly as it always was," she finally answered him. "It probably needs some work before we sell it."

"Sell it?" Nate asked, sounding surprised.

She explained about Grandma Vera's terms to willing the house to her three granddaughters, and that there was no way all three of them were about to move here and live in the house together.

"Well, you could just move in, Jules. Em and Nora could come visit you. That would work too." He smiled a little, like he was joking, but maybe only half, because his acorn eyes flickered across her face as if he was waiting to gauge her reaction too.

She laughed; the prospect of it felt ridiculous. But that was exactly what Nate had done after he'd inherited his mother's house. After a brief, failed stint in medical school on the East Coast, he'd dropped out, moved his whole life back here. It was different for him though. He'd grown up here. The Pacific Ocean had always been his home, surfing almost as natural to him as walking. Julia, who had barely even dipped her toes in the surf since the stingray incident, could not move here. Besides, she had a whole life in DC. "That's a nice thought," she said. "But I have to finish law school."

"After law school, I meant. They have lawyers in San Diego, you know," Nate said.

She nodded. He wasn't wrong. So why did the prospect of living out here still feel so outlandish? Coronado Island, Grandma Vera's house, had always been her happy place. But it couldn't be her home. "Ted hates the beach," she told him. "He doesn't like the feeling of sand on his toes."

Nate raised his eyebrows, and she wondered if inwardly he was having the same reaction Nora did when she'd mentioned this detail about Ted to her sisters last Christmas. *What kind of a monster doesn't like the beach?*

But even if he was thinking it, Nate was at least kind enough not to say it out loud. Instead, he finished off his beer, then stood and grabbed two more Bud Lights from the fridge. "Ted," he said, as he handed her one. "The boyfriend you mentioned?"

Normally Julia wouldn't drink more than one of anything—she hated feeling out of control. But in this particular instance, she took the second can without argument, took a sip before answering him. "Ted's great. Really smart," she said. "You'd love him." At least half of that was true. Ted was brilliant and articulate. He'd gotten his op-ed analysis of President Clinton's impeachment trial published in the *Post* last month, and he'd clerked for Justice Scalia all fall. Julia liked the law; she liked rules and order, writing oral arguments. She knew she would be a good lawyer, but she wasn't in the same universe as Ted. In fact, she often felt dazzled by him. Ted was going places. Julia was attracted to men driven by their ambition. Nate, who had moved into his childhood home and now worked odd jobs on the island, felt like the exact opposite of a man chasing his ambition. So why could she not stop staring at his lips now, wondering what would happen if she kissed him, the way she did when she was seventeen? The beer, that was probably why.

"So it's serious, you and Ted?" Nate asked.

Julia tried to decide whether he sounded annoyed or happy for her. But his voice was so steady, maybe he was indifferent? Maybe he was just trying to be kind and strike up conversation, get her mind off Grandma Vera.

"Are you gonna marry the guy?" Nate added.

"Maybe," Julia said. It wasn't something she and Ted had discussed yet exactly, but who had time as they were both worrying about finishing law school, preparing for the bar. But if Nate had asked, instead, if she was in love with Ted, she would've said a truthful *yes*.

"You know," Nate said suddenly. "What if you rent it instead?"

It took her a minute to realize he'd moved away from Ted. *The house.* He was talking about the house. "How would that help?" she asked.

"Turn it into a weekly rental, I mean. You could reserve one week a year for you and Em and Nora. It would keep you good with Vera's terms, and you'd all have a little extra income on the side."

"One week in May," Julia said. "Just like we always did. I wonder if we could make that work?"

Nate considered it for a few seconds. "There's a city ordinance around rentals. It is a little tricky. You'd have to get it rezoned as a hotel to be able to rent weekly." He paused and finished off his shrimp skewer. "But I could help you figure it out. My friend is on the zoning board now. I could help you manage all the tenants and day-to-day operations too, since I'm just right here next door."

The thought of having Nate's help made her want simultaneously to sigh with relief and run away and hide. She actually loved his idea of keeping the house, coming one week every year with her sisters to this place, their favorite place, in honor of Grandma Vera. It would be a lot to manage from across the country, though, and Nate's help would make the logistics significantly easier. Except for the fact that this might mean she'd have to talk to Nate on a regular basis from here on out. And emotionally, that felt like a heavy lift. Two beers deep, she considered whether this would make sense to him if she said it out loud. But what she said instead was, "I don't know . . . That's a lot to ask, Nate." Of him. Of herself.

"I don't mind. Vera was like family. And you . . ." He paused for a moment, ran his fingers through his hair, making the curls disheveled, making her want to reach up and organize them. Her fingers twitched, wanting to feel the coarse texture of his hair again, and she clasped her hands together in her lap. "And you and Emily and Nora were always like my little sisters growing up," he finally added.

Little sisters? His words flamed up in her chest, like an insult, though she knew that wasn't how he'd meant it. But if that was how Nate thought of her now, if he'd forgotten all about those teenage summer nights between them, then there would be no problem with accepting his help. Why shouldn't she take him up on it? "Okay," she said. "But we'll pay you. I mean, we don't have anything right now, but once we start making income from the rental . . . we'll pay you. I wouldn't ask you to do all this for free."

"That sounds fair enough," he agreed. "But Jules . . ." He hesitated for a moment, and he stared at her so intently. This was not the way a man stared at his younger sister. She closed her eyes. "Jules," he said again.

"Yeah?" she said softly, her eyes still closed.

"Look at me," he said.

She listened, opened her eyes. He gave her a lopsided smile, then reached up and tucked a stray hair that had fallen from her loose ponytail back behind her ear. The warm brush of his fingertips against her forehead, her earlobe, made her shiver a little.

"It's just . . . I hate seeing you like this."

But somehow the word *hate* sounded more like *love*, and after a few seconds had passed, she wasn't entirely sure which word he'd actually said out loud.

CHAPTER 6

2000

THERE WAS ONE DETAIL Emily had failed to share with her sisters since she'd come home from France: She didn't have a job. And not only that, but she seemed entirely incapable of getting one. Not for lack of trying either. She'd interviewed at every museum in Boston, for every single open position, all to no avail. So the entirety of her income, at the moment, was the checks Julia sent monthly for her share of the Ocean Boulevard rent. After all their expenses to redecorate, refurnish, pay property taxes, and pay Nate to manage, and after they split what was left three ways, her monthly check was barely enough to cover the rent on her shitty studio apartment.

It wasn't really that she'd meant to lie to them. At least, not at first. She'd told her sisters about an interview at the Museum of Fine Arts a few months back, and for whatever reason Nora had (wrongly) assumed she'd gotten that job. Then Nora mentioned to their father in front of everyone at Julia and Ted's wedding that Emily had gotten an amazing new position, and Emily couldn't just blurt out the truth. All she'd done was sip her amaretto sour and nod.

Months later, Emily realized she might have to come clean to her sisters when they started emailing about their flights for their first annual sisters' week at Grandma Vera's in May. That's when it occurred to her: She couldn't afford to buy the plane ticket. She was going to have to ask their father, or God forbid Julia, for help. Or maybe she could email her sisters and say she couldn't go at all? She could lie and say that week no longer worked for her, even though they had, months ago, very specifically coordinated all their schedules to make sure all of them could go in May like they'd always done. Julia might take the train up from DC just to strangle Emily with her bare hands if she suddenly bailed on them now. And besides, she couldn't risk it. What if Julia decided her not coming for the week meant she wasn't doing her part to get the monthly share of the rental income?

"What are you sighing about?" Helen rolled over in bed, propped herself up on her elbow, and stared deeply at Emily, as if her face would give away the answer. Helen took a drag on her cigarette and then held it out to Emily. "You look like you need this more than me right now."

Emily shot her an appreciative smile and took the cigarette.

Actually, scratch that. There was more than one thing she'd been keeping from her sisters since she'd returned from France. They didn't know she smoked now. And they didn't know about Helen either.

She took one slow drag on the cigarette and then handed it back to Helen. "What am I always sighing about?" she finally said. "Money. What else?"

"How much do you need?" Helen asked.

Emily shook her head, unwilling to give Helen an answer. Helen was a senior at Tufts, on a full scholarship. She didn't have any money either. They'd met in Paris, at a bar, two American girls abroad from Massachusetts. Being in Paris together had given them this sort of ethereal connection, but now that they'd been back in Boston for six months, sometimes Emily wondered if they actually had anything real in common. And even with Helen here, in her bed, lying next to her naked, wisps of smoke trailing up around her pretty cherubic face, Emily already understood that whatever existed between them was fleeting. She couldn't take her money.

"Don't worry about it," Emily finally said. "I'll figure something out."

When Nora stepped out of the taxi on Ocean Boulevard, she was surprised to see a strangely familiar car parked out front: the 1988 red Pontiac Sunbird that all three sisters had learned to drive in. Dad had given it to Emily her senior year at Smith when Nora was a freshman at Northwestern. Julia hadn't needed a car in law school in DC. Nora had nowhere to park it on campus as a freshman, and Dad said it was taking up too much space in the driveway. That was how the sisters' car had become Emily's by default. Nora had long planned to try to get Dad to buy her a car when she graduated. *If* she graduated.

But she shook that thought away. Nora hadn't told her sisters what she was considering, and she couldn't this week either. Not unless she wanted it to immediately get back to Dad. Neither Emily nor Julia could keep a secret.

She ran her hand lightly across the familiar hood of her former high school car. What was it doing here? Parked on Ocean Boulevard? Emily couldn't have possibly driven it all the way from Boston. Could she have?

For some reason, that unexpected thought made Nora feel unsettled as she wheeled her roller bag up the front walk. But it wasn't really the sight of her old car that disturbed her. She understood that much as she walked up the steps, onto the porch. It was more the sight of Grandma Vera's house, which technically was no longer Grandma Vera's but a weekly rental for tourists that was now one-third hers. From the outside, the house appeared exactly the same as it always had her whole life: a stately white Victorian with a large lattice porch, sitting just across the street from the beach. But now, Grandma Vera was no longer inside.

She took a deep breath as she opened the unlocked screen door and walked in. She'd glanced through the pictures Julia had emailed of the interior refresh and new furniture, but somehow seeing it in person felt different. Grandma Vera's pink-and-blue-seashell walls had been turned neutral and beige; there were modern white leather couches where the old blue velvet tufted ones had been, and even the kitchen cabinets had been repainted white. Nora bit back tears as she looked around. It suddenly felt as if Grandma Vera had not only died but also been erased.

"You're here." Emily's voice cut into her thoughts, and Nora looked up and saw her walking down the steps just off the kitchen. Emily sounded irritated, as if Nora had shown up late, though her flight had landed exactly on time.

"Where's Julia?" Of her two older sisters, Nora would take Julia over Emily most days of the week. Except for maybe Saturday nights. Emily liked to go out and have fun. Julia was always tucked in bed before ten.

"I'm right here." Julia walked out of the kitchen.

"I saw the Sunbird outside. Did you drive?" Nora said, turning back to Emily. "From Boston?"

Emily shrugged. "I wanted to do a road trip."

"Why? That's a really long road trip," Nora said.

Julia nodded. "Not to mention dangerous. All that distance by herself."

Emily rolled her eyes. "Jul, it's a new fucking millennium. Welcome to the twenty-first century, where a woman can even drive across the country on her own."

Julia frowned. "Am I not allowed to worry about your safety, Em, when you decide to drive *three thousand* miles all by yourself? You know I read recently that driving tired is worse than driving drunk."

Emily rolled her eyes again.

Nora already felt bad she'd even asked. The last time she'd seen her sisters had been at Julia's wedding four months earlier, and sometimes she forgot how an innocent question could potentially be a spark that quickly became a flame. When they were younger and all lived together in Dad's house, they were close, bound by their shared experience, but they had bickered through most of their teen years, and were still doing so now that they were all in their twenties and out in the world. Sometimes it felt like they had more differences than common ground. "We're not going to fight all week, are we?" Nora asked.

"Probably," Emily said, plopping herself down at the dining room table. A large rectangular glass table, not the oval chestnut one Grandma Vera had had forever, Nora noticed now.

Julia shook her head. "I certainly didn't come all this way to argue."

"Then what are we going to do?" Nora asked, sitting down at the table.

"Give me a minute." Julia stood and ran up the stairs.

When they had come here to visit Grandma Vera when they were younger, Nora's favorite activities were exploring the beach, digging holes and burying each other, roasting crabs and marshmallows, and singing by the backyard firepit when it grew chilly at night. They'd sit on the porch early in the mornings when the sky was still gray and the sun hadn't quite burned through and read books, stopping to identify the military planes as they burst through the low cloud cover overhead, landing at the base just down the island. Grandma Vera, having once been married to a navy admiral (her second husband), was quite the expert. But none of that sounded vaguely appealing to Nora now. Maybe it was because she was no longer a little kid, or maybe it was because Grandma Vera had made being here fun.

Julia ran back down the steps, clutching a manila folder. She removed two papers and handed one each to Emily and Nora. "I made us a schedule," she said.

"Of course you did," Emily murmured under her breath.

Nora glanced at the paper. Julia had written down every meal, who was in charge of it, what they would be eating. And there was an activity for each day of the week and night. Runs down Ocean Boulevard beginning at nine a.m. Beach time in the afternoon, weather permitting. Shopping on Orange Avenue and at the marketplace on the other side of the island by the ferry landing. Grill-ing crabs at night and fish taco Tuesday, which Nora noticed she was assigned to. She suddenly felt exhausted.

"Do we need all this?" Nora asked. "I mean, we don't have to be doing things together every single second that we're here, do we?"

Julia gave Nora a look but then picked up a pen from the table and scratched off tomorrow afternoon's walk to Dog Beach. "Fine. Do whatever you want tomorrow afternoon. But tonight and the boat ride tomorrow morning are nonnegotiable."

Nora glanced at the schedule again. The first thing on it was s'mores at seven p.m. Nora felt herself tearing up, remembering what it had been like to be a little kid and anticipate exactly that moment, that gooey, marshmallowy, chocolaty moment, soon after she arrived at this house each May. Julia had noted in the schedule (of course she had) that Nora was responsible for getting graham crackers, Emily chocolate, and Julia marshmallows.

"And tomorrow morning we have to be out on the water exactly at ten a.m." Nora realized Julia was still talking, and she glanced back at the schedule.

10 a.m., Monday: Scattering Grandma Vera's ashes in the Pacific.

"Nate already borrowed a sailboat from his friend to take us and he needs it back after lunch tomorrow," Julia added.

Nate. Was he coming with them to scatter the ashes? The last time Nora had seen Nate, she'd been barely seventeen, a kid. Now she was in her early twenties, the same decade he was.

"You know what?" Emily said, interrupting Nora's thoughts. "I'm actually down with this whole schedule." A slow smile erupted on Julia's face, and Nora fought the urge to roll her eyes. "Seems like an easy enough way to manage the week," Emily continued. "Keep our promise to Grandma Vera. And probably not kill each other, since we won't have the time."

"Exactly." Julia full-on smirked, annoyingly pleased with herself. She and Emily nodded at each other like they had been in cahoots all along.

And Nora felt it again, that cold, hollow feeling in her chest of always trying to catch up to her sisters and perpetually feeling left out.

After a shared takeout pizza for dinner (per the schedule), which Julia only picked at, pulling off the slices of pepperoni and stacking them on the side of her plate in a neat little pile, they roasted their s'mores by the firepit. Then Julia excused herself and went upstairs to bed. Nora glanced at her watch—it was not even seven thirty. Time changes and travel aside, she was not at all ready for sleeping.

"Wanna smoke a joint with me?" Emily asked Nora as soon as Julia had disappeared inside the house.

"You traveled with pot?" Nora whispered, worried Julia would somehow hear and scold them.

"I drove, remember."

"Still, isn't it like illegal to carry it across state lines or something?" Nora didn't distinctly know if this was true, but it seemed like a dumb thing to do, even for Emily.

Emily shrugged. "Only illegal if you get caught. And anyway, medical marijuana is legal in California now."

"Is that why you have it? There's something medically wrong with you?" Nora raised her eyebrows.

"I'll be right back," Emily said, ignoring Nora's question. She stood and wandered inside the house.

Nora did not smoke pot. Except for once, at a frat party last year. The getting high part was fine, even preferable, maybe, to getting drunk. Because getting drunk always made her have to pee in places that did not have the nicest bathrooms. It was the smoking part she didn't enjoy. The way it burned her lungs and had made her cough until she'd almost gagged. It'd made her voice feel froggy, made her hoarse, and she cherished her singing voice more than anything. Still, she tried to recall a time in her life when Emily had invited only her to do anything. She came up blank.

Emily walked back outside and lay down on the lounge chair next to Nora's, in front of the still-lit firepit. She lit her joint, the tip glowing an orangey yellow, like a firefly, and Nora was hit with the sudden overwhelming odor of pot. If Nate was home, if he had his window open, would he notice? Or would the smell waft upstairs to Julia's open window?

Nora didn't say any of that out loud, though. When Emily handed her the joint, Nora took it, inwardly begging her lungs to be cool for once. She took a slow drag and immediately sputtered into a coughing fit.

Emily giggled and took the joint back. While Nora patted her chest, trying to remember how to breathe.

"Want to know a secret?" Emily said when Nora finally stopped coughing.

When she could breathe again a lightness came over her, and it hit her how much she loved this backyard, this house, this island. Owning part of this, committing to come here every year for the rest of her life with her older sisters. It was pretty goddamn amazing.

"Well, do you?" Emily prodded.

A secret. Right. "Yeah," Nora said. "Tell me your deepest, darkest secret."

"I like women," Emily announced. "I'm dating a woman."

Nora laughed, a giant bubbling laugh that welled up inside her hollow chest and burst up uncontrollably through her throat.

"What the fuck is wrong with you?" Emily spat. "I am baring my soul and you're laughing at me?"

Nora waved that notion away with her hand. "No, no, I'm not laughing at you baring your soul . . . I'm laughing because . . . because . . ." she sputtered. "You think that's a secret. A deep, dark secret?"

"It is a secret," Emily said. "I haven't told anyone."

"I have literally known you liked women since the summer I was ten. When we came here and you met that girl from Spain on the beach, remember? What was her name?"

"Olivia," Emily said. "And we were just friends! I was like thirteen."

"Okay," Nora said. "But it has not occurred to me once in the last eleven years since that you would ever fall in love with a man. It's not a secret if it's already obvious, dumbass."

Emily chuckled and passed over the joint for Nora to take another hit. "So all it takes for you not to be a total uptight bitch is getting a little high," Emily mused as Nora's lungs sputtered into another choking fit. "Good to know."

Nora probably should've been offended, but now she was just feeling light. "Don't you have a real secret you can tell me? You know, like something I don't already know," she said as she handed Emily the joint.

Emily chewed on her bottom lip, then opened her mouth to say something, as if maybe she did have a real secret and was considering spilling it. But then she shook her head and took another hit on the joint.

Nora was already high enough that she let the moment pass. "What's your girlfriend's name?" she asked instead.

"Helen," Emily said. "But I'm probably gonna break up with her when I get back to Boston."

"Break up with her? Why?"

Emily didn't say anything for a moment, and Nora watched the joint glow orange, the wisps of smoke trail delicately above her sister's face. "You know how Julia said at her wedding in her speech that Ted dazzles her or whatever?"

Nora nodded, though she didn't remember this particular detail about Julia's wedding. She had turned twenty-one just a few weeks before and had had one too many mixed drinks at the open bar.

"Well," Emily continued. "Helen doesn't dazzle me."

No one had ever dazzled Nora, man or woman, with maybe one exception. She glanced toward his house now, but it was completely dark. Nate didn't appear to be home. Or he was already fast asleep. And even in her strange amorphous state, she felt grateful he wasn't sitting in his backyard wondering where the pot smell was coming from.

"Okay, your turn," Emily said, passing the joint back to her one more time.

"To dazzle you?" Nora asked, eyebrows raised. She inhaled and coughed again, and even though she could feel herself smiling, she vowed she would never smoke anything ever again. She had to protect her lungs, her voice.

"No, I mean tell me a secret," Emily said.

"I don't think I'm going back to school in the fall." Nora blurted it out before she could stop herself.

"What? Why not?" Emily asked.

"I'm moving to New York instead. I want to be on Broadway."

Emily snickered. "Dad is going to kill you!"

She was not wrong. But it had taken Nora three years of college and processing Grandma Vera's death to realize that maybe that wasn't the worst thing in the world. Maybe it was worse to be living a life someone else wanted for her. She'd been saving up the rent checks Julia had sent all year, her share of Grandma Vera's legacy, and maybe that extra bit of security was what she needed to take this leap.

"But you wanting to be on Broadway is hardly a secret," Emily continued. "I've known that since that visit when Grandma Vera taught you all the songs from *Funny Girl*." She smiled a little at the memory. "The two of you stood here in the yard belting out 'Don't Rain on My Parade' like you were twin goddamned Barbra Streisands. What were you, seven?"

"Eight," Nora corrected her. "And I still maintain my secret is more of a secret than your secret."

Emily sighed. "Fine, if we're trading secrets Dad would kill us for, then mine is I can't get a job. I'm completely unemployed."

"Wait, what? What happened to that museum job you mentioned at Julia's wedding? I thought you'd been working there for months already?"

Emily shook her head. "You misunderstood. And I didn't correct you."

"I have a secret too." Julia's voice suddenly came from somewhere behind them. Nora turned, and her oldest sister was a shadow on the brick patio just outside the kitchen.

"Shit," Emily said, and she dropped the joint, grinding it out with the bottom of her flip-flop.

"I know you're smoking pot," Julia said. "Did you think I couldn't smell it with my window open? I'm pretty sure you've already given me a contact high."

For some reason that struck Nora as ridiculously funny. The thought of Julia, accidentally high! And then Emily started laughing too. "You could've just come out here and joined us," Emily said. "I would've shared with you the normal way."

"I can't smoke pot!" Julia exclaimed.

"Why not?" Emily asked. "Because you uphold the law?"

"No," Julia spat back quickly. "No," she repeated, her voice echoing softer. Then she said it almost no louder than a whisper, so at first Emily and Nora both weren't sure they'd actually heard her right: "Because I'm pregnant."

"Shit," Emily said again, softly.

"A baby?" Nora said after a minute, thinking about how Julia always managed to one-up them at everything, even at this secret-telling. Unemployed. College dropout. None of that beat the fact that Julia was about to be the one thing none of them had ever known or understood: a mother.

Later that night, after the high had worn off, Nora was restless in bed, unable to fall asleep. Even with the cool ocean air drifting in through her slightly open window, the sounds of the waves in the distance that, as a kid, had lulled her instantly to sleep—none of that put her at ease. Worry for Julia coursed through her veins, making her heart beat too fast.

Julia was twenty-seven, only six years older than she was. She was much too young to face the one thing Nora had always feared most. Their mom had died of undiagnosed eclampsia having Nora, and she had known her whole life she never wanted that for herself or her sisters.

She and Julia and Emily had discussed it once, in this very house. That summer they met Olivia from Spain on the beach, when they were ten and thirteen and sixteen and were playing Truth or Dare while roasting marshmallows over the firepit.

When Emily chose Truth and Olivia had asked her how many kids she wanted to have, she answered: zero.

Nora and Julia had echoed the same.

"Well, that's just ridiculous!" Grandma Vera had exclaimed, listening through the open window in the kitchen as she washed the dishes. "Your mother wouldn't have wanted you to live in fear. At least one of you girls will have to make me a great-grandmother."

The three of them had looked back and forth between one another, pressed their lips tightly together. A silent, all-knowing promise passed between them. It was the one thing they had all always fully agreed upon. Julia, Emily, and Nora planned to grow up to be adults, women, maybe even wives. None of them ever wanted to be mothers.

But Nora couldn't remind Julia of this now. It was too late. Julia was already pregnant. Nora's heart raced on, and she wasn't sure she'd be able to sleep all night.

Julia was extremely nauseous the next morning, before they even got on the boat with Nate. It was true, her stomach didn't do well on boats even on her best day, and this was not close to her best day. She'd already thrown up once and was trying to quell her nausea by nibbling on a pack of saltines on the porch while she waited for her sisters to finish getting ready.

As she forced a dry cracker down her throat, she eyed the urn on the table. And she wished Grandma Vera were still here so she could ask her all the things a woman was supposed to ask her mother when she was ten weeks pregnant, twenty-seven, and terrified. Like, was she ever going to feel normal and not queasy again? How could birth control that was supposed to be 97 percent effective just . . . not work? And, now that she'd gotten herself into this situation, how was the baby ever going to get out of her? It just didn't even seem in the slightest bit possible that it could work the way she'd read in all the books.

"Women have been doing it for thousands of years," she imagined Grandma Vera saying. "And you, my darling, are a goddamn rock star. You've got this." She imagined Grandma Vera would then follow this up with an offer to accompany her to doctor visits for extra support.

But the imagined words didn't feel real enough, or in the slightest reassuring now.

"Hey, Jules." She looked up and Nate was standing in front of her.

She'd been focusing so hard on chewing the damn cracker, she hadn't heard him walk up the porch steps. But now that he was standing so close, she suddenly noticed his smell. Oh my God, his smell. The sandalwood was so strong, she felt the bile rise in her throat, and she tried to swallow it back.

"Where's the rest of the Trouble Trio?" Nate asked.

She held one hand over her mouth and tried to breathe deeply as she pointed with her other hand toward the house.

"You okay?" he asked. "You look a little green."

"You know she gets seasick even thinking about boats," Emily announced, walking out onto the porch. She was still in her plaid pajama bottoms and wore giant sunglasses. How much pot had she smoked last night? But suddenly Julia was grateful for Emily's brashness. For some reason, she really didn't want Nate to know she was pregnant. Emily was a good distraction.

"You want me to grab a Dramamine? I think I have some in my house," Nate offered.

She shook her head. And he put a hand on her shoulder, as if to steady her. But as he moved closer the smell of his aftershave returned and another wave of nausea crested in her stomach.

"I'm here." Nora suddenly breezed through the door, wearing a white bikini with a sheer cover-up dress over it. "Nate! Oh my God, I haven't seen you in ages."

"Nora!" Nate said. "Jesus, you're all grown up."

Julia eyed her youngest sister's perfect body, every inch of it visible through that ridiculous cover-up. Nora was the shortest of the three of them, but also the curviest, and her large breasts were on full display in this getup. Did Nora not remember how chilly the Pacific mornings were? She was going to freeze.

As if on cue, she shivered, and Nate grabbed her in a half hug, rubbing her shoulders to warm her up.

Nora shot him a grateful smile. Was she wearing lipstick? And eyeliner?

"Don't you want to go get a sweatshirt, Nora?" Julia said.

As Emily said, "Can we please get this fucking show on the road?"

Nate stared at Nora just a beat too long before letting go of her, with a look on his face that made something uncomfortable thrum in Julia's chest. "There's a blanket on the boat," Nate finally said. "Shall we?"

"Hold on a second," Julia said. "I forgot—" But she didn't finish her sentence. She was already running inside, up the steps.

She barely made it to the upstairs bathroom before she threw up again.

As Julia disappeared into the house, Emily picked up the urn off the porch table. Even once Julia returned and they all walked down the long stretch of beach, got on the tiny sailboat sitting by the edge of the chilly water, Emily was the one who clutched the urn tightly against her chest.

Emily had only been sailing here once before, when she was

still in elementary school, the summer before Grandma Vera's second husband, Grey, the retired navy admiral, died. They had never met their real grandfather, but Grey loved Grandma Vera so much, they sometimes forgot she had ever been married to anyone else.

He'd rented a boat that summer and insisted on taking them all out. But the water was choppy. Julia puked over the side. Tiny Nora was crying in Grandma Vera's lap. And Grey had shaken his head, dismayed, and taken Emily to the front of the boat. It was a rare moment in her childhood, when an adult had paid special attention to her. Neither the youngest nor the oldest, the prettiest nor the most vocal, Emily had a way of being overlooked amongst her sisters. But that day, Grey had shown her, and only her, the secret to finding the wind. He'd even let her turn the till and steer the boat. It was remembering that specific moment that had made her so devastated when he'd died six months later.

The memory resurfaced now as Nate pushed the boat into the water and then hopped on and took over the till. The water was remarkably calm today, but the morning was gray and cool, the marine layer not yet quite burned off even though it was already midmorning. Nora sat shivering, her knees huddled to her chest. Julia looked pale and clung to the edge of the boat. Emily gently stroked the urn with her hand. "I hope you're dancing to Madonna with Grey right now," she whispered, letting the wind take her words the same way it was taking the sail.

Nate sailed only a little offshore, just far enough, he told them, so any onlookers from the beach couldn't really see them. He took his hand off the till for a moment to throw a blanket to Nora and she wrapped it around her shoulders.

"Oh God," Julia said, as it suddenly dawned on her. "We were probably supposed to get a permit for this, weren't we?"

"You're not hurting anyone," Nate said gently.

And Julia pressed her lips tightly together, trying to keep herself from explaining to him that that was not the way the law worked.

"Fuck a permit," Emily said. "Grandma Vera paid taxes on this island for forty years and she wanted her ashes here."

Julia frowned deeply, and Nate slipped a stick of gum out of his pocket and handed it to her. "Spearmint," he said. "It'll help with the seasickness."

She held the foil-covered stick in her hand for a moment, wondering if this was okay to chew. Or if the artificial sweetener would harm the baby. But her stomach roiled, and she slowly put the gum in her mouth and focused on chewing it. She would spit it out as soon as her legs were back on dry land.

Nora wrapped herself tighter inside the blanket and she suddenly felt six years old again, like she was the first summer their dad had let the three of them fly out alone to visit Grandma Vera. And only because Julia was twelve and, as Dad used to say, highly responsible. Nora, at the age of six (and also now), was not at all responsible. That was why her teeth were chattering, because she clearly hadn't dressed properly for this outing, and staring at the urn in Emily's hands, thinking about the fact that this was all that was left of Grandma Vera, she started to cry softly. Nora had always hated being the youngest, the smallest, the slowest. She lost every crab race on the beach, she was the only one who'd cried and had to go to the ER that summer of the stingray. She sometimes had nightmares sleeping at Grandma Vera's just because she was away from home, and the loud military planes landing just down the island on the base used to scare her. But Grandma Vera had never made Nora feel small. She'd given her a hug when she got scared and asked to sing a song with her. Grandma Vera had been the one who'd first encouraged Nora to sing, who had called her *my tiny songbird*, a nickname that had felt just as endearing at sixteen as it had at six.

Emily removed the top from the urn, and the three of them huddled in close, each taking a handful to scatter in the water.

And Nora thought, *I'm going to sing for you.*

And Emily thought, *I'm going to find someone who loves me as much as Grey loved you.*

And Julia thought, *I hope I have a daughter.*

CHAPTER 7

2001

JULIA HAD PUMPED EXTRA milk for the entire month of April in preparation for the sisters' trip to Coronado in May. She meticulously labeled each tiny plastic bag with the date and time before lining them up in order on a reserved shelf in their freezer. Sometimes as the pump whirred at her desk, and she felt conspicuously like an overworked cow, she considered whether she might also use her Sharpie to note what she had been working on each time she pumped. *Wednesday, April 11, 3:45 p.m., the Greenwell divorce. Thursday, April 12, 9:30 a.m., the Horner mediation.* But by the time the pump had finished cycling and the bag was full, she found herself rushing to snap her nursing bra back together and button her shirt, scribbling the date as fast as she could. It's not like Ted would care or notice what she had been working on anyway when he pulled out a bag to thaw. Or more likely, Janet, their nanny. Ted had already hired her to stay on 24-7 the week Julia would be away, rather than her normal eight to six during the workweek.

"Veronica is six months now," Janet said to Julia, as Julia stood in front of the freezer, showing her the stash of milk the Friday evening before she left. By then, there were close to fifty tiny bags, and the rows went back four deep.

"Not until the end of next week." Julia would, in fact, miss

Veronica's six-month birthday while she was away, a thought that had almost made her reconsider going, or ask her sisters if they could switch their week. But remarkably, the Ocean Boulevard house had grown quite popular with tourists and was rented out every single other week all summer. And Julia couldn't just not go. This was only the second annual sisters' week. If she did that, then they might as well give up on the whole thing right now—Em and Nora would never be able to keep things together without her. And she couldn't abandon Grandma Vera's wishes just like that.

"I've arranged the milk front to back," Julia explained to Janet now, brushing her fingertips along the icy bags. "The oldest milk is in the front, and it's all labeled, so it should be very easy. Self-explanatory, really."

Janet grinned. "Like I said, Veronica is six months. I'll start introducing some rice cereal when you're away. Maybe a little yogurt."

Julia took a deep breath before replying. They'd hired Janet because she was experienced, older, in her sixties, and had once been a preschool teacher. She knew children in and out. Ted called her *Mrs. Peace of Mind.* Julia secretly thought of her as *Mrs. I'd Like to Give Her a Piece of My Mind.* "Don't introduce anything new while I'm gone." Julia forced her tone to remain calm, even, like she was in court. "She'll be six months and one day when I get home. I'll introduce rice cereal then. For now, milk should be enough."

Mrs. I'd Like to Give Her a Piece of My Mind raised her eyebrows into tiny silver arches. "If that's your preference. I can always supplement with a little formula while you're away," she tsked. "She did just fine with it last week."

"What? Veronica isn't supposed to have formula. That's why I pump!" *Breast is best.* Every child-rearing book she had read (and she had, of course, read them all) had said that. The upcoming week away had her pumping at least twice a day, sometimes three, at her desk. Even before April, she'd been pumping at least once at her desk, and at home in the morning and night too. She had turned herself into a goddamn cow because *breast is best*. All so that Janet could just . . . give her daughter formula.

Janet laughed. "It's your first child, Julia. Wait until the next one. You'll throw that darn pump away."

And then Julia, perhaps egged on by hormones, or the feel of her raw nipples suddenly and inconveniently leaking milk on her shirt, unleashed every bit of frustration she'd felt since Veronica was born.

"Janet," Julia said in her calm, even lawyer tone. "You're fired."

Nora marveled at the New York City skyline from afar, the way the Twin Towers gleamed like beacons of hope on the other side of the Hudson as she caught a glimpse of them out the taxi window on her way to Newark Airport. The city felt, from here, like the dollhouse she'd had as a little girl. Everything that was supposed to be big turned small.

On the highway in New Jersey, she felt suddenly, weirdly boundless. Empty. Nora loved the noise and lights of the city, the way the tall buildings and people surrounding her always made her feel like she was a part of something. She had left it only once since she'd moved here last summer, to go to DC to meet baby Veronica after she was born in November. But it had been six months, and now from the back seat of the taxi, she found herself staring at the skyline, feeling like leaving it behind was the same as giving up.

But she wasn't giving up. It was just a week. Just seven days with her sisters in Coronado. Still, she felt this weird sensation in her gut, like the moment she left this grind she wouldn't ever be able to bring herself to go back to it. The truth was, a singing-waitress job at the Moonlight Diner was the best role she'd been able to get this past year. It was so far from Broadway, or even off-off-off-Broadway. She'd told herself at least she was singing every day. For money! But every night she was exhausted and came home to her tiny apartment in Brooklyn with swollen ankles, her hair reeking of French fries. If that was living the dream, she'd started to question the dream to begin with.

As she got to the airport now, her cell phone jingled inside her backpack, and she dug it out. Dad's number ran across the small front screen, but she refused to actually flip open the phone and talk to him. They had agreed to her moving to New York under the condition she would try it for one year. A year ago, she'd believed that was all the time she needed. She would show him! But now, she wasn't sure she knew anything. And she'd been ignoring Dad's recent calls, as his voicemails and emails were both imploring her to go back to school in the fall. *At least get a degree to have in your back pocket.* Deep down she knew that if she picked up the phone now, she was going to have to admit that he was right.

The phone finally stopped jingling and then a few moments later the voicemail icon popped onto the tiny screen.

Nora listened to it: *Nora, honey, why don't you take this next week and talk to Julia about how important her education was to her.*

Then she powered her cell phone totally off and threw it in her backpack.

Emily did not drive to Coronado this year. She had been tempted to, but the car needed brakes, and new tires, if it was going to make it all the way across the country and back. And in the end, buying a plane ticket was the cheaper option.

In the last nine months, Emily had broken up with Helen, quit smoking, and gotten an extremely boring but decently paying job as a teller at Fleet Bank. She had enough money saved for the plane ticket now, and she had enough vacation hours saved up to take the whole week off.

But still, as she waited at Logan, the little red letters next to her flight number flashing "Delayed," she wished she had just used her credit card to fix up the car and driven after all. It was too late now, and then she decided since she had nothing to do for the next three hours while she waited for her delayed flight, she may as well get a drink. She wheeled her bag across the terminal and took a seat at an empty table at the bar.

It was just past nine in the morning, but she ordered a glass of Chardonnay. If she had a few, maybe it would help her sleep on the flight, make the time pass more quickly. Come to think of it, maybe she would have to adopt this plan all week. Wine, wine, wine. It would dull Julia's and Nora's whine, whine, whine. As she sipped her Chardonnay, she giggled at that thought.

"I also find a nice dry white hysterically funny." Emily turned at the sound of the woman's voice coming from behind her, suddenly embarrassed that someone had noticed her laughing into her wine, alone in an airport bar in the morning.

The owner of the voice raised an eyebrow, then her glass of white wine in a mock toast. She was older than Emily, or she at least gave off the vibe of being more elegant. She had olive skin, bright green eyes, and shiny jet-black hair that hit at an angle just above her shoulders. She was wearing a long, flowy emerald-colored dress that complimented her eyes, while Emily's light brown hair was pulled back in a messy bun, and she was in her travel clothes: old gray yoga pants and her ratty Smith sweatshirt.

"I don't normally sit alone drinking and laughing, I swear," Emily finally said. "My flight's delayed. I'm headed to spend a week with my sisters, and I guess I'm just . . . pregaming."

"Ahh, sisters." She grimaced. "I have three. I totally get it. I'm Cara by the way."

"Emily. And I only have two. But I'm the middle sister."

"Oh, the dreaded middle sister! Same!" Cara laughed, stood, and wheeled her bag next to Emily's table. "Can I?" she asked, gesturing to the empty chair. Emily nodded.

Cara took a seat, and Emily had this weird flash of déjà vu. She suddenly thought about Monica, the Cal student she'd met sort of randomly this same exact way, at Clayton's Diner in Coronado when she was seventeen. The first girl she'd ever gotten drunk with *and* kissed.

"So where are you headed, Emily?" Cara asked, interrupting her thoughts.

For some reason Emily interpreted this as "What are you doing with your life?" forgetting that she was in an airport. "I have a degree in art history. My eventual goal is to become a curator, but at the moment, I work at a bank." She took a big gulp of her wine.

And now it was Cara's turn to laugh. "Your flight," she sputtered in between laughs. "I meant where are you flying to?"

"Oh, right, of course." Emily felt her cheeks turning hot and she pressed the backs of her hands against them.

"But now I'm much more interested in why you work in a bank."

Emily shook her head. There was nothing interesting about it, not the job, nor the reason behind it. It was the first job she had actually gotten since she'd finished college. Money was money. "San Diego. That's where I'm flying to," she said instead, and she explained briefly about Grandma Vera's house on Coronado Island, their one sisters' week every May.

"Well, that sounds nice actually," Cara said. "My sisters and I just bicker when we all see each other at my parents' house near LA where we grew up."

"My grandma grew up there too," Emily said, as if she were the expert, though she had only been there once as a kid, and it was before Nora was born so she'd been too young to truly remember it. And these days, she only sometimes, briefly, thought about Santa Monica and the return address.

"That's actually where I'm headed now." She sighed. "My mom is in the hospital."

"I'm so sorry," Emily said.

Cara shook her head. "She'll be fine, I think. All three of my sisters live in California. But I still felt I had to go there and see her with my own eyes, you know?"

Emily nodded, like she did know. But when you don't grow up with a mother, you actually don't know stuff like that. She resisted telling Cara all of that, though weirdly it felt like maybe she would understand.

Cara glanced up at the flight screen. Then gulped down the rest of her wine. "Shoot, my flight was canceled. I should go figure out how to rebook." She stood and grabbed her bag.

"Actually, wait," Emily called after her. "Can I get your number? I'll call you when I'm back. We can get a real drink." She paused for a moment. "You can let me know your mom is okay. And I can let you know why I work at a bank." She would need the week to come up with something entirely interesting to say.

Cara hesitated for a moment, then pulled a pen from her black leather purse, grabbed Emily's hand, and quickly scribbled her number across Emily's palm.

"Make sure you write it down before you wash your hands!" she called behind her as she ran down the terminal.

On Tuesday morning, Julia had her eyes closed while nursing Veronica on the white leather couch. The TV was on mute in the background, *The Price Is Right*. Though it was almost ten, and the schedule she'd made had included a morning walk at nine, Nora and Emily were still upstairs, likely asleep. Truth be told, the schedule of activities she had meticulously planned for them was already, two days into the week, too hard to keep with a baby in tow. Nora and Emily hadn't complained that she'd brought Veronica, but neither sister had seemed thrilled when the baby had woken them all up crying in the middle of the night.

Still, her sisters had been kind enough not to say anything about it, but there was a tacit understanding that no one was expected to follow Julia's schedule.

And Julia had not had it in her to explain to her sisters the circumstances that had led to her bringing the baby in the first place: firing the nanny on Friday and the huge fight that ensued with Ted the next day. All the milk she'd been pumping and freezing for a month be damned. (All Ted's talk of being an equal co-parent when she first found out she was pregnant also be damned.)

Julia had told them only the briefest of truths: "I'm nursing . . . it's just easier."

And though it didn't quite tell the whole story, it wasn't a lie. Being with the baby the entire day felt infinitely easier than pumping at her desk. Her mind felt clearer. Her chest felt lighter (literally and metaphorically). But it irked her that if all this was true, then maybe Ted had been right when he'd told her she should quit her job and be a stay-at-home mom after she fired Janet. *No one will ever do things as perfectly as you want them,* Ted had said—not meanly, but matter-of-factly. *I know you, Julia. We'll never have a nanny who lasts longer than six months. Why even hire a new one? Why don't you just quit your job and do it yourself?*

At that point, Julia had stomped out of the kitchen and then slept on the daybed in Veronica's room, before heading off to the airport the next morning with Veronica in tow. Not that she'd had much of a choice—Ted had already left for work by the time she'd woken up, so she either had to take Veronica or not go to Coronado at all. But now, a few days later, her anger with him had dissipated. Maybe Ted had been right, and instead of still being mad at him, she felt more irritated with herself.

A knocking on the front door suddenly startled her, and she opened her eyes, sat up. Veronica protested and fussed as Julia unlatched her from her breast. The knocking came again and now Nora was running down the steps in an oversized Brooklyn T-shirt, her long curls matted and messy.

"Julia, Nora, Emily!" Nate's voice came through the door now.

Julia had somehow managed to avoid him the first two days she was here. In fact, every time she'd glanced at his house it had been dark, quiet. She'd wondered if he was away somewhere.

He knocked again on the door. And finally, Julia stood. But by the time she had Veronica settled against her hip, Nora had gotten there already, opened the door.

Nate walked inside the living room, still in his wet suit, his hair damp, his usually messy curls slicked back. His eyes moved past Nora, straight to Julia, and then settled right on Veronica. He knew about the baby, of course. Julia had sent him a birth announcement, and they periodically spoke on the phone about the business of the rental, and Nate was always polite enough to ask how Veronica was doing. But still, his face registered a look of surprise seeing her now, like he could not believe this tiny, flailing creature had somehow come out of Julia. And Julia suddenly, in that very moment, realized only half her shirt was buttoned. Her cheeks flamed as she fumbled one-handed with the buttons, but Nate's eyes stayed squarely fixed on Veronica.

"I didn't know you were bringing the baby," he finally said.

"Neither did we," Nora said.

"It was kind of a last-minute . . . I just . . . I couldn't leave her." The words rang in Julia's ears for a moment, and she swallowed back the weight of them.

Nate nodded. "Well . . . I didn't mean to interrupt, but . . . Mike let me borrow the sailboat and I wanted to see if you all wanted to go out for a little bit this morning. But I guess with the baby . . ." His voice trailed off.

"Julia gets seasick anyway," Nora said cheerfully. "And Em is still asleep. But I'll go. Just let me get dressed."

Nate nodded but his eyes went back to Julia's face. It was only a little over two years ago that she had come to clean out Grandma Vera's house and had spent more time with him alone than she had since they were teenagers. And yet, that felt like a lifetime ago.

She was married now. A mother.

But somehow, Nate was standing here before her, still very much . . . Nate.

Nora climbed up onto the sailboat, and then Nate pushed it into the water and hopped on himself. She'd been smarter this year and had thrown a sweatshirt and sweatpants on over her bathing suit, but still the morning was gray and chilly, and she felt herself shiver.

Nate turned and offered her his gorgeous lopsided half-smile, then threw her a flannel blanket. "So here I got the Trouble Trio down to one."

Nora smiled. "I was always the only one getting in trouble, you know. Even that summer when you started calling us that, I stepped on the stingray first, I was the one who cried and had to go to the ER because my foot swelled so much."

"I remember that." Nate laughed.

"I was always trouble. Still am." Nora sighed dramatically.

"Oh, come on," Nate said. "You're living your dream in New York City. That's not trouble. That's brave."

"I feel like I'm actually kind of blowing the dream and failing big-time." She finally said it for the first time out loud. *Failing.* That's what she was really doing in New York City.

"Is there something I can do to help?" he asked, his voice thick with concern. "Do you need money?"

His worry for her hit solidly in the center of her chest, and it warmed her from the inside out. She shook her head. Between her waitress job and the money from the rental, she had enough to get by and pay her rent. "Not that. It's just . . . what am I even doing in New York if the best I can do is sing at a diner? A diner in Queens for heaven's sake." Dad had implored her over voicemail to talk to Julia about going back to college, but Julia had been consumed with the baby, and here she was, pouring her heart out to Nate instead.

He nodded and didn't say anything for a moment. Then he said, "Anything worth having takes hard work. You can't give up."

"But you did," she said. "You left medical school and came back here. Do you regret it?"

He shook his head. "I quit because I didn't really want to be a doctor. It was some stupid thing I thought up when my mom was sick, and my head was a mess. The truth was, everything about medicine made me miserable." He paused for a second and put his hand gently on her shoulder. "But this, this is different. This is your dream, Nora."

"Maybe it's a stupid dream," she said softly. "A million other people have the same dream as me and most of them don't make it very far."

Nate chuckled a little. "I still remember when you were maybe ten years old, the first time I heard you singing with Vera."

"Eight," she corrected him. "I was eight years old." That was the year Grandma Vera taught her how to harmonize. Taught her that perfect pitch ran in their family. She still knew all the lines of *Funny Girl* by heart. "I don't remember you being there," she said.

"I was right next door." He smiled. "And you and Vera were never quiet."

She blushed, about fourteen years too late, thinking about Nate listening to her and Grandma Vera belt out "Don't Rain on My Parade." Then she laughed and buried her face in her hands. "Oh God, you heard us?"

"You're not trouble, Nora. You're a star," Nate said. "You were always going to be a star."

Nora smiled, trying to soak in what was probably the nicest compliment anyone had ever given her, unsure what to say.

He paused for a moment, ran his hand through his messy curls. "You can't give up, okay? Don't ever give up on the one thing you truly want."

Nora nodded, and for a little while, all the doubts in her head were drowned out by the sound of the waves hitting the side of the boat.

"Do you have a joint?" Nora asked Emily later that night. It was almost ten, but Nora didn't feel remotely tired. Her conversation with Nate was still running through her head. And Dad had left her another voicemail, asking if she'd talked to Julia and if he should pay her tuition deposit for the fall.

"Why would I have a joint?" Emily asked. "I quit smoking pot. And anyway, I flew this year." But the truth was, she had been thinking about Cara, from Logan Airport. Emily had saved her number in her flip phone and had been wondering if—and when—it would be okay for her to call it. She sighed. "I could really use a joint too actually."

"There's a bottle of wine in the fridge," Nora said. "I bought it yesterday at Vons when I picked up my graham crackers. Should we invite Julia to join us?"

"Nah. It's late. She must be asleep. And she wouldn't drink with us anyway. She'd probably complain it would go straight to her boobs and make the baby drunk."

Nora giggled. It was funny only because it felt so accurate. That was exactly what Julia would say. Only she wouldn't use the word *boobs*. And she'd have some scientific fact from some book she read to back it up.

Julia was not, in fact, asleep.

She put Veronica down in the Pack 'n Play, and then she noticed something unusual. The light was on in Nate's childhood bedroom, directly across from hers. After Nate had moved back into the house as an adult, he'd taken over the master bedroom downstairs. Julia hadn't seen that light on from here in years, even since before Grandma Vera died.

She went to her window and opened it, and then Nate did the same across the way. She had no paper to make an airplane, and anyway, it had been so long, could she still remember exactly how to make one fly into his window?

They stared at each other for a few moments, doing nothing at all, and then Nate made a come-over-here motion with his hand. She hesitated, glancing at the Pack 'n Play. But Veronica was sound asleep, and if she left the window open a bit, she'd still hear her cry from next door.

She ran quietly down the steps, but when she reached the living room, the sound of her sisters' laughter trailed in from somewhere out back. She paused for a moment and wondered if they were smoking pot again. But she didn't smell it, and she wanted to go next door and see Nate more than she wanted to know what they were doing, so she kept on moving toward next door.

Nate opened his front door before she could reach up to knock, as if he had been standing right there, waiting.

"Hey," he said softly.

"Hey," she said. But neither one of them moved. They just stared at each other for another minute.

"It's a nice night," Nate finally said. "I was thinking maybe we could take a walk, down Ocean Boulevard to the Del. You know, like we used to."

She thought about that walk, the first summer they dated, when she was seventeen. They took that walk every night that week, except the day she'd gotten stung by the stingray. How many times they had stopped, leaning against the stone seawall along the way to kiss. How greedy, how hungry they were for each other. The thought of it now made something ignite in her that she'd forgotten about. Desire had all but vanished in the second half of her pregnancy, in the first six months of Veronica's life. And weirdly, something stirred inside of her again, here, face-to-face with her teenage boyfriend. As she stood before him, sleep-deprived and in a milk-stained oversized T-shirt! It was that thought that made her laugh.

Nate smiled. "It's nice to hear you laugh. You looked so . . . so . . . earlier, this morning, I mean." He didn't finish the thought, as if he wasn't exactly sure how to describe the terrible way she looked. Like a tired, overworked, flailing cow, that's how she'd looked. And poor Nate didn't have the vocabulary to figure out a way to say that nicely.

He stepped out of his house and shut the door behind him, standing next to her on the porch. "Come on," he said. "Walk with me."

"I shouldn't. Veronica is next door asleep. She could wake up."

"And your sisters are there if she does," Nate said.

"Both are probably high," she said. "Or drunk," she added.

Nate chuckled. "They can't be that drunk. At least not Nora. And we'll be back in an hour. It'll be okay."

He bounded down the steps to the sidewalk and then turned back to her expectantly, waiting for her to join him before he crossed Ocean Boulevard to the sidewalk on the ocean side of the street.

He was right. Veronica was asleep. Emily and Nora were at the house. The cool evening air, the sweet scent of honeysuckle, standing here, being with Nate, it all made her feel a little bit alive again. She couldn't help herself; she walked down the steps to join him.

They walked down the sidewalk together in silence for a few moments before Nate said, "I can't believe you actually have a baby."

Julia laughed. Nate sounded like he was still sixteen years old.

"I mean, what's that even like, Jules?"

It was one of those things, like anything else, she supposed, hard to believe or imagine until you were actually living it day to day. And then it just became . . . strangely normal. Julia had felt that way about being a wife, a lawyer. And now a mother too. "It's nice," Julia said. "I mean it's hard, of course. I've barely slept in six months. And my body is a mess."

Nate shook his head. "You look the same to me. You look great."

She blushed. Maybe her oversized milk-stained T-shirt somewhat hid her giant sore breasts and her still-bulging belly? "You're such a liar."

"I'm not!" Nate insisted. "I think motherhood agrees with you."

She nodded. "Veronica's amazing, and sometimes I just stare at her after she falls asleep, and I can't believe I made her. I made this new, beautiful tiny person somehow, out of nothing. If that's not a miracle, I don't know what is."

"Well, technically you *and* Ted," Nate joked. "I remember high school health class."

Julia blushed again. "Right. Ted was involved." Veronica was half him, so why did it feel like he didn't do half the work in taking care of her? Sure, there was the biological aspect of Julia having carried the baby in her womb, breastfeeding her now that she was here. But since Veronica was born, Ted had gotten a promotion after being part of a team working on *Bush v. Gore*. He was swamped and worked longer hours. It's not that Julia wasn't happy for him, it was more that she could no longer totally understand him. She felt like she was drowning every second she was at work and away from Veronica. He'd been working even more.

"In all seriousness, though, you're happy, right, Jules? I was really worried when I saw you this morning. And now you're frowning," Nate said, interrupting her thoughts. Was she frowning? She made an effort to turn her expression more neutral. "The baby. Ted. They make you happy, right?" Nate asked.

She nodded, though the truth was what she'd been feeling lately wasn't anything that resembled *happy*. She loved Ted. She loved Veronica. Of course she did. But she wasn't exactly radiating joy these past few months trying to balance everything on her own. But that felt too complicated to explain to Nate, so all she said instead was, "Ted and I actually got in a huge fight right before I left."

Nate was silent for a few steps, and then stopped at the B Avenue crosswalk, turned, and faced her. "If you need me to fly to DC and beat the shit out of him, let me know." He said it with all seriousness, but Nate was the last person who would ever beat anyone up. Rescuer of spiders and crabs since childhood.

Julia burst out laughing. "I don't believe you have it in you to do that, one. And two, I can take care of myself, thank you very much."

Nate grinned. "I know you can, Jules. That's not what I meant to imply."

"Anyway, it's kind of my fault," Julia admitted quietly as they continued walking. "Ted said something very honest about me that I couldn't quite process. It's why I got so mad at him."

Ted was right. She would never be happy with the way anyone

else watched over Veronica. But at the same time, she had no idea what the hell she was doing as a mother on her own. She wanted to be everything for Veronica that she'd never had as a kid herself. Except, she wasn't even sure exactly what that entailed.

"The real problem isn't Ted, it's me. I didn't have a mother growing up. What if I don't even know how to be a good mother?"

"You had Vera," Nate said quickly.

Julia nodded. And she chewed on her bottom lip, considering telling Nate more, what was really bothering her, deep down. But she hadn't ever told anyone this particular truth, and if she said it out loud to Nate now, well, then maybe it would be real. All this time, she hadn't ever quite admitted to herself it *was* real. So instead she said, "Ted and I are going to be fine. I'm going to be fine. You don't need to worry about me."

"I do though," he said softly. "I can't help it."

"Of course you do. I'm like your little sister." She repeated back the words he'd said to her a few years earlier. If there was one thing Julia knew that could sum up almost the entirety of her life, it was that the more times you repeated a lie, the more true it began to feel.

Nate didn't say anything in response. Up ahead, the Hotel del Coronado came into view, twinkling, the red triangular roofs of the towers lit with white string lights for the summer. Grandma Vera had told them once that L. Frank Baum had written some of *The Wizard of Oz* series in Coronado, living in a house just a few blocks from hers, by Star Park, and that some people would say this hotel, with its grand red turrets and beautiful white towers, was his inspiration for Emerald City. *There's no place like home*, Julia thought, staring at it up ahead of them now.

Nate suddenly reached for Julia's hand, and then they held on to each other as they walked up closer to the hotel.

"If you're ever not okay, though. You'll tell me?" Nate said, squeezing her hand gently. "Promise me, Jules."

"I promise," she said.

CHAPTER 8

2019

NORA WOKE UP TO the sound of someone knocking on the door, and she was drenched in sweat, disoriented.

It took her a moment to remember where she was. *Coronado.* Emily had gone next door to look for Nate, and Nora had been so consumed by jet lag, she must've sat down on the couch and fallen asleep.

Emily had been right, it was hot in here without the AC working. But maybe that wasn't why she'd woken up sweating—maybe it was the strange dream she'd been having. Something hazy that mostly escaped her now. Julia yelling at her, telling her she'd ruined everything. How long had she been asleep?

"Julia, open the door!" Mallory's voice rang through from the porch, and Nora sat up and wiped the sweat off her brow with the back of her hand. *Was Julia here?*

Nora looked around and didn't see her suitcase, coat, or any signs that she was. She checked her phone and in the sisters' chat there was one new text but it was from Emily: Taking a walk. Text when you bitches are ready for dinner.

Nora got up and opened the front door, and was surprised by the woman-child standing before her. In the year between eleven and twelve, Nate's daughter, Mallory, had somehow blossomed into someone entirely new. She was taller than Nora now and appeared to have boobs too.

She took one look at Nora and made a face. "You're not Julia."

"Exactly, I'm your favorite May sister, and you're in luck. Because I'm the only one here."

Mallory giggled, and for a second she sounded like a little girl again. Of course, Julia was her favorite. Julia was everyone's favorite. It didn't mean that Emily and Nora didn't still try to bribe Mallory by bringing her gifts each May. This year Emily had brought a stuffed manatee from her museum that Nora had inwardly thought was much too babyish for a twelve-year-old, but of course she hadn't said that out loud. That reminded her. "Oh, I have something for you in my bag!" Nora exclaimed. "And it's better than what Em brought you."

"What did Em bring me?" Mallory's face lit up.

Nora distinctly remembered Emily leaving for Nate's with that silly stuffed manatee before she'd fallen asleep. "You didn't see her earlier?"

Mallory shook her head. "I just got home from my friend's house and found a note on the door about your air conditioner. I figured it was Julia who'd left it."

"Julia's not here yet," Nora said. "That note was from Emily. I fell asleep." She cleared her throat. And then she asked the question that had been running through her mind since she'd stepped off the plane. "Where's your dad?"

"Where's Julia?" Mallory asked, ignoring Nora's question. "She's usually here first."

Nora chewed on her bottom lip. "I'm guessing her flight got delayed." There was no other possible explanation for it, really. Still, it did bother her that Julia hadn't texted to communicate that, or anything else, for that matter. That small trickle of doubt nagged at her. Something was off. She just wasn't sure what it was yet.

Mallory frowned, looking worried, and Nora felt the urge to cheer her up. "Wait here a second, Mal. Let me go grab your gift."

Nora walked into the dining room and picked up her Louis Vuitton carry-on off the chair. She rifled through it for a moment before pulling out the signed *Playbill.* The actor who was playing the lead in her new show was the same actor who had played the beloved Will the Wizard in Mallory's favorite childhood TV series. She would not tell Mallory that, in real life, she could barely stand to look at him, and that she'd had to beg one of the swings to get his signature for her.

Mallory's eyes widened as Nora handed her the signed *Playbill* now. "Nora! This is really for me? This is so cool."

Nora smiled and gave Mal a hug, and she almost felt a little bad for Emily's stuffed manatee. "I'll get you tickets if your dad will bring you to New York," Nora said, tucking a few stray wisps back into Mallory's thick braid.

"You know how Dad feels about the East Coast." Mallory sighed, and Nora realized that she did not, in fact, know how Nate felt about the East Coast. "Anyway, I'll ask Dad when he gets home from LA."

Oh. *LA?* Nora wondered what he was doing there without Mallory. Was twelve old enough to be left home alone? As a forty-year-old woman with no kids of her own, Nora had no sense of such things.

"Thanks again for this, Nora." Mallory held up the *Playbill* and started walking toward the door.

"Wait, do you want to hang out until your dad gets back?" Nora asked.

Mallory shook her head. "It's hot in here. But come get me when Julia gets here?"

Nora nodded, trying not to feel hurt that Mallory didn't want to stick around to hang out with her.

Emily walked slowly down Ocean Boulevard, clutching the stuffed manatee in her hands, thinking the breeze off the Pacific would cool her down. Calm her down. But the truth was, her favorite walk, even her favorite ocean breeze, wasn't going to be enough to do it today. The heat was coming from somewhere inside of her—resentment that had built up over time, that wasn't going to be able to subside here, thousands of miles away from her wife.

Emily never should've left Florida the way she did. Their fight rattled through her brain now, repeating itself on a loop. The way Cee's face had crumbled when she had said the word *betrayal.* Then, the defensive *fuck you* Emily had sounded off in response.

Nearly twenty years of sisters' week be damned—Emily definitely should not have left for the airport this morning without making things right with Cee. But Emily wasn't exactly sure *how* to make things right. They came to Coronado every May, no matter what. She had to come, despite how mad Cee was about what she'd done last year. Cee knew that!

Emily stopped walking and glanced at her phone. It was already past dinnertime in Florida, and she knew Cee would be overseeing homework with the boys at the dining room table. She wouldn't be able to talk now, even if she had cooled off. *You know the routine,* Cee would say, right before hanging up on her. She did know the routine, and maybe that was part of the fucking problem.

Emily considered texting her instead, but the right words escaped her. No, she would call later. After the boys were asleep. She didn't have it in her to talk to them tonight, to pretend like everything was okay.

She looked up and the sun was an orange ball at the end of the horizon. It would be dark soon, time for dinner and then s'mores. She glanced at her phone again, but neither Nora nor Julia had responded to her in their sisters' chat. Was her stupid phone not working? Julia had to be here by now.

When Emily got back to the house, she found Nora sitting out on the patio by the firepit drinking rosé from a Solo cup. "You want some? Help yourself." Nora pointed to the bottle of wine and stack of red cups on the table next to her.

Emily had quit drinking six months ago (after Cee had learned what she'd done while very drunk last May), promising Cee it was for good this time. But Emily really needed a glass of wine right now, and Cee would never know. Emily took a red cup and poured herself a little. "Julia's still not here?"

Nora shook her head. It was dark now, and Nora's pretty face was lit up by the twinkle lights Nate had strung for them a few summers before. In the nearly twenty years of coming here, Julia had never arrived later than midafternoon. The first sunset meant it was time for s'mores, the official kickoff to their week.

"Should we . . . do our s'mores?" Emily asked, sounding uncertain as she sat down on a lounge chair.

Nora shook her head. "We can't without the marshmallows." Besides, she was starting to get worried. "She should be here by now," Nora said.

Emily agreed. "Was there bad weather in DC or something?" she asked.

"I don't think so." Nora had taken off from Newark into a cloudless sky. "Maybe we should call Ted? Something doesn't feel right."

Emily sighed. She'd rather chew glass than talk to her brother-in-law. But she also agreed with Nora that something wasn't right. It was weird that Julia wasn't here, and that she hadn't communicated with them. It was not at all like her. "I went over to Nate's, so now it's your turn. You call Ted," Emily said.

"But Nate wasn't even there," Nora protested. "You didn't actually do anything."

"I left a note. He'll come over when he gets home. I did do something. You call."

Nora sighed heavily, put down her rosé, and picked up her phone. She was tired and didn't have it in her to argue with Emily. Where was Julia and her damn schedule anyway? There was no time to argue when they were busy, busy, busy.

She scrolled through her contacts until she found Ted's number. It rang a few times and she exhaled a little, thinking he was not going to pick up. But then suddenly his deep voice: "This is Ted."

Did he not even have her number saved?

"Ted . . ." She floundered momentarily. "It's . . . Nora. Julia's sister."

"Oh, hi, Nora," Ted said. "How are you?"

"Good, I'm good. How are you?"

Emily raised her eyebrows and motioned for Nora to get to the point.

"Oh, you know." Ted laughed. "Busy with work. What else is new?"

"Right. So . . . um . . . Em and I are at the Ocean Boulevard house for sisters' week and Julia's not here yet. It's probably just a flight delay, but do you have her flight number?" The other end of the line went so silent for a full minute that Nora thought the call dropped. "Ted, are you still there?"

"I'm here," he said softly. Then he added, "Julia didn't tell you?"

"We haven't talked in a while," Nora said. She had not, in fact, spoken to Julia since this time last year. Emily had, though. At least Nora assumed she must've.

"I'm sorry," Ted said. "This is really awkward."

"Ted, you're scaring me," Nora said, and suddenly her heart was pounding too hard against the walls of her chest. Five minutes ago, it had seemed almost ridiculous to call Ted, and now it felt like she should've called him weeks ago. Emily's eyes widened and she moved in close enough to Nora that she could hear Ted's voice coming through the phone too.

"Julia and I are getting a divorce," Ted finally said. "I moved out a few months ago." He paused for a moment and then he added: "We haven't talked since then. I wanted a cooling-off period before we hashed it all out legally. I'm sorry, Nora. I don't have her travel information."

"Oh, I see," Nora said, but she felt the rosé roiling in her stomach, and she was worried it was about to come back up.

Emily grabbed Nora's phone. "What the fuck, Ted? Julia is a fucking goddess. And you're trash."

"Emily, hi, you don't know the whole—"

She angrily poked the red button to end the call and then handed Nora's phone back to her. Nora stared at Emily with her mouth slightly open. "What?" Emily said. "Ted is a piece of shit."

A giggle burst out of Nora. She covered her mouth with her hand, but then she couldn't stop it from pouring out of her as an all-out body-shaking laugh as she imagined what Ted's face must look like right now. She agreed with Emily: Ted was a piece of shit. But he was Julia's piece of shit.

"Are they really getting *divorced*?" Nora said after her laughter subsided. Then a heaviness sunk in her chest: disbelief, worry. "Did you know?"

Emily shook her head. "Julia never mentioned it to me."

Nora felt guilt wash over her. She had been so stupid last May. And she had let a whole year go by without trying to fix things with Julia. But Emily and Julia weren't mad at each other, and she hadn't told Emily about the divorce either. Did Veronica know?

"Maybe we should call Ronnie," Nora said.

Emily shook her head. "No. We shouldn't worry her. Not unless something is really wrong. And it's probably not, right?"

"Probably not," Nora said, but now she really wasn't so sure. It felt almost preposterous to think that Julia, planner, organizer, the glue, had something, *a marriage*, she wasn't able to hold together. Nora was certain her sisters wouldn't be shocked if they knew the mess she'd made of her own love life. Julia, though, was different. And the fact that she hadn't told either of them? None of this was sitting right with Nora. "But it's weird she's not here and we haven't heard from her," she said. "*And* she's getting a divorce and didn't even tell us?"

Emily nodded to agree, then picked up the bottle of wine and poured more into her Solo cup. She drank it down before saying anything else. "Okay, this is what we're gonna do."

Nora leaned in closer, wanting someone, anyone but her, to make a plan.

"We'll drink the rest of this shitty wine, order some dinner, go to bed, and Julia will almost certainly be here by the time we wake up in the morning."

"And if she's not?" Nora said softly.

"If she's not . . . then we call Ronnie," Emily said.

"And her office," Nora added.

"But when we wake up and she's here all chipper with her goddamn schedule, then we kill her for making us worry like this," Emily added.

"Don't even joke about that," Nora said solemnly, feeling the wine coming back up in her chest now. "It's not funny."

"I mean, it's a little funny," Emily said.

But the truth was, Emily was putting on a front, the way Cee complained she always did. It was what Emily did best. And worst. *How can I ever see the real you if you refuse to show me?*

Deep down, Emily had a sinking feeling. As she sipped her rosé, she couldn't stop thinking about another thing she had pushed beneath the surface of her carefully constructed facade. Pushed it down so deep and let it fester there, until sometimes it felt like it was burning up her very soul, as if that alone were responsible for every single bad decision she'd made.

CHAPTER 9

2002

"DO YOU REALLY HAVE to go?" Ted whispered the words into Julia's hair as they were lying in bed together, the night before her flight to San Diego. Unlike last year when she took baby Veronica with her, she would be going to Coronado for the week on her own. She'd already made an extra-full schedule for sisters' week, filled with adult things that she would do with her sisters, actual adults. It would be her first adults-only time away from Veronica in almost a whole year, since she'd quit her job to be a stay-at-home mom last June.

The year had somehow blended into one long, similar day after another, and Julia had lately been feeling a little restless. She'd weaned Veronica promptly after her first birthday, stored the pump and her nursing bras on the high shelf of her closet for future babies. The reality was, now that Julia was done breastfeeding, she was, in a way, untethered again. Ted had agreed, months ago, to take a week's vacation from work to take care of Veronica while Julia would be away with her sisters.

"Do you?" Ted said again now. His arm, which had been lazily draped around her waist, clung around her tighter now, and he pulled her toward him. His thumb skimmed the top of her pajama bottoms, teasing at the elastic. Though she had lost most of her pregnancy weight and gotten back in shape after buying a jogging stroller earlier this spring, she still felt self-conscious about her stomach, and fought the urge to push Ted's hand away.

"Do you really have to go?" he murmured, rolling her over to kiss her neck.

"I do," she whispered back. "You know I do." Aside from her promise to Grandma Vera, and the fact that she missed her sisters, Veronica had recently learned the power of saying the word *no*, and Julia really, really needed a break. She'd been counting the days until this trip, marking them off one by one on the wall calendar in the kitchen.

Ted moved his hand away, rolled over on his back. "Grandma Vera." He sighed.

Annoyance flooded her chest. Grandma Vera was an imaginary person to Ted, a theoretical idea that inconvenienced him. "I wish you'd met her," Julia huffed. "And anyway, I can't just cancel on my sisters." As a practical matter that was true, a more logical argument than her promise to Grandma Vera, or even her own desperate need for a break. And Ted was always swayed by logical arguments.

"But I was thinking," Ted continued, seemingly unswayed. "It's just such a shame to use my vacation week this way. We could all go on vacation next week instead. The three of us. Drive up to Montauk."

Ted's parents owned a house in Montauk, and Julia had been only once, the summer after Grandma Vera died, just after they'd gotten engaged. It was a beautiful white, three-story house near the water: gleaming, cold, and immaculate on the inside, much the way Ted's mother herself was. It didn't feel like the kind of place you could relax on vacation, much less with a toddler. And anyway, it was a moot point. She wasn't canceling on her sisters!

"Why don't you take Veronica to Montauk," she told him. Though the idea of it made something strange thrum in her chest. Veronica, being with Ted's mother, without her there. The judgment that would surely follow, that Julia was, due to her absence, somehow a bad mother.

"I mean there's two of them." Ted was still trying to convince her. "Emily and Nora can survive just this one week without you, can't they?"

She chuckled. "You've met them."

"They'll understand. You're married. You have a family. You're just in a different place now, that's all."

"My flight leaves in the morning. Let's not argue," Julia said, rolling back closer to Ted, moving her hand slowly across and down his stomach, reaching beneath the elastic of his boxers until she heard him moan softly.

She tried to remember the last time they'd had sex, and she couldn't put her finger on it. *Valentine's Day?* No. That had been the first time she'd drunk wine in over two years, and she'd fallen asleep right after dinner. *Ted's birthday in March?* No. He'd been in the midst of a trial and had come home late that whole week. *New Year's Eve?* Yes, that was it. Julia had just weaned Veronica a few weeks before and it was the first time in two years her body felt like her own again. She wasn't a vessel to grow a baby, she wasn't a milk machine. She had been feeling giddy inside her skin at the mere thought of it.

Ted stopped talking, pushed her underwear down, and rolled on top of her all in one smooth, practiced motion. It had been so long, they both finished quickly, and then Ted kissed her gently on the lips, rolled back off her, and promptly fell asleep.

She heard the soft sound of his snore, but now she was wide awake. Her body felt relaxed but her brain wouldn't stop. She suddenly felt a little nervous about flying—it would be her first time since September 11th, and everything she'd read about the new security sounded stress inducing. And how was she really leaving her daughter for a week? *A whole week!* They had been together every second of every day for the last year. What if Veronica needed something that Ted couldn't anticipate?

She tried to shake that thought away. Ted was Veronica's father. And they had always agreed they would be equal partners, co-parents. Whether it truly shook out that way or not, Ted had to be able to manage for one week.

Besides, she had left him a detailed printed schedule and notes of everything Veronica needed, at every time of day, when and what she ate, when and how she napped. All Ted had to do was follow all the instructions she left him.

She repeated the lists in her head now, the schedule. The order of it finally soothed her enough to fall asleep.

But when she got out of bed the next morning, Ted and Veronica were already gone. Her neatly arranged packet of instructions was still sitting in a folder on the kitchen table, next to it a sticky note that said: *Gone to Montauk. Join us?*

Nora was the first one of them to spot the strange, beautiful woman at Nate's house. As she got out of the cab and wheeled her roller bag up the front walk, Nora caught a glimpse of her on Nate's porch. A leggy woman in a lime-colored bikini, with vibrant strawberry-red hair and pale skin, was reading a book in a lounge chair. She didn't look like the kind of woman who took kindly to the beach, and she definitely didn't look at all like she belonged on Nate's porch.

"Who the heck is that?" Nora said to Julia after walking inside, abandoning her roller bag in the entryway and running to the side dining room window to try to get a better look through the slats of the mini blinds.

"Who is what?" Julia asked. She handed Nora a thick, stapled packet. The weight alone told Nora that Julia had spent extra time on their schedule this year. *Great.* Nora already felt annoyed as Julia stood on her tiptoes and peered over Nora's shoulder.

"That woman, on Nate's porch." Nora pointed, but from this angle, they could only make out the shock of red hair.

"I can't tell," Julia said. "And anyway, why do we care?" she added breathlessly.

Nora was seeing someone in New York. She was waitressing at Joe Allen now, and she'd met Leo when she was his server one night when he'd come for a late-night steak. It was March, the night Halle Berry had won an Oscar for *Monster's Ball*—they'd been playing the Oscars on the TV back in the kitchen and Nora was feeling inspired by her acceptance speech. "You look like you're ready to be someone," Leo had said to her after she'd taken his order. And then he'd handed her his card: *Leo Marks, producer.*

It was only later, after she called him and met him for a drink, that she realized he had a wife. A wife he was planning on divorcing, after which she would tell her sisters about him. Emily might not care that he was married, but she would probably care that he was forty. Julia, she was certain, would care about both things because she was Julia.

She supposed Julia was right about the woman on Nate's porch. She should not care in the slightest about her, whoever she was. So why did she still feel a twinge of jealousy in her chest? She was positive she'd outgrown her girlhood crush on Nate now that she was dating a real grown man back in New York, but she still felt strangely possessive of him. "I don't care," she said now, perhaps a bit too emphatically, so that it both felt and sounded like a lie as it popped out of her. "I'm just curious, that's all. She doesn't look right for him. Does she?"

Julia pulled the string to tighten the blinds all the way closed. "Nate's a big boy," she said. "Did you bring the graham crackers?"

Nora glanced at the thick schedule in her hand and saw Emily would be arriving in an hour. Then there would be a walk to the Del, drinks (since when did Julia encourage them to drink?!) by the water, fresh shrimp for dinner that Julia would cook here, and s'mores at seven. She turned the page and saw tomorrow morning started at seven with a bike ride before coffee at Clayton's at eight and a packed day from there.

She had brought graham crackers, but now realizing she only had an hour until Julia's intense schedule began, she lied and told her she had forgotten. She could use a quiet walk to the store. "I'll walk to Vons and buy some right now," she said.

"Seriously, Nora." Julia shook her head and smiled. "Sometimes I wonder how you manage the rest of the year without me."

She was joking, of course, but Nora felt irritated by the implication, nonetheless. Though she was twenty-three, Julia still saw her as that little girl she had to look after when the three of them had flown to visit Grandma Vera on their own and Dad told Julia she was in charge. But Nora had grown up, become a woman of the city, a woman of the world. Leo had even promised he would be setting up an audition for her for a new show he was investing in when she got back. She was starting to feel certain that soon, she would be someone. Then, even Julia would have to see that.

Nora changed out of her airplane clothes into jean shorts and a sweater, put on a little makeup, and left to go to Vons to buy graham crackers. But as she walked out the front door, she suddenly heard Nate's voice from across the yard.

"The Trouble Trio's back in town!" He stood and bounded down the porch steps, across the grass, and wrapped her in a giant hug. He smelled like the ocean, like her childhood, like if happiness itself had an actual deep, woodsy scent. That was all Nate.

He pulled back, held her at arm's length for a moment, and then broke into a smile. "Nora, you look great! How have you been?"

She felt her cheeks redden, at not only his gaze but his comment that she *looked great*. "Well, I've been great." She laughed. Maybe that was a slight exaggeration. But she imagined by this same week next year, she might be living with Leo in his Upper East Side apartment, after having secured a role in his new show.

"Hey, come meet Becca." He grabbed her hand and pulled her toward the redhead on the porch lounger. Becca was listening to music on one of those fancy new iPods Nora had started seeing pop up all around the city. "Bec, this is one of the May girls I told you about that I practically grew up with."

Becca pulled off her headphones, raised her sunglasses to the top of her head, gave Nora a once-over, and smiled. "Is this the one you dated? Or the one you taught to surf? Or the other one?"

She was, of course, *the other one*. Was she not even memorable enough in Nate's stories to get some kind of distinction?

"This is the singer, the actress," Nate said. "Nora's the one making it big in New York City."

"Well, trying to make it big." Nora laughed again. "Working on it."

"Oh!" Becca smiled. "That's adorable."

Nora didn't like the way she said *adorable*, like she was patronizing Nora for being young, easily dismissed.

"Nora, Becca moved in a few months ago," Nate said. "Maybe we could all go out on the boat sometime this week while you three are in town. I want her to get to know all of you."

Moved in? So Becca was serious.

"Oh," Nora heard herself saying. "Wow. Yeah, of course. The boat would be . . . so much fun," she stammered.

And before she knew it, she'd signed them up for sailing later in the week with Nate and Becca. A slight deviation in their schedule. She hoped Julia wouldn't kill her.

That old stupid saying about muscle memory, that it was like riding a bike, didn't apply to Emily. The truth was, she never really learned how to ride a bike. She could never quite get the hang of how to balance and pedal at the same time.

She reminded her sisters of this fact as they roasted their s'mores over the backyard firepit and browsed the schedule Julia had handed her for the week.

"Anyone can ride a bike," Julia said in response. She'd had half a glass of wine two hours earlier, after their walk, and still sounded a little woozy.

"You don't do boats," Emily retorted. "I don't do bikes. If you're forcing me to bike, maybe I'll see if Nate can get us out on the sailboat."

"Um . . . actually," Nora said, her mouth full with a gooey bite of a s'more. "I told Nate we'd go on the boat with him and Becca Friday morning, so we have to edit the schedule."

"What?" Julia said, sitting up.

As Emily said, "Who the hell is Becca?"

"Nate's live-in girlfriend," Nora said, licking marshmallow off the side of her thumb.

"She lives there?" Julia raised her eyebrows.

Emily looked back and forth between her older and younger sister. Nora was focusing very hard on her s'more and Julia looked like she'd just tasted something sour. She suddenly longed for the freedom of last summer, when Julia had shown up with Veronica and they'd pretty much ignored the schedule and had done exactly what they'd wanted all week. "How about no bikes, no boats," Emily said. "We could all just sit on the beach and read, and then drink and eat s'mores out here at night? You know, relax."

Nora and Julia simultaneously glared at her.

"I already told Nate we would go," Nora said.

"I already paid for the bikes," Julia said. "And besides, I spent a lot of time making the schedule this year. We have to make up for last year when we missed out on everything."

"It's great you're both so flexible. I can already tell this is going to be a super fun week," Emily retorted. She popped the rest of her s'more in her mouth and stood, walking back inside the house.

"You don't have to be such a bitch!" Nora called after her.

"Nora!" Julia said. "Be nice."

But Emily pretended not to hear, walking up the stairs to her bedroom.

It wasn't that she was all that annoyed by her sisters. It was more that she hadn't been in the best mood these last two months, and even here, in her favorite place in the world, she felt stretched thin, weary. She'd waited for the calm to hit her from the back seat of the taxi as it drove over the bridge to Coronado a few hours ago, the way it had her whole life. But so far, she still felt tense and annoyed.

After she'd gotten back to Boston last summer, she had called Cara. They'd met for a drink, then a movie, then dinner. By the fall they were up all night, talking on the phone, and by the winter, up all night exploring each other's bodies in Cara's apartment. They were dating. Though it was only in hindsight that Emily realized, not *officially*. They'd never actually agreed it was anything exclusive. But this wasn't high school! They were together all the time for six months. And for the first time in her life, Emily thought she understood what it meant to really be in love. Like what Julia had said when she married Ted: Emily was *dazzled*.

In March, Cara's mom suddenly took a turn for the worse. She went out to California again to see her, promising Emily she would call as soon as she got back into town. And two months later, Emily still hadn't heard a word from her.

After the first week passed, she was worried. *Is her mom okay? Is Cara okay?* She tried to call her. Just once. But when Cara sent Emily to voicemail she tried again. And then again. And then it was too many times to count. A number maybe verging on making her look like a stalker.

Then, she did actually become a stalker, as she found herself on Beacon Street at ten o'clock one oddly balmy night in April, walking slowly by Cara's apartment. She stopped in the street outside: The light was on. So she was back from California? Emily could see Cara's frame through the kitchen window. She was sitting at the table with another woman, a woman Emily didn't even recognize, talking. They leaned in close. *Were they laughing? Hugging?*

Emily explained this all to Ben, who worked the teller window next to her at the bank, on one very slow Thursday morning a few weeks ago.

Ben had nodded, not even pausing from counting the ones in his drawer before saying, "I'll tell it to you straight, Em. It's a classic asshole move guys do all the time. She got tired of you, met someone else, and didn't feel like going through all the drama of breaking up."

Emily wondered if Ben had done this, *all the time*, if that's why he sounded so versed in it. He was nice enough to work next to, but she already understood that people were different when they were dating. Was it that they became their true selves or the opposite? That part she wasn't sure of. "She wouldn't do that to me," Emily insisted. "There must be a reasonable explanation. I should call her again."

"Do *not* call her again," Ben had said firmly. "Not unless you want her to take out a restraining order."

She'd listened and she hadn't called her or walked by Cara's apartment again. But it still didn't stop her from checking her phone a few times a day to see if Cara had finally called her back. So far she hadn't, and even Coronado, the old familiar house on Ocean Boulevard, her sisters—none of that was making her feel any better. In fact, for some reason, it all was only making her feel worse.

Julia didn't like the sound of Becca's laugh.

Objectively speaking, it was too high-pitched, she did it too frequently, and it came off as disingenuous.

Emily was sipping a mimosa—her second—and quizzing Becca on what she liked about Nate, as she picked at the edge of the Band-Aid on her knee with her thumbnail, covering up the small scrape sustained bike riding the day before.

"Where do I even begin?" Becca said. Then laughed again.

Julia felt queasy as the sailboat lurched over a wave and Becca's laugh penetrated her ears like nails on a chalkboard.

Nora was sitting off the edge of the boat, her toes dangling in the chilly water. Leo had called last night with amazing news. He'd gotten her an audition for a late open spot in a new musical called *Hairspray*, starting previews in July. They were already in rehearsals, something hadn't worked out with the original casting—Nora was unclear what and she didn't ask. The only problem was, the audition was tomorrow afternoon, and Nora wasn't set to fly back until Sunday. "Just switch your flight," Leo had implored her. "This is too big an opportunity to pass up, kiddo."

She had rebooked her flight for tonight and would have to leave right after this boat ride. She felt guilty about leaving early, missing their annual last-night dinner out at the historic boathouse restaurant on the bay. Grandma Vera used to take them there, and even last year they'd kept up the tradition, bringing baby Veronica. But Emily had already mentioned she'd noticed the restaurant had a new name; it had a new owner and was no longer the Chart House. It wasn't going to be the same, Nora had told herself, whether she flew home early or not.

"Jules, you don't look so great," Nate was saying, and Nora turned back to look at her sisters. Nate was right, Julia looked like she was going to throw up. Emily's eyes were glassy as she sipped her mimosa.

"We should head back," Nora said. She hesitated for a moment and then considered that this might be the safest place to tell Julia and Emily she was leaving early. On a boat, out in the water. With Nate and Becca as witnesses. Or human shields. "I actually, um, had to change my flight to go back a little early and have to, um, get to the airport soon anyway," she mumbled.

Emily raised her eyebrows and downed the rest of her mimosa. Julia grimaced and clutched the side of the boat. And only Becca said anything in response. "Is everything okay, Nora?"

Nora nodded and smiled. "Yeah, I just got a last-minute audition tomorrow, so I have to get back to New York a little early."

"Oh, how fun is that!" Becca said, and she raised her champagne glass in a mock toast before laughing and taking a sip.

Back at the house, Nora quickly finished packing her suitcase. And when she carried it downstairs, Julia was sitting on the couch. Her color was back to normal, but her arms were crossed in front of her chest, and she was frowning deeply. Emily was lying on the other side of the sectional, her eyes half-closed. Per the schedule, they were supposed to be reading on the beach now, followed by grilled cheese and strawberry jelly sandwiches and an afternoon ice cream sundae bar, just like Grandma Vera used to set up for them. Before Leo had called with the news, this afternoon had been what Nora had been looking forward to most. She wanted to tell Julia that now. But Julia was shooting daggers with her eyes, and Nora bit her lip and said nothing.

"So you're really leaving early then?" Julia said crisply, sounding personally offended.

"I have to," Nora said.

"One week a year, Nora," Julia said quietly. "Is that really too much to ask?"

"But this could be my big break!" Nora exclaimed, annoyed that Julia didn't seem to care or understand that in the slightest. "And what difference does it make if I miss one day?"

"It makes a big difference! We can't finish the schedule if you leave now."

Emily opened her eyes. "God, Julia. Calm the fuck down."

"No one asked you," Julia snapped, offering Emily an icy stare.

Emily stood up. "Well, since I don't count . . . then maybe I should go too."

"Sit down, Em," Julia said curtly.

"Hold up, Nora," Emily said, walking toward the stairs. "Let me grab my stuff and we can share a cab to the airport."

"Let's not fight," Nora said weakly, but both of her sisters ignored her.

Julia raised her arms. "Why did I bother leaving my kid and coming all the way out here if no one wants to be here?" She shouted toward Emily, who was already halfway up the stairs.

"Grandma Vera," Nora said, thinking how Grandma Vera would understand exactly why she was leaving early, that she would, in fact, be pushing her out the door, with last-minute notes on what song to use for her audition.

"Grandma Vera isn't here," Julia said. "And we're all adults now. No one is forcing any of us to be here."

"Exactly!" Emily shouted from the top of the stairs.

"Great." Julia threw her hands up in the air again. "Well, this is just great." Julia turned back to Nora and glared at her. "Now look at what you've done."

Nora felt her cheeks flaming as Julia chastised her, like she was still a child. "Why are you being such a bitch? It's one stupid day. If we're supposed to be honoring Grandma Vera this week, well, she would want me to go do this. Unlike you, Grandma Vera believed in me."

Emily ran back down the stairs, her roller bag in one hand, which she plopped down next to Nora's. "Nora's right," Emily retorted to Julia. "And you are being a bitch."

"Fine," Julia said. "Go. Both of you. Far be it from me to stop you. In fact, I'll just tell Nate to book this week for next year so none of us ever have to come back here together." Her voice was rising now, and color splashed across her cheeks, the way it did when she got truly angry.

"Fine by me," Emily said.

Nora wanted to say that it wasn't what she wanted at all. That she was sorry she was making them all fight. That she would make it up to them next year, when she was certain her life and her career would finally be in a better place. But all she said instead was, "I have to go. Or I'm going to miss my flight."

Julia changed her flight and left a day early too.

The truth was, she was missing her daughter desperately. She'd thought she'd needed the adult time away from Veronica this past week, but once she actually got it, she'd felt all week like she was walking around with a hole in her chest. A hole that seemed to grow and grow, no matter how many activities she had crammed into the schedule each day. In her head she had been checking it all off, one by one, counting down until she could get on the plane, fly back home, walk into her house, and kiss those sweet toddler cheeks. She even longed for the sound of Veronica's voice as it shouted a defiant *no.*

Had she overreacted about Nora leaving early? That thought floated in her head the whole long flight home, but she pushed it aside as soon as she got to her house and unlocked the front door. She was, at last, where she was meant to be: home!

It was quiet inside her two-story Colonial, the front living room dark. Her stomach dropped as she realized that Ted and Veronica might not even be back yet.

But the kitchen light was on, and she walked past the foyer toward it, finding Ted sitting at the table with a glass of red wine in front of him.

"Julia!" Her name burst out of him like sunshine, and she smiled, the first genuine smile she had allowed herself all day. Maybe all week. He stood and walked quickly to her, wrapping her in a hug. "I thought you weren't coming back until tomorrow."

"I wasn't," she said. "But I missed you. And V. So much." She swallowed back the rest of the story, because this much was also true. She had missed them both terribly. And now that she was back home, where she belonged, she suddenly felt like crying.

"We missed you too," he said, pulling back and gently kissing her forehead, then her lips. "And I'm sorry. I felt bad all week about the way I behaved. You should be able to take a week with your sisters. Of course you should. You love them. They're important to you. Please accept the humble apology of a daft only child."

Julia let out a small laugh as she guiltily remembered the way she'd left things with her sisters yesterday. "No one would ever accuse you of being *daft*. And I'm sorry too," she said. "Where's V?"

"Asleep." Ted put his finger to his lips in a weary way that made Julia understand bedtime might have been a battle.

She smiled. "I think the terrible twos are upon us. All the

parenting books say they can start at eighteen months. So I guess . . . here we are."

Ted nodded and pulled her back toward him. Her head hit the top of his chest in that perfect place it always felt like it fit, and they swayed together for a moment in the kitchen, like they were dancing slowly to a song only they could hear. "So maybe this is gonna sound crazy," Ted said quietly. "But I was thinking while you were gone, how much your sisters mean to you. How those relationships were so formative for you."

Julia nodded, suddenly biting back tears. *Her sisters*. She would never love anyone in quite the same frustratingly wonderful way that she loved Emily and Nora. They'd bickered their whole lives. But being sisters always transcended everything else. Their shared history, their shared trauma, their shared DNA. It was all irreplaceable. And she knew, no matter what she might've said in anger yesterday, that she would find her way back to Coronado each May, to Emily and to Nora, no matter what else happened between them.

"And I really want Veronica to have that too," Ted continued. "I think we should give her a sister, Julia."

She leaned close into her husband, enjoying the warm and comforting scent of his evergreen aftershave. "I don't think that sounds crazy at all. In fact," she added, "I think maybe we should give her two."

CHAPTER 10

2003

WHEN THEY WERE YOUNGER, whenever the May sisters would fight, Nora would be the peacekeeper. As teenagers, Emily and Julia seemed to disagree on just about everything. Every movie they watched or pizza they ordered turned into an argument, until Nora would distract them by doing what she did best: being cute or funny. Endearing. Once she got them both laughing, any unkind words or tense feelings were suddenly forgotten.

Her sisters pulled themselves apart; she pushed them back together. Again and again and again. Maybe Grandma Vera hadn't been that far off when she'd called Nora the graham crackers.

But after Nora left Coronado early last year, she wasn't quite sure *how* to fix things. For maybe the first time in her life she was the cause of their fight, not the antidote, and that left her at a loss. She considered calling Julia and apologizing, but when she ultimately didn't get the part, it all felt like a waste, and she didn't know how to justify that she'd left early.

Then, six months later, just like that, Nora finally got a break. An offer for a spot in the touring production of *Beauty and the Beast*!

Leo had a friend who knew about a sudden opening, and one quick, last-minute audition later, Nora suddenly found herself with the job. She hadn't spoken to either of her sisters in months, but suddenly, their fight evaporated from her mind. Her sisters were the first people she wanted to tell her happy news to, and she quickly dialed them both in on a three-way call.

"Nora? Are you okay?" Julia's voice was imbued with worry.

Emily didn't say anything for a moment after saying hello, but Nora could hear her breathing through the line, which felt oddly reassuring.

"I'm good," Nora said. "Actually, I'm great! Guess who just got cast in the national tour of *Beauty and the Beast*? Ahh!" She squealed, unable to contain her excitement.

"Wow!" Emily said, breaking her silence. "Nora, that's really cool!"

"Oh my God!" Julia exclaimed. "That's V's favorite movie right now. When and where can we come see you?"

"I mean, it's just a small part, in the ensemble. You don't have to come," Nora said. But she suddenly felt warm from her sisters' words, from their belief in her. From the way they'd just cheered her on.

"There are no small parts. Only small actors," Emily quipped. "Isn't that what Grandma Vera used to tell us whenever she was rehearsing for auditions?"

Nora smiled at the memory. "Remember that one May when she worked a French word into every other sentence? Then she got that part, and she wrote me a letter telling me all about it. She only had ten lines in the whole show."

Emily laughed. "That sounds about right."

"Well, she was perfecting her craft," Julia said. "Just like you've been doing all this time." She paused for a moment and then she added, "Grandma Vera would be so proud of you, Nora."

"She would be singing and dancing, jazz hands and all, by her firepit right now to celebrate," Emily added.

Nora felt a sharp pang in her chest, and oh, how she wished Grandma Vera were still here. Why was it that her loss never really felt easier?

You did it, my tiny songbird! If she focused hard enough, she could almost hear the tinkling sound of Grandma Vera's voice in her head.

"We're all still going to Coronado . . . the last week in May, right?" Nora asked.

"Of course we're going," Julia said quickly. As if she didn't remember she had threatened to have Nate book out their week. Then she added, "I shouldn't have ever said we wouldn't. We'll go every year, no matter what. Right?"

"Right," Emily agreed.

"Okay, good. Then I'll request that week off from the show now," Nora said.

"And email me the show's schedule so I can see if I can find a weekend to take V," Julia said.

"Yeah, and send it to me too. I also want to try and come," Emily said.

And suddenly, all was right with the world, with the May sisters, and Nora's heart felt full again.

At the end of April, when the show was in Detroit, Julia and Veronica and Emily flew in to watch the Saturday matinee, and Dad drove from Chicago.

They waited for her backstage afterward with flowers and hugs, and Veronica stared at her aunt in awe and asked if she could touch her dress.

"Of course!" Nora said, bending down and holding on to her niece's tiny hand before gently pulling it across the green taffeta. She had quickly gotten used to the rhythm of being on the road, the exhausted joy that put her soundly to sleep in a new hotel room after singing and dancing again and again, night after night. But nothing had yet felt as special as this moment, when she'd managed to wow her two-and-a-half-year-old niece.

Veronica pulled back after a moment and clung shyly to Julia's pant leg before asking Julia if she could whisper something in her ear. Julia bent down and listened to her daughter, pressing her lips together tightly, clearly trying not to laugh. "V wants to know if her aunt is a real princess now?"

"Last time I checked, Miss Ronnie," Dad said, leaning his tall frame down to pat his granddaughter on the head, "no royal bloodlines on either side of the family. My girls got the big brains from me. And Nora, you got your voice from . . ." Dad's voice trailed off, as if for a moment he wasn't sure how to finish his sentence.

"Grandma Vera," Emily chimed in. "Duh."

"Right. I forgot that Vera could sing," Dad said softly.

"Duh!" Veronica mimicked, and Julia shot Emily a look.

"What?" Emily shrugged. "There are much worse things I could've said. Be grateful."

Julia rolled her eyes, and Nora half snorted a laugh.

Julia, Veronica, and Emily went straight to the airport after the show, but Dad asked if he could buy Nora a quick dinner before making the drive back to Chicago.

They went to a diner down the street from the theater, and Dad stared at Nora, looking pensive, after they both ordered. "What?" Nora finally said. "I can tell you want to say something, Daddy. Spit it out!"

"It's just . . ." The waitress plunked down his black coffee and he took a slow sip before continuing. "I worry this is a hard life, Nora. Traveling day after day, week after week."

"I love traveling," Nora said emphatically.

He nodded. "You're young now. But what about in ten years or twenty?" He took another sip of coffee. "Maybe after this tour ends, you go back to school. I can help you out with the tuition."

Nora fought the urge to roll her eyes and wished she had ordered something stronger to drink than a Diet Coke, even though she had another show to do in two hours. "This is just a stepping stone," she said. "After this tour ends, I'm hoping I can get a bigger role. And then eventually something on Broadway. In New York City. I won't be traveling like this forever."

"Still," Dad said. "An actor's life is a hard life. And a degree never hurt anyone to have in their back pocket."

Nora sighed. If he mentioned her *back pocket* one more goddamn time, she was actually going to lose it.

"Just think about it, all right?" he urged.

Nora finally promised she would, though even as she said the words out loud, she knew they were a lie.

On the last Sunday in May, Julia was the first to arrive at the Ocean Boulevard house.

She put her bag of marshmallows on the dining room table before changing into shorts and a sweatshirt and taking a long walk on the beach.

An hour later, Emily arrived and put her Hershey's chocolate bars on the dining room table right next to the marshmallows, before going out back to take a nap on a lounger on the patio.

And thirty minutes after that, Nora walked in, clutching a box of graham crackers.

At six o'clock, they walked to the Brigantine for dinner, and at seven thirty they made their s'mores by the backyard firepit.

They all three stayed the entire week, strictly keeping to Julia's meticulously prepared schedule. And not one of them mentioned their fight from the year before.

CHAPTER 11

2004

THE CARD FROM NATE happened to arrive in the mail the same afternoon Julia started bleeding. She had just picked up Veronica from her morning at preschool, stopped at the mailbox at the bottom of the driveway, and noted the cream-colored envelope with Nate's return address on top. But right after she started unhooking Veronica from her car seat, she felt the trickle of something warm against her inner thigh. And then the sudden sensation of a menstrual cramp she definitely should not have been having.

"Ronnie, sweetie, can you put the mail on the kitchen desk? Then go wash your hands for Mommy?" Julia tried to keep her voice even as she planted a soft kiss on Veronica's forehead, finished unbuckling the straps, helped Veronica hop out of the back seat of her Lexus SUV, and then handed her the pile of mail.

Having made it (mostly) through the terrible twos, Veronica, at the age of three and a half, now listened and followed directions, at least 90 percent of the time. She was a competent little person who reveled in doing things all on her own. She clutched the mail now and skipped inside the house. Julia watched her go and felt something constrict in her chest.

After Ted had brought up having another kid, she'd found

herself wistful, thinking about her own childhood. She'd gone off the pill, and they weren't really *not* trying for a while. But months passed and then Julia read every book on fertility she could find, working diligently to time sex with her exact ovulation window, month after month. It had taken almost another year of real trying, but here in the beginning of May, she was nine weeks pregnant.

Then she felt it again, the warm, sticky trickle, and she ran toward the bathroom. She lowered her jeans, sat down on the toilet, and there was a jarring bright red splash of blood in the toilet water. She knew instantly, this wasn't right. This had never happened to her when she'd been pregnant with Veronica.

In that moment, all the hope of so many months of trying, of a sister for Veronica, left her body, and she suddenly felt chilled. The so-far easy pregnancy that lacked the morning sickness of her last had always felt too good to be true. Maybe it was.

And Julia forgot all about the cream-colored envelope she had seen on the top of the pile of mail with Nate's return address.

Nora found the card in a large cardboard box that her roommate, Kim, had stuffed full of mail and sat waiting outside her bedroom when she finally made it home to Brooklyn after six weeks out on the road. After *Beauty and the Beast* had ended, she'd joined the national tour of *Hairspray*. She'd spent a good part of the last year traveling with the show as a member of the ensemble and understudy for Amber Von Tussle. And now she was making a quick three-day stop home in Brooklyn before she would fly to meet her sisters in Coronado.

She picked up the cream-colored envelope from the top of the pile and noticed the return address on Ocean Boulevard. *Nate?*

She tore the envelope open and pulled out the photo card—Nate and Becca, standing out on the beach, their arms wrapped around each other, Becca's red hair blowing sideways from the wind.

The sky was cerulean, and the sun was an orange ball, just about to drop behind the horizon. *Save the Date*, it read just below that. *We're getting married! Five is our lucky number: 5-5-5.*

Well, that would be adorable if it didn't suddenly hit her in the gut with a small wave of nausea. Nate, who had always strangely been theirs, the keeper of the Trouble Trio. He was going to be Becca's starting next May. Till death do they part?

She stuffed the card back into the envelope now, sighed, and fell back into her bed. Then, for the first time in weeks, she thought about Leo.

They hadn't exactly broken up before she went out on the road on this latest tour, but they hadn't been keeping in touch either. His wife, it turned out, was pregnant, so not only had they stayed married all this time, but that bit of news had made it abundantly clear to Nora that Leo and his wife weren't any closer to getting a divorce.

I'll call you, Nora had told him the night before she left for *Hairspray*, after a goodbye drink at Playwright, and months later, she still hadn't reached out. Although he knew her number and hadn't called her either.

She picked up her cell phone now and thought about it. She was in the city for three days. They could meet for a drink later, reconnect. But instead, she found herself dialing Julia's number.

"Nora?" Julia answered without a hello, and her voice sounded strange, timid, underwater. But maybe it was just a bad connection.

"Five is their lucky number," Nora said. "I mean, give me a break, right?"

"What are you talking about?" Julia's voice sounded oddly strained.

"Nate's Save the Date card. I just got back from my tour, and I'm going through all my mail."

"Oh," Julia said. "Right, I think maybe I did get that. I

haven't . . . opened it yet." Why hadn't she opened her mail? Julia was the type to immediately open every envelope, file the important things, and shred the rest. Was it possible Nate hadn't sent it to her? They had dated a million years ago, but he and Julia now seemed to have an easy enough relationship managing the details of the rental.

"Are you okay?" Nora asked her.

"Of course, why wouldn't I be? Ronnie, get down from there! Mommy's on the phone and you're going to fall. Sorry, we're at the park," she said.

"Oh, I'm bothering you," Nora said. Nora remembered the last time they'd spoken on the phone, back in early March when she was trying to discuss the ridiculousness of Nipplegate with Julia, and Veronica had suddenly grabbed the phone and shouted: *What's a nipplegate?* Julia had not been happy with her, and now Nora felt like she was interrupting.

"No, no, you're not bothering me," Julia said, sounding somewhat disingenuous. "How's the show? Ronnie, I said get down! I'm sorry, Nora, can I call you back later?"

"Yeah, of course," Nora said. "Or . . . I'll just see you on Sunday in Coronado."

"Email me your flight," Julia said before hanging up.

Nora considered for a moment calling Emily, but Emily probably wouldn't care about the Save the Date. She might even, annoyingly, be happy for them.

Instead, Nora found herself dialing Leo's number.

In fact, Emily didn't know about Nate's upcoming wedding. She was the only one of the Trouble Trio who hadn't gotten a Save the Date card in the mail. Which, to be fair, was not Nate's fault. She'd moved to Florida to start graduate school last fall, and she had either subconsciously or intentionally or just out of a lack of interest never figured out how to forward her mail. For one thing, she never got any mail of importance, and for another, in a way, it felt like a giant fuck-you to Cara. If she could disappear, just like that, well, Emily could too. Of course, Emily would be easy enough to find in Florida and had kept the same cell phone number. But still.

Seeing Nora finally start to achieve her dream onstage last year had inspired her to quit her job at the bank and find something better to do with her own life. Then she had applied and gotten accepted into the museology master's program at the University of Florida on a whim after randomly catching an episode of *CSI: Miami*. Florida felt like it would be a different world—everything that Boston was not: lush and tropical and warm and fifteen hundred miles away from the temptation of walking by Cara's apartment on Beacon Street. She could not work at Fleet Bank forever (unless she wanted to literally die of boredom), and a master's degree might finally help her get that elusive job at a museum.

In reality, though, Florida was more swamp than beach. Emily's hair seemed to have puffed out three times its size and her ankles had been covered in mosquito bites for months. At first, she weirdly missed the cold, the white of snow, the bright red scarf she used to wear walking to the bank each morning in Boston. But by the spring she had become more accustomed to the sight of towering palms, spraying down with bug spray before she left her apartment. She had chopped off all her hair, dyed it blonde, and found a decent frizz serum.

And she realized she felt vaguely happier being back in school again. Being with other people who loved art and history. Spending her days contemplating things aside from the crisp, boring bills in her teller's drawer. Learning, studying, memorizing, writing. *Thinking.*

She would have her master's degree in two years, just in time to turn thirty, and it occurred to her that maybe she was finally on the path to getting her shit together.

On her flight to San Diego for sisters' week, she amended her silent promise to Grandma Vera again in her head. She didn't need to find a person to love, she needed to find a job she loved. And maybe that's what would finally set her on the course toward being happy.

It had been two years since the May sisters had seen Becca or Nate, but this year, Nate invited the three of them over for dinner on Wednesday night so they could get to know Becca better and toast their engagement.

The invitation came through Emily, who ran into Nate in Vons on Sunday afternoon when she was buying chocolate. And when she mentioned it casually to her sisters, later that night over s'mores, Nora made a face, and Julia picked up a pen and her schedule and crossed off her original Wednesday night dinner plan—fish tacos at Miguel's. Then wrote in pen: *Nate.*

If it was on the schedule, in pen, no less, it was happening, so Wednesday, after a two-mile morning walk, afternoon beach yoga, and shopping on Orange Avenue, all three of them showered and changed into clothing that in varying degrees showed something off: Julia picked a pale pink maxi dress and wore a little pink lipstick that reminded everyone she might be a mom and in her thirties but she was still cute, Nora dressed in fitted jeans and a crop top that showed off her sculpted abs from a year of intense dance routines, and Emily put on denim shorts and her Florida sweatshirt, a reminder that she was killing it in graduate school.

Julia pulled a bottle of rosé from the fridge and Nora shot her a look. "Em and I were gonna drink that later," Nora protested.

"Well, we can't show up empty-handed," Julia insisted, wishing she'd thought ahead to buy some fancy champagne, something that appeared celebratory, while they were out shopping earlier. But the truth was she had blocked this little get-together from her mind until about an hour ago, when she'd found herself rooting through the clothes she'd packed for the week, deciding if she had anything suitable to wear.

"It's fine, bring the wine. Nora, I'll buy you a margarita at Miguel's after dinner," Emily said. "You too, Jul."

"We're all going to need it," Nora muttered under her breath. But if Julia and Emily heard it, they'd ignored her; they were already walking down the porch steps, across the front lawn.

Julia reached Nate's front door first and raised her hand to knock, but then she heard the sounds of voices, shouting, from inside. *You never do!* a woman's voice said.

Well, you never give me a chance! Nate sounded angry, an emotion the May sisters had rarely, maybe never, heard in his voice in all the many years they'd known him.

Julia and Nora exchanged looks, but Emily walked past them and rapped hard on the metal part of the screen door. "Nate," she called before trying the handle. It was unlocked and she let herself in. "Nate, hello," she called out again. "We're here."

It suddenly got very quiet, and then Nate appeared from the kitchen, Becca trailing a few steps behind him, barefoot and wearing a tiny yellow sundress that, in Julia's opinion, didn't leave enough about her (fake?) breasts to the imagination. Nate suddenly broke into a smile and gave Emily a big hug. He patted Nora affectionately on the shoulder and then offered Julia a wave.

Julia handed over the bottle of rosé, placing it in his raised hand. Nate tried to pass it off to Becca, but she shook her head and didn't take it.

"I'm so sorry," Becca said flatly. "I have a migraine. Can we reschedule dinner?"

"Reschedule? They're only here one week a year." Nate's voice rippled with irritation.

"Migraines suck," Nora said sympathetically. "I get it."

Julia didn't know Nora got migraines, and she stared at her youngest sister for a moment, trying to figure out whether she was being sincere or acting.

"I should go lie down. I'm so sorry to be rude," Becca said, not actually sounding very sorry.

"No, not at all." Julia waved away her concern. "Please, go rest if you don't feel well. And we can always have dinner here . . . next May?" She looked at Nate, and his frown creased deeper.

"We'd been talking about Miguel's for tonight anyway," Emily said. "Julia needs her yearly oversized margarita fix."

Nora giggled. Julia had never been able to drink more than half of their giant house margarita, and even that made her loosen up to the point of verging on being hilarious.

"No," Nate said firmly, turning toward Becca. "Bec, you should go upstairs and lie down. But I have enough shrimp to feed all of us." He turned back to look directly at Julia. "You're all already here. Please don't leave."

Becca's face fell a little, like maybe Nate had just failed some test the May sisters didn't quite understand, but then she quickly reversed course into a small smile. "Of course. Go on ahead and eat without me. I'll catch you next year, girls."

Girls? The three May sisters all exchanged a look. "Feel better," Nora called out as they watched Becca walk up the stairs.

"Let me go throw the shrimp on the barbecue," Nate said evenly. "I'll be right back to open this wine."

"Nate, are you sure you don't want us to go?" Julia asked. "We don't want to impose."

"Absolutely not," Nate said. He was already walking toward the fridge, where he pulled out a giant tray of skewered shrimp.

Julia suddenly thought about the shrimp he'd grilled for her that time she'd come over right after Grandma Vera died, when they first talked about renting the house. The way she had felt that night, flooded with grief and the sudden, sharp longing to be a teenager again. How far she felt from that girl now. But still, somehow, even at thirty-one, being here in Nate's kitchen, like this, that same longing rose up in her chest.

As they ate Nate's shrimp, no one mentioned Becca. Instead, Nate told his favorite Grandma Vera story (which was the time he'd watched her perform onstage as Sally Bowles in *Cabaret* with his mom when he was a little kid). Nora wanted everyone's thoughts on the series finale of *Friends*—which only Emily had actually watched, and Nora acted offended when she said it was just *okay*. Emily pointed out that she now had something in common with President Bush, who fell off his bike the week before, which made Nora giggle and say, *I saw that and I immediately thought of you*. And Julia wanted to know whether everyone thought Scott Peterson was guilty or innocent. (Everyone said guilty, except for Nora.) Then Nora and Emily left to go get their margaritas at Miguel's, and Julia asked Nate if he wanted to take a walk down Ocean Boulevard to the Del.

He hesitated for a moment before saying yes, that he would just run up and let Becca know and meet Julia by the street. Outside, the night air was ripe with the scent of freshly bloomed honeysuckle. But an evening fog had rolled in across the water and the sweet-smelling air was also surprisingly chilly. Julia shivered as she crossed the street and waited for Nate, and she considered going back for a sweater.

But then Nate was running down his porch steps, heading toward her, and she couldn't move. A wave of nostalgia rolled over her, warming her from the inside out. In that moment, Nate looked exactly the same as he had at fifteen, nineteen, twenty-seven. The scent of honeysuckle and the ocean. The chill of the night air. It was all so achingly familiar. And she suddenly felt the way she had at all those ages too. For a moment she was overcome with some emotion she couldn't exactly put her finger on.

"Thanks for suggesting this, Jules. Getting out of the house is exactly what I needed," Nate said as he reached her.

She smiled at him. "Becca okay?"

Nate nodded but didn't elaborate. He unzipped his hoodie, took it off, and handed it to Julia. "Here—you look cold."

She hesitated for a second but then took it. She was swimming in the long sleeves, in the way it smelled like him, like the ocean and sandalwood. And the summer they first started dating when she was seventeen. "Thanks," she said softly, as they walked down Ocean Boulevard toward the Del, side by side, the way they had so many times over so many years.

"You know," Julia said after a few silent moments. With her sisters gone, suddenly she felt like she wanted to say something *real.* "If you need me to go back there and beat her up for you, I will. If it would help."

Nate laughed, a full-bodied genuine laugh that shook in his chest. "You sound even dumber saying that than I did a few years ago."

Julia smiled, glad to hear Nate sounding more like Nate than he had all night. She wanted to say something else then, something about how even the name Becca sounded so harsh, and Nate himself was so soft and comfortable, like this sweatshirt of his she was borrowing. But she didn't know how to articulate that without it coming off wrong. Finally, she said, "Are you happy?"

"Do you want the truth?" he asked.

"Of course," she said. "Always." It was funny how the years could pass, but once she and Nate slipped back here, walking on this path just by the roar of the Pacific Ocean, everything that had happened, everything that would happen, it all felt so far away and out of reach. It was just the two of them, again, every thought and hope and fear drowned out by the rush of waves so close.

"I'm really not sure," Nate said. "I don't even know if I understand what happy means."

Then you should not marry Becca, she thought. But what she said instead was, "I don't think anyone really does."

Nate bit his lip, and maybe he wanted to ask her if she was okay again, or why she wasn't trying to explain the definition of happiness to him. Wouldn't a happy person know how to explain it? "How's the baby?" he finally said.

She thought of the bright red blood pooling in the toilet, but of course he didn't know about that. That wasn't what he meant. *It'll be okay. We'll try again*, Ted had said, kissing the top of her head gently later that night in bed. And she knew they would. But trying for the past two years had already felt like so much work. Ted had processed the miscarriage as a blip, something that could easily be fixed, redone. While she had been feeling hollow for weeks, feeling—when she first woke up in the morning and remembered what had happened—like the sense of loss could swallow her whole. She hadn't told anyone that though, and she couldn't bring herself to tell Nate now either. "V is a little person now," she said instead, because of course that's what he meant when he'd asked about the baby: *Veronica*. "Three going on thirty. The parenting books say *threenager* for this phase."

Nate laughed. "That's awesome," he said. "Now I'm picturing her like a tiny teenage version of you."

"A little bit." In some ways she was, but Veronica had gotten Nora's thick brown curls and flair for the dramatic, and in a lot of ways, she reminded Julia most of teenage Nora.

"I can't wait to be a dad," Nate said.

"You'll be great at it," she said, and she meant it. Though she felt something like disappointment catch in her chest when she thought about Nate's future *threenager* looking and acting something like Becca.

Up ahead the Hotel del Coronado started to come into view, the red triangular roofs of the buildings laced with white twinkle lights. It was amazing the way this historic hotel had been here for over a hundred years, and how every May she had been coming here, it still looked exactly the same. Beautiful. Twinkling. Majestic. Emerald City. Vacation spot to kings and presidents and movie stars. The white-and-red hotel never changed. If nothing else in her life was constant, at least this was. She said that to Nate now.

"I heard there's actually a major renovation in the works." He nodded up ahead toward the hotel. "Probably long overdue."

"Well, no matter what they do to it," she said, "I hope they don't change the character. It's beautiful just the way it is."

Maybe she was just talking about the hotel or maybe she was saying something about Nate and Becca too.

Nate nodded. "Everything and everyone changes, Jules. That's just life."

CHAPTER 12

2005

NORA WAS THE ONLY one who could make it to Coronado for Nate's May 5th wedding.

Emily couldn't come because it was during her finals. Julia couldn't come because it was too hard to manage the details of leaving Veronica for Coronado twice in May. They'd considered switching their week from the last week in May to the first, but the Ocean Boulevard house was already rented. Nora, who had recently left the *Hairspray* tour and didn't have all that much going on other than trying to figure out her next move, said she didn't mind going out there twice. She was used to traveling now. Besides, it was Nate! At least one of them had to show up as the May sister representative for his wedding. And Nate had very kindly offered that Nora could stay in his guest room so she wouldn't have to pay for a hotel, since he and Becca would be away on their honeymoon anyway.

Still, it felt odd to get out of the taxi on Ocean Boulevard a few weeks earlier than normal, to see two children she didn't know playing with a soccer ball out on Grandma Vera's porch, like it belonged to them. She supposed that for the week it did, that unfamiliar families and strange, tiny children rotated in and out all year long. Her head had long known this information, of course. But her heart lurched actually seeing it like this, before her.

She knocked on Nate's front door, steeling herself for Becca. Taking a deep breath and trying to get into character the way she did before a show. Happy, supportive, longtime friend/little sister. That was right. She was here because she was thrilled for Nate and Becca. *Thrilled.*

When no one answered the door on her first knock, she tried again. "Nate! Becca!" she called out, making her voice higher-pitched than usual, overly cheerful. "You lovebirds home?"

There was still no response, and she sat down on a porch rocker and rifled through her backpack. She had neglected to bring either the wedding invitation or her address book, and she hadn't called Nate enough times to have his cell phone number memorized.

She had Julia on speed dial, though, so she called her instead. But her cell phone went straight to voicemail. She tried her house number next, and that went straight to Ted's voice on the answering machine. Before she could wonder too much about where Julia could possibly be at dinnertime on a weeknight, Nate's front door suddenly swung open. And then she heard his gravelly voice: "Oh, shit. Nora. You're here."

She stood from the rocker. "Nice to see you too, buddy."

But in that moment she actually *saw* him. He was unshaven, days-old stubble across his chin, and his usually sexy and somewhat tousled wavy hair was sticking straight up in the back. He was wearing plaid pajama bottoms and a tattered UCLA sweatshirt. This did not look like a man two days away from his dream beach wedding. The last time she had seen Nate looking close to anything like this, it was the summer his mom got sick.

"What's going on?" she asked, her voice hitching. "What's wrong?"

"Shit," he said again. "I emailed Jules and asked her to tell you and Em."

"Tell me what?" She was suddenly registering it as strange that Julia had somehow both forgotten to tell them something from Nate and that she wasn't answering her phone.

"Becca and I broke up last week. There's no wedding," he said flatly.

"Shit." Now it was her turn to curse, and she focused her full attention on him. "Nate, I'm so sorry—"

He held up his hand to stop her from saying any more. "It's fine. I'm fine," he said.

Nora put her hands on her hips. "You don't look *fine*."

He stared at her for another moment, but he didn't try to argue. It probably made her a bad person that she was feeling the smallest sense of relief building up inside of her. *Nate and Becca aren't getting married!* Nate would still be here, next door each May, just the same Nate he always was. But she swallowed this selfish feeling back. Even thinking it made her feel like a horrible person, like she was secretly reveling in his grief. "I can get a hotel," she said instead. "And I'll . . . see if I can get a flight out in the morning." And also, she was going to kill Julia for not telling her this before she flew all the way out here. Once she finally got ahold of her.

Nate shook his head, opened the door wider, and ushered her inside. "Don't be ridiculous," he said. "You're already here. I told you that you could have my guest room. Stay until Saturday morning like you'd planned."

She hesitated for a moment. "I'd be bothering you. You don't look like you're up for company right now."

He reached up to run his hand through his hair and it caught in a tangle of knots. He frowned, as if he suddenly realized how bad he actually looked. Then he shook his head. "You're not company, Nora. You're family. Why don't you come in and get settled? I'll shower and then we can get something to eat."

Nate was looking more like Nate after a shower, dressed in a clean pair of jeans and a well-fitting T-shirt. But when Nora offered to buy him a drink, he said he'd rather have sugar than alcohol. Nora suggested ice cream, and they walked toward town in silence, heading to MooTime. This charming old-fashioned ice cream place opened in the late nineties, so it hadn't been here when they'd visited Grandma Vera as kids, but if it had, she imagined she would've begged to come every night. As adults, they'd stopped in only a handful of times, as usually there was a long line that went out the door and down Orange Avenue a block or two.

But today it was the grayest of May days, when even late in the afternoon the sun hadn't managed to penetrate the low cloud cover and the air felt chilly. It was the first time Nora had ever seen MooTime completely empty, and they walked inside, straight up to the ice cream counter. No line.

"Get whatever you want," she said to Nate. "My treat." And though it was silly and just ice cream, saying this made her feel like maybe she was finally a grown-up in his eyes. Or at least, she hoped she was.

"Maybe I should get vanilla," Nate said to no one in particular. "Because that's how Becca sees me. But I don't even like vanilla. I like chocolate."

"So get chocolate," Nora said.

"But chocolate can be boring too," Nate said. "It's plain. *Unoriginal. Uninspiring.*" He accentuated every syllable in such a way that Nora was pretty sure Becca had said those exact words to him before dumping him the week before their wedding. What a bitch! Nate was better off without her.

Nora kept those thoughts inside her head and instead said: "I love chocolate." Grandma Vera always used to say Emily was the chocolate of their trio because she was the perfect blend of bitter and sweet, and that always seemed more interesting than her own assigned graham crackers, which were frankly plain, and always tasted a little stale to her.

"No," Nate said. "I want the flavor of the month. Rocky Road. Now, that sounds fitting, doesn't it?"

"Two small Rocky Roads," Nora said to the bewildered-looking teenager behind the counter.

"Cup or cone?" The teenager sighed.

Nora glanced at Nate, who no longer seemed to be paying attention. "Cones," she finally said.

"I'm really sorry you came all the way out here," Nate said as they licked their ice creams before they could melt and walked down Orange toward the Hotel del Coronado. "I feel like such an ass for not messaging you, separate from Jules."

Nora's annoyance over the whole thing had softened now that this trip had turned into her and Nate, like this. Spending time together. She'd told herself she'd long outgrown her girlhood crush on him, but after being so on-again, off-again with Leo, she had started to wonder whether any man would ever live up to the perfection of Nate in her head. "You don't have to be sorry," Nora said. "I'm between jobs anyway, and you know I love it here. I'm just sorry you're sad."

"I'm not sad," Nate said. "I'm more angry. And not even at her. At myself."

"Did you . . . do something wrong?" Nora thought about Leo, his now one-year-old son, and the fact he still called her sometimes. But she could not imagine any universe in which Nate would act like him.

"I knew it wasn't right between us," Nate said. "But I kept thinking I could make it work. If I tried hard enough, I could fix everything, you know?"

"Sure," Nora said, thinking about Leo again. She no longer believed he would ever leave his wife, or imagined herself moving into his place on the Upper East Side. She still met up with him occasionally, but now it had nothing to do with her thinking they had any kind of future together. It was more that Leo still believed that she was going places, and she enjoyed this perception of herself. It was as if, every time she was with him, she could imagine her own success through his eyes. She inwardly cringed even thinking about this now; it felt so self-serving. If she were to try to explain this to Nate now (which she definitely would not), she wasn't even sure she could pin down her own logic. "I get it," she finally said. "But you should give yourself a break. Don't be angry with yourself. You fell in love. You put yourself out there. It doesn't always work out."

She finished off her cone with one last satisfying crunch, wiped her fingers on a napkin, and then stood up on her tiptoes and patted Nate on the shoulder.

"Little Noradora." He used her earliest nickname and grinned at her. "When did you get to be so wise?"

Later that night, after they shared a takeout white pizza from Village Pizzeria, Nate popped popcorn on the stove, and he brought it to Nora in a giant bowl on the couch. He had an old copy of *Some Like It Hot*, and he popped it into the VCR. There was still something thrilling about watching Marilyn Monroe, right here in Coronado where it was filmed, at the Hotel del Coronado.

"I haven't seen this in years. Not since . . ." She thought about it for a moment. "God, I think it might've been like 1996?" Nora distinctly remembered now that she and Grandma Vera had last watched this movie together when she was sixteen or seventeen, then talked about her mom's acting in high school. It was one of the few times Grandma Vera had ever said anything substantial about her mom to Nora.

"Well, I'm pretty sure it hasn't aged well." Nate laughed as he plopped down on the couch next to her, reaching into the popcorn bowl to take a handful.

"I always loved Marilyn's voice though." Grandma Vera did too. Watching this movie usually ended with Nora and Vera doing their own rendition of "I Wanna Be Loved by You."

As the opening credits cued now, Nora teared up, missing Grandma Vera, wishing she could hold her close and sing with her again.

"You okay?" Nate asked, noticing as Nora wiped her eyes.

She nodded and sniffled a little. "I know it's already been . . . six years. But sometimes it still feels like she died yesterday."

"Vera would be so proud of you," Nate said. "A real Broadway actress! You made it, Nora."

She didn't correct him; she hadn't actually been *on* Broadway yet but traveling in two different national tours. As a member of the ensemble and as an understudy. That barely felt like it scratched the surface of her dream. "I don't know." Nora sighed. "Sometimes I think if she were here, she'd agree with my father by now. That I should go back to college and find a respectable career, and that I'm pretty much wasting my life with acting."

Julia had a law degree, a husband, and a kid. Emily was almost finished with grad school now and would probably soon have some fancy museum job. What did she actually have to show for herself?

"I disagree," Nate said after a moment. "I actually think Vera would be thrilled with your career. And, that she would tell you to follow your heart."

She warmed at the compliment from him, at the thought that maybe, just maybe, he could be right. If her grandmother were still here, maybe she would still understand Nora completely. Maybe she would cheer on every tiny role and tell her to keep on going, keep on trying. *Rome wasn't built in a day*, she might say. Or, *The heart wants what the heart wants.*

Then she thought about what Grandma Vera had told her the last time they watched this movie—that her mom had loved to act too. It apparently had been her mother's dream, and maybe the very least she could do was to somehow make it as an actress, for both their sakes.

CHAPTER 13

2019

EMILY WOKE UP EARLY on Monday morning with a start, sweating. She wiped her neck with her hand, and for a moment she was hit with a sudden overwhelming sense of doom. She had the sense she'd been having a terrible dream, but she couldn't quite remember it. Something was wrong, everything was wrong. *What's wrong?* She couldn't exactly put her finger on it in the first moments after waking.

Right. She had really fucked everything up: Cee had read through all her texts and was angry with her for still coming to Coronado this year. Julia was late to arrive and was getting divorced. The air conditioner was broken, and it was unusually hot for May. Was that true, or was she falling into early menopause on top of everything else?

She'd read an article somewhere that said your age at menopause was mostly genetic. Whatever age it hit your mother, it would probably hit you too. But how would she ever have any way to know that? It wasn't something that had occurred to her to ask Grandma Vera as a teenager. She wondered if Julia was already having hot flashes, and maybe that would be something to ask her. If she ever showed up.

She got out of bed, briefly thinking maybe Julia had snuck in in the middle of the night. But her body didn't quite believe it, and the doom pervaded her, making her limbs feel heavy as she lumbered down the hall toward Julia's room and gently pushed open the door. The room was dark and quiet, the bed was still made. No suitcase either. No sign of Julia.

Emily needed fresh air, and outside on the porch, she was greeted by the cool burst of the gray morning. A chilly breeze blew off the ocean; she was suddenly surrounded by low clouds that made the island, and ocean, look almost white. But she exhaled with relief at the temperature change, with the way the cool air instantly made her feel a little lighter. And then she walked slowly into town, to the Clayton's to-go window to order a double Americano and a jelly donut.

Back on the porch a half hour later, she sipped her tall espresso, letting the caffeine slowly seep into her veins and wake her up. It was six thirty here, but nine thirty in Florida. The boys would be at school. Cee would already be at work.

Now didn't seem like the right time to call her wife. Instead, she picked up her phone and typed out a text, staring at it for a moment, deciding if she should hit send: I know you're mad at me, but I didn't cheat . . .

The word *cheat* made her feel sick to her stomach, even typing it like this in a text, and she paused. She heard her wife's angry voice in her head: *An emotional affair is still an affair!*

The sudden squawk of a seagull interrupted her thoughts, and she looked up. A beautiful large gray-and-white bird sat on the top porch step, staring up at her. "Hey, Vera," she said. The bird cocked its head and stared at her hard, like it too agreed with Cee.

"Thanks," Emily said. "Obviously, you would take her side over mine."

It was Julia who had first insisted Grandma Vera was coming back to them as different birds. A few months after Vera died, the night Ted proposed to her, Julia had found herself stalked by a red-tailed hawk that had recently relocated to the tree outside her apartment. She'd noticed it peering in her open window that night, just as Ted got down on one knee. Later, Nora would be walking up Seventh Avenue, to her very first audition in New York City, when a pigeon would poop on her head. Though Julia insisted that was supposed to be good luck, Nora hadn't gotten the part, and then Nora believed Grandma Vera had been trying to tell her it wasn't the right part for her. When Emily first moved to Florida, there was a gorgeous heron that she would often find standing outside her apartment building, eyeing her as she'd walk to class. In a way, it had started as a joke between the sisters, but then, over the years, it had started to feel a little bit real too. Sometimes the three sisters didn't text for months, and then one of them would send a picture of a bird they'd spotted. Grandma Vera says hi!

Emily moved away from the half-composed text to her camera and took a picture of the seagull now. She popped it into the sisters' chat: Grandma V is ready for sisters' week to begin.

No one immediately responded, which told her Nora was likely still asleep and Julia was . . . well . . . she really didn't know. She swallowed back that feeling of doom again as it started rising up in her chest, to her throat, and then she went back to the text she'd typed out to Cee and reread it.

"This isn't right, is it?" she said to the seagull, who continued to stare at her from the step, its head tilted.

She deleted the text and simply typed instead: I miss you.

She hit send quickly before she could change her mind, and then she watched three dots appear briefly, then disappear. She stared at her phone for a few minutes, willing Cee to respond. Something. Anything was better than nothing. But she didn't. At least not right away.

And when Emily looked up again the seagull was gone.

Nora arguably had always had the best bedroom in Grandma Vera's house. Though it was the smallest of the three upstairs bedrooms by far, which was why her sisters had probably stuck her with it in the first place, it was the only one that sat directly in the front of the house, which meant when she opened her blinds each morning, she was looking straight out at the ocean. As a kid, she hadn't really appreciated that, and she hadn't liked the way being in the front of the house had magnified the noise of the military planes and helicopters flying drills just off the beach. But over the years, even the noise had become a thing of comfort. Although she had fallen asleep last night worrying about Julia, she had slept remarkably well, the way she always did in this room, this bed.

But then as she stretched, got up, cracked the blinds this morning, she noticed not the Pacific Ocean but Emily sitting out front on the porch. Alone. Was Julia still not here? What was going on?

Nora went and picked up her phone and saw the text Emily had sent to the sisters' chat nearly an hour earlier: a seagull picture. Julia hadn't responded there. Or to the text Nora had sent her directly yesterday. Nora liked the picture of the bird, and then felt her heart thudding in her chest as she grabbed her robe and ran down the hallway toward Julia's room. But Julia's bed was still made, the room looked untouched, empty. It was now Monday morning. Nora could think of no logical reason why Julia wasn't here, and plenty of terrible reasons ran through her brain instead. She tried to push them away as she ran downstairs, outside to the porch.

"We should call the police," she blurted out, breathless, as she tumbled outside.

Emily turned from her spot on the steps, looked at Nora, and frowned. "What?"

"What if something terrible has happened to her?"

Emily forced herself to take a slow, deep breath, trying not to succumb to Nora's panic. "Why don't we try Ronnie first?" She glanced at her phone. "It's ten thirty on the East Coast. Reasonable time to call a college student, right?"

Nora shrugged. She had no idea. She'd texted Veronica on her birthday last November and sent her a Starbucks gift card, but hadn't interacted with her niece since then.

"I'll call her," Emily said.

"Put her on speaker," Nora said. Unlike Ted, whom Nora had no desire to ever talk to, the sound of her niece's clear, sweet voice always made her happy. And she was worried Emily wasn't going to handle this right. "Let's try not to freak her out," she added.

"Says the one freaking out," Emily retorted.

"Well, maybe the seagull came because she knows something's wrong," Nora said softly, as she listened to the line ringing through Em's speaker. "Vera is trying to tell us something."

Emily gave her a look. "The seagull came because the beach is across the street and seagulls live at—"

"Aunt Em, is that you?" Veronica's sleepy voice suddenly came through the phone, and they immediately stopped arguing about the seagull. "What's wrong?"

"Hey, Ronnie!" Emily said, her voice pitched with false brightness.

"Hi, Ron, I'm here too," Nora chimed in, too cheerful.

"Oh!" Veronica said. "It's the last week in May." Like it suddenly dawned on her exactly where her aunts were and why they were together, calling her. "Is Mom there too?"

Emily and Nora looked at each other, and they locked eyes for a moment, as if battling out who was going to speak next. What exactly they were going to say. Nora sighed and finally spoke. "Well, actually, sweetie, that's why we're calling. Your mom is a little late getting here and we haven't been able to get in touch with her. Do you know where she is?"

Veronica was silent on the other end of the line for what was probably only a few seconds but felt to Nora like an hour. "That's weird," she finally said.

"Right," Emily said. "Your mom is almost always the first one to arrive in Coronado."

"No, I mean . . . I had her on Find My, but now she's just . . . gone."

"What do you mean *gone*?" Emily asked.

Veronica cleared her throat. "Well . . . to be honest. We kind of got in a fight about Find My a few weeks ago. She kept tracking me and like was a little obsessed about knowing where I was. You know how she is." Emily and Nora both murmured in agreement. They did know. "And I um . . ." Veronica continued. "I might have told her to get a life and stop looking on Find My. So, I guess maybe she did?"

Nora tried to decide if Veronica's voice was thick now with alarm or sadness or just sleep. Then she wondered if Veronica even knew about her parents' impending divorce or whether Julia and Ted hadn't told her yet either.

"So she just like didn't show for sisters' week?" Veronica said.

"Well . . ." Emily floundered. "Aunt Nora and I only got here yesterday afternoon. But yeah, she's not here yet."

"And she's not answering our texts," Nora added. "Has she been texting you at least?"

Veronica sighed. "It's been a few weeks. Like I said . . . we kind of got in a fight. And I told her I needed some space."

Nora felt herself flinching, for Julia. She wasn't a mother, and she would probably never understand the complicated mother-daughter relationship, not having had a mother herself. But she knew how much Julia loved Veronica. When she thought about the last thing Julia had yelled at her the previous May, she immediately understood one thing about Julia with her whole heart. That Veronica telling her she needed space had hurt Julia pretty badly. Was that enough to explain her disappearing act now? Or was Nora herself the one to blame? Her entire life she had brought the sisters together whenever they'd fought, and then she'd let this whole year go by without reaching out to Julia to try to fix things. It wasn't that she hadn't wanted to, it was more that she hadn't known how.

"Did you guys ask my dad?" Veronica said.

Nora and Emily exchanged a look. "He wasn't really sure about her travel arrangements," Emily finally said.

"That tracks. They hate each other," Veronica said matter-of-factly.

Hate each other? That felt both strong and unexpected. And Emily and Nora exchanged another look that was part *fucking Ted* and part a newly genuine worry for Julia. Where was she that she hadn't told any of them? How bad had things really been between her and Ted?

"You know, she did this once before," Veronica was saying now. "I think I was like five or six?"

"Did what?" Emily asked. "She has always shown up in Coronado on Sunday for sisters' week. Since we started doing it in 2000."

"Yeah," Veronica said. "But you know about that one year where she just didn't come home *after* your sisters' trip, right?"

Emily raised her eyebrows and Nora shook her head. No. Neither of them knew about this.

"What do you mean *didn't come home*?" Emily asked.

"She came home eventually. But it was like three or four weeks late. I was five or six at the time, so I don't know the whole story. But I just remember there was like this gap of time where it felt like she had disappeared into thin air."

"Disappeared into thin air," Emily repeated softly, suddenly thinking about the secret that she'd accidentally stumbled upon herself when she was a teenager. It threatened to rise up, to spill out of her now. "Your mother would never do that," Emily added. Veronica had been young. Whatever had happened, she was probably remembering it wrong now.

"No, she did," Veronica insisted. "Ask Dad if you don't believe me."

Emily rolled her eyes and Nora chewed on her bottom lip. There was no way in hell either of them was going to call Ted back.

"I asked her about it once, a few years ago. And she said she just needed a little time alone to think. That she kind of freaked out and didn't mean to leave me, but she needed that time to herself. I mean . . . that's probably what's happening now too . . . ?" Veronica's voice trailed off into a question, as if she was suddenly considering the possibilities of where Julia could be. That something more sinister, more terrible could be going on.

"Probably," Nora said too brightly, a lame attempt to reassure her niece.

"I bet if you call her office, they'll know where she is," Veronica said. "She might disappear on us, but she would never do that to work." Nora thought she detected a trace of bitterness in Veronica's voice, but maybe she was imagining it.

"Okay. We'll do that," Emily said. "And if you get in touch with her, will you let us know? Even if she's not planning on coming here this week . . ." She stopped talking, as if saying it out loud could make that a reality. How could Julia just not show up? After all this time? Without even telling them. They had promised each other they would come every year, no matter what. "Nora and I at least want to know she's okay."

"I'm sure she's okay," Nora added, again too brightly. "But, it would be great to know where she is."

"Knowing Mom, she'll probably just . . . show up in Coronado today with some very reasonable and logical explanation," Veronica said. But then she added, her voice a little softer: "Tell her to text me when she does, okay?"

CHAPTER 14

2006

A BROWN SPARROW FLITTED ONTO a wood plank of her back deck while Julia sat out there, the pregnancy test in her shaking hand. She was willing it to turn positive, while also simultaneously terrified that it would finally, actually turn positive again. After two miscarriages in the last two years, she was not yet sure whether a third pregnancy now would be the charm, or another emotional disaster.

Then the sparrow flew up and landed on the patio table, sitting just across from her, staring at her. And she had the brief, ridiculous, hopeful thought that it was Grandma Vera. That she had come to tell Julia that everything was going to be okay.

A plus sign suddenly appeared in the tiny test window, Julia let out a little squeal, and then the sparrow promptly flew away. But Julia knew it in her heart: Vera had come to her just now for a reason. This time the pregnancy would stick. She was going to have another baby!

Still, she took a deep breath and tried to caution herself that it was too early to feel this hopeful. Or to call her sisters and let them know the news. She hadn't had a chance to let them know about the pregnancy before she'd started bleeding, almost two years ago. And then, pregnant again last year, she had felt superstitious enough not to tell anyone except for Ted. She'd made it all the way to ten weeks last time, only for it to fall apart the first week in May, the week Nate was supposed to get married.

But this time it was going to be different, and she felt an urge to tell someone, right now. Or else she might burst. She ran inside the house, her hands still shaking, and picked up the phone in the kitchen to dial Ted at work. After a few rings, it popped to his assistant, Jane. "Oh, hi there, Mrs. Gilbert. Ted isn't at his desk. Can I help you with something?"

Julia cleared her throat. She hated it when people who should know better willfully ignored her choice to keep her own last name. It felt like an insult wrapped inside some veil of stupid politeness. But all she said was, "Can you page him for me, Jane? I really need to talk to him."

"Is everything all right?" Jane asked.

Julia was not about to share this news with Ted's assistant when she hadn't even told her sisters! "Jane, please," she said. "Can you page him?"

Jane hesitated for a moment, like maybe Ted had asked her never to page him, but then she told Julia to hold on.

"Julia?" Ted's voice came through sounding breathless a few moments later. "What's wrong? Are you hurt? Is Veronica okay?"

"Yes, oh my gosh, V is fine. I'm fine. I just . . ." Julia hesitated for a second, realizing the moment she said the words out loud they would be real again. And once this was real, it was, also, tenuous. "We're pregnant," she finally blurted out. Then she tried to tell him about the sparrow that suddenly appeared on the back patio when she was taking the test.

"A what? A sparrow?" Ted interrupted, sounding confused. Of course, the bird thing was between her and her sisters. She'd told Ted once, and he'd laughed her off. Now it seemed he didn't even remember.

"Never mind," she said. "Just a good omen, that's all."

"Julia, that's great. I'm so happy. But can we talk later when I get home? I was in the middle of a—"

"Of course," she cut him off. Her heart suddenly felt like it was in free fall, and she gripped the edge of the kitchen counter, a little dizzy. It was too early for these symptoms to be pregnancy related. This was something else. Maybe she shouldn't have called Ted after all. Maybe she should've just waited until later tonight, when he was home, in front of her, when she could see on his face that he was just as excited or nervous as she was. "I didn't mean to bother you," she said. "I just thought you'd want to know right away. The second I did."

"I did," Ted said gently. "I do. We'll talk more tonight at dinner, okay? I promise."

Julia nodded. "I'll go to the grocery store and get some chicken breasts to make that marsala recipe you like. Before the morning sickness kicks in, and I can't stomach the smell of chicken—"

"Sounds good," Ted said quickly. "I really have to go. Love you."

"Love you too," she said. But he'd already hung up.

Julia held the dead phone in her hand for a moment and focused on her breathing. Ted's career was thriving, and he was busy all the time. She understood that. She had the vaguest longing for what it felt like to be so consumed with work that everything else rushed and swirled around you in a haze. *We're pregnant*, she'd told him. But the truth was, the *we* felt sort of like a joke. *She* was pregnant. And this time, no matter what, *she* was going to make sure it stuck.

Right, Vera? she whispered, glancing out toward the back deck, wishing for just one more look of the sparrow.

Emily had gone out of her comfort zone in her final semester of grad school and was taking a class called Museums and Oceans. Not because she had any particular interest in oceans, but because it was being taught by a visiting professor, Dr. Daniels, who was also the director of America's biggest aquatic museum in Tampa.

Her advisor had suggested it might help Emily stand out to have the personal connection and to learn from someone with real-world experience before graduating.

And as it turned out, it was one of the best decisions Emily had made. Dr. Daniels was young to have her PhD (maybe just a few years older than Emily?), well-spoken, and already established in her field. Still, Emily had no interest in oceans, and so she couldn't quite explain why she found herself in Dr. Daniels's office during her Thursday morning office hours every week, discussing marine life.

Okay, maybe she could explain it.

Dr. Daniels was gorgeous. She had smooth, honey-colored skin; beautiful thick, black, curly hair; and hazel eyes that always seemed to be infused with laughter. When Emily sat in the chair across from her in her office, she felt like she was in the presence of a star, and she couldn't keep herself from smiling. Every time Dr. Daniels laughed, which was pretty often, Emily felt like she was a part of some special inside joke. Dr. Daniels was the kind of person whom her father would refer to as magnetic. Or Julia would call *dazzling*.

When Dr. Daniels invited Emily for coffee at the end of the semester, the week before Emily's graduation, it didn't feel all that strange. It wasn't something any of her other professors had done, but after all the hours they'd spent together in her office, grabbing coffee before Dr. Daniels moved back to Tampa felt only natural. It didn't actually strike Emily as odd, until she showed up at Starbucks and suddenly found her stomach coiling with nerves.

She ordered a decaf latte and found a table by the window. It was ridiculous, to feel nervous before meeting her professor.

But then Dr. Daniels walked in, and the air inside the Starbucks shifted, as if everyone in the room noticed this tall, confident, beautiful woman walking inside, lifting her sunglasses up, laughing that relaxed laugh as she ordered and joked around with the barista. She got her drink, walked over, and sat across from Emily.

"Okay," she said with a smile as she sat down. "So I hope this isn't wildly inappropriate. But I had an ulterior motive in asking you to coffee today."

"Oh?" Emily gulped down a small sip of her decaf latte, wishing it was infused with something stronger that could calm her. She put her coffee down on the table and suddenly had to resist the urge to reach across, to tuck back a curl that had fallen out of her professor's hair clip and in front of her eyes. Emily's fingers twitched and she clasped her hands together.

"Well, I was wondering . . ." Dr. Daniels said slowly.

And Emily thought, *Yes, I want to kiss you too.*

And then she said, "I was wondering how you might feel about coming to work for me?"

Work for her? An aquatic museum wasn't at all what Emily had in mind for her career, but working alongside Dr. Daniels each day suddenly felt like a dream job. "I'd love to," Emily heard herself saying.

Nora was opening in her first show in New York City in the middle of May. A one-week run as Juliet in an off-off-Broadway musical adaptation of *Romeo and Juliet.* When she found out she'd gotten the role, she'd immediately called both her sisters and invited them to come to opening night.

"I'm sorry, I can't this time," Emily said. "I'm going to start a new job in Tampa, and I need to move before we go to Coronado."

"Sorry," Julia said flatly. "You know I can't leave Veronica twice in May."

"Bring Veronica," Nora suggested. "She loved *Beauty and the Beast.*"

"But is this show really kid-appropriate?"

Nora didn't like the way Julia sounded, like she was chastising her. But she was also probably right. A show ending in double teen suicide likely wasn't *kid-appropriate* at all.

"It's just a short train ride for you, Julia," Nora wheedled. "If you can't make it for opening night, then at least come for the Saturday matinee when Ted can watch Veronica."

"Ted works most Saturdays, and I just . . . I really can't right now, Nora." Julia breathed the words softly across the line. "I have a lot going on. I'll catch your next one."

Nora vacillated from joy to seething with rage in the twenty minutes since talking to her sisters. She considered for a moment calling Dad, inviting him to opening night. But she remembered what a downer he'd been after he'd come to see her in *Beauty and the Beast*, and she didn't want him to dim what was left of her excitement. She worried he would focus on the *off-off* part of her news and not on the fact that she'd actually gotten a starring role in a very hip and inventive take on Shakespeare.

And besides, she told herself, it didn't matter. It didn't matter if no one came to support her. She would make her dreams come true all on her own.

Nora was still telling herself this by opening night a month later. It became something like a chant as she repeated it in her head, slowly, rhythmically. Even after the first performance ended to a standing ovation and the rest of the cast wandered outside to greet family members who gave them hugs and flowers. Even then. *It doesn't matter. It doesn't matter.*

She snuck out of the back entrance, suddenly wanting to avoid everyone. She rushed out without removing her stage makeup and was eager to get home to wash her face and undo her hair from the braided buns. It was a chilly night for May, and rainy on top of that. She pulled up the hood of her raincoat and let herself out onto the cool, wet sidewalk. And then as she walked back toward the front of the theater to catch her train, she suddenly saw a woman walking out the front exit who looked remarkably like Julia.

Had Julia come to surprise her last-minute?

Nora sloshed through a puddle to catch up to her, but when

she touched the woman on the arm the woman turned her head, and it was clear, up close, that she was much too old to be Julia. Maybe she bore a small resemblance, but she had wrinkles around her eyes and her mouth that Julia wouldn't have for at least twenty more years.

"I'm sorry," Nora said. "I thought you were—"

"Nora?" The woman said her name softly.

"How do you . . . know my name?" Nora suddenly felt chilled from the rain and she shivered.

The woman stared at her for a moment. Then she held up her program from the show. "I should be more polite—Ms. May. I read it in your bio. You were really great up there. You should be proud."

Nora thanked her and slowly let go of her arm.

And then the woman turned and walked away before Nora could ask her anything else, before Nora could say the crazy thought that was running through her head: If their mother were alive, she imagined she would look just like this woman. Sound just like this woman. Show up for Nora on opening night of an off-off-Broadway play, even if no one else in her family would.

But of course, that was ridiculous. Because her mother had been dead for over twenty-six years. Exactly the same amount of time that Nora had been alive.

Still, Nora actually thought about saying something to Emily and Julia about this strange encounter when they all arrived in Coronado a few weeks later. She had it there on the tip of her tongue as she got out of the taxi, that there was a woman who'd come to her show who, if she hadn't known better . . . *if she hadn't known better*, she might have thought was their mother.

But Nora was the last sister to arrive, and the moment she walked in the door, Julia held out a schedule. "You're late!" she exclaimed, like it was Nora's fault the flight had landed with an almost two-hour delay. She shoved the schedule into Nora's free hand before she had even let go of her suitcase. Nora glanced at it, and they appeared to have already missed the first few line items on Julia's agenda:

Ice cream cones from MooTime.

Walk on the beach.

Dinner reservation at the Brigantine at 6.

S'mores at 7:30.

(Dammit, Nora had forgotten to bring the graham crackers this year—she'd have to stop at Vons and buy some.)

"If you hurry, we can still make our dinner reservation," Julia said, glancing nervously at her watch. Nora fought back the urge to tell her that the world wasn't going to end if they missed it.

"I'm starving," Emily grumbled. "Nora, put your stuff upstairs and let's go."

Nora swallowed back the words that she had wanted to say to them for weeks. "Just let me change really quick," she said instead.

"Do you ever think about Mom?" Nora asked Julia later that week.

The morning clouds had burnt off early, by nine, the sky was a brilliant blue, and Julia had even agreed to cross off the day trip to the San Diego Zoo from her schedule in favor of pulling the sand chairs and umbrella out of the small shed and lugging them down to the edge of the water.

Julia and Nora sat there now, toes a safe distance from the cool stingray-laden Pacific, staring out at the sparkling crested blue. Nora was sipping a mimosa she'd made up at the house, and Emily had wandered off down the beach alone for a walk with hers. Julia sipped just orange juice.

"What?" Julia asked, like she had misunderstood Nora's question over the rush of the tide. Though, she had heard Nora perfectly well. She just needed a minute to form an answer. A trick from her attorney days. Ask them to repeat the question while you worked on formulating the best thing to say.

"Mom," Nora repeated. "Do you ever think about her?"

"Well . . ." Julia still floundered and tried to ignore the slight cramping in her abdomen that had been there off and on since she'd woken up. "I mean, of course, I think about her sometimes. I'm sure we all do."

Nora nodded. "But do you think about what she might be like now? You know, if she were still alive."

Julia shook her head. "Why would you ask that?"

Nora shrugged. "No reason, really. It's just . . . I wonder what Mom would have thought about my show. Like if she would have come up to me afterward and told me she was proud or something?"

Shoot. Her show. Julia had been in such a trance of hope and wonder and worry, of prenatal vitamins and fretting over every small pang, that she had forgotten about Nora's show after Nora had called to invite her. She should've at least sent flowers or a fruit basket or called her after opening night or something. "She would've definitely been proud," Julia said emphatically now. "We're all proud of you, Nora. I was really sad to miss this one. I'll for sure catch your next one."

"Sad to miss what?" Emily asked, plopping back down into her sand chair and setting her empty Solo cup down in the sand.

"Nora's show," Julia said.

"Yeah, I was too." Emily pulled her sunglasses down and put her head back against the chair like she was about to take a nap.

"I mean it," Julia said, realizing it made her sound even more disingenuous to say that. She wanted to tell Nora and Emily right then, why she had been so spacey and distant, why the last two years had seemingly slipped away from her, outside of her. But then she felt that small cramp in her stomach again, and she bit her lip. She was scheduled for a twelve-week ultrasound next week. She would wait and call them both with the news then, and she would explain everything.

"And not that either of you asked yet," Emily said. "But my new job seems really great."

Shoot. Julia had forgotten about that too. Though at least she'd remembered to send a card for Em's graduation from grad school. And she'd replied all to the email Dad had sent with pictures from the ceremony saying how great Emily looked in her cap and gown.

"That's really awesome, Em." Nora picked up her Solo cup of mimosa and held it up in a toast now. "To your new job," she said.

"And to our little baby sister becoming a bigger star," Emily added, raising her own empty cup to tap Nora's.

Julia picked up her cup of orange juice and tapped it gently against each of her sisters'. "And to May sisters and many more May weeks in Coronado," she said. In her head, she silently added: *And to the new niece or nephew I'll introduce you to by this time next year.*

Julia's flight was the last to leave this year, and so the house was already quiet and still when she felt that awful familiar trickle as she stood from the breakfast table. She ran to the powder room, hoping against all hope that she had mistaken the sensation for something else. An accidental spill of water from God knows where, or milk from her cereal. Or that it was her imagination, that it wasn't happening. *It couldn't be happening.*

But as she sat down on the toilet she heard, and felt, the rush of liquid, and when she looked down, the toilet water was completely red, and she heard herself let out a small scream that sounded like it came from somewhere else. Somewhere outside of her. Shrill and distant and ethereal.

This can't be happening again. Here. Now. What about the sparrow?

She knew she needed to go to the hospital, but her sisters were already gone. Ted was thousands of miles away. She was all alone. In this house, in this realization about what was happening to her body. Again.

She tried to stand and was struck with a wave of dizziness. Then, another rush of blood, into the toilet water. She hadn't bled this much the other times. Something was very wrong. How was she even going to get out of this bathroom, much less to the hospital alone?

Her mind felt foggy, but in some distant space in her head, she had the thought that if she stayed here, bleeding like this, she might die. But what was she supposed to do?

Get to the phone. Call an ambulance.

The window next to the toilet was half-open, letting in the damp morning air, and then she heard the sudden squawk of a seagull.

She looked up, and the large gray-and-white bird sat on top of the white picket fence that divided their backyard from Nate's. It squawked again before it flew away, and then she could see that Nate was outside, just beyond where the seagull had been. Hanging his wet suit to dry.

"Nate." His name croaked out of her, too soft for him to hear it at first. "Nate!" She said it louder.

He stopped for a moment, turned, looked around.

"Nate!" she screamed as loud as she could.

"Jules?" He looked around, still unsure where the sound was coming from.

Then everything felt hazy, dark.

I'm not okay! she cried out. Or maybe she didn't manage to say that part out loud. Maybe she just thought about that time he'd told her once, if she was ever not okay, she had to promise to tell him.

But the next thing she knew, Nate was wrapping her in a beach towel, picking her up, carrying her over his shoulder.

She woke up sometime later, in a hospital.

She was certain of that. It was definitely a hospital room, white and sterile and bleak, and there was the sound of a monitor beeping somewhere close by.

What hospital she was in, how she had gotten here, exactly, she wasn't entirely sure.

"Jules?" Nate's voice. She turned her head, and he was sitting in a chair across the room. Then she vaguely remembered: Nate carrying her into an emergency room, her signing off that he could talk to the doctor on her behalf.

He offered a sad smile. And stood and walked toward her bed.

"What happened?" she asked him, though she knew. She felt it in her gut. The baby was gone. Again. For the third time. Nothing else mattered but this.

"You've been out for a little bit . . . You should talk to the doctor," he said gently. "I can go find him."

He started to move toward the door, but she reached out to grab his arm. "No, just tell me what happened."

"I . . . I'm not a doctor," Nate said weakly.

"Tell me!" she demanded. "The baby didn't make it, did it?" He hesitated for another moment, and then nodded slowly, his face looking grim. Was there more? "What else?"

"Do you want me to get Ted on the phone?" he asked gently.

"No, I want you to tell me every last goddamn thing the doctor told you." Her voice shook. She never spoke like this, never lost control. But she felt her whole body trembling and she couldn't get it to stop.

Nate exhaled slowly, sat down on the side of the bed, and gripped her shoulders gently. "It's not good, Jules," he said softly. "You lost a lot of blood. They had to give you two pints. You're going to be fine with some rest, but the doctor said there's too much scarring to . . ." His voice trailed off, and he couldn't or wouldn't finish the thought.

"Too much scarring to what?" she whispered, though maybe deep down she already knew the answer. She already understood that she had wanted too much, she had asked for too much. She had a child, a beautiful, healthy five-year-old child. But why did it have to be too much to give her a sister? To want an Emily, or a Nora, for her too?

"He said you can't get pregnant again." Nate was still talking. His words soft, precise. She heard them and they cut right through her, making her feel chilled. "That next time it could be worse," Nate said. "You could . . . die."

"No," she said. "That can't be right."

"Do you want me to call Ted?" he asked again.

But she didn't answer him. She couldn't find any more words to speak. All she could do was grab on to him, bury her head in his chest, and sob.

It wasn't that she intended to not go home, not at first.

She spent a night in the hospital and then she was too weak to even think about flying home by herself. Nate took her back to his house and she slept through several days in his guest room while he cooked her bone broth and brought it to her in bed, begging her to take small sips.

She was still bleeding, and for those few days she felt pale and listless enough to wonder if she still might die. If she needed more blood. But it felt easier to sleep than to ask those questions. And so, she kept on closing her eyes and going back to sleep. Waking, sipping soup. Sleeping again.

Before she knew it, a week had passed. She had mostly stopped bleeding except for spotting here and there. She finally got up out of bed to eat a bowl of soup at Nate's kitchen table, and then she noticed, through the open living room window, that a new family had come to stay for vacation next door at Grandma Vera's house. She watched them—a mom, a dad, and two perfect red-haired girls bouncing around on the porch. *Sisters.*

She didn't forget about Ted and Veronica, not exactly. Nate told her that he had called Ted right away to let him know what had happened. Then called him again when she left the hospital, told him that she was safe and just needed a little time to get herself together before she flew home. She just nodded blankly at Nate, because she couldn't face Ted. Worse, she couldn't truly face herself. And she pushed all thoughts of reality to the back of her mind. As long as she stayed in Coronado, in Nate's guest room, with Nate making her soup, then reality didn't have to truly exist.

When she felt strong enough, she walked along the beach early each morning, for days and days, listening to the rush of the waves and squawks of the seagulls, and in these small moments, she could maybe remember how to breathe again, how to live without the all-consuming guilt and grief she felt pushing down in her chest.

Somewhere in the back of her mind it occurred to her, it was June, her first time ever in Coronado in June. But it seemed the June gloom was much like the May gray: cool mornings with low clouds hovering across the water. Somehow this made it feel like no time was passing, as one gray day rolled lazily into the next.

Nate insisted on walking with her along the beach, like he was afraid if she went alone, she would walk into the ocean and never come back. She wouldn't have. (At least, she didn't think she would've.) But it was nice to have his quiet company by her side, to have his hand gently reach for her arm when she suddenly felt weak and would have to slow down or stop to catch her breath.

It was nice to hear him say *Jules*, first thing in the morning when she walked downstairs and last thing at night before she walked upstairs to go to bed.

It was nice to sit on the couch next to him and watch *Some Like It Hot*, to see right there in black and white the way this island hadn't changed in so many years. The ocean still beat back against the shore, the Hotel del Coronado still sat like a white-and-red gem. Nate was still here too, warm and full of light, the way he had been her entire life.

And when the movie ended, when Osgood says, *Well, nobody's perfect*, Julia knew it was supposed to be a joke, but she heard it this time like it was directed at her, a rebuke. A lesson.

Nobody's perfect.

She suddenly thought about Emily, about Nora. About disappearing into herself.

And then she turned to Nate and asked him, "Can you drive me to Santa Monica?"

"What's in Santa Monica?" he asked.

Julia just stared at him, and his brown eyes held on to her face, etched with worry. She knew she had to tell him the truth, that after he had been so kind to her these last two weeks, she trusted him more completely than she had ever really trusted anyone.

CHAPTER 15

2007

NORA WAS THE FIRST sister to spot the announcement in her mail.

She'd been sending out headshots, trying to get a new agent, and frequently checking her mailbox for responses that had yet to trickle in. When she saw the envelope in her mailbox, with Nate's return address in the top-left corner, it felt weirdly reminiscent of the Save the Date that had arrived a few years earlier. *Oh God*, she thought. *Please don't let him be engaged again.*

She tore open the envelope on her walk back up the stairs to her apartment and pulled out the thick white card from inside:

NATE AND HEIDI ANNOUNCE THE BIRTH OF THEIR DAUGHTER:

MALLORY GRACE

6 LBS 6 OUNCES, 19 INCHES

5/2/2007 AT 11:53 P.M.

Nora ran the rest of the stairs, and she was out of breath, her hands shaking as she picked up the cordless phone and punched in Julia's number.

"Who the hell is Heidi?" she said as soon as Julia picked up.

"What?" Julia asked. "Nora? Is everything all right?"

"Nate had a baby, with a woman named Heidi?"

"What are you talking about?" Clearly, she hadn't gotten her mail yet.

"I got a birth announcement in the mail. Nate and someone named Heidi had a freaking baby. You didn't already know? Don't you talk to Nate about the rental and stuff?"

Julia cleared her throat. "Not in a . . . few months. I haven't spoken to him lately . . . Nothing has come up that we've needed to talk about."

Somehow more surprising than Nate having a baby with a woman she'd never heard of was the fact that Julia didn't know a single thing about it. Nora wondered if Julia was telling her the truth. "So Nate really didn't tell you, about any of this?"

Julia sighed so deeply in response that Nora sensed she was being honest.

"You really didn't know?" Nora repeated.

Julia was silent on the other end of the line for another moment and then she said softly, "Nate has . . . a baby? This isn't some kind of a joke?"

"Go check your mail," Nora said. "And then call me back."

Emily sat at her desk, in her tiny office in a small upstairs room above the aquarium portion of the Museum of the Ocean. She was trying to figure out how to use the museum's new online system to request PTO for the whole last week in May for her sisters' trip, when her boss, Dr. Daniels, walked in without knocking. It wasn't unusual, as they had formed an easy sort of comradery in the last few months, and Emily often forgot that her boss was actually her superior.

She plopped down in the folding chair on the opposite side of Emily's desk and sighed deeply. "Do you have any Tums?"

"Tums?" Emily opened up her bottom desk drawer, rifled around in the mess, but came up with only a half-empty bottle of Motrin. She held it up as an offering, and her boss shook her head.

"No, it's not cramps. It's full-on nausea, Em."

"Maybe you're pregnant?" Emily joked. She knew, even as the words popped out of her mouth, that it wasn't a wholly appropriate joke. With her boss. But not much had been appropriate between the two of them these last few months. It's not that they were sleeping together, or, God, even anything close. Her boss was married, and any attraction (which Emily would deny altogether, if pressed) was one way. Still, there had been many moments like this: walking in without knocking. Or the accidental brush of a hand as they walked by each other, or the very intentional hug. And Emily knew that her boss's marriage was rocky at best, she had confided that much to her. They'd gotten married young straight out of college, high school sweethearts, and twelve years of marriage later things didn't quite have the same shine.

Emily never had many close female friends in her life, aside from her sisters. Her acquaintances from high school and college had come and gone, and years later, there was no one she cared enough about to keep in regular touch with. So, she had told herself, again and again, that that's what this was. That's what she was feeling every time her boss walked into a room and suddenly made her feel warm: friendship. Here, at thirty-one years old, Emily had made her first bona fide friend.

"God, maybe I am pregnant," her boss said now, standing up and clutching her stomach. "I've been telling myself it was food poisoning, but . . . I've been off all week."

Emily raised her eyebrows, suddenly finding the whole idea of what she would've done to have gotten pregnant vaguely annoying. "You could take a test," she said, opening and then closing her bottom drawer again quickly. She definitely did not have a pregnancy test stashed away among this mess. It was more that she suddenly felt the need to do something with her hands.

Her boss nodded. "Would you go out and buy me one? I know it's not your job . . . but you don't mind, do you?"

Emily shook her head, though she actually did mind. Not

doing the favor, but somehow the act of being complicit in whatever this eventually turned out to be. A baby, a stomach flu. She didn't want any part of either one. But she didn't say that out loud. Instead, she stood up and said, "Sure . . . is there like any specific kind I should buy or . . . ?"

Her boss shrugged and then slunk back down in the chair and sighed. "Just get the cheapest one. Or, I don't know, maybe get the most expensive. Is that more accurate?"

Emily let out a dry laugh and shook her head. "I'll get the priciest one and expense it."

"Ha, you're hysterical. My purse is downstairs on my desk. Grab a twenty out of there and use that."

Emily put her hands on her hips and just stared for a moment before moving toward the door.

"What?" her boss asked, and raised her eyebrows. "Am I breaking labor laws by asking you to do this for me?"

Emily shook her head. "I mean . . ." she started, and then hesitated. "I thought you and Rick weren't even getting along?"

"We're not."

"So how could you be . . . ?"

"Oh, Em, you really were born yesterday, weren't you?"

Emily reddened at the teasing insult. "Never mind," she said. "I'll be back in twenty minutes."

"Everyone is having babies!" Emily bemoaned a few weeks later, stretched out on the large white leather sectional in the Ocean Boulevard house. Nora was peering through the window in the dining room, trying to get a glimpse of Heidi, who was walking back and forth on Nate's porch with what allegedly was a few-weeks-old baby but sounded, from here through the open window, more like a squawking goose.

"Not everyone," Julia said quietly from her place at the other end of the sofa. Neither of her sisters picked up on the weight of her words, or noticed as Julia turned away. She pulled her laptop from her bag and powered it on, pretending she had to urgently check her emails.

"Damn!" Nora squealed from across the room. "She's cute!"

"All babies are cute," Julia said flatly.

"Not the baby, dumbass. Heidi."

Emily got off the couch and walked to the window to take a look; Julia stared at her laptop screen and scrolled through her inbox.

"Julia, get over here," Emily commanded her.

But Julia didn't move. She had no desire to see this *cute* woman whom Nate had somehow met, gotten together with, and had a baby with all since she'd left him in the middle of the night in Santa Monica last June. They'd been avoiding each other ever since, having communicated only through a few emails about the rental over the course of the entire year. Still, Julia felt hurt. She knew she deserved this, after the way she'd left him. But the fact that Nate's entire life had changed in a whirlwind of nine months, and he hadn't even called her to tell her about any of it, made her stomach ache. She felt it viscerally, deep in her core, in the empty space inside of her that would never grow another baby. She'd had no idea a *Heidi* even existed, much less that Nate had made a baby with her, before Nora had called about the birth announcement a few weeks earlier.

"Let's go over there," Emily said. "I'm dying to meet her. She looks nicer than Becca, thank God."

Nora nodded in agreement and grabbed her flip-flops from by the door. "Jul?" she said, casting a look at Julia, who had not budged one inch from the couch. "Aren't you coming?"

Julia shook her head. "I'm tired from the early flight. I'm gonna rest." Emily and Nora exchanged a look, and Julia forced a smile. "I'll meet her later this week, I'm sure."

Nora frowned for a quick second, but Emily slipped her feet into her bright orange Crocs and opened the front door. The two of them ran down the porch and across the yard, and through the open window Julia could hear the sound of an unfamiliar woman's laughter. Pure and high and sweet-sounding. *Cute?* From her laugh, Heidi sounded glamorous and beautiful. Julia wondered how they'd met, and then she quickly shook the thought away. *It doesn't matter.*

With her sisters out of the house for a few moments, Julia got off the couch and picked up their schedules from the dining room table. She took a pen from her purse and then added activities to all the free time that could've potentially gone to Nate the rest of this week. She could not withstand a dinner at his house, smiling at Heidi and their baby. A trip out on the sailboat, seeing the glow on his face now that he was in love again.

Outwardly, a year after her final miscarriage, Julia looked whole again, healed. *Normal.* But inside, she often still felt ripped in two, like maybe she'd left her real self with Nate back in a hotel in Santa Monica, and only her bloodless shadow had been walking around her real life ever since.

She had done it before, put something that had happened between her and Nate in the vault. Then she saw him again the next year and pretended like nothing had ever happened. But she couldn't bear to do that right now. Every emotion still felt too raw, and she didn't have it in her to pretend this week.

Julia added in extra walks. A dinner at Peohe's on the bay side of the island, which they had never tried. A day trip to SeaWorld, which they also had never been to but it seemed somehow relevant to Emily's new job. An afternoon stroll through Balboa Park to see the beautiful jacaranda trees in full purple bloom this time of year. Followed by an evening jaunt up to the La Jolla Playhouse to watch the world premiere of *Carmen*, which she knew Nora would be thrilled about. She had this strange feeling that if she kept her sisters entertained, neither of them would think to ask her about why she was avoiding Nate.

And avoid him was exactly what she did that week. Julia went out of her way not to go next door. Nate didn't come over to say hi either, or ask her to take a walk, like he usually did.

Nora and Emily would report back that Nate seemed tired and that Heidi seemed very nice. But Julia would not witness any of this for herself.

And by the time she saw Nate again the following summer, she would have convinced herself that she had almost forgotten what had happened just before she'd left him in Santa Monica. Almost.

CHAPTER 16

2008

EMILY WAS SITTING AT her desk at the museum when her cell phone rang with an unfamiliar Los Angeles number. Emily briefly thought, *Santa Monica*. She hesitated a moment before answering.

"Emily, it's me." A woman's voice came through her new smartphone, and Emily knew it sounded familiar. Her heart beat wildly in her chest for another moment before she placed it.

"Cara?" she said softly, suddenly wishing she hadn't answered the phone, or that she had taken the time to transfer all her old flip phone contacts into her new iPhone.

"It's been a while, huh?" Cara's easy laugh breezed in through the phone, and Emily swallowed back the bile rising in her throat.

"What do you want?" she said.

Cara didn't say anything for a moment, and then she said, "Can we meet?"

"I don't live in Boston anymore," Emily said quickly.

"Oh?" Cara sounded surprised. Emily resisted the urge to cry out that she hadn't, in fact, lived in Boston in years! "So where are you right now?"

"I went to grad school in Florida and now I work at a museum down here. Tampa." Emily realized she was giving away too much information. Telling Cara things she didn't need to know. But it all popped out nonetheless. Then she repeated herself, trying to keep her voice stern: "What do you want, Cara?"

"I just wanted to see you before I move back to LA," Cara said. Emily let that knowledge sink in for a moment. Cara was moving back to LA. She wondered how her mom's health was but she couldn't bring herself to ask. "I know what I did . . . was wrong," Cara added.

"It was years ago," Emily said brusquely. "Water under the bridge." That wasn't true. When she thought about the way Cara had just disappeared and started ignoring her, it still felt fresh enough to sting, like no time had passed.

Cara was silent on the other end of the line for a moment. Then she said, "Do you still go to San Diego every May with your sisters?"

Emily considered whether she should lie. But Cara had known her well enough for a brief period of time that she didn't think lying about this would be believable. "Yes," she said. "Of course."

"I'll be back in LA by then. I could drive down and meet you," Cara said.

"I don't think that's the best idea," Emily said.

"Are you with someone else?" Cara asked.

Emily suddenly thought about her boss, who was currently out on maternity leave, at home with her twins. They'd talked on the phone every night this week. Her boss said she was calling about work, but then no words had been exchanged about the museum. "No," Emily said. "I'm not with anyone else. Not that it's any of your business."

"Of course not," Cara said softly. "So how about you just let me buy you lunch then, in May?"

Julia's BlackBerry buzzed on her desk, but knee-deep in preparing for her first hearing, she ignored it. She had only very recently come back to work in family law part-time, in an effort to still be able to pick up Veronica from school at a reasonable hour each day and then be there to make her dinner too. But a hearing, especially her first custody hearing, meant all bets were off.

Her BlackBerry buzzed again, and she finally grabbed it if only to make it stop. *Shoot. Veronica's school.* She quickly answered the call and the school nurse promptly informed her that Veronica had thrown up, just after lunch, and needed to be picked up. Julia said she would be right over.

Ted had been supportive about her going back to work, encouraging even, about her new desire to focus on custody cases, but still, he'd never quite offered to pick up any of the slack at home. Not that Julia had asked him to either. In her own mind, working *part-time* meant she could still be a full-time mother to Veronica like she wanted.

But now, today, she had this hearing to prep for. He'd said at breakfast he had an easy day, a golf outing with a client in the afternoon. He could probably leave that now to get Veronica at school.

She called him but he sent her straight to voicemail, and Julia sighed.

She considered trying him again, knowing he would pick up if he suspected a true emergency. She knew he cared, even if his work often seemingly came first. But things had felt strained between them in this new reality where they were no longer trying for a baby. It wasn't Ted's fault—he'd tried to initiate sex a few times in the first few months after the last miscarriage, and she'd pushed him away, not ready. But by the time she maybe was ready again last year, he'd stopped trying. And she'd felt too shy to initiate things with him. Recently they'd fallen into a place where it felt like they swept by each other rather than toward each other.

Her phone buzzed with a text: Everything okay? I have bad signal and just saw I missed your call.

Yeah. V threw up at school and the nurse called me. One of us has to pick her up.

Oh god, vomiting 😫

When she'd had terrible morning sickness, Ted had sometimes

thrown up right along with her. That's how sensitive he was to puke. Hopefully just something she ate, Julia texted back.

Do you want me to go get her? Ted texted. I know you have a busy afternoon.

She hesitated before she responded, having a rush of mom guilt, suddenly picturing her poor baby feeling sick. What if Ted felt too sick himself to rub her back, or hold a cool washcloth to her forehead? Or clean her up if she needed him to? No. I'll figure it out. I just wanted to let you know what was going on.

Are you sure? Ted asked.

Yeah, I can go get her and then I'll work at home with her. How exactly that was going to work, she wasn't sure, but first hearing be damned. She couldn't let V down. She would figure it out. She always did.

And then she grabbed her purse and her jacket and she ran out the door.

Nora cursed as she dropped her flip phone running up the steps of the Union Square subway station on her way to an audition. The back of the top half of the phone popped off, and she ducked into Duane Reade to buy duct tape to reattach it. She hastily taped and walked with purpose toward the tiny theater on Thirteenth Street, hoping this wasn't some sort of pre-audition bad omen. It wasn't bird poop on her head, she told herself. It wasn't spraining her ankle running for the train (as she had stupidly done six months ago). Still, since her role as Juliet two years ago, she'd had only dribs and drabs of real theater work. This audition was the best shot she'd had in a while.

She'd most recently been earning money giving voice lessons to middle and high school students. It was better than waitressing, and it was (mostly) paying her bills along with her supplemental income from the Coronado rental. It had only taken her mentioning music lessons for Dad to suggest maybe returning to college for a music education degree. She'd told him she'd think about it, but even rehashing it in her mind now, again, felt like giving up. She often clung to the words that Nate had said to her once on a sailboat just off Coronado years ago: *Anything worth having takes a lot of hard work. And you can't give up on your dream, Nora.* Still, she was only one year shy of thirty now, and she knew she couldn't keep doing this hustle for work forever. If enough time passed, she'd quite simply be too old to get her big break.

She pushed that thought aside, shoved her taped-up phone in her purse, and entered the theater. She was auditioning for a small off-Broadway revival of a little-known Barbra Streisand role from the sixties. It would be a perfect fit and would've been a dream role in Grandma Vera's eyes—something that gave her just the littlest bit of hope as she pushed on the glass door and walked inside. Nearly running right into Leo.

"Nora." He caught her elbows, righting her so she didn't trip, and stared at her for a moment. It had been a few years since they'd seen each other, or even talked for that matter. Their last communication was a voicemail he'd left her the May week she was in Coronado with her sisters, just after Nate and Becca had broken off their engagement. Spending that week with Nate had somehow refocused her to want more, to expect more from any man she would be spending time with. And she'd never returned his call upon getting back to New York. Well, shit, was he the producer her new agent, Stella, had mentioned, who'd asked if she'd come in to audition?

She cleared her throat. "Leo!" She forced enthusiasm. "Gosh, it's been a minute. You look . . . great."

Annoyingly, he did, in fact, look great. Aging agreed with him, the way it seemed that age could only agree with men. The tiniest threads of gray running through his beard, peppering his thick, wavy brown hair, made him look distinguished, kind. Smart. Nora had thus far in her life found one gray hair in her own scalp, freaked out, and promptly plucked it out. That's all she needed, to go gray early.

Leo smiled at her now, and she felt something ping in her chest, remembering how he'd always made her feel good about herself. "You look great too," he said. "How have you been?"

"I've been good," she lied. "You know, getting by. Still trying for that big break."

"I'm so glad you made it in to read today. I thought you would be the perfect Miss Marmelstein."

So he *was* the producer who'd called her agent. She bit her lip, wondering if he'd brought her here because he'd missed her. He let go of her and she noticed, as he lowered his arms, that he wore the thick gold band on his ring finger. *Still married.*

"I'm really pulling for you to get this." Leo was still talking. "Go in there and give it your all, but I have your back, kiddo." He shot her another easy smile.

And then she struggled to recall why she hadn't called him back three years ago. Why in the hell shouldn't she audition for him or let him help her now? She suddenly remembered what had attracted her to Leo in the first place, that in spite of everything he had working against him (and the fact that he had a wife and a kid), he always, deep down, truly seemed to believe in her in a way no one else did or could.

"Thanks," she told him. "I really appreciate this. It was so nice of you to think of me for this part."

He nodded. "I've missed you a lot, kiddo," he said.

And then she walked into the audition, trying to push that comment out of her mind. She told herself this was about her. Not him.

A month later, Julia sat on the white leather sectional in the Ocean Boulevard house, watching Nora's eyebrows knit together as she reviewed a script. Nora had sent both her and Emily an email to let them know that rehearsals on her new show were set to begin the week she got back from Coronado, and so she would need time in the schedule this week to prepare.

Emily hadn't responded. Julia had replied all: No problem. We can work it in—congrats, superstar!

But Nora had only been here an hour, and she already seemed a million miles away. Julia had tried to sound super supportive over email, still feeling guilty about the way she'd totally missed Nora's last big stage role. But now she wished Nora would put her script away, at least for a few days. And she hoped she could convince her after Emily got here. Julia had arrived in Coronado feeling oddly unmoored and she needed Nora to be her normal fun self.

Ted and Veronica had gone to the Hamptons for the week, and Julia had silenced her BlackBerry. She'd decided she would check it only periodically, just in case any family emergencies should arise. (Ted promised her they would not. And Julia did feel he had this one week a year down pretty well at this point.) Then Ted, half-serious, had said to her right before she left to catch her early-morning flight: *Don't disappear on us again, Julia.*

He'd said it like it was a joke, but she'd found it entirely unfunny on all fronts. That wasn't what had happened two years ago, and Ted knew it. He'd known where she was the whole time she was gone. Nate had called him from the hospital, and then again from his house the following week. Ted had known she'd needed the mental, emotional, and physical space to process the way her body had betrayed her. Two years later, his joke about it made it all feel raw again. And it irritated her that he could find humor in her falling apart.

"Well, you neither," she'd chided back earlier this morning, trying to keep her voice light. "Don't you fall in love with the Hamptons and leave me."

Ted had groaned and rolled over in bed, pulling the covers over his head. They both knew he hated the beach, and that he didn't even remotely love the Hamptons the way Julia loved Coronado—he loved that his mom would dote on Veronica for the week while Julia was away. And that's why he went. And that's why Julia hated that he went. And that's probably why he made sure he *definitely* went.

"Have a good week. Love you," Julia had said as she'd wheeled her suitcase out of their bedroom.

He'd probably said *Love you* back, but she was already down the hallway and didn't hear him say anything.

"Have you guys talked to Nate yet?" Emily said later that night, as she roasted their marshmallows over the backyard firepit.

Nora had finally put her script away. Julia had had a glass of wine at dinner and her cheeks were red now, her face more relaxed as she sat wrapped in an afghan on the outdoor sofa, waiting for Emily to prepare their treats.

Nora shook her head. Julia said, "A few weeks ago. Why?" But the truth was she hadn't actually *talked* to Nate in almost two years at this point. They'd emailed. Mostly business about the rental, with the exception of a few pictures he'd sent of Mallory's first birthday a few weeks earlier, and one she'd sent him last fall of Veronica's first day of second grade. It felt safer that way. Email.

"Did he tell you about Heidi?" Emily said, squishing a melted marshmallow and chocolate in between two graham crackers. She handed the first one to Nora.

"What about Heidi?" Nora asked, licking the melted chocolate off her forefinger before taking a bite.

"She left," Emily said, lowering her voice to a whisper, so on the off chance Nate walked out into his backyard he wouldn't hear. They all glanced next door briefly, and the house was dark and quiet. He didn't appear to be home.

"Left how?" Julia frowned.

"Like moved out in the middle of the night, note on the kitchen counter that she wasn't equipped to be a mom, *left*." Emily handed the second s'more to Julia. But Julia's stomach churned and she suddenly wasn't hungry.

"How do you know this?" Julia felt stunned in disbelief and did not immediately take a bite of the s'more.

"I ran into him earlier, when I was walking on the beach, and he told me." Emily shrugged. "So neither of you knew?" Emily made a pained face.

Julia thought about Mallory, what it would be like for her to grow up without her mother around, and then, later, to know that she had a mother who'd once abandoned her. She thought about Nate, who was suddenly, deeply in the trenches of parenthood all alone. She put her s'more down on a napkin, unable to take even the smallest bite.

"What kind of a woman would do something like that, abandon her own daughter?" Nora sounded aghast, but she finished off the last of her s'more with one final bite. Julia averted her eyes, focusing on her magenta polished toenails, and Emily was concentrating very hard at assembling the final s'more for herself.

"A selfish fucking bitch," Emily said sharply. "That's who."

The harshness of the words made Julia feel even more uncomfortable. She squirmed a little, curling her toes. But the truth was, Emily wasn't wrong. Julia knew that better than anyone.

On Friday afternoon, Emily spotted Cara standing at the corner of Orange and B Avenues. They were supposed to meet for lunch at Miguel's, and as Emily walked there down Orange, suddenly, she saw Cara's lithe frame in a floral sundress, standing beside the B Avenue sign, as if that's where she'd been planning on meeting Emily all along so they could walk the rest of the way to the restaurant together. She raised both her arms up to wave, and a smile erupted across Cara's pretty face.

Damn it. Why does she still look so good?

Emily had agreed to meet for lunch, but only at the end of the week. Thinking that if she saved this for last, she'd get it over with quickly, fly back to Florida, and forget all about Cara. And yet, seeing her standing there again, Emily felt something erupt in her chest, something painful, different from what she'd been expecting. She'd thought she would be angry, but instead all she felt was deeply hurt. Cara had abandoned her, once. Why was Emily so easy to walk away from?

"I love your hair!" Cara exclaimed, walking toward her now, then reaching a hand up to touch Emily's short, blonde crop. Emily had almost forgotten about the boring shoulder-length brown hairdo she'd once sported, a lifetime ago, back in Boston. "Can I give you a hug?" Cara asked. "Is that all right?"

Before Emily could answer, one way or another, Cara had wrapped her arms around her and squeezed her tightly. "God, it's great to see you. I'm so glad we made this work."

Cara still smelled like strawberries and summertime, and for the moment it took for Emily to extricate herself, she struggled to breathe. "I don't think I can do this," she said abruptly, stepping back. She was thinking about poor baby Mallory, about her own mother, about the way she had felt that cold Boston winter walking back and forth on Beacon Street below Cara's apartment. Alone. Unworthy. Left behind.

"You can't do lunch?" Cara laughed.

Emily shook her head. It wasn't lunch. It was people who disappeared. Cowards, liars. The kind of selfish people who didn't stick around when things got hard. That was what Emily couldn't and wouldn't do. And maybe Cara had a perfectly reasonable explanation for all of it. She'd driven all the way here from LA just to see Emily! But Emily suddenly didn't care; she couldn't hear it. She didn't want to hear it. "I'm sorry," she said instead.

And she really did feel a little bit sorry as she turned around and walked in the opposite direction down Orange, leaving Cara standing all alone at B Avenue, her pretty mouth agape.

Julia spotted Nate struggling to make it down his porch steps with a stroller. It looked like a Bugaboo from her spot across the yard on Grandma Vera's front porch swing, but she decided that it must be a knockoff. Nate didn't seem like the type to spend $1,200 on a stroller. Unless Heidi did. But damn, did a woman really spend that much on a stroller and then just abandon her kid?

"Jules, hey." Nate had seen her and now that he'd gotten the stroller down the steps, he'd stopped on the path, called out to her, and waved.

She blushed, wishing she hadn't been staring at him so intensely. She wanted to tell him it was the stroller she'd been staring at, not him, but instead she said, "Long time no see."

It had been two years, but somehow Nate looked exactly the same as he always had. Maybe a little more tired. More worry lines crinkling around the corners of his mouth, his eyes. But for the most part, he still looked like the messy-haired teenager she'd gleefully run to meet on the beach.

"You want to join us for a walk?" he asked. "It's the only way I can get her to nap in the afternoon," he added, sounding apologetic.

Julia hesitated for a second, wondering if two years was enough time to soften the blow of what had happened between them in Santa Monica. Nate's entire life had changed in the two years since, been turned around and now upside down. Nate was someone's father now. A single father, at that. And she would be leaving in the morning anyway. Maybe a walk would do them both good. Reset the Nate and Julia clock to make everything steady and normal again, the way it had been for so many years.

She got off the porch swing and jogged down the path to meet him, and then she offered to push the stroller, which she noticed on closer inspection was a Bugaboo. Well, that brought up so many questions that she swallowed back.

It was the middle of the afternoon but the sun hadn't quite made it out today, the sky a misty gray and the air cool. It was emptier than usual on the sidewalk by the beach, and Julia pushed the stroller with ease.

"I know this is weird," Nate said softly as they walked.

"Lucky for you, I'm an expert stroller pusher," Julia said. But in her head, she kept repeating the word *baby* as she walked. She was thinking about how she would never again have another one of her own who would need a stroller like this. Veronica didn't even need a booster seat in the car anymore.

Nate chuckled. "That you are. But you know what I mean. You and me. The baby. My baby."

"I've been doing much better this year," Julia said, and it almost didn't sound like a lie. "I went back to work part-time."

"Do you enjoy it?" he asked.

"I do. It keeps me busy," Julia said, and that was the truth. She'd been wallowing in self-pity for so long that it felt good to have another purpose. She liked her new position focusing on custody cases, essentially, as she saw it, helping kids who needed her. Plus, it was exhausting working, mothering Veronica, trying to keep everything easy and good with Ted in between. Exhaustion made it so much easier to fall asleep each night.

"I don't want this to be weird between us," Nate added, interrupting her thoughts. "I mean Santa Monica . . ." His voice trailed off, like he couldn't quite finish the thought.

"It's not weird," Julia said emphatically. There would be many more May weeks and more Ocean Boulevard walks. Mallory would bloom and grow, and Julia would love her because she was a part of Nate, not in spite of that. "And Santa Monica is in the vault," Julia said firmly.

"Thank God for the vault." Nate laughed wryly.

They walked on for a few minutes in silence. Mallory's thumb migrated slowly into her mouth and then she closed her eyes and drifted off to sleep. "Success," Julia said quietly, pointing into the stroller.

"I've really missed you, Jules," Nate said in response.

She had missed him too, but she didn't let herself say that. Instead, she looked at his beautiful, peaceful sleeping baby and said, "You should work things out with Heidi."

He shook his head. "Heidi isn't interested in that."

"Still, you could co-parent. I could help you with some kind of legal agreement." Her short time in custody cases had already taught her that this was generally the best option for any kids involved in a parental split. "Mallory deserves to have her mom, no matter what happened between—"

"Don't you think I want that too?" Nate cut her off, sounding rattled in a way that was out of character for him. "But Heidi isn't interested. She fell in love with some guy at the base, and when his unit got sent overseas, she left and went with him. She left me a goddamn note to explain herself."

Julia felt the pain in Nate's voice in her own chest, and she sharply drew in her breath. "I'm sorry," she said. Heidi came into Nate's life like a whirlwind and left that way too. Now Julia was glad she'd never actually met Heidi, because in her head she pictured her like the Wicked Witch of the West, Veronica's new favorite movie villain, being swept in and out of Coronado in the eye of a tornado. "You know, I'm here," Julia said. "If you ever need me."

"One week a year," Nate said evenly, neither a revelation nor a disappointment. Just a fact.

Julia wanted to tell him that the rest of the year she was only an email, call, or text away. That the space between them wasn't as huge as it used to be when they were kids and barely had a way to communicate. But instead she said, "This little girl is lucky to have you."

Nora was packing her suitcase Saturday afternoon when her cell phone rang. Miraculously, duct-taped and all, the old flip phone still managed to jingle through half of the speaker when someone called her. Thank goodness. Because she didn't have the money to replace it.

"Hey, kiddo," Leo's voice came through the line, sounding staticky and far away.

"Leo! Hi! Don't worry, I've been practicing all week, and I'll be back in the city before five tomorrow. Ready for rehearsals first thing—"

"Nora," Leo cut her off. "We lost funding."

"What?" The words were unexpected, and therefore made no sense. "What do you mean *lost funding*?"

"I mean, the show isn't happening anymore. I'm so sorry."

Isn't happening? "What?" she said again, still not totally comprehending.

"It's canceled," he said.

But she'd spent the whole week steeped in Miss Marmelstein. Running lines in her head as she'd jogged on the path with her sisters. Singing lyrics into the ocean when she was out on the beach early mornings alone and also in the shower, much to Emily's chagrin over their shared bathroom.

"Do you want me to pick you up at the airport tomorrow?" Leo was still talking. "Which one? LaGuardia?"

She shook her head, forgetting for a moment he couldn't see her. She was flying to JFK and had planned on taking the train. And anyway, she didn't want to face Leo under these circumstances. "No, I'm good," she lied. "I'll just . . . call you next week once I'm back."

"Okay. I'll buy you a drink. Chin up in the meanwhile," Leo said. "Something else is going to come up soon."

But as Nora disconnected from the call, she started to really doubt that it would, that it would ever happen for her the way she and Grandma Vera had once dreamed. She was never going to make it.

Nora was set to fly out last the next morning, and after Emily and Julia left in a cab together for the airport, and Nora was throwing all their linens in the washing machine (as Julia had reminded her three times before she'd left), she suddenly heard Mallory's screams coming from Nate's porch. If Mallory had sounded like a goose as a newborn last year, this May, as a one-year-old, she sounded more like a possessed alien. Bigger, stronger, louder. Bossier. And entirely unearthly. Poor Nate. Nora worried he was in over his head.

She abandoned the wash and walked outside, across the front yard. Mallory was standing up in a Pack 'n Play on the porch, screaming her head off, and Nate was sitting on a chair across from her, his head in his hands.

He looked up when Nora walked up the porch steps. "I don't know what to do," he shouted. "I don't know why she keeps crying."

Nora had absolutely no experience with one-year-olds and on top of that, very little interest. She planned to stick to the promise she and her sisters made to each other as kids—she never wanted a baby. She would never have a baby of her own. But she opened her mouth and did the only thing she could think of: She started to belt out "Miss Marmelstein," the song she'd been rehearsing into the ocean all week, and which now she would never actually get to perform onstage.

As she belted out the very first Miss Marmelstein lyric in the very first line, Mallory suddenly and all at once stopped crying, stared at Nora, and Nora did the only thing she knew how to do: She kept on singing.

"Damn," Nate said when she finished the whole song, and he and Mallory were both staring at her wide-eyed. "Damn, Nora. You're so unbelievably talented."

She felt her cheeks turning hot with the compliment. "Yeah, well, I was supposed to start rehearsals on Monday for this show, but it suddenly lost funding." She sighed. "So now I'm about to fly back home to absolutely nothing."

Nate stared at her for another moment. "What if you didn't?"

"What if I didn't what?"

"Fly home. I could really use some extra help for a few weeks. What if you stay here with us instead, just until I can get my shit together," he pleaded.

What was he asking her, exactly? To stay with him, here, in his house, for a few weeks? "I don't even know the first thing about babies," she heard herself saying. But she was thinking, no matter how much time passed or how much her girlhood crush had faded, she would still, always, have a hard time turning Nate down.

"I don't know how to do this alone." Nate's voice broke, like it was the first time he'd spoken this particular truth out loud. "Please, Nora."

Nora thought about the few days she'd stayed here with him, after Becca canceled their wedding, the way he had slowly come back to life as they'd spent time together, and how for once, Nora had felt like maybe she was the glue. And as she stood here now, Leo and the sting of another career disappointment suddenly felt a million miles away. "I guess I can stay for a little while," she finally said.

"You're a lifesaver." He grinned, that classic Nate lopsided grin. And now she felt that he was looking at her like she was this talented, powerful woman whom he *needed,* not like she was just little *Noradora.*

He wrapped her in a quick hug, and she suddenly worried he'd feel the rapid pounding of her heart in her chest. Then he pulled back, pointed to Mallory in the Pack 'n Play. "Do you mind watching her while I go make up the guest room? God, no one has stayed there since Julia—"

"Since Julia?" Nora cut him off, confused. "When?"

Nate hesitated for a moment. "Never mind, I misspoke. I haven't been sleeping much."

"But when did Julia ever stay in your guest room?" Nora pushed, feeling somewhere between curious and annoyed.

He bit his bottom lip, not answering for a few seconds. "I guess . . . um . . . right after Vera died, and she came to clean out the house."

Nora, relieved, let out a laugh. "So I've stayed here since then, silly."

Nate stared at her for another moment, and then he nodded. "Like I said, haven't been sleeping much. Time got away from me."

CHAPTER 17

1999

AFTER GRANDMA VERA DIED, Julia had saved cleaning out the large chestnut armoire in the dining room for last.

Bagging up and donating the contents of Grandma Vera's closet, kitchen, and living room had been one thing. She'd set aside the videocassette of *Some Like It Hot* that they'd watched at least ten summers in a row (which she would give to Nate for safekeeping), the Barbra Streisand records (which she would ship to Nora), and Grandma Vera's poetry collection (which she would ship to Emily). For herself, she had set aside Grandma Vera's favorite crocheted orange-and-green afghan that they had used to warm their legs on chilly nights out back by the firepit. But all the rest of Vera's clothes and possessions had been bagged, boxed, and easily loaded into the back of a Goodwill truck.

Everything, that is, but the contents of this armoire. The miscellany of her life, the entirety of her life. You couldn't donate old birthday cards and business cards, bills and letters. But how did you just . . . throw them out? Julia stared at the top-left drawer, the memory of what she'd seen within vivid even now, many years later. What if she'd been wrong? *What if she'd been right?*

One thing she'd come to admire about Ted in the few months she'd been dating him was his fearlessness, and she imagined, if he were sitting here, he would tell her just to open up the damn drawer, methodically sort through the contents. He would tell her not to run away, or hide from, or, worse, fear the truth.

Easy for him to say, though, when he had two very alive and still married parents on Long Island, whom he talked to precisely once a week, every Sunday afternoon at two o'clock for twenty minutes. She knew Ted could never understand this part of her, this wanting. This longing. She knew, also, that she would never tell him about this. Even the thought of mentioning it to him felt embarrassing, her biggest weakness.

Still, she had to face it. She took a deep breath, stood, and opened the top-left drawer.

It was more filled than she'd remembered it, stuffed full with stacks of letters. But the sender, the return address, all seemed to be the same one in Santa Monica that she had glanced nine years earlier when Grandma Vera had sent her to the armoire in search of her ob-gyn's card. Julia quickly rifled through the letters now, and it appeared the postmarks went back at least fifteen years.

Julia felt the sudden sting of betrayal. It ripped through her belatedly, years, or decades, too late. It felt hot building up inside her chest, suddenly indistinguishable from grief.

What was she supposed to do now?

She could shred these, throw them away. Make sure Nora and Emily never knew anything about them. Push this down and hide it inside of her, the way she had already for years.

But the budding lawyer in her would never throw away evidence. And she decided in that moment, that's exactly what these letters were: *evidence.*

What if one day she wanted to read them? What if one day she needed to read them?

Before she could change her mind, she quickly packed them up inside a small box, and then walked to the post office and shipped them back to her DC apartment.

The night before she left, the house was totally empty. She'd had all the remaining furniture hauled away to be donated earlier that afternoon, and then, just around dinnertime, she realized, she didn't have a place to sit and eat or lie down and sleep. It was unlike her, not to plan for such a thing, and that's when the grief suddenly crested in her chest, and she sat down in the middle of Grandma Vera's empty living room and began to cry.

She heard a sudden knock on the front door, and she knew without even getting up. It had to be Nate. Could he somehow intuit every little thing she was feeling, as if it traveled to him in paper airplanes across the short distance between the two houses?

But no, that was ridiculous. She'd told him her flight was in the morning. He'd probably just come over to say goodbye.

She stood and wiped her tears away, straightened her ponytail, and then she walked to the door. As soon as she opened it, his face dropped. "Jules," he said. "What's wrong?"

"Nothing," she said. *Everything.* Grandma Vera was dead, and her entire house was empty, as if she had been completely and irrevocably erased in only a few days and a few donations. But perhaps the most pressing issue at hand, if not totally what had brought her to tears, was that she hadn't considered spending one last night in this completely empty house. "I don't have anywhere to sleep tonight," she finally said.

He held out his hand, then patiently waited for her to take it, while she hesitated. *I have a boyfriend,* she thought. But Nate was her family. He'd said the other night that she was like a sister to him. It wouldn't do her any harm to take his hand now, to hold on to him and steady herself for just a moment.

"Go get your things and come stay the night at my house," he said softly. "Come on," Nate urged her, his hand still outstretched. "You can sleep in my childhood bedroom. I've been wanting to turn it into a guest room—I haven't had the chance to fix it up yet. But my old bed is still in there. You can sleep there."

Nate's bed, where he'd slept as a teenager. Seventeen-year-old Julia, twenty-year-old Julia would've burned up in agony (or was it ecstasy?) at just the very thought. But here, twenty-six-year-old Julia was so long over Nate. She had a serious boyfriend! She was almost a lawyer! Nate was offering her his old bed to crash in for the night, because her alternative was sleeping on the floor. Case closed. Of course she should take him up on it. She should take his outstretched hand. There was no reason not to.

But—

The bedsheets smelled like Nate. Or maybe it was this whole entire room. He said he hadn't slept here since he'd moved back in, remodeled the master for himself. But she pulled the covers up to her head and sandalwood and the ocean invaded her nose. She pulled them down, kicked them away, and still, the smell lingered.

She stood up, went and opened the window, hoping some fresh air would cool the heat that smell had suddenly injected into her limbs. She stared straight into the now empty, dark space across the way, where she had once stood and thrown paper airplane messages to Nate as a kid. They would refurnish Grandma Vera's house to make it suitable for a rental, and she still planned to come back to that very room once a year, every single May. She thought again about the letters in the box. Maybe she should've just shredded them. Let the past stay buried.

"Jules?" Nate's gravelly voice came through the closed door. "You need anything? I'm headed to bed."

She suddenly noticed a tiny hummingbird, flitting in between her window next door and this one, like it was connecting the two with an invisible thread. Like she had always been connected to Nate with that same invisible thread.

She knew what she should say, what she should do, but the hummingbird flew close enough for a moment that she felt like it was trying to tell her something, before it flitted away altogether into the night. Then, for once, her body and her mind disconnected. Julia turned away from the window and walked to the door, opening it quickly.

Nate raised his eyebrows, surprised. "Do you need something?"

When Nate's mother had gotten sick, he'd pushed her away. Now her own body felt heavy from grief, but Julia had the opposite response. She suddenly needed to pull Nate close.

"You," she heard herself saying in barely a whisper, so for a moment, while Nate stood in the doorway frozen, she wasn't actually sure she'd actually said anything out loud. "You." She repeated it a bit louder.

"You don't mean that, Jules," Nate finally said.

"I do," she insisted. Though maybe she didn't. It was hard to tell. This was the very first time she'd ever been in Coronado without her sisters and Grandma Vera. No one would know what happened right now, tonight. No one except for her and Nate. And it was hard to feel anything except for this nostalgic twist of desire in her stomach, incited by the smell of everything she'd wanted in her teenage years.

"What if we just put tonight in the vault," she said. It was the same phrase Nate had used when he'd broken up with her six years earlier. She'd been twenty, desperately in love with him, desperately sad for the way he was suddenly losing his mother. She had pulled him out of his house, attempting to pull him out of his grief, held his hand as they'd walked out to the beach, down to the edge of the ocean early one morning. Nate had leaned down and kissed her, slowly, deeply, more passionately than he ever had before. And then he'd told her he wanted to break up. *I can't love you anymore*, he'd told her. *Let's just be friends.*

What about that kiss? she'd said, suddenly annoyed that his mouth seemed to be saying two totally different things at once.

A goodbye kiss, Nate said.

But why had goodbye felt so much to Julia like desire?

No, Julia insisted, stupidly certain she could still change his mind. *What am I supposed to do with everything that kiss just made me feel? I know you're hurting, but I can help you. We don't need to break up!*

And that's when he'd said it: *Can we just put that kiss in a vault?* He clarified he didn't want to lose her as a friend. So why couldn't they just lock up any remaining sexual tension, lock it away. Why couldn't she return the next May and the next and the next, and still act normal, like his best friend next door, like she had for years before they'd ever kissed to begin with. Why couldn't mistakes, *teenage slips*, he'd called them, be corrected, reversed, even forgotten?

Nate just stared at her now, as if he too was remembering that moment on the beach. That last kiss that had meant nothing and everything at once. "The vault is some stupid thing some stupid hurt kid made up a long time ago," he said.

"I don't care," she said.

"You will tomorrow."

"I won't," she insisted. (Though he was right. She would care the next afternoon when she walked back into her apartment, her lips still feeling swollen, and found Ted sitting on the couch waiting for her with a surprise box of welcome-home chocolate chip cookies from Reeves.)

But that night, she really, truly didn't care. She couldn't think or see beyond what was right in front of her: *Nate.* He was still staring at her, standing firmly in the doorway, and then she reached for him, grabbing a fistful of his T-shirt in her hand, and pulled him closer to her, into the room, up against her chest. He moaned softly, like he had been waiting for her to do just that for years.

He leaned down and kissed her, gently, hesitantly at first. "Are you sure?" His mouth moved close enough to hers that she felt the words on her own lips more than she could hear them.

But instead of answering him, she kissed him back.

CHAPTER 18

2009

THE THING ABOUT THE vault was, Julia's heart wasn't actually foolproof.

She supposed she had known this all along. Years passed and memories faded. Grief crested in waves but never truly went away. She was twenty. She was twenty-six. She was thirty-three. She was thirty-six.

All year long, she was a busy wife, a mother, an attorney.

But then every May, for one week, she came to Coronado. Nate was still next door, and he still knew all her secrets. They rose up inside of her again, mistakes, or wishes, lost, then found. She would get out of the taxi on Ocean Boulevard and find herself glancing just across the yard at Nate's house. Wondering if he had remembered she was coming. If he was just beyond the front door, still waiting for her.

This May, though, ten years after Grandma Vera died and they had put their one night in the vault, Nate was sitting on his porch when she arrived. He sat in a rocking chair reading a book. Two-year-old Mallory sat in front of him, playing quietly with oversized Legos. Julia's heart swelled, and she had to work very hard to breathe as she pulled her suitcase from the trunk of the cab.

"Jules!" he called her name, and she remembered what he had

said to her last May when she'd pushed Mallory in the stroller, that he didn't want this to be *weird*. Still, it did feel *weird* to see him again now for the first time in a year, to have all those old buried feelings suddenly rushing back up to the surface. No matter how much she wanted it to be, her heart was never truly a vault.

She shut the trunk of the cab and waved back, then walked to his porch, dragging her suitcase behind her. Mallory glanced up from the Legos, but then quickly went back to her tower. Nate grinned widely, looking happier, more relaxed than he had last year.

Julia thought: *Fatherhood really agrees with him*. But she didn't say that out loud. She suddenly remembered that she owed her own father a call. He'd left her a voicemail last night when she'd been busy packing. Her own father, who had raised three times the Mallorys, all on his own.

Mallory reached up to hand Nate a block, and he put his book down on the table to build part of her tower.

"What are you reading?" she asked him, glancing past them to take a look.

He fastened his block to the top of Mallory's tower, Mallory clapped with glee, and then he held his book up. Now she could see it was a textbook. Educational psychology. "Studying," he said. "I'm going back to school to get my teaching degree."

She smiled. Nate had been in and out of careers since his mom died. From a failed stint in medical school to pharmaceutical sales to real estate to handyman jobs. But teacher finally felt exactly right. Nate was patient and gentle and clearly good with kids.

"I should go get myself settled," she heard herself saying, her voice sounding ethereal, far away. "Nora and Em will be here soon. I have to finish making our schedule for the week."

Nate nodded. "Walk later, to catch up? Put me on the schedule this week, Jules."

She nodded again and pressed her lips tightly together, suddenly afraid if she spoke any more, the vault would blow wide open.

After dinner and s'mores, when Emily and Nora stayed on the back patio to drink wine, Julia said she was tired and went upstairs to go to bed.

But the truth was, she wasn't tired at all. She opened her laptop and caught up on some emails. Then she finally called Dad back and chatted with him for a little while, telling him about V's latest third-grade exploits and her participation in the end-of-year school play (which was adorable despite her lacking any requisite rhythm for the singing and dancing portions).

"So she and Nora aren't actually related then?" Dad said with a chuckle.

"Shh, don't say that too loud. Nora is just downstairs. And she thinks V is her mini-me."

"They look alike and yet, they couldn't be more different." Dad was still chuckling, overly amused in that nerdy way he always had when it came to anything having to do with his daughters or his granddaughter. "And how are you doing, Julia?" Dad asked gently. "Not working too hard."

"I'm only working part-time, Dad."

"Still, you're in a field with a lot of stress, and raising a kid isn't easy either."

"I'm good," Julia said. "You never have to worry about me."

"Okay, sweetheart. Give Em and Nora a hug for me. And have a lot of fun together this week."

"We always do," Julia told him before she hung up.

Usually, it calmed her to talk to her father, to hear his steady voice that seemed endlessly unchanging, across years and miles. But tonight, even after they talked, she just couldn't squash the feeling of unease that rose in her chest.

She got into bed, but she tossed and turned for a while, and at ten o'clock, she was still wide awake. It was one a.m. at home—she should be sound asleep. The house was quiet—even Nora and Emily had already gone to bed.

But Julia felt deeply unsettled. *I'm good. You never have to worry about me*, she had told Dad. Yet, now that felt like a lie. She didn't feel *good* at all.

Perhaps it was simply because of the illusion of Nate. Her forever *what-if.* Just next door. Her vault filled up with things she should forget, feelings that never should've happened in the first place. But Nate was both a hologram and a time warp.

Across the country, there was her real life. Her husband and her daughter. And that's what was keeping her awake now. The truth was, what was really bothering her were five simple words from an unknown number flashing across Ted's BlackBerry screen earlier this morning: *Can't wait to see you.*

They'd both had their BlackBerries charging in the kitchen, and just before she'd left for the airport, she had accidentally grabbed Ted's by mistake. As soon as she realized, she'd put it back on the counter, but not before she saw that message flash up. *Can't wait to see you.* Was it something innocent? His mother texting from the Hamptons on someone else's phone? Or something else? Something she shouldn't have seen.

She got out of bed now and walked to the window, opening it to let in the cool sea air. Nate's childhood bedroom just across the side yard was dark, the window closed. Of course. Nate didn't sleep there anymore, and anyway, he was likely sound asleep by ten.

But out of habit, or out of nostalgia, she ripped a piece of paper off the yellow legal pad in her bag, folded it carefully into a paper airplane. On one of the wings, she wrote in her trademark neat cursive: *What if we opened the vault?*

But of course, the window was closed. There was nowhere for her to throw it now anyway, even if she'd wanted to.

"How was Grammy and Pop-Pop's?" Julia asked Veronica a week later, as she was driving her to summer camp drop-off before work. "Did you and Daddy have fun without me?"

Julia glanced in the rearview mirror for a reaction, and Veronica shrugged in the back seat. Julia had pleated her curls into neat braids, one on each side of her head, and she looked different, older, without their wildness. "Daddy didn't stay the whole week, and then Pop-Pop was golfing and Grammy and I made tiny sandwiches for afternoon tea. But they had cucumbers." Veronica made a face.

"Ah yes, the dreaded cucumbers. How did you survive it?" Julia deadpanned.

"I spit them in my napkin when Grammy wasn't looking, and then I threw them in the trash."

Julia chuckled, remembering Nora doing the same thing as a kid any time Dad would make lamb chops, which to this day Nora insisted were the most vile thing she'd ever tasted. Julia was going to have to tell her this story the next time they talked. "So where did Daddy go?" Julia asked, trying to sound nonchalant. Ted hadn't mentioned anything about leaving Veronica in the Hamptons alone.

Julia glanced in the rearview mirror again and Veronica shrugged again.

"He had work?" Julia spoon-fed Veronica an answer that she hoped was true.

"He always has work." Veronica sighed. "And so do you."

"I only work part-time," Julia reminded her as she pulled up at the curb for camp drop-off and stopped the car. "I'll be back to pick you up from camp at three, V."

But Veronica didn't immediately unlatch her seat belt. "I hate camp," she said instead.

"You *love* camp," Julia reminded her. "Last summer all you

could talk about was how much you love camp! Remember all the art projects? You had so much fun!"

Veronica made a face and sighed dramatically. "That was last summer."

"You're just nervous because it's the first day," Julia said. "That's normal. Go on ahead and you'll see your friends and you'll remember how much you love it again."

"Do I have to?" Veronica asked.

"Yes," Julia said.

Veronica sighed again, and then opened the car door.

"Have fun, sweetie. I love you," Julia called out.

But Veronica shut the car door without saying anything else.

Julia popped in her headset and called Ted on the drive to work.

"V says she hates camp now," Julia said as soon as Ted picked up.

Ted snort-laughed. "It's just another phase," he said. "I forgot to tell you, last week she also decided she hates tennis. Mom tried to get her to play. Remember last summer that was her favorite camp week?"

Julia nodded, remembering, also, the expensive lessons they'd paid for all last fall. "Well, what if it's not a phase. Maybe we should listen to her. Could there be a reason why she suddenly hates things she used to love?"

"So, what then . . . she doesn't go to camp? And does what all summer?"

It was a good question, and one Julia was not immediately prepared to answer. "I guess we could hire a college kid to hang out with her?"

"She'll be happier at camp," Ted said, and Julia knew he was right. Even though Veronica's sudden swing still nagged at her.

"Hey, V said you didn't stay in the Hamptons all week." Julia blurted it out before she could lose her nerve.

Ted cleared his throat. "Yeah . . . uh, work emergency."

Can't wait to see you.

What would he say now if she confronted him about seeing those words on his BlackBerry screen just before she'd left for Coronado? She opened her mouth but she couldn't bring herself to say it. "I figured," she said instead. "Work never stops, does it?"

"Never stops," Ted repeated. Then he added, "Hey, have a good day. I'll try not to get home too late so I can talk to V about camp before bed."

"Sounds good," Julia said.

And when they hung up, and it was totally quiet and still inside her car, she thought about the way her life now had such an easy rhythm.

Where would Veronica go if she didn't go to camp?

What would Ted say if she confronted him with something that might be difficult?

And maybe it was just better, easier, if she kept on. Steady, steady.

One warm night that fall, Emily's iPhone rang in the middle of the night, waking her out of a deep sleep. She felt around blindly for it on her night table: 1:46 a.m., and her boss was calling.

There couldn't possibly be a work emergency at this hour. The museum was long closed, and any security lapses or alarms went straight to the security team. She quickly swiped to answer.

"Em, I'm sorry if I woke you. I didn't know . . . who else to call." Cecile's normally smooth voice sounded fractured. Was she crying?

Emily sat up and opened her eyes all the way. "What's wrong?"

"Mikey's fever won't come down no matter what I do. I think it might be swine flu. It's running through day care right now."

Emily had seen headlines about the outbreak, how it was particularly bad, even deadly, for kids, and she swallowed hard.

"I . . . I don't know what to do. Rick is still in Minneapolis. I'm here all alone with the boys."

"How's Jim?" Emily asked. "Is he sick too?"

"No, he's fine. He's asleep." Emily heard a little cry, a whimper in the background and Cecile's soft, *Shhh, it'll be all right, baby.* The twins were fraternal, but Emily had not yet met them enough times to tell them apart. She knew their names, of course, but she was having trouble picturing exactly which one Cecile was jostling against her hip, comforting now. "He's really burning up!" Cecile exclaimed.

Emily hugged the phone between her shoulder and her ear as she got out of bed and quickly threw a pair of pants on. "Okay," she said firmly. "I'm coming over and then I'll stay there with Jim while you take Mikey to the ER."

"I can't ask you to do that," Cecile said.

"You didn't," Emily said, grabbing her keys off her dresser. "I'm offering."

Emily had been to Cecile and Rick's house a few times before. Once for the baby shower, another when she'd stopped over briefly with some papers to sign for work. It was a cute redbrick ranch, in a sprawling suburban neighborhood twenty minutes away from Emily's condo near the beach.

But now it felt strange to be inside their house all alone after Cecile left in a rush for the ER. Emily sat down on the couch in a small living room cluttered with objects foreign to her: toddler toys and babyish things, a pile of folded diapers and sippy cups. A half-eaten bowl of Cheerios sat on the coffee table in front of her, the milk bubbling in a suspicious way, so she was almost certain it had gone rancid. And Emily thought, again, *God, I am never having kids. Never.*

Worse, she read more about the swine flu on her phone while waiting. Forty-three kids had already died in the last few months, a handful of them under five years old, and suddenly worry crept up inside of her, making her feel hot and a little nauseous. She threw her phone down on the couch, picked up the bowl of soggy

Cheerios from the coffee table, and started scrubbing in the kitchen.

By seven a.m., when Cecile walked back in the door, Mikey asleep on her shoulder, Emily had cleaned the entire living room and kitchen. She'd even found a mop and washed the floors.

"What are you doing?" Cecile let out a muted laugh. She looked tired, but her normally smooth voice, her composure, was back. "Did you . . . clean my damn house?"

"Is he okay?" Emily asked.

Cecile nodded. "They gave him some fluids and his fever broke. Thank God."

"Thank God," Emily repeated.

"Thank you so much for staying here. Really, you were a lifesaver. Was Jim okay?"

Emily nodded. "I think he's still asleep. I haven't heard a single sound." Thankfully, because she had no idea what exactly she was supposed to do had Jim started crying or woken up.

Cecile sighed heavily. "Great. He's probably getting sick too. The kid never sleeps this long."

Suddenly, Emily understood the burden of motherhood, of twins in particular. Any relief, relaxation was fleeting, and worry was a constant undercurrent.

"I'm gonna go try and lay Mikey down. You should go home and get some sleep," Cecile was saying now. "Don't go into work today. I'll call Maria and tell her we're both out sick."

Emily nodded and watched Cecile walk off down the hall. But then, instead of leaving, she brewed a pot of coffee.

When Cecile walked back into the kitchen thirty minutes later, Emily handed her a steaming mug.

"You're still here." Cecile sounded surprised, but did she also sound pleased? She took the coffee and offered Emily a weak smile. "You definitely deserve a raise."

Emily laughed. "I do." She knew the museum's budget better than anyone, and so she also knew that there was no reasonable way she was getting a raise anytime soon. "Should I hold you to that at our budget meeting next week?"

Cecile smiled and took a sip of coffee. "Seriously, though, I really owe you, Em."

Emily shook her head. "Don't be silly. We're friends, aren't we?"

Cecile put down her coffee, suddenly reached across the table, and grabbed Emily's hand. She held on to it for a moment before offering a light squeeze and another smile. "Go home. Go get some sleep."

CHAPTER 19

2010

SOMETHING HAPPENED TO NORA when she turned thirty. Other women might have said they felt a biological clock ticking when they hit this age, but Nora had never felt the urge to have kids, and perhaps even less so now. No, she felt something else. It was the pulse of her dream, ringing constantly in her ears. She was about to fail spectacularly, or she was about to finally make it happen. She realized this quite suddenly on New Year's Eve as the clock turned to midnight: 2010. It was months after her thirtieth birthday, but when the ball dropped at midnight, when Leo pulled her into a dark corner of the bar to kiss her, it hit her. She would do anything, anything to finally make it before it was too late. *Anything.*

She whispered this to Leo in the dark, as if saying it out loud would manifest something new: *This is my year. It has to be.*

I believe in you, kiddo. He gave her shoulder a small squeeze and then, at 12:05 a.m., he walked out of the bar and took a cab home to his wife.

Nora was used to this by now, but still, as she pushed past a crowd of drunk people on the street to get to the train, she hated the way she always felt a little lost, a little empty when Leo tossed her aside for his real life.

But when he called her three days later with what he promised was a way to make her New Year's pledge come true, she remembered again that it was all worth it.

At the end of April, Nora flew to LA for three weeks. Leo's bit of January hope had been an audition for a very small supporting role in an original musical movie. The script wasn't very good. LA wasn't her scene. Film wasn't her medium. But Leo had set up the audition through a friend of a friend, and she'd gotten the part. It would pay well, and Devlin St. Claire, Hollywood's up-and-coming It man, was the lead.

The truth was, Nora hadn't exactly known who Devlin St. Claire was when Leo first told her about this movie. His breakout was a role in a TV series based on some children's books she had never read. But when she mentioned it to Julia, Julia said she and Veronica had read all the books and they'd seen every season of the series so far. "Nora!" Julia had exclaimed over the phone. "How cool is this?" Then she'd added, "Do you get to meet Will the Wizard? Or um, I mean, Devlin? He is, objectively, very nice-looking."

Julia wasn't wrong. (Julia was never wrong.) But when Nora first caught a glimpse of Devlin St. Claire on set, her immediate reaction was that Julia had severely undersold him. He was, objectively, extremely fucking gorgeous.

He was medium height and build, with wavy brown hair, and deep blue eyes that reminded her of the color of the ocean on that rare sunny May afternoon in Coronado. There was something magnetic about him, the velvet sound of his voice, the bright sound of his laugh. Nora watched him for a few moments and she immediately felt her skin growing hot.

He suddenly seemed to notice her standing off to the side, all by herself, watching him, and he jogged over and introduced himself. "Oh!" he said when she told him her name. "Nora May. You're the one playing Rosie. I love your song." She enjoyed the way he said the word *love*, like it was both sweet and a little salty on his tongue.

"I love it too." She laughed.

She had one song, and only a few short scenes, but he was right, the song was a good one. It was, above anything else, what had ultimately excited her about this job. This feeling, that if this one song could be her breakout moment, she could show people what she was made of, maybe finally go somewhere in her career.

"I was just about to get out of here and get a coffee down the street. Do you want to come along?" Devlin asked.

"Sure," Nora said, trying hard to sound cool, to keep her voice steady and pretend like she got invited to coffee by famous gorgeous actors every day. No big deal. "I had a really early flight this morning. So coffee would actually be great right now."

He grinned and bit his bottom lip in this incredibly sexy way, so she felt it like a jolt in her thighs. Then he fastened a Dodgers cap on his head and motioned for Nora to follow him out the back door of the set. She followed him through a parking lot, down a hill, and then they cut through an alley filled with trash cans. "I am not kidnapping you," he said. "I promise."

Nora laughed. "I didn't think you were." (There was honestly no way kidnappers were this hot.)

"Too many cameras out front," Devlin said. "And sometimes I just want a cup of coffee without someone taking my picture, you know?"

Nora nodded sympathetically, like she did know. But of course, she might die of happiness if someone ever cared enough to take her picture while she was simply going for coffee.

They finally hit the glass door of the coffee shop, and as Devlin reached for the handle Nora heard a man's voice yelling: "Hey, Dev! Who's the girl?"

Nora spun around, and a paparazzo stood across the street, camera around his neck, waving to get Devlin's attention.

"Jesus," Devlin said quietly to Nora. "They're relentless." Then he turned and shouted back: "Hey, man, we're just trying to take a break from set to get a cup of coffee, okay?"

Devlin opened the coffee shop door and ushered her inside

first, hovering behind her to shield her from the paparazzo's camera across the street. "Sorry about that," he said softly. He stood close enough that she could feel his breath against her hair as he spoke. "I make the worst first impression these days."

"Don't be sorry," Nora said. Truth be told, she was finding this all a little thrilling, and for the first time, she actually felt truly excited about the prospect of shooting this movie, of spending the next few weeks in LA.

They walked farther into the shop and when she turned around to see if the paparazzo was still out on the street, Devlin's face was right there, and he smiled.

The bright afternoon sunshine streamed in through the front glass windows of the shop, making his beautiful features temporarily awash in yellow light, glowing. Nora suddenly understood what it meant to feel *starstruck*.

"How was your first day on set, kiddo?" Leo asked over the phone later that night. He spoke in hushed tones—Nora realized it was already after midnight in New York and he'd probably snuck down the hall while his wife and kid were asleep to call her.

Back in her hotel room, Nora was bingeing the first season of *The Wizards of Central Park* on pay-per-view. She was three episodes in by the time Leo called and already considering herself a Devlin St. Claire superfan. Devlin was not only, objectively, very gorgeous, but also, objectively, a very good actor. She could see why both her sister and the paps were obsessed.

"It was good," she told Leo, struggling with the remote, trying to figure out how to pause the show so she wouldn't miss anything. "The most LA thing already happened to me today." She recounted following Devlin out the back of the studio, through the trash can alley, and still somehow being followed by a paparazzo.

"Nora, that's brilliant," Leo said.

"What do you mean? Getting coffee with Devlin?"

"No. Yes. I mean, keep hanging out with him while you're there, get photographed as much as you can, and we can capitalize on this."

Nora suddenly felt dirty hearing how Leo wanted her to take advantage of Devlin's kindness. "He actually seems like a nice guy," Nora said. "There's something weirdly genuine about him, considering how famous he is."

"Even better," Leo said, his voice thick with excitement. "Get close to him. Get your name and your face out there. It could be really great for you!"

"So what are you, like my pimp now?" Nora said abruptly, feeling annoyed with Leo, this conversation. With herself. Why was she even still talking to Leo after all these years? What was wrong with her?

"Hey, kiddo." Leo's voice softened. "I didn't mean it like that. I'm just thinking about your career. You said it's your year, remember?"

Nora sighed. She had said that to him, on New Year's. And she supposed he wasn't wrong. But still, she fought the urge to tell Leo to go back to bed and fuck his wife. "I should go to sleep," she said instead. "I have an early call tomorrow."

But when they hung up, Nora did not go to sleep. Instead, she stayed up way too late, bingeing the rest of the first season of *The Wizards of Central Park*.

On Nora's last day of shooting, Devlin invited her to have dinner at his house.

Doing a movie had turned out to be both more stressful and more exhausting than she could've imagined. Nora had barely thought about Leo's advice, much less had the time or energy to really hang out with Devlin or be photographed.

"Nothing fancy," Devlin said. "Just my little way to say goodbye and good luck before you head back to New York."

Nora hesitated for a moment, thinking about the way Devlin's blue eyes were bright, his smile sincere, even after a long day on set. Did the man ever look anything less than perfect? She'd spent a lot of time in makeup this morning as they'd worked on the dark circles under her eyes.

"I don't mean to sound like a creep, inviting you to my house," he continued. "But dinner there is more private. It's also Tuesday, and I make very good tacos."

Nora laughed. "You sound a little bit like a creep. But I do love tacos."

"Worth the risk," Devlin joked. "I promise you won't be disappointed."

"Okay," Nora said. "It would be a shame to leave LA without at least trying your tacos."

"I'll send a car to your hotel in an hour? Gives you time to shower and change if you want?"

Nora nodded. "I actually haven't had a home-cooked meal in . . ." She couldn't quite remember when. She certainly never cooked in her shoebox kitchen in Brooklyn. Maybe last Christmas, when she'd gone to Julia's house? "Well, it's been a really long time. This sounds great. Thanks for the invitation."

Two hours later, full from his delicious tacos, a little tipsy on her second glass of sangria, Nora sat in Dev's kitchen and laughed when he asked her to name her favorite Broadway show.

When she had first arrived, she'd been acutely aware of how large and expensive-looking his Malibu house was, how famous he was, but now, three carne asada tacos and almost two sangrias later, she felt oddly comfortable sitting across the small kitchen table from him. She wasn't putting on a show, or overthinking her answers, she was just . . . being.

"Favorite show?" Nora repeated, giving it some thought. How was it that no one had ever asked her that question? Not Leo. Not her agent. Not any casting director she'd auditioned for. She thought about it for another moment. "*Rent*," she finally said.

"My dad took me to New York as a high school graduation gift, and it was the first show I ever saw on Broadway."

"So it's as much the show as the memory of the trip?" Dev said.

Nora nodded. That was true. She'd done theater in high school, marveled over movies and productions with Grandma Vera her whole childhood, but she would never forget the experience of being in the rush of New York City for the very first time at the age of eighteen, walking inside the Nederlander and seeing Idina Menzel perform live onstage.

"Well, then for me it would have to be *Cats*," Dev said.

"*Cats*?" Nora snort-laughed.

"My grandma Claire took me to see it on Broadway when I was ten. First show. First trip to New York City."

"Ooh, she corrupted you at the age of ten," Nora joked. "I like this Grandma Claire." She suddenly thought about Grandma Vera introducing her to Barbra Streisand when Nora was around that same age, and she had the urge to tell Dev everything about her.

Dev smiled. "Yeah, she was the best. She raised me after my parents died in a car accident when I was eight. *Saint Claire*, my cousins and I always called her."

"Wait—*Saint Claire*? So that's not your real last name?"

Dev shook his head. "Stolarski. Mom, and Grandma Claire, were of Irish descent. Dad, Polish."

"Devlin Stolarski," Nora said softly. Then she held out her hand across the table. "Well, it's nice to meet you. The real you."

Dev stared at her for a moment before he reached out his hand and took hers, clasped it in his own for a moment before letting go.

"What's he like? Tell me everything," Julia said to Nora a few weeks later in Coronado, pulling a bag of marshmallows from her travel bag and throwing them across the patio to Emily.

Emily tore open the bag with her teeth and then delicately pulled marshmallows out one by one, lining them up at her usual s'mores-making station by the firepit. "What who's like?" she asked. If Nora was dating someone, she would be the last to know. Not that she had told her sisters anything she'd been up to lately. So, maybe it was fair, if not also annoying, to be out of their loop.

"Devlin St. Claire!" Julia exclaimed. "Em, didn't Nora tell you that she just filmed a movie, costarring with him?"

"Who?" Emily repeated as she started layering the s'mores. She vaguely knew Nora had been in LA, filming something Nora had called *small*, but hadn't paid that much attention to the details.

Nora tucked her legs underneath her on the lounger and said, "Costarring is an overexaggeration, Julia. I have a very small part in a movie that he's starring in."

"You're in the same movie. I will not rephrase when it's technically, factually true."

Nora laughed. "Okay, whatever, legal eagle."

"Is he that guy from *The Wizards of Central Park*?" Emily finally seemed to be catching on.

"You've watched it?" Julia raised her eyebrows, surprised.

Emily shook her head, but she didn't explain that Cecile had watched most of the series last fall when she'd been up late at night, as Mikey, and then Jim, had both gone into sleep regressions after getting sick with, and then recovering from, swine flu. She'd recounted the episodes to Emily every morning at work, popping into her office without even knocking, often with Emily's favorite pumpkin spice latte in hand. Maybe not a raise, but Emily accepted the free coffee. (*I don't get what everyone sees in Devlin St. Claire*, Cecile had said then. *He's so . . . ordinary.*) Emily had googled him, and the show after that, and she had agreed that he didn't really appear to be anything special. In fact, she couldn't exactly remember what he looked like in any sort of distinct way.

She was going to need to google him again now that Nora obviously was infatuated.

"I don't know. He's . . . nice," Nora finally said. "You know . . . we had three scenes together. We had dinner once." She shrugged, trying to appear nonchalant. It wasn't that she didn't trust her sisters, it was more that she had gotten used to hiding stuff from them over the years. The way she had felt about Nate in her teens and most of her twenties, for one thing. Her on-again, off-again affair with Leo, who was married, for another.

Nothing had even happened between them, but the truth was Nora hadn't been able to stop thinking about him since she'd left LA a few weeks earlier. She had poured her heart out to him while drinking sangria her last night there, and now he knew everything about her: her mother's death, her love for Grandma Vera. He'd nodded with such understanding in his eyes, she had never felt closer to a man in her life. But the night had ended with a chaste goodbye hug before she'd gone back to her hotel after midnight.

Then, the next morning, she'd flown home. And when she'd arrived back at her apartment and checked her email, there was one waiting from Devlin with the subject line Miss you already.

Set isn't the same without you. —xD

She'd written back, to let him know she missed being on set too and that she'd gotten home safely. And they had been emailing each other a few times a week ever since.

The truth was, she was starting to think she might actually *like* Dev, for real. And that was exactly why she was scared to admit any of this out loud to her sisters now. "Dev is just . . . a nice guy," Nora finally repeated, which also was not a lie. "Like really genuine for an actor."

"*Nice? Genuine?*" Julia raised her eyebrows. "I've been married for ten years. Let me live vicariously through whatever you have going on, Nora." She let out a little sigh, and Emily and Nora exchanged a look.

"Everything all right with you and Ted?" Emily asked, handing Julia the first s'more.

"Of course," Julia said quickly. "It's just . . . ten years of marriage and we have a kid and busy jobs and it's not like we're, you know, jumping each other's bones all the time."

Nora shook her head, feeling embarrassed for Julia. "Oh my God, Julia. No one says that."

"So the two of you aren't fucking anymore? That's what you're trying to say," Emily said, handing the second s'more to Nora, who promptly took a bite, realizing if her mouth was full with gooey marshmallow and chocolate, she would not be able to say anything to her sisters for a few minutes. Thank God.

"Em!" Julia admonished. "Don't say it like that. You make it sound so . . . so . . . crude."

Emily shrugged unapologetically. "Have you gone to counseling?" she asked.

"We don't need counseling," Julia said emphatically. "We're just normal boring married people."

Cecile and Rick had been in counseling since the twins were born, but Emily decided not to cite that as an example, especially because she also knew it hadn't done much to improve anything between them. Plus, it would open her up to a lot of questions she didn't want to answer about why she knew so much about their marriage. "Hmmm," she said instead, then took a bite of her own s'more. "Nora, did you buy any wine earlier when you picked up the graham crackers?"

Nora shook her head. "Let's go walk to Vons and get some now," she said, happy to be off the subjects of both her and Dev, and Julia's sex life.

Julia yawned, stretched, and pronounced herself ready for bed. "You two go on without me," Julia said as she stood, and gave each of her sisters a quick hug. "But don't stay up too late. There's a lot on the agenda tomorrow."

Yes, there was a run on the beach starting at seven, followed by breakfast at Clayton's. At least Emily and Nora knew they would have pancakes to look forward to in the morning.

An hour later, Nora and Emily were back by the firepit, each with a Solo cup of cheap grocery store Pinot Noir. Though neither of them had ever admitted it to each other, this was their favorite part of their Coronado weeks. The night was quiet. The sea air was cool and familiar. The wine was smooth. Julia was asleep, and they were both feeling loose, easy. It was the moment of truth. The one moment a year when Nora and Emily remembered how to understand each other again.

"Tell me a secret," Emily said after she finished the first cup and poured herself a little bit more wine.

Nora finished off her cup too, considered pouring more but then decided against it. She already felt warm, relaxed. She put her empty cup down on the patio, lay back in the lounger, and closed her eyes. "No," she said to her sister. "You tell me a secret first."

Both of them were silent for a few moments, and then Emily finally spoke softly. "I think I'm in love with her," Emily said.

Nora didn't have to ask with whom. She had already known for at least two years that Emily had a crush on her married boss. "That's not a secret," she said, opening her eyes. But then she added, "I think I'm in love with him."

Emily laughed wryly. "Well, that's not a secret either."

"But I don't think I've ever been in love with anybody before," Nora blurted out. What she had with Leo was never love. What she'd always felt around Nate was a one-sided teenage crush. This felt altogether different in the way it completely consumed her, and even thinking about Dev now, she suddenly found it harder to breathe. "And Dev is like . . . Hollywood royalty. He can't possibly ever love me back."

"Why not?" Emily asked. Then she added, "At least he's not married."

"Married people get divorced all the time," Nora said, though she thought about Leo and she was suddenly glad she'd never told Emily about him. She sighed. "Honestly? I might be more terrified of what could happen if he does love me back. I wouldn't even know what to do or how not to mess it all up."

Emily nodded. She had, in fact, been in love before. And she understood the terrifying part. Loving someone meant that it could destroy you if they abandoned you, *when* they abandoned you. It was so much safer never to love anyone than to risk your heart. But Nora didn't know what Emily knew; Nora wasn't haunted the way she was. "Nora," Emily finally said. "That *Hollywood royalty* would be the luckiest fucking man alive to have the privilege of loving a gorgeous, talented bitch like you."

Nora laughed. "Takes one to know one." She picked up her empty Solo cup and tapped it to Emily's. "And it doesn't matter anyway," she said. "Filming is over. I'll probably never even see him again."

But in September, Dev was in New York to do a press junket in Central Park for the special-edition DVD release of the final season of *Wizards*. Though they had emailed a bunch in the last few months, Nora was still surprised when Dev showed up unannounced at her apartment. It was nearly midnight, and they had tentatively planned to have dinner the following day, after he was done working. She knew for a fact that the studio had paid for his hotel. What was he doing outside her door now?

"Can I come in?" he asked, smiling widely as soon as she greeted him.

For a moment, she forgot to be embarrassed by the shabbiness of her apartment, because she was just so shocked to see Dev standing right here, in Brooklyn Heights.

She nodded, opened the door wider, and suddenly she realized she was wearing ratty sweats, her curls piled on top of her head in a messy bun. She put her hand up in an awkward attempt to do something (anything) with her hair.

Dev closed the door behind him, then reached up and gently caught her hand. He smiled and brushed a wayward curl off her face. "You look beautiful, Nora," he said gently.

She laughed. "I definitely do not. But you actually look beautiful." And that wasn't a lie. Somehow even after a cross-country flight, Dev's wavy hair looked perfectly styled, his face was smoothly shaven, his skin wrinkle-free and flawless.

"My God," he said, leaning in closer, touching his forehead gently to hers. "You are everything."

No more perfect line could've been written for him, even if someone had tried. And some screenwriter somewhere probably had. Nora felt her breath suspend in her chest. She wanted to say something, but every coherent thought escaped her.

And then he kissed her. His lips felt warm, electric, like Nora was suddenly being kissed for the first time in her life at the ripe old age of thirty.

CHAPTER 20

2019

As soon as they hung up with Veronica, Emily dialed the main number for Julia's law firm on speaker and was connected to Julia's assistant, a woman named Robin.

"Who did you say this was?" Robin asked skeptically before answering Emily's very direct and immediate question, if she knew where Julia was.

Nora cleared her throat and took over in her stage voice. "Julia's younger sisters, Nora and Emily May. She was supposed to meet us in California yesterday but she hasn't shown up yet."

Robin didn't say anything for a moment, and then she said, "I'm not sure where she is right now. Julia hasn't been in the office for almost three weeks. She took a scheduled leave, so we're not expecting her back here until after July Fourth."

Scheduled leave? Nora and Emily exchanged a glance. Nora thanked Robin and asked if Julia checked in, to please have her call her sisters.

"So she took off work for a while," Emily said after she hung up. "Wherever she is . . . this isn't unexpected, is it? She planned this?"

Nora chewed on her bottom lip. Something still felt off, but Emily was also right. This didn't feel like a call-the-police kind of situation, as she'd thought it was when she'd first woken up. Julia had told work she'd be gone for eight weeks. She'd clearly gone . . . somewhere on purpose. Just not here. But was it possible that was very much on purpose, that Julia was avoiding seeing her? Nora inwardly kicked herself for not picking up the phone just once over this last year and apologizing for what had happened last May. Would that have made a difference?

"I think this might be all my fault," Nora suddenly blurted out. "Julia must still be mad at me for last year."

"What?" Emily looked confused. "Because we took Veronica out on the last night?"

There was more to it than that, of course, a very mortifying piece that Emily didn't know. But Nora felt so embarrassed thinking about it now, how stupid she'd been when she was drunk, that she didn't say anything for a few seconds.

Emily shook her head. "I don't think that's it," she said. "I've talked to her since then and she never brought that up. And besides, you know her, she'd show up just to yell at you in person if she really was still mad about it."

But would she? All bets were off with Julia whenever it came to Nate. Nora knew that, which made what she'd done even dumber.

Just then, the sound of a truck pulling into the driveway next door startled them and they both turned. It was like he'd somehow intuited what Nora had just been about to spill to Emily. Nate was home.

He parked in his driveway, hopped out of his truck, and spotted Nora and Emily sitting on the porch step. He looked around them, as if searching for the missing member of the Trouble Trio. But before he could walk over, Mallory ran out of his house, right into Nate's outstretched arms, and gave him a huge hug.

"Their air-conditioning is broken!" Mallory told Nate as he gave her a kiss on the forehead.

"Were you good for Mrs. McAllister?" he asked.

"It's really hot next door," Mallory said, extracting herself from Nate's embrace. "You should go fix it before they all die of heatstroke."

Nate laughed and tousled one of her braids. "It's in the seventies this morning. No one is dying of heatstroke, Mal."

As if on cue, Emily fanned herself with her hand. It may have only been in the seventies, but the cloud cover had already burned off, and the sun beat down on them.

"Dad, I'm serious," Mallory said. "Go help them. Nora might melt."

Emily was, in fact, the one who was melting, but Nora was the one who blushed. Nate just laughed, gave Mal another kiss on the forehead, and then walked over. He glanced around again, clearly looking for Julia.

"She's not here yet," Emily said flatly. "We don't know why. We're working on figuring that out."

Nate frowned deeply, and Nora noticed how much older he looked, how the wrinkles and worry lines had bloomed around his acorn eyes. In her head, she always pictured him as that same twenty-five-year-old she'd had a crush on as a teenager. But up close, he appeared believably now only a few years shy of fifty.

"She didn't say anything to you about not coming this week, did she?" Emily continued.

Nate shook his head. "I've . . . had some . . . um, stuff I've been dealing with recently. I haven't talked to her since . . ." He paused, like he was trying to remember the exact last time they'd spoken. "She texted me after she moved Veronica to college. I got a picture."

"That was January," Nora said, and her voice came out more accusatory than she meant it to. Considering she had also gotten a picture and had never responded to that text.

"Everything okay with you?" Emily asked Nate, and then Nora felt like a total bitch for not picking up on that part of Nate's answer.

Nate nodded. "Yeah, of course." He ran his hand through his brown, messy hair, sprinkled, Nora noticed now, with not a small amount of gray.

"But you know Julia," Emily continued. "It's not like her to disappear. Although Ronnie just told us it happened once before, years ago . . ."

Nate averted his eyes and didn't say anything for a moment. "Let me go take a look at the AC," he finally said, and Nora and Emily exchanged another look. Nate walked the rest of the way up the porch, toward the front door. "Okay if I go inside?"

They nodded, and as he went inside, Emily turned and whispered to Nora: "Evasive much?"

Yet again, Nora considered telling Emily the whole truth about what she had done last year. But instead, she nodded. She agreed with Emily on this much: Nate was acting like he was hiding something.

CHAPTER 21

2011

FOR NORA, 2011 BEGAN with a *Page Six* article that identified her as Devlin St. Claire's new mystery woman.

On the first morning of the year, she started a group text to her sisters from her new iPhone: a picture of the small blurb about her in *Page Six*, which appeared underneath a grainy photo of her and Dev in baseball caps, wandering through the farmer's market in Malibu. Figured. It was one of the first times they'd been out in public together, and the paparazzi were still relentlessly hounding him. *Nora May, the 31-year-old Brooklyn-based actress, appears in DSC's new movie musical and also in his heart?*

Damn, Emily immediately texted back. You're famous now.

Nora!!! Julia texted a few minutes later. V and I are dying over you potentially dating Will the Wizard. Is this for real? Do we trust Page Six?

Yep, she responded. Dev and I are together now.

And if her heart could beat outside of her chest, suddenly she felt it right there. It pounded furiously as everything she had ever wanted, and everything she hadn't even understood she'd wanted, enveloped her. *Brooklyn-based actress! Devlin St. Claire's girlfriend!* Well, yes, yes, she was.

After they'd seen each other in New York last fall, they'd been keeping their relationship on the down-low and she hadn't even told her sisters. They knew she'd gone out to LA last month, but they'd believed it was for work, until now.

Sorry I didn't tell you sooner, she typed out, feeling a little guilty that they were just finding out now, alongside the rest of the world. It's only been a few months, and it was just so new . . . we were waiting to see where it was going. I didn't want to jinx it.

Bitch please, Emily responded. We all knew where it was going last May.

If you're happy, then I'm so happy for you! Julia wrote.

I'm happy!!!!

She texted a picture of the *Page Six* blurb to their father too and said, Look, I'm getting some press for my upcoming movie! And this is the actor I told you about. We're dating!

Not even a moment later, her phone rang, *Dad's number*. Was he finally, finally ready to admit that maybe, just maybe, she was going to make a real career for herself, the way she had always dreamed? She was feeling both smug and happy.

"Daddy!" she said brightly as she picked up the phone. Then she inwardly chided herself for how she still immediately turned into a little girl with him.

"Nora," he said softly. "I'm so sorry."

She sighed and braced herself for how he was about to find fault with her. She cleared her throat. "*Page Six* is a pretty big deal, Daddy. And my agent already said she was getting a ton of calls since this story broke." Okay, technically not true. But also, technically today was a holiday. Stella would be getting calls. Nora would be getting attention. Next week.

"Nora," he said again. "I have to tell you something."

Then her heart froze, and she tried to remember how to breathe. "What's wrong?"

"I'm sick," he said.

"Oh no! Do you have the flu?" Dev had the flu last week and it had meant they weren't able to spend Christmas together like they'd planned. Instead, she had, last-minute, taken the train to DC to have dinner with Julia and Veronica and Ted.

He was silent on the other end of the line for a moment. Nora could hear him breathing, and that reassured her momentarily. "There's a malignant tumor in my lung," he said.

The words *malignant tumor* sounded strange, like something foreign she had never been taught the meaning of. She repeated them once back to him, as a question, and didn't like the way the words felt on the tip of her tongue. Then she said, "How could there be a tumor in your lung? You never smoked."

"I don't know," he said quietly. It was strange to think that her father, who had always seemed to know everything, didn't have the answer to this.

"Well, you'll get treatment and be okay, right?" Nora asked hopefully. "There's lots of things doctors can do these days."

"I'm starting chemo next week," he said. "Best case, I go into remission by the summer."

Nora didn't ask what the worst case was; she didn't want to know. She couldn't fathom knowing. "That's good," she said instead. "Do you need anything? How can I help?"

"No, I just wanted you to know what was going on with me, honey." Then he paused. "I'm visiting Emily now and I saw Julia in November. It's been a while since I've seen you. Maybe you pick a good weekend to fly out here. I'll buy your plane ticket."

It occurred to her in that moment that she was the last one he'd told, that Emily and Julia had probably already known about this for days, if not weeks. Had Julia known when she'd been at her house for Christmas dinner last week? If she had, she hadn't let on in the slightest. "I'll check my schedule and visit in the next few weeks, okay?" Nora promised.

"Good. I can't wait to see you." He paused for a moment, and then he said something that really made her worried about his health. "And if you want to bring that actor boyfriend, I'd love to meet him."

Nora called Julia as soon as she hung up with Dad. "Hello there, *Page Six*!" Julia said cheerfully as she answered the phone.

"When did you know about Dad?" Nora asked quietly.

"Oh, Nora." Julia sighed. "What does it matter *when* I knew?"

It mattered to Nora. She'd hated being last her whole life. "Julia," she whined. "You always do this to me. You and Emily still treat me like I'm five years old."

"Come on, Nora, that's not true. Dad said he wanted to talk to all of us on his own timeline. And the important thing is he's getting treatment, and he's going to be fine."

Julia would never tell Nora that she had known for six weeks that something was wrong. That Dad had mentioned it casually over Thanksgiving when he'd come to visit, that there was an upcoming biopsy. And that she had spent most of her lunch breaks throughout December researching lung cancer at the Georgetown library. Ever since, she'd had a sinking feeling in her stomach.

Emily hadn't seen their dad in almost a year when he had called her out of the blue and told her he was coming to Florida between Christmas and New Year's. He'd already bought his plane tickets. Luckily, Emily had no other plans.

Usually, he went to Julia's house for the holidays, to spend them with his one and only granddaughter, but this year, when he called Emily, he'd told her that he wanted to start his 2011 off with sunshine. "And I want to see the ocean again," he'd told her.

Emily hadn't clarified that in Tampa, it was actually the gulf. Instead, she'd told him she would make up the guest room in her condo and take him to Clearwater Beach. Give him a tour of her museum.

"I'd love all that," he'd said. "And I want to finally meet this Cecile too."

Emily briefly wondered if Nora had given up her secret. But when she pressed Dad on why he wanted to meet her boss, he'd only said that he always liked to know his daughters' friends. She supposed it was true in high school and still true now. And she accepted that answer, whether it was the actual truth or not. It was the only way she had maintained a good relationship with him over the years, accepting his word as good, even when deep down she didn't believe him.

Dad told her about his diagnosis two days before New Year's, when she took him to the beach. They had met Cecile for lunch, and Dad had fawned over her in a way that Emily had found strangely embarrassing. But Cecile had already texted her to say how great he was, how lucky Emily was. Two hours later he and Emily sat next to each other in folding sand chairs, toes in the gulf, and Dad blurted it all out stoically, staring straight ahead at the water.

"What do you mean *sick*?" Emily asked, unable to process the gravity of it. Dad was a tall man, who towered over all three of his daughters. Emily's big bones and height came from him. But he was thin and fit and still had a full head of wiry gray hair at sixty-eight. When she was in college, he'd been hospitalized with a bout of appendicitis, but Emily couldn't remember any other time in her life that he wasn't the perfect picture of health.

Still, Dad told her about his treatment, and she managed to keep herself together for the next few days, until she dropped him at the airport to fly home on January third.

Then she found herself driving straight to Cecile's little red-brick house, as if on autopilot. She didn't know where else to go. Who else to talk to. Her sisters' text chat had been oddly silent since Nora had sent her *Page Six* news two days earlier. It was unclear to her whom Dad had told first, or why he had chosen to come tell her in person and not Julia or Nora. In hindsight, it almost felt unfair that Emily had gotten to ring in the New Year with him, watching the ball drop on TV from her couch. That she had taken him to the beach, shared a grouper plate with him for dinner. That she had gotten to hug him goodbye at the airport and inhale the very Dad earthy scent of him. As the middle child, Emily wasn't used to getting special treatment. Why now? Why her?

"It's because you're so calm," Cecile said, pouring Emily a glass of Cabernet, then pouring one for herself. She moved aside a pile of picture books to sit down on the couch next to Emily, tucking her long legs underneath her. Her long hair brushed Emily's arm, making her shiver.

"The fuck I am calm," Emily said in response, downing a large sip of wine, hoping to erase the chill.

"Nora sounds dramatic, and I gather Julia is type A. Maybe he just needed you to take him to the beach and make him feel like everything would be okay in that soothing, practical way you have about you?"

Soothing, practical way? She shook her head. Did that really describe her? Had she done that? She wasn't sure. "What if everything isn't okay?" She whispered her deepest fear out loud to Cecile now, and Cecile leaned in closer, wrapping Emily in a hug.

Emily could feel the beating of Cecile's heart, close to her own, hear it vibrating into the stillness of the moment. Or maybe it was her own heart she was hearing, feeling. Thumping. "I wish everything were different," Emily heard herself saying, her own voice coming from some faraway place she couldn't quite control.

"He's going to be just fine," Cecile said. "I know it."

But that wasn't entirely what Emily meant.

In May, Nora left a few days early and flew to LA first to spend time with Dev. He picked her up at LAX in his BMW convertible and put the top down as they drove out of the city, onto the windy highway and into the hills of Malibu. Nora breathed in the salty Pacific air, Dev reached for her hand and squeezed it, and suddenly she exhaled, feeling lighter than she had in months.

"This bicoastal thing is hard," Dev said as they got out of his car. He grabbed her suitcase from the trunk and wheeled it inside his house.

Nora nodded in agreement. They'd seen each other only twice all spring. Once when Dev had met her in Chicago to visit Dad just after he'd started treatment. And another time when Dev had come to New York and they'd spent Easter weekend at the Plaza. Phone calls, emails, texts, and a weekly Sunday Skype were not the same thing.

Dev put her suitcase down inside his neat, contemporary-styled living room, and then he grabbed her in a hug. Nora clung to him, inhaling the strong, woodsy scent of his aftershave. A smell that always reminded her of Christmas. "I know you need to go see your sisters on Sunday," he said softly into her hair. "But what if you come back here after that and stay for a while?"

Was he asking her to move in with him? Nora froze for a moment, unsure what to say, how to react. Her body wanted to lean into him more. Her mind sounded with alarm bells. She needed to be in New York to keep auditioning.

But what if she didn't? Stella had been fielding movie and TV offers for her all spring.

"At least stay until the premiere," Dev added. Their movie was out in the middle of August, and Nora already had plans to fly back out here then, for the premiere. "What if we tried this for real, Nora? For the summer."

Nora didn't answer right away, and Dev tilted her chin up toward his with his forefinger, then leaned down and gently kissed her. "I'm tired of missing you," he said.

Nora felt his words, his kiss, deep in her chest. It was a feeling she never had before she'd met him, a warmth, like she was glowing from the inside out. She couldn't give up her career for a man. She wouldn't. But maybe she owed it to herself, to him, to give them the summer and see what might happen. "Okay, let's do it. I'm tired of missing you too," she finally answered.

On Wednesday in Coronado, Julia woke up when it was dark still. She checked the clock: 4:30 a.m. It was seven thirty at home. *Close enough*, she thought. She had too much on her mind to try to go back to sleep, so instead she crept out of bed, went quietly down the steps, and brewed a pot of coffee.

She grabbed a blanket and went and sat out on the front porch, sipping slowly from the warm mug, trying to calm herself down by listening to the waves lapping the shore, just across the street. The moon was full and bright, and hung low enough over the water that it illuminated everything. The beach looked long and lovely and almost blue, the water both black and pearlescent.

She heard the front door creak open next door, and she turned—there was Nate, tiptoeing out onto his porch. She was expecting him to be in a wet suit. But no, he wore plaid pajama bottoms and an oversized Penn sweatshirt, and had his own steaming mug of coffee in his hand. Of course. Mallory was asleep inside. He wasn't about to leave her all alone to go jump into the ocean like he had in his former life, even if he wanted to. Wasn't that part of what being a parent was? Leaving the old pieces of who you once were behind, embracing who you were now, a keeper and nurturer of this entirely other being.

He noticed her watching and motioned for her to sit with him. She hesitated—her mind was clouded with so many thoughts, worries, she wasn't really in the mood for conversation. Her father. And, also, what were Ted and Veronica doing right now in the Hamptons? She wanted the ocean air, her coffee, the predawn quiet to steady herself, alone. But Nate kept on staring at her, so she finally wrapped herself in the blanket and walked over to his porch.

He reached out to hug her, but then the blanket made it difficult, and he patted her awkwardly on both her shoulders instead. "You look tired, Jules," he said. "You should go back to sleep."

"So should you," she said pointedly.

He shook his head. "Nah, I've needed this early-morning time to study and get stuff done. And now my body just naturally gets up at this hour."

"How's school going?" she asked him.

"Good, I'm student-teaching in the fall. Mal will be in preschool. Hopefully next year when she goes to kindergarten, I can get a full-time teaching job. Good, steady hours with a kid at home, you know?"

She nodded. Like she did know. But the truth was, she didn't know at all. Part-time law was never as part-time as she wanted, and Julia often felt like a full-time failure as both a lawyer and a mother. It didn't help that Veronica, at not quite eleven, had already begun acting like a full-blown ungrateful teenager. At first, she just hated camp, tennis, a girl from school who'd been her friend since the pre-K years. But now that was blossoming into what seemed like a permanent chip on her shoulder directed squarely and specifically at her mother. Julia had kissed V goodbye Sunday morning before she'd left for the airport, told her to enjoy her week in the Hamptons with Ted and her grandparents, and Veronica had rolled over from a half-sleep to tell Julia that she *hated* her for leaving every May. All the parenting books decried this mom-hate as normal, but still, it was hard to hear. It felt unfair that exactly none of V's wrath ever seemed directed at Ted. The two of them were thick as thieves.

"But you're on vacation." Nate was still talking, and Julia tried to shake away the thoughts of Veronica's new preadolescent mean streak. "Why are you up?"

She shrugged and paused to take a sip of her coffee. "Time change," she lied. Nate gave her a look like he could see right through her. She sighed. "My dad has a big doctor's appointment today. To find out if the chemo worked."

She had made the schedule for this week extra busy, every moment packed, hoping to keep all of their minds off what felt like impending doom. But that still hadn't stopped her from waking up early, from tossing and turning all night. From worry running through her veins, hot and thick.

"I'm sure it worked," Nate said.

But of course, he couldn't know that. And Julia suddenly remembered the way his face had looked when they were sitting out here the summer his mom had gotten diagnosed. And how he had insisted that she couldn't help him and that he couldn't love her anymore. As she thought about it all these years later, it still stung a little.

"It had to have worked," Nate added.

"I hope so," she said, and for the first time she really felt in her bones how hard it must've been for Nate to go through this at twenty-one. At the time, she knew, theoretically, that it was difficult. But now she really understood it, viscerally, in a way that momentarily took her breath away.

Nate reached out and gently patted her thigh, and the warmth of his hand made her slowly breathe again. "I definitely didn't handle it well when my mom was going through it," Nate said. "I thought pushing everyone away was the only way to survive. Stop feeling altogether."

She nodded, understanding now the way she hadn't back then. Nate had been desperately trying to protect his heart.

"But if you need anything, Jules . . . even if you just need to talk. I'm here for you," Nate added softly now.

One week a year, she thought, remembering how he'd said that to her when she'd offered him the same solace.

They both noticed headlights at the same time—a car driving slowly down Ocean Boulevard. Nate quickly moved his hand back from her thigh, like he'd been caught doing something he shouldn't have. Julia didn't dare look at him and peered out toward the street instead. One lone BMW rolled toward them. It stopped right in front of Nate's, parked by the curb.

"You expecting company?" Julia asked. It occurred to her that Nate could be dating someone again. That if he was, he probably wouldn't have mentioned it to her in the emails and texts they shared throughout the year. But Nate shook his head.

The driver door opened, and then a man in a black baseball cap hopped out. She didn't have her contacts in yet, and the glasses she'd traveled with were an old prescription. She squinted, trying to get a better look in the low light. "Is that . . . is that Devlin St. Claire?" Julia whispered to Nate.

"Who?" Nate asked.

It was almost unbelievable that Nate didn't know who Devlin was, until she remembered Mallory wasn't old enough yet for *The Wizards of Central Park*. So she didn't explain about him being a celebrity, the momentary feeling of being starstruck herself. Instead, she simply answered him: "Nora's boyfriend."

Nora was in a deep sleep when Dev showed up in Coronado. Her head was thick from the wine she'd drunk with Emily on the patio the night before, where after two glasses each, they both admitted that they weren't ready to lose the only parent they had left. She had drunk enough that she crawled into bed just before midnight and quickly fell asleep. When Julia gently shook her awake, she was in the middle of a dream. A dream she had from time to time where she sees her mother in the middle of Fifth Avenue, standing right in front of Bergdorf Goodman. Nora sees her there and instantly, suddenly, freezes, unable to move to cross the street even though the light is green.

"Nora." Julia's voice shook her out of the dream, and she opened her eyes. The light was pale gray in the room, barely dawn.

"What time is it?" she croaked. Her throat felt dry. She hadn't drunk enough water. "Did Dad call already?"

Julia shook her head. "Not yet. But Devlin is downstairs."

"Dev?" She sat up quickly. "Here?"

Dev wasn't supposed to be in Coronado. He was supposed to be in LA. She was supposed to rent a car and drive back up there herself on Sunday, and anyway, today was only Wednesday.

"I offered him some coffee." Julia frowned. "But he asked me to wake you. He seems . . . upset."

"Upset?" Nora croaked. Her mind felt thick, everything around her hazy, and for a brief moment she wondered if she was still dreaming.

But Nora blinked, and Julia was still hovering above her, frowning. No, she was awake. And she got out of bed and quickly pulled on yoga pants and her old Northwestern sweatshirt before running downstairs, Julia following behind her.

Dev turned and glanced at her from the couch as soon as she hit the living room. Julia was right. He did look upset. His normally animated features were weirdly stoic.

"What's going on?" Nora said.

Julia moved toward the couch, her eyes trained intently on Dev, her lips pursed to form a question as if ready to cross-examine him.

Before Julia could say a word, Nora said: "Dev, let's go take a walk."

"I didn't expect you to show up here," Nora said as they crossed the street to the path that ran down Ocean Boulevard. It was just barely dawn, the sky an almost eerie blue-gray. "But now I can show you everything I love about this island." Nora kept talking as Dev's pace sped up, and she struggled to keep up with him. "Sunrise for one. We can make it to the bay side of the island in about twenty minutes, and by then the sun should just be coming up over the bay. It's usually gorgeous. Of course, I've only seen it a few times because I'm never awake early enough—"

Dev suddenly stopped walking, and Nora came to a skidding halt. He turned abruptly on his heels to face her and put his hands on her shoulders—not gently, like he had last weekend in Malibu, but firmly, holding her at arm's length. "Dammit, Nora. I thought you really liked me, that this was real," he said.

"I do," Nora insisted. She reached up to grab his hand on her shoulder but he jerked away. "Dev, what's going on?"

He pulled out his phone and handed it to her. "Explain this to me."

She looked at what was on the screen. It appeared to be an article of some sort, with a headline that read: "Nora May Speaks Out: The Truth About Devlin St. Claire."

Nora shook her head. "I don't understand. Some fake hit piece?" People wrote shit about Dev all the time—she'd never seen it bother him before. But to see her own name? This was something unexpected. And she briefly felt excited, until she remembered again how mad Dev had seemed.

"Read it," he said gruffly. "It's not fake."

She glanced through the first few paragraphs, and it did appear to have quotes from her. Or, rather, an *inside source* who was *close* to her, who said that she had pretended to have feelings for Dev to get publicity for the movie. But that what she really thought was that Dev was too self-absorbed to ever really love someone. That he was nothing at all like Will the Wizard. *Not a kind bone in his entire body.* She actually physically flinched when she read that line, and she stopped reading and looked back up.

"I never would've said that . . . it's not true. And I don't even know who this *inside source* is," Nora stumbled. "This is all made up, Dev."

"Keep reading," he insisted.

She scrolled down. *The Devlin St. Claire affair was all smoke and mirrors. Nora May has actually been in a relationship with an unnamed Broadway producer for years.*

And then it hit her. *Leo?* She remembered his eagerness for her to get close to Dev, get photographed, his insistence that he would make it work for her career. She hadn't talked to him in months. Was this all him? She suddenly felt like she was going to throw up, and she sat down on the sidewalk and tried to catch her breath.

"Which producer?" Dev asked.

Nora focused on breathing. *In and out. In and out.*

"Goddammit, Nora," Dev said. "You've been in a relationship with a producer this whole time?"

"No," Nora said. "I mean . . . yes. I mean . . . I was sort of . . . before. But not since you and I got together. Leo and I were never—"

"Leo fucking Marks?" Dev reached down to grab his phone back. "You sold me out for that asshole?"

"How do you know Leo?" she asked dumbly.

"Is that really what matters now?"

Nora shook her head, and suddenly it felt like anything else she said was going to make everything worse. So what if she and Leo had been in an on-again, off-again relationship for years? She hadn't spoken to him in at least six months. She did love Dev. She had nothing to do with this article. She just had to figure out a way to explain so Dev would understand.

"You thought this was all a fucking game." Dev spoke quietly but his voice bubbled a little, like he was about to explode. "And I thought, for once . . . you and I, this was real life."

"It was," Nora said. "It is. You know how I feel about you. You know what we have is real."

"I don't know anything," he said.

"Dev, please." She hated the way her voice sounded so small, desperate. She stood up and tried to reach for his hand, but as soon as she touched him, he yanked away and started walking back toward his car.

"Dev!" she called after him. But he kept on walking. "Devlin Stolarski!"

He flinched, stopped walking for just a moment, but he still didn't turn around. And then he continued and got in his car.

When Nora made it back to the house and got her phone

from the nightstand, she saw she already had a text from Leo: You're welcome, kiddo.

Dad, as it turned out, needed a second round of chemo, and when Veronica went back to school in the middle of August, Julia called her sisters and asked what they thought about going out there to check on him. He lived alone (he'd lived alone for years, since Nora left for college), and she knew he had a close-knit group of friends nearby, but still, she didn't like thinking about him in that great big house all by himself going through so much chemo.

"Someone should go," Nora agreed. "But I don't know if it can be me. I have a full travel schedule to promote this movie."

Julia had recently spotted her sister on a billboard off the beltway (advertising the film) and she had pulled off to take a photo to send to the sisters' chat. Even V had been impressed when she'd shown her that.

"I mean, I guess I could see if there's anything I could skip . . ." Nora's voice trailed off.

"No way. Dad wouldn't want you to miss any of that," Julia assured her.

"I don't think I can do it either," Emily said. She told them about the two baby orcas, a new exhibit at the museum that was opening in September. "By Thanksgiving things will be calmer, and I'll make sure to see Dad then. But I can't take the time off right now."

And so, after a moment of quiet on the line, Julia stepped in, stepped up, as she always had her whole life: "Well, don't either of you worry, I'll do it. I'll go out there myself."

"I told you, you didn't have to come. I'm doing just fine," Dad said a few weeks later, as he opened the door and ushered Julia inside.

It was chilly, considering it was still technically summer, and Julia was only wearing a light jacket. Freaking Chicago, she really hadn't missed it.

"Can't a daughter come for a visit? I wanted to see you," Julia insisted as she walked inside. It was funny how their childhood house never seemed to change. Same furniture, same carpet, same neolithic gas stove Nora had spent her whole life being afraid to light. She hadn't been back in a few years, as Dad had routinely come to visit her in Maryland for holidays, birthdays, celebrations. But now, stepping inside, it felt like a time capsule.

"Yeah, but you're so busy, sweetheart. I know how hard it is for you to get away."

She shook her head. She'd actually left Maryland with little fanfare—Ted had told her to take as much time as she needed in Chicago, and that he would manage V's schedule (with the help of the neighborhood moms who said they'd run the carpools without Julia for a few days). Veronica had barely shrugged when Julia mentioned she was leaving to check on Grandpop, as well as shot down Julia's suggestion that she make him a card to cheer him up (*What am I? Like five?*). "It's really fine, Dad," she insisted now. "I can take a few days away."

She put her bags down and gave him a hug. Her arms fit around his usually big frame too easily. She could feel what his thick sweater was hiding—he'd lost a lot of weight. "I'll make you a bunch of food while I'm here and we can freeze it," she said. "Do you still have the old freezer in the garage?"

"Of course I do! Where would it have gone?" Dad asked, and Julia laughed.

The next afternoon, in the midst of Julia making her fourth lasagna to put in the garage freezer, Dad woke up from a nap on the couch.

"Julia?" he called for her, his voice sounding thready.

"Can I get you something?" she asked, walking into the living room. "Are you cold? Do you need a blanket?" Her whole life, Dad had complained about the cold in Chicago, and now that he looked so frail, she worried it might feel even worse.

He patted the spot on the couch next to him. "Sit."

"I have one more lasagna to put in the oven," she said.

"Forget the lasagna." His eyes stayed fixed on her face, and he patted the seat next to him again.

She complied and sat next to him.

"My Julia," he said gently. "You never sit still, do you?"

"I'm sitting now," she said.

"Okay." He gently patted her thigh. "But you have to remember to sit, even when I'm not right here to insist." Julia smiled, and then he said, "It's funny how sometimes I feel like I blinked and all you girls grew up, just like that."

She nodded. "It's what all the parenting books say: The days are long, the years are short." That had yet to feel true with Veronica, though. Sometimes it felt like she was trapped inside some kind of preteen parenting hell that she might never make her way out of.

"But you're all grown up. You need to remember to sit, to take moments for yourself. I'm not going to be here forever to remind you."

"Don't say that!" Julia said quickly.

"Why not, it's true. The only thing certain in life is death."

"And taxes," Julia added.

Dad chuckled. "You get that sense of humor from me, you know."

She nodded. She did know, or at least thought she did. She didn't know what she inherited from her mom by comparison. She stared at him for another moment, hating how frail he looked. She hated cancer and the ability it had to make a person you loved wither right before your very eyes. And then she wondered if she would ever again have the chance to ask him the one thing she'd been trying to for twenty years.

"Dad," she said, forcing herself to voice it now. "Since we're talking about death . . . will you tell me the truth now?"

"The truth?" His face turned, confused.

But she kept on staring at him. "About Mom," she said softly. And then his face fell. *Understanding.* He shook his head.

"Please?" she said.

He didn't say anything for a few moments, and he twisted his thin fingers together in his lap. "I love you three girls so much," he finally said. "I made a promise, a long time ago, that I would do whatever it took to protect you."

CHAPTER 22

2012

"ALL PUBLICITY IS GOOD publicity," Stella reiterated to Nora, as the two of them sat inside Gramercy Tavern sharing lunch on a Thursday in the middle of February. Outside it had started snowing, and Nora glanced out the large window to her left, watching the way the white flakes looked peaceful, even beautiful, from here. When she had to go back out on the street and walk to the train after lunch, it would be a different story. She had forgone boots for impractical pretty heels for this lunch meeting. Just thinking about the trip back to Brooklyn made her toes feel cold.

"Nora," Stella said. "Are you listening to me?"

Nora nodded, turned away from the window, and smiled. Though she had truthfully only half heard what Stella was saying. *Blah-blah-blah.* She'd been saying it for months, ever since Leo's hit piece on her and Dev had gone viral and their low-budget movie musical had sold wildly beyond anyone's expectations at the box office. Six months later, Stella was still trying to get Nora to do yet another movie. Nora had at first listened and spent most of November filming a straight-to-video Hallmark rom-com in Toronto. But Nora had been begging Stella to turn this name recognition, her fifteen minutes of fame, or whatever it was, into a bona fide Broadway role instead.

"So look," Stella said now. "Leo called me this week."

Nora made a face. She refused to talk to Leo. It didn't matter how much Stella proclaimed what he had done as *brilliant*, the space inside Nora's chest where her heart once was had felt strangely numb since Dev had left her standing on Ocean Boulevard last May. Then he'd rejected all of her calls, blocked her on social media, and circulated a counter piece to the press saying that all the rumors of their relationship had always been false. That they had met on set and briefly become acquaintances, nothing more. *Nothing more.*

"I don't want anything to do with Leo," Nora insisted.

Stella raised her eyebrows. "Not even for a role in this crazy amazing new musical based on Greek mythology, where you could play the lead opposite Brett Booker?"

Nora opened her mouth, then closed it again without saying anything. Brett Booker had been one of her idols since she saw him in *Hamlet* in the Park the first summer after she'd moved to New York City. And then, last year, he'd won a Tony for his role in a smash-hit Sondheim revival. "Are you serious?" Nora finally said.

"As a heart attack," Stella replied. "They want you to come in and read, but Leo has already talked you up and they all watched *Bright Spaces* and were super impressed with 'Rosie's Song' so they already love your voice. This one is yours for the taking, Nora. All you have to do is reach out and grab it."

Nora nodded. "Tell me all the details."

"*Hera* is slated for a two-month tryout up in Boston this summer. If all goes well, they're hoping for Broadway by next spring." Stella paused and took a slow sip of her dirty martini. "I told Leo you would do anything he wanted to make this work. Was I wrong?"

Nora slowly shook her head. "No," she said. "You were right." She would, in fact, do anything, *anything*. Even if it was going to have to mean ingratiating herself with Leo again.

Outside the streets were slick from the snow, and Nora's toes were almost instantly numb as she trudged toward Union Square. She pulled her phone out of her purse, and she called the person she wanted to tell the most in the world about this new, exciting opportunity.

"Daddy," she said as soon as he picked up. "I think it's finally happening."

He was newly in remission, after enduring a second round of chemo last fall, and when Nora and Emily had both gone to Julia's house for Christmas to spend the holiday with him there, he'd told them all the good news. He'd looked weak, thin, bald at Christmas, but he'd assured them he was feeling strong. That he was ready to get back to normal. Cancer was in the rearview mirror.

"Nora," he said now. "I see on the Weather Channel it's snowing in New York. You're supposed to get twelve inches in the city."

"Daddy," she repeated. "I think I'm about to get everything I ever wanted." Well, maybe not everything. But all she had to do was just lock up all thoughts of Dev, hide them in the far corners of her mind, and never, ever again take them out.

"Do you have boots that fit you?" Dad asked. "I can order you some new ones. I just got the L.L.Bean catalog in the mail."

Nora laughed. "Daddy, I haven't ordered from that catalog since high school. And my feet are warm!" Her feet were definitely not warm as she trudged through a pile of gray slush crossing Park at Eighteenth. "But listen to what I'm saying right now. I just had lunch with my agent and there's this role. A dream role. It'll be in a tryout in Boston in the summer and if all goes well, on Broadway next spring." She repeated what Stella said, noticing now as she spoke how far away that all must sound to her father's untrained and suspecting ears. But this was *it*. She felt it in her bones, and that feeling alone was keeping her warm even as she walked through this wintery slush.

"That's wonderful, Nora," Dad finally said.

"I mean, it really is. I'll be playing opposite one of my Broadway idols. Brett freaking Booker, Daddy."

"I liked that movie you were in with Dev," Dad said quietly.

"He was such a nice young man, that time I met him in Chicago with you."

She suddenly remembered the way Dad had binged all of *The Wizards of Central Park* before they'd shown up, and how Dev had so kindly sat across from Dad on the couch and patiently answered all his plot questions. "I told you we're not together anymore," Nora said, her voice sharper than she meant it to be.

"I know," Dad said. "It's just . . . a shame, that's all. I liked the way he treated you."

They were both quiet for a moment, and Nora wanted to ask if he liked the way Dev had dumped her in May. Or how he had publicly lied and privately blocked her. But she swallowed back those feelings. She didn't want to talk about Dev. If she didn't talk about him, didn't think about him, then she would be okay. And besides, she wanted to focus on the happy news from Stella. Forget Dev. She was finally, finally going to have her big break.

She wasn't quite at the train yet but she told Dad she was, that she was about to walk down the steps, about to lose him underground.

"Okay, call me later, honey. Be careful in this snow."

As soon as they hung up, she texted her sisters about *Hera*, before getting to the train.

You're going to rock this and get the part, superstar! Julia replied immediately.

Omg, you're for real going to be too famous for us now, Emily texted a few seconds later.

And then, Nora was suddenly smiling again.

The night before Emily left for Coronado, her phone rang around midnight.

She had booked an early flight and had gone to bed at nine, but at the sound of the ring, she suddenly jumped up, wide awake, instantly worrying something had happened to Dad. But then she remembered again: *remission*. He was okay now.

Her heart still thudded in her chest as she grabbed the phone from her nightstand. *Cecile?*

"I didn't wake you, did I?" Cecile's gentle voice came through the line, soothing Emily's racing heart like a lullaby.

"Not at all," Emily lied, trying as hard as she could to sound wide awake. "What's up?"

"I couldn't sleep," Cecile said. She paused for a moment, and Emily just listened to the soft sound of her breath on the other end of the line.

"It's not the orcas still, is it?" Emily asked, referring to the new exhibit that had been the bane of both of their existences all year long as one thing after another had gone wrong, from the marketing mishaps that called them *killer whales* to one of them developing a stomach ulcer.

Cecile didn't answer for another moment. And then she said, "What if I told you I didn't want to be married anymore. That I might . . . love someone else."

"What?" Emily asked, confused. What exactly was Cecile trying to tell her? Was it what she thought, or was that ridiculous? She *loved* someone else. Maybe she was talking about Marty, who did the books for the museum and often brought them Starbucks when he stopped by once a month. But Emily vaguely remembered him mentioning a girlfriend last month . . .

"What would you think of that?" Cecile pushed.

"Why do you care what I think?" Emily said.

"You know why," Cecile said. Emily suddenly understood she wasn't talking about Marty.

"I think . . . I think . . ." she stammered, uncertain. What did she think? She knew what she felt, but she was too terrified to commit her thoughts to actual words. "What about Mikey and Jim?" she finally said.

"What about them?"

"Divorce is really hard for kids. Wouldn't they be better off growing up in a house with both their parents?" Emily said.

"Even if their mother loves someone else?" Cecile asked softly.

Emily didn't say anything for a moment or two and time felt suspended, weirdly frozen. "I should go to sleep," she finally said, which she understood was no kind of answer. Cecile sighed on the other end of the line, which prompted Emily to keep talking, even though words suddenly didn't seem to make sense. "I have an early flight in the morning," she heard herself saying.

"Okay," Cecile said after another moment of silence. "Travel safe."

The next night, Emily was still drowning in that conversation, repeating it over and over again in her head as she sat out on the back patio drinking wine with Nora. Had she done the right or wrong thing? What if she had just said to Cecile: *I love you too.* Why hadn't she said that?

But Nora seemed fixated on her own thoughts and didn't notice or comment on Emily being unusually quiet. She finished off her second glass of cheap grocery store rosé and set the empty goblet down on the bricks. Emily poured the remains of the bottle into her own glass and set the empty bottle on the bricks too.

Nora sat up to warm her hands over the firepit. The night air in Coronado never failed to surprise her, even after all these years. The chill that cut across the water after dark always felt weirdly unexpected, and for some reason she thought about how cold she was last year, running after Dev on Ocean Boulevard before sunrise. Even with the warmth of the fire now, she shivered.

"No body fat," Emily said.

"What?" Nora asked, rubbing her hands close to the fire.

"You have no body fat, Nora. You look like you lost some weight since Christmas. You should eat more."

"I eat plenty," Nora protested, though it was true she had lost a little weight in the last month. They'd had to take her costume in just before she'd left. "It's all the dance rehearsals for *Hera.* I'm burning so many calories." Maybe it was that, or maybe it was that she was filled with this overwhelming joy that kept threatening to burst every time she even thought about the role. It was happening! It was really happening! Nora had been burning up with nervous energy. She had, in fact, until now not even thought about Dev for months.

"You do look a little thin," Julia agreed, walking back out from the kitchen, where she must've been listening as she'd loaded the dishwasher. They often got takeout pizza the first night, but she'd arrived early enough this year that she'd gone and bought crabs at the bayside market and cooked them for dinner. Julia picked up the bottle of wine now and frowned upon seeing it empty.

"There's more wine in the fridge," Nora said, brushing off her sisters' comments about her weight. Maybe they'd needed to mother her when she was five, but they did not need to now that she was in her thirties. She, in fact, had a very healthy diet! "And I can take care of myself. I don't need either of you to be my mother!"

Julia frowned again, sat down on the ledge by the firepit. She crossed her legs and wrung her hands. "You're right. I'm sorry, Nora. And anyway, don't listen to me, I'm a terrible mother."

"Bullshit," Emily said. And she thought again about Cecile, and how Emily had said that she should stay married, for her boys' sake. Is that what *good* mothers did? That felt all wrong. Why had she said that?

"You are like the world's best mother to Veronica," Nora affirmed—not that she would have any real way to judge such a thing. But in the glimpses she got at holidays and over texts and email, Julia seemed super involved in Veronica's life. Isn't that what a good mother was? "I just was trying to remind you that I don't need you to do that for me."

Julia shook her head. "Veronica truly hates me right now. She'll barely even talk to me. And then Ted recently bought her a phone—without asking me, of course. And now I think she just blocked me over text. Either that or she's been ignoring my messages."

Emily suddenly chuckled. "Don't you remember what I was like at her age?"

Julia made a face and Nora nodded. "Yeah, you were such a bitch, Em. I mean, you still are." Nora giggled. Emily poked her hard on the shoulder. "Ow!" Nora exclaimed.

"Takes one to know one," Emily said.

"Veronica is so different from us," Julia sighed. "She's an only child. Ted spoils her way too much." She was quiet for a moment while she nervously chewed on the skin around her thumbnail. "My biggest regret is that we were never able to give her a sister."

Nora didn't say anything, but she stood, walked into the kitchen, and returned a moment later with a third glass and another bottle of wine. She unscrewed the cap, did a large pour into the glass, and held it out to Julia.

"Do you want to talk about it?" Nora asked gently. She didn't know why Veronica was an only child, but she'd always assumed it was because Julia and Ted both worked a lot. And that Julia's career was important to her too. It made sense.

Julia shook her head, accepted the wine, and took a large sip.

"Jul, you're a great mother," Emily said emphatically. "Preteens are just assholes. It's like a requirement at that age or something."

"Total assholes," Nora agreed.

Julia took another sip of wine. "We all grew up without a mother," she finally said in a quiet voice. "What if I don't know how to do this right? What if I can't ever get through to her and she hates me forever?"

"Mommy died," Nora said. "You're here and you're healthy, and Veronica is just in some weird adolescent phase. You'll figure it out. History won't repeat like that."

Julia stared very hard into her wineglass, and Emily took a very large sip from hers.

"I don't believe history repeats," Julia finally said when she looked back up. "It rhymes."

CHAPTER 23

2019

"I'M STILL STUCK ON what Ronnie said, that Julia *disappeared* like this once before," Emily said after Nate was out of earshot, checking the AC. "What if this is all related?"

Nora shot her a skeptical look. "But we didn't even know about her disappearing at the time. How would we figure that out now, all these years later?"

Emily chewed on her bottom lip, still thinking it through. "Well . . . Ronnie said she didn't come back from Coronado like she was supposed to. Let's say she stayed here on the island a few extra weeks. Who else might know about it?" She cast her eyes toward the house, the living room, where a clanking sound suddenly arose, causing Nora to jump a little. "Why don't you go in there and ask him?"

The truth was, the last thing Nora wanted to do was talk to Nate, about anything. "No, you ask him," she whispered, nudging Emily with her elbow.

Julia and Nate had been thick as thieves for most of their lives. It was entirely possible she'd told him something years ago that she had never told her sisters.

"Well, do you want the good news or the bad news?" Nate suddenly stepped back out onto the porch, wiping his hands on the sides of his jeans.

"Good," Nora said, as Emily simultaneously said, "Bad."

Nate chuckled. "You two never change, do you? Okay, I'll say them both quickly. Bad news is the unit is totally dead and you need a new one. Good news is a friend of mine at school, her dad owns an AC company, so I can probably get him out here this afternoon, even though it's a holiday."

Right, Memorial Day. Nora had completely forgotten. She had always loved the years their week here overlapped with the holiday, and they could walk to Glorietta Bay and watch the fireworks lighting up the sky across the water, over downtown San Diego. Or sit on Orange Avenue and watch the parade in the morning.

"Thanks," Nora said shyly, and shot Emily a look. Her eyes were daggers that said, *Ask him! Ask him, dammit!*

Emily sighed, and Nate started walking back toward his own house. "Hey, Nate!" Emily called after him. He stopped and turned around. "Um . . . Nora and I were just wondering. That thing Ronnie said about Julia disappearing one other time, years ago. Well . . . do you have any idea what she was doing then?"

Nate ran his hand through his hair and looked down at his sneakers for a moment, but he didn't immediately say anything.

"I mean, Nora was thinking," Emily continued. "And I guess I agree . . . that maybe if we knew that information, it might somehow give us an idea of where she is now."

Nate shook his head. "I don't think—"

"Dad!" Mallory ran out of his house next door and skipped across the lawn. "Mrs. McAllister made blueberry pancakes!" She wrapped her arms around Nate and gave him a hug.

She was still sweet for twelve. Or maybe just so entirely different from Emily's stepsons, who were about the same age but wouldn't dare be seen hugging their mom, or their *Emma*, in public, much less in front of other adults they knew.

"Blueberry pancakes!" Nate said. He flashed a quick grin at Emily and Nora. "I'm sorry. Gotta run. They're my favorite and breakfast is the most important meal of the day. I'll let you know what time they can stop by to install a new window unit, okay?"

Mallory skipped back across the yards and Nate jogged to keep up with her.

Nora shook her head. "Damn. Saved by the blueberry pancakes."

"But he was acting sketchy as hell, right?" Emily said. "It wasn't just me?"

Nora nodded, though she wondered if the weirdness they were sensing was because of her.

"So, what this all boils down to," Emily continued, "is that Julia has had a secret for the last ten or fifteen years that she never told us about?" Emily suddenly felt irritated, both at Julia for keeping something from them and at herself for not noticing.

"But Nate knows something," Nora said. "And maybe we're grasping at straws here, but we have nothing else to go on, do we?"

Emily nodded in agreement.

Nora glanced at Nate's house, swallowed back the shame she felt every time she thought about last May, took a deep breath, and walked down the porch steps.

"Where are you going?" Emily called after her.

"I'm suddenly in the mood for some blueberry pancakes," Nora said resolutely as she strode across the front yard.

CHAPTER 24

2013

IN THE THIRTEEN YEARS the May sisters had come to Coronado since Grandma Vera's death, not one of them had stepped foot inside her former bedroom. Per the pictures Nate used for the rental listing, the downstairs master had been tastefully redecorated with a king-sized bed, pale blue walls, and prints of seashells hanging around the room. The bedroom didn't look at all the way it had when Grandma Vera had actually lived there, or when Julia had cleaned it out in 1999: warm, messy, filled with splashes of bright colors. And in the years since, none of the sisters had been able to bring themselves to go in when they visited. The three bedrooms up the stairs were smaller, but were the same three they had stayed in when they'd come to Coronado as girls, teenagers, and now, adults. The master had, thus far, been for the renters' use only.

But two weeks after Dad had called all three May sisters that March, to let them know that the cancer had spread to his brain, Emily had an idea.

"You said you wanted to see the ocean," Emily reminded him over the phone. "Come to Coronado with us in May. There's an extra bedroom just for you."

Robert May had been to his mother-in-law's house in Coronado only once before. It was sometime in the early seventies, when Vera and Grey got married in a small ceremony on the beach. The girls hadn't been born yet. Meredith had been pregnant with Julia at the time, but it was still early enough that she'd been hiding it, and they hadn't even told Vera yet.

Then Julia was born, Emily three years later, Nora three years after that, and suddenly Meredith was gone. He was a single father to three small girls. And he and Vera seemed to disagree on everything. Well, except for maybe the girls' well-being. Vera, he was certain, understood that he would do anything, *anything*, to keep them safe. And Bob was certain that Vera had loved them fiercely, loved them as her own. Which was why, after she had promised to keep his secret, he had promised her he would send the girls to Coronado every May for one week. It was a promise he'd kept until she'd died, when she'd taken his secret to the grave.

Though rationally he knew that Vera had been gone almost fifteen years, when he stepped out of the cab and onto the sidewalk in front of her old house, he felt her in the air. It all looked exactly as he remembered. The staunch white Victorian with the large front porch, nestled on a tree-lined street of similar Victorians. The great, wide blue Pacific just across from them, roaring in his ears as he walked up the front path. The ocean seemed to whisper her name: *Vera, Vera, Vera.*

And before he walked up the steps to the porch, he stopped for a moment and whispered back: *I'm sorry.*

"Dad!" Julia bounded out the front door. "Let me help you with your bag."

He waved her away. "I can carry my own bag." He was dying, he knew that fact somewhere in the rational portion of his mind. But largely, he still felt good. His body still mostly moved the way he wanted it to, and somewhere in the irrational part of his mind, he couldn't believe that he was *actually* dying. Maybe it wasn't even true.

"I'll take it," Julia insisted, pulling the suitcase from his hand. She never did take no for an answer. Not when she was five years old; certainly not now.

"How's my granddaughter doing?" he asked as he followed her inside. "Did you bring her?"

Julia shook her head. "Veronica's good, and no, she always goes to the Hamptons with Ted to visit his parents this week. It's just a sisters' week, Dad."

"So then I'm intruding?"

"You are *not* intruding," she said. "We all wanted you to come this year. We want to spend some time with you."

The inside of the house looked very different from how he remembered it, and he supposed his daughters had done a nice job turning it into a rental. Making it into a business and still making it out here every May to spend time together. *Sisters' week.*

We did something right, Vera, he thought.

"This is where you can sleep," Julia said, gesturing around the bedroom. "It's the biggest one and on the first floor so you don't have to worry about steps."

"I can climb steps," he said. "I'm perfectly fine." Julia gave him a worried look. "Like I told you on the phone, this is just something I'll have to manage. Stay on top of."

That was, in fact, what he had told her, Emily, and Nora on the phone. It was not, in fact, the truth. His oncologist had offered him two options: more chemo, which would maybe give him another year, two at the most. Or forgo treatment and let nature take its course, which would give him another six months, or maybe even a year. Possibly two if he was really lucky. To him that sounded the same both ways. Right now, he felt perfectly fine. No more chemo. And he would hope for the best. Magical thinking was still, after all, thinking.

"I printed you a copy of our schedule. It's on the bed," Julia said.

"A schedule?" He raised his eyebrows.

"I always do a schedule for sisters' week," Julia said. Of course, he would expect nothing less from his eldest daughter. "But if you don't feel up for anything on there, you can always stay here and rest instead."

"I feel good," he said. "I'm here to spend time with the three of you. Count your old dad in. For all of it."

"Okay." Julia looked at him and smiled a little, like maybe she too had caught his magical thinking, even though that wasn't at all Julia's style.

"But can I make one request?" he asked. Julia nodded. "I want to meet your dear friend Nate while I'm here."

"Nate?" Julia raised her eyebrows.

He nodded. "All these years, I've heard so much about him, but I've never met this Nate the Great you love so very much."

"Um . . . okay," Julia said. "He's actually on the schedule already. Taking us out on the boat on Saturday with his daughter, Mallory. So you'll meet him then."

"Daughter? Nate's married?" Bob asked.

"No . . . he's a single dad."

"Oh." Bob perked up. "Like me. Well, then I want to meet him even more."

Julia thought for a moment and stared at him without saying anything. "Why don't you get some rest," she finally said. "We do s'mores on the back patio at seven thirty. We'll order pizza around five thirty for dinner, once Nora and Em both get here." She pointed to the schedule on the bed.

"Sounds great, honey," he said. "You know I love pizza. And s'mores. What a treat."

"I'm worried about Dad's memory," Julia whispered to her sisters later that night, out on the patio. After s'mores, Dad had gone inside to go to sleep, but all three of them had remained outside.

Emily got up, brought the wine from the fridge and two glasses. Julia walked to the kitchen and came back with a third glass.

"What's wrong with Dad's memory?" Nora whispered, as Emily poured the wine into all three glasses and then handed one to everyone.

"He seemed weirdly obsessed with meeting Nate while he's here," Julia said. "Called him 'Nate the Great' and talked about how much I *love* him, like he was stuck back twenty years in the past or something."

Emily laughed and took a big sip of her wine. "I'm sure Dad just fondly remembers your lovesick teenage years the way we all do."

Julia frowned. "But that was such a long time ago."

"So let him meet Nate. Who cares," Nora interrupted. She gulped down her wine. "Nate probably would want to meet Daddy anyway. He always says we're like his sisters."

Julia nodded. "I'm just telling you guys, I'm worried. I don't know if he's totally with it."

Emily waved away her concerns. "Dad has been like that since we were little," she said. "Saying Dad things. Being nostalgic about us growing up. You know, he was probably just saying he wants to meet your friend, like when we were back in high school, and he was so annoying about wanting to meet every single person we hung out with."

"Nate is friends with all of us," Nora said.

"True," Emily said. "But we all know he and Julia have a special connection."

Julia felt her cheeks turning red, though she wasn't sure why. Maybe it wasn't Dad's memory that was bothering her, but those old feelings toward Nate he had reminded her of.

And then Julia thought, *No, no, no*. Whatever she thought she was feeling right now, she was going to have to put it in the vault.

Bob woke up earlier than all three of his daughters the next morning and fumbled around with the coffee maker in the kitchen, which was one of those newfangled single-brew ones he could never quite manage to figure out at the hospital. Something resembling brown sludge made it into the mug, and he took it out on the front porch.

It was barely dawn; a pink light crept over the horizon; and Bob sat down on a rocking chair, sipped his coffee-like-sludge, and took in the pale gray first-light beauty of the Pacific Ocean just across the street. It rushed in his ears and he heard it again: *Vera, Vera, Vera.*

Look how great all three girls turned out, he whispered back. *Even Nora.*

Especially Nora, the Vera-ocean roared.

"Excuse me." A man's voice interrupted his conversation with the ocean, and Bob looked up, startled. A tall, young guy with messy hair who looked like he'd just rolled out of bed stood on the porch steps with his arms crossed.

"Who are you?" Bob asked. He didn't look like an intruder, but he wasn't exactly sure what an intruder would look like.

"Who are you?" the man asked.

"I'm staying here for the week," Bob said.

The man frowned and pulled his cell phone out of his pocket, double-checked the date. "No, you're not. You need to leave."

And then it hit Bob. This disheveled . . . gentleman was Julia's . . . "Nate?" He said it out loud. "My daughters own this house," Bob continued. "I got invited to sisters' week this year. I'm Bob May."

Nate put his phone back in his pocket, straightened out his sweatshirt, smoothed out his hair. Then he stepped forward and put his hand out for Bob to shake. Bob took it and liked the way Nate's grip was firm, his movements intentioned. This was a man who knew what he wanted and wasn't afraid to get it. Much like Julia. "Hey, Mr. May, sorry about that. Julia hadn't mentioned you were coming. I know it's their week, so I was a little alarmed to see a man sitting out here on the porch. Nice to meet you."

"Nice to meet you too," Bob said. He gestured to the other rocker on the porch. "Have a seat. I'd offer you a cup of coffee, but this one turned out terrible. You wouldn't want it."

Nate laughed and sat down. "Nora ordered that fancy machine for the house a few months ago. None of the renters can figure it out either."

That seemed about right. His baby. His impractical dreamer. Of course she would purchase an impossible coffee machine she likely couldn't afford. She kept saying her show was going to transfer to Broadway soon, that it was going to change her life. But it hadn't quite happened yet. He hoped he would live long enough to see it.

"What brings you out here?" Nate asked. "It's your first time to Coronado, right?"

Bob nodded. "Well, first in about forty years. Before your time."

"Close," Nate said. "I'm forty-one. And I've lived in that house next door pretty much my whole life."

Bob wondered if his parents had been at Vera and Grey's beach wedding, a baby Nate in tow, but that was all a blur.

"So what brings you back after all this time?" Nate asked.

"Emily invited me to join them this week. And I rarely get to see all my girls in one place, for a whole entire week. How could I turn that down? Especially now . . ."

Nate nodded and rocked slowly in the chair. "Julia told me, about the cancer," Nate said gently. "I'm really sorry. Cancer sucks."

Bob nodded, remembering that Nate's mom died of cancer, and the way Julia had sat at the dining room table and sobbed when they got the news.

"Nate," Bob said now. "I want you to do something for me."

Nate turned and shot him a quizzical look. Maybe it was a big ask, considering they had never met before now. But then Nate said, "Sure. Whatever I can do to help, I'm happy to."

"I want you to take care of Julia," Bob said.

Nate shook his head. "With all due respect, sir, Julia takes care of herself. She wouldn't want me or anyone else to take care of her."

"Sure," Bob said, and he felt warmed by the way Nate seemed

to understand Julia. "But I don't mean now," he clarified. "I mean, later on. If things ever get bad." He paused. "Julia doesn't know how to ask for help when she needs it. She never did. She pretends everything is fine, until she breaks. And that's when she'll need you. That's when I'm asking you to help her."

Nate nodded with recognition, like this made perfect sense. And Bob wondered exactly when Nate had seen Julia break in the past, or how many times it might have happened.

"So you'll do that for me, son?" Bob said.

"I always have," Nate said. "Always will."

At the end of the week, as Emily boarded the plane to fly home, she got a text from Cecile. Just about to sign my divorce papers!

Let's celebrate soon, Emily typed out in response. Then she agonized over whether *celebrate* was truly the right word, deleted the text, and wrote instead: Let me know if you need anything.

Aren't you in California?

Just boarded my flight home. I'll be home later tonight.

Okay, then call me later, Cecile wrote. Then added: Have a safe flight xx

Emily felt the strangest sensation as she switched her phone to airplane mode, years of feelings she'd been suppressing, that she hadn't truly been allowing herself to feel, suddenly flooded to the surface. What-ifs and never-gonna-happens.

When she'd land in Tampa in a few hours, Cecile would be single for the first time since Emily had met her.

And then she had the strangest thought that she wished she could get off the plane, go back to Coronado, and tell Dad how happy she was that Cecile was about to be single. That he would understand exactly how she was feeling in this moment, that he would look at her, smile, give her a hug, and simply say: *Honey, I know.*

CHAPTER 25

2014

JULIA AND TED WERE not quite speaking to each other on the day they boarded the flight to Chicago in February. Julia didn't want Veronica to catch on and so she decided, sitting at the gate at the airport, that she would resume speaking to Ted, cordially, for at least the next seventy-two hours, while they were away from home and would be in the constant company of their daughter, and also her sisters.

It was unfortunate timing that Julia had finally gotten up the courage two days earlier to pick up Ted's phone when he was in the shower and read through *all* his texts. Her act of confidence that morning—or idiocy—was due to the fact that he had finally gotten an iPhone and had been grumbling about transferring over all his contacts from his ancient beloved BlackBerry. Julia had the stupid thought that she would do it for him while he was in the shower, surprise him. Congratulate him on finally joining the rest of the smartphone-using world in the late, great year of 2014. But then, in the process, she'd inadvertently, or (if she was being honest with herself) on purpose, ended up scrolling through all his old texts.

Ten minutes later, when Ted had walked out of the bathroom, wrapped in a towel, Julia was trapped somewhere between shock and anger. "I was trying to help you set up your iPhone and I saw your texts," she said.

Ted nodded and pulled the towel from his waist, then strode across the room stark naked to grab his boxers from his chest of drawers. In that moment, it suddenly bothered Julia that he was still so at ease in his forty-year-old body, fit from running most mornings, trim from being overworked, forgetting to eat lunch. He still looked good naked, not in the slightest old or saggy, or even *middle-aged.* Had she not been fuming about the texts, Julia might've stared at her husband naked and remembered why exactly he'd dazzled her in the first place, almost twenty years earlier, back in law school.

He pulled on his boxers, walked over to the bed, and plopped down next to her. "What about my texts?" he asked.

Julia seethed at the way he was always so goddamn calm, and then, suddenly, her phone rang.

Hospice.

The call she'd been dreading for weeks, as Dad had made a rapid decline since the start of the year.

She'd ignored Ted's question, answered the call, and then had immediately thrown herself into organize mode. There were so many details to take care of and people for her to call that she and Ted never finished their conversation about his texts. (To be fair, they'd never actually started it, really.) But they hadn't spoken to each other either. At all. About anything. Julia had compartmentalized whatever was happening in her marriage and had booked Ted a flight to Chicago alongside her and Veronica. Her father was dead, and nothing else really mattered. There wasn't time, there wasn't space in her brain to process all the things she had read on Ted's phone.

Still, it gnawed at her, there, in the back of her mind. Those texts resurfaced in small moments, in between ordering flowers and deli trays. Who was EM? Julia couldn't think of anyone she knew with those initials, aside from her sister (and certainly, those texts were *not* to Emily). Why was Ted texting this EM constantly, telling her she was *beautiful*, and making plans to meet her for drinks, dinner, a weekend (a goddamn weekend!) in New York City back in December? Ted had told her he was on a work trip at the time. The idea of him having some torrid affair with some woman he worked with, whom Julia had never even heard of—it all felt so cliché that Julia actually disdained him even more for his lack of creativity.

"Julia." Ted said her name gently now, touched her on the shoulder. She flinched and drew back. "We're boarding."

"Right." She stood and doled out the boarding passes from her purse. "I'll take the aisle. V, you're in the middle, and Dad can have the window."

"But Dad hates the window," Veronica protested.

"Does he?" Julia was in no mood to argue with V. Or try to placate Ted. Or obsess over why their daughter always seemed to take his side. "Well, so do I."

"Mom can have the aisle this time, Ron." Ted winked at their daughter in a way that made Julia's stomach clench. Had he always been this way, and she just hadn't noticed it before? So calm, so smooth. So full of shit.

Emily was still in bed when Julia called to tell her the news.

It was a Saturday morning in February. The sun was shining in through her large bedroom window, and normally she would be up and getting ready to go to the museum. But it was a rare Saturday off. And besides that, the first time Cecile had spent the night.

Emily had woken up first, and for a little while she'd been turned on her side, watching Cecile sleep. She looked so peaceful, so beautiful. So very at ease. *I can't believe she's actually here*, Emily thought. *With me.* Years of longing had finally surfaced, been given room to breathe over the last few months. And, for the first time in her life, Emily actually felt light. Even, dare she say, happy?

Emily had waited until last October, a few months after the

divorce was final, to finally work up the courage, admit to Cecile how she really felt. Even then, she'd worried it was too soon. Too much. Cecile was her best friend. (Let's be honest, her only friend.) She didn't want to ruin it or lose her. All of that, and all of her feelings, had finally tumbled out of her, a confession, then a rambling apology, one night over a bottle of wine.

"Em." Cecile had said her name softly. Then when Emily kept on rambling, Cecile had put her forefinger up gently to Emily's lips. "Stop. I feel it. You know I feel it too."

The rest, as Julia might say, if she were trying to tie it up into a neat little bow, was history.

Of course, there wasn't really anything neat about dating a newly divorced woman who had shared custody of her seven-year-old twin boys. No matter how Emily felt about Cecile, she remained strong in her conviction that she could not and would never be any kind of mother. Something she had yet to actually mention to Cecile.

But on that bright morning in February, with Cecile sleeping so peacefully next to her, Emily couldn't bring herself to worry about that yet. She could only feel. *Warmth. Happiness. Relief.*

Then her phone rang.

"He's gone," Julia said as soon as she picked up.

"Fuck." Emily had known it was coming. They all had. But still, actually hearing the news felt like a punch to the gut and she momentarily struggled to breathe. Cecile sat up, mouthed: *Are you okay?* Emily shook her head. She wasn't okay. She might never be okay again.

As soon as she hung up, she got out of bed and grabbed her suitcase out of the closet.

"Your dad," Cecile said sadly, hugging her knees to her chest. "I'm so sorry, Em."

Emily didn't know what else to do but start packing her suitcase, so she went into the closet and blindly grabbed a handful of clothes off hangers. When she walked back out, Cecile had gotten out of bed, thrown on a sweatshirt. She gently grabbed Emily's shoulders. "Put the clothes down," she said.

"I have to pack," Emily insisted. "I have to go to the airport."

"Let me make you a cup of coffee," Cecile said. "Then I'll get your laptop and find a flight to book for us first. Then we can go to the airport."

"Us?" Emily asked. "We?"

Cecile nodded. "I'm not going to let you go alone."

"But the boys . . ." Emily protested.

"The boys can stay with Rick for a few days."

Emily had never been an *us*, a *we*. Not in any way that counted. Not in any situation like this, and even though, under normal circumstances, that might've scared her, all she truly felt right now was grateful.

Nora was floating when Julia called her.

Hera was finally, at long last, going to transfer to Broadway in June, and the news had just been announced on *Playbill*'s website. Nora had clicked to refresh, but before she could actually read the full story, her phone was buzzing with Julia's call.

Then Daddy was dead. And Nora was sinking.

She didn't understand how the world could be so cruel and so kind to her all at once. She was about to have everything she'd always dreamed of! How could Dad no longer be here to share it with her?

"Dad knows," Julia assured her when she blubbered all of this over the phone, through tears. "Dad was super proud of you, Nora."

Nora had last talked to him a week ago. He'd called her in the middle of the night, sounding more lucid than he had in months. The last thing he'd told her was that she should use some of the money she'd inherit from him to go back to school, and to invest the rest wisely.

"Don't talk about things like that," she'd said, half-asleep.

"Honey, I'll be gone soon."

"You can't," she'd insisted. "I won't let you. I'll be on Broadway by the summer, and I want you to come to opening night."

It turned out, they were both right. She would be on Broadway by the summer, and also now he was gone.

A few days later, Nora was numb from cold.

She suddenly remembered how much she hated Chicago in February. But it felt colder than she remembered from her childhood, her three years at Northwestern, and the chill went straight to her bones.

The ground was frozen so solid, Julia told them, that the funeral home said they'd needed a jackhammer to dig the hole at the cemetery. Nora hated thinking of her father being put into the ground when it was this cold. Even standing under the heated white tent at the grave site now, she shivered.

"Is he being buried next to Mommy?" Nora asked her sisters, trying to recall if she had ever been taken to this cemetery as a kid. She couldn't remember if she had. But if he was being laid to rest near her now, somehow she felt that would bring him peace.

Julia was attempting to smooth her staticky hair with her fingers, to no avail, while Nora noticed Ted stood off to the side, hugging Veronica, trying to warm her. Emily clung tightly to her new girlfriend's hand. Julia didn't say anything as she was still trying to fix her hair, and it struck Nora that it was a slightly different color than usual. Julia's natural medium brown had new red overtones.

"Mom was cremated, remember?" Julia finally said.

Nora shook her head. She didn't remember. She didn't remember a cemetery, or an urn of ashes. Who'd kept them? Dad, most likely, but maybe it had been Grandma Vera.

"And Dad left behind wishes that he wanted to be buried here, near Grandma and Grandpa May." Nora realized Julia was still talking.

Nora nodded. "Where is Mommy now?" she asked.

"Like Julia said," Emily said sharply. "She was cremated."

"But where are her ashes?" Nora asked.

"Lake Michigan," Julia said. "Dad scattered her ashes in the lake the summer after she died."

"How do you even know that?" Emily asked.

Julia shrugged as if to say, how *didn't* she know that?

Nora sighed. Julia always knew everything. A function of being the oldest, or maybe just of being Julia.

Then Nora thought about that time on the sailboat in Coronado when they'd scattered Grandma Vera's ashes in the Pacific, how it had felt healing, in a way, to know she was being left in a place she was most at peace. And how the frozen tundra of Chicago felt like the worst possible place to leave Dad now.

"We can't leave Daddy here like this. He hated being cold." Tears sprung up in Nora's eyes and stung as they rolled down her frozen cheeks. She might not remember exactly what had happened after her mother died, but she did remember a lifetime of Daddy wearing two pairs of socks and a wool cap in the house in the winter. The way he still worried if she had a heavy enough coat and the right boots when it snowed in New York, even when she was in her thirties, because he'd wanted her to be warm too.

"Nora," Julia said gently. "This is what he wanted."

As if on cue, the funeral director walked over to talk to Julia to ask if they were ready to begin. Emily let go of Cecile's hand and walked with Julia and the director to the edge of the tent. But Nora remained firmly in place, crying. They wouldn't start without her. They couldn't put him in the ground without her.

She suddenly felt a hand on her shoulder, and she turned. Cecile, Emily's girlfriend, was standing behind her. "It's hard to lose a parent," she said gently, rubbing Nora's shoulder. "I know it is."

"They still think I'm the baby," Nora sniffled. "But I'm right. Dad hated being cold."

Cecile nodded and offered Nora a sympathetic smile. It struck Nora how opposite she was to Emily. Warm where Emily was cold, bright where Emily was dark. Kind where Emily was snarky. She thought about two pieces of a jigsaw puzzle that appeared to be vastly different shapes and colors, but somehow still fit together seamlessly to build something whole.

"Come on." Cecile put her arm around Nora's shoulders, offering her physical support. "Let's walk out there together and stand with your sisters. I think you'll regret it if you stay back now. If you don't take this chance to say goodbye to him . . ." Her voice was soft, sweet, like a lullaby.

As much as she wanted to resist, rebel, she also knew, deep down, that Cecile was right. Julia wasn't going to budge, and she would regret it if she refused to participate.

"Em is really lucky to have you," Nora said with a slight smile. Then she added, "Just make sure you don't ever put up with any of her shit."

Three months later, Emily was up before dawn for her flight to San Diego, trying to sneak out of bed quietly so she wouldn't wake Cecile.

"Em." Cecile's voice cut into the darkness and Emily froze.

"I was trying so hard not to wake you," she whispered. "Go back to sleep."

"You should tell them the truth in Coronado this week," Cecile said into the darkness. "Nora and Julia, I mean. They both deserve to know what you saw."

Emily grabbed her roller bag from the end of the bed, where she'd left it after she'd packed last night. "There's yogurt and fruit in the fridge for you for breakfast," she said. "I'll see you next weekend."

"Em!" Cecile called after her as she wheeled her bag into the hallway, toward the front door. "Imagine how much better you'll feel if you tell them, after all this time."

In Coronado, the ocean roared on as it always had. The sea churned and rushed. High tide, low tide. The sound of it, the blue-green sight of it from the porch, reminded all three May sisters that life went on. Over the years, the gray stone seawall across the street from them had been built up higher and higher, but the ocean itself remained this perfect, beautiful force, unchanging.

Mallory wore her hair in pigtails this year and was missing both front teeth, which she proudly showed all three May sisters, bragging about how the tooth fairy had brought her ten dollars for each one. "Twenty whole dollars!" she exclaimed.

Julia raised her eyebrows. "Oh my, you have a very wealthy tooth fairy in Coronado. Veronica only got one dollar a tooth!"

Emily wondered how much Cecile had left for the boys, and before now, that thought had never occurred to her. They'd lost teeth. She'd seen them in pictures with their adorable toothless grins, but she didn't understand this kind of minutiae. This nitty-gritty of parenting. She never would. It was why she'd recently broken down and told Cecile her deepest secret. Because she'd needed Cecile to understand why she could never be a mother. Yet, Cecile had, in response, simply handed Emily her therapist's card.

"When I had to get braces in eighth grade," Nora was saying now, "I had to get four adult teeth pulled. And the tooth fairy left me a hundred-dollar bill."

Mallory's eyes widened, and Nora's suddenly welled with tears.

"Inflation," Julia said. "I got like fifty cents a tooth or something ridiculous."

"You're aging yourself, Jul," Nora said, wiping her eyes.

Nate scooped Mallory up, gave her a giant kiss, and told her it was time to get ready for bed. She ran next door, and then Julia whispered, "Seriously, Nate. Twenty dollars?"

He shrugged. “I didn’t know the going rate.”

Nora laughed and swatted him on the arm. “Pushover.”

“Guilty as charged.” Nate laughed. “Anyway, it’s late. I should go read Mal a book. I’ll catch you later in the week?”

“Dinner on Friday!” Julia called after him. “It’s on the schedule.” He waved and nodded as he walked away. “He’s such a good dad,” Julia said, turning to her sisters as they watched him.

Nora nodded and sighed thinking about how much she missed her own dad, how it felt almost impossible now that he had been here with them just a year earlier. “Mal is really lucky,” she said. “She failed out in the mom department but Nate more than makes up for that.”

Opening night of Hera is June 30th, Julia texted Emily a week after they got back from Coronado. I’m buying tickets now so we can go and surprise Nora. Do you want a seat with us too?

Yeah . . . I need to check flights but I’ll figure something out. Her fucking Broadway debut! I’m going.

One ticket or two?

Let me think about it . . . Actually, hold on. I’ll go ask Cee.

Okay. I have them in my cart . . .

Two. Cee says she wouldn’t miss it. Tell me how much I owe you and I’ll Venmo you after work.

Don’t worry about it. Excited you’re coming and we can get to know Cee better too. Just buy us dinner before the show and we’ll call it good.

Okay, loser. But joke’s on you because dinner is . . . Mickey D’s. No, wait . . . Taco Bell!

Lol. Awesome. V loves their nachos. 😉

Yeah, but Ted doesn’t strike me as a Taco Bell guy . . .

All good. Ted can’t make it.

CHAPTER 26

2015

"HOW'S THERAPY GOING?" CECILE asked Emily in the beginning of January. It had been months since Cecile had gently pushed her therapist's business card into Emily's hand, and Emily had promised she would make an appointment. Last fall, she'd even lied and told Cecile she'd started going weekly, but the truth was, she'd never even called to schedule something. She didn't want to go to therapy. She didn't need therapy. She was doing just fine. Better than fine.

"It's good," Emily lied again. "Great!"

Cecile grabbed her hand and squeezed it. "Good. Because I think we should get married."

"What?" Emily leaned against the back of her couch to keep her balance, totally caught off guard by the not-quite proposal.

Cecile nodded quickly. "It's newly legal again in Florida. And I think we should do it before they can reverse it. What if, God forbid, something were to happen to one of us. I want the legal protections marriage could provide us."

Emily frowned.

"And of course, most important of all. You know how much I love you, Em. I want to marry you!"

"But the boys . . ." Emily murmured. This was exactly the reason why Cecile had suggested therapy in the first place.

"The boys love you too!" Cecile said, immediately considering their perspective, forgetting all about Emily's worries.

Emily nodded. Sure, maybe Mikey and Jim did like her, but in that way you might like your fun, unmarried aunt who brought you gifts every time you saw her. It wasn't the same thing as becoming a permanent fixture in their daily lives, their *stepmother*. Cecile had the boys every other weekend and most nights of the week, and both Christmas and fall break last year. She and Emily had taken them to New York City for fall break to see Nora's show, then to Disney World for Christmas. There were now framed pictures sitting on Emily's mantel of the four of them in Times Square, and then another of the four of them with Mickey and Minnie. Cecile pointed to those pictures for emphasis right now: proof that they could actually be a real family.

Emily felt something rattling deep inside her chest. But she wasn't sure if it was joy or terror. As a little girl she had never imagined some elaborate future wedding the way Nora and Julia had. She'd had trouble envisioning even dating someone until she'd gotten to college. But she loved Cecile more than she had ever loved anyone—she knew that much for sure.

"If you don't want to," Cecile continued, her voice quivering in a way that made Emily's heart clench. "I understand."

The thing was, Emily suddenly realized she did want to, and maybe that was the thought that terrified her most of all. "Yes," she finally said. "Yes, Cee! Let's get married."

Since *Hera* had opened on Broadway, Nora had been indulging in retail therapy. Half the road to fake it till you make it was, Nora decided, dressing the part. And running up her credit card balance on Fifth Avenue wasn't quite as bad as it used to be. She had money coming in from the show now, and she'd split the proceeds from the sale of Dad's house in Chicago, as well as his remaining IRA balance, with her sisters. A few hundred thousand that she should've kept as a nest egg or invested wisely like Dad had told her to do. But what she needed right now was to look good and to keep on moving up. Never mind that Emily said she wanted to use the money for a house after she and Cecile got married. And Julia said it would cover Veronica's college costs. Nora had only herself to worry about.

Still, it hit Nora when she was in Coronado with her sisters that maybe money, designer clothes, and a dream role on Broadway somehow weren't enough to make her truly happy.

Across the table, on their last night in Coronado, Emily looked like she was practically radiating joy. Her normally stoic features appeared softened; her face was downright glowing. This was the effect Cecile had on her—and maybe she had also gotten too much sun this week? Either way, Nora could never figure out how to make herself look like she glowed from within, no matter how much money she spent on facials and makeup. "I can't believe I'm the last one of us to get married," Nora said after they did their annual last-night cheers, toasting to another successful sisters' week and to Emily's upcoming nuptials.

"Believe it, bitch," Emily said with a small cackle before she took a sip of wine.

The three sisters were sharing a bottle of Pinot Noir at their annual last-night dinner at the restaurant in the old boathouse on Glorietta Bay, which was now the Bluewater Boathouse. The restaurant ownership had changed several times since the Mays had been coming to the island, but the beauty of the location had not. As they sat out on the deck, a cool breeze flitted off the bay beside them. Sharing a bottle of wine, here, with her sisters, Nora always thought that if her life had one perfect night each year, it was this one.

Nora took another sip of her wine and turned to her oldest sister. "Julia," she said. "You're the old married lady here. You should give Emily some advice."

"Old?" Julia protested.

"Yeah, like remember when you texted us about your mammogram last month? *Old*," Nora emphasized.

Emily chuckled into her wine. Julia had sent a very detailed text into their sisters' chat about said mammogram.

"It's very important to get screened after forty, Nora. Mom wasn't around at my age for us to know what our family history might be."

"Okay, okay, I know." Nora smirked. "In another *five* years I'll worry about that. So go on, give Emily your best marriage advice."

Julia made a face, buttered a piece of bread, then used a napkin to delicately wipe her hands. "Always tell the truth, Em," she finally said.

Emily frowned. "What's that supposed to mean?"

"I mean. That's the number one rule of making a marriage work in my opinion. Just . . . be honest."

"I am honest," Emily said.

"The lady doth protest too much methinks." Nora chuckled and took another sip of wine. Emily shot her a look.

Julia was on a roll now and kept on talking: "The second you stop telling the truth, that's when it's over."

"Everything all right with you and Ted?" Nora asked.

Julia forced a smile. "Of course! I'm saying this from my decades of experience as a family law attorney, not as an *old married lady*."

"I was just teasing," Nora said. "You might be old, but you're still super hot. Some dude was totally checking you out yesterday on the beach."

"Oh my God, no one was doing that, stop." Julia's cheeks instantly turned red and she put her hands over her face. "I have a teenage daughter for heaven's sake."

Nora shrugged and smiled. It was always fun to tease Julia, but she was also telling the truth. "I'm just saying, Jul, your skin is flawless and your boobs still look great. Who cares about honesty. Ted probably can't keep his hands off you with that hot bod."

"Nora!" Julia protested.

"And that would be my marriage advice, Em," Nora continued. "Stay hot for as long as you can."

"Wow, Nora, that's so deep." Emily rolled her eyes. "It's no wonder that you're the last one of us to get married."

The truth was, Julia shouldn't have been giving anyone marriage advice. Her own marriage hadn't been in a good place for a while. Maybe not since that point in Julia's life when her body, her perception of family and motherhood, had fractured nine years earlier. Maybe then it had started as a hairline crack between her and Ted, until over time and space it had bloomed into a full-blown break.

But the marriage counseling they'd been going to for the last year was something Julia hadn't mentioned to anyone. Not her coworkers, not her sisters, and certainly not Veronica. The idea of counseling itself felt like an admission of some kind of grievous failure. But worse was the fact they'd been going so damn long, and deep down she felt she was still losing control. Of her truth. Of her marriage. Of Ted. Of herself.

The truth was, she had started going to Zumba classes on her lunch hour because exercising was the only thing that eased that crushing sense of being so out of control. Nora wasn't completely wrong—Julia was actually in the best shape she'd been in in years.

Julia and Ted sat in the therapist's waiting room one humid Friday afternoon in July, six weeks after Julia had returned from Coronado and had given Emily that ingenious advice. She hoped her sister's marriage, years down the road, would be in better shape than her own.

She glanced at Ted now—he looked annoyed, probably about leaving work early, as he was fervently checking his phone. Julia turned to her own phone, remembering the promise she'd made to Veronica that she would take her shopping for a dress for Emily's wedding this weekend. She hoped they could make it through the endeavor without having a huge argument over what constituted an appropriate dress. She started scanning through the juniors' section online at Nordstrom, wondering if she should preselect ones for Veronica to try that weren't egregiously short. (No small task.)

And then, suddenly, Ted turned to her, touched her gently on the arm, in a way he hadn't touched her in a long time. The feel of his fingers on her arm like that made her jump. "Let's stop paying for this bullshit and make a deal," he said.

She looked up from her phone. Looked at her husband. He looked strange. Not quite put together. His collar was unbuttoned and he'd loosened his tie. His brown eyes were watery, and his expression looked defeated.

"I mean, why are we still doing this?" Ted said with an air of frustration. "Why are we even here?"

Julia shrugged. "This is what married people do when they hit road bumps. They go to counseling."

"I don't think we've hit a road bump," Ted said. "I think it's a sinkhole."

Ted had apologized for his texts with EM (Eva Martin, an associate at his firm) but swore nothing had happened that wasn't (mostly) work-related. Julia believed him, sort of. She'd vaguely remembered seeing the word *beautiful* in his texts, but maybe, with all that had happened, she'd embellished that specific detail in her mind. When she'd asked to review the texts again to see, he'd told her he'd already deleted them and retired the old BlackBerry to a drawer at work. Then she'd wondered: Why the hell did he do that if he'd done absolutely nothing wrong?

"It's not a sinkhole," Julia said now, but even as she said it, she wondered if maybe Ted was right. It wasn't just the texts either. Last week, they'd been given the homework assignment to list five things they loved about each other and Julia had really floundered. She admired Ted, as an attorney, as a father. He had aged beautifully and gracefully. She had loved him deeply once, when they were in law school, when they were first married. But now she struggled to remember the exact reasons *why*.

"Julia," Ted said gently. "Why don't we just make a contract right here, today."

"A contract?"

"We'll stay together until Veronica goes to college. I don't want to screw up her teen years by splitting up now. I know we both agree she's the most important thing in all of this. But after she moves out, we'll separate."

"Separate?" Julia repeated. The word reverberated in her brain, sounding like *failure*.

"I mean, we're paying this therapist a small fortune to fix a marriage neither one of us want to be in still."

Was that true? All of their problems aside, Julia had never actually considered *giving up*.

"Let's just write up a contract here and now," Ted continued. "We stay together until Veronica leaves for college four years from now. Then, after she moves out, we get an amicable divorce." Ted opened up the notes app on his phone and started typing.

"Do you really have to write it up?" Julia asked, feeling oddly the most offended by that last part. "You wouldn't even trust me on a verbal?"

He hesitated for a moment and then put his phone down. "So, you agree then?"

Did she? Julia didn't know if she really wanted to get divorced. But she did agree that this therapy wasn't getting them anywhere and was costing a fortune. Four years from now was a long time. Ted might change his mind. She might figure out how to fix things between now and then. Or maybe, once their nest was actually empty, their relationship would revert to what it was like when they were younger. But out loud, all she said was, "If you really want to do this, I have some terms."

"Of course," Ted said. "I would expect nothing less."

She had the sudden memory of him verbally sparring with her during mock trial in law school, and then she remembered, yes, *this* was one of the things she loved about him.

"Go on," Ted said, folding his arms across his chest. "Tell me your terms."

"No cheating," she said emphatically. "And that includes texting, flirting, dating, or anything else. Nothing I would find offensive if I looked and saw it on your phone."

Ted nodded.

"And we don't ever tell Veronica or anyone," she continued. "Ever. Even later if we get . . ." She couldn't bring herself to say the word *divorced* out loud. "Even in four years from now. No one knows we planned this in advance."

"Fine," Ted said. "Anything else?"

Julia wished she could think of more terms, but she was breathing hard, sweating, and suddenly all logic escaped her. She shook her head.

"Well, I have one," Ted said. "Fire Nate."

"What?"

"Hire a professional management company to deal with your house in Coronado and don't see him or talk to him while you're there either."

"He lives next door," she argued. "Of course I'll see him. And he manages the house for such a small fee. It would cost too much to use a professional company." Suddenly Nora's words rang in her ears: *The lady doth protest too much methinks.*

"You don't want me to cheat," Ted said smugly. "I'm just asking you for the same courtesy."

"You're being ridiculous," she spat at him.

"Am I?" He raised his eyebrows.

Julia thought about the vault, and how if she allowed herself to open it, all the things, all the truths, might come flooding out and drown her. But the truth was, she had never cheated on Ted in their entire fifteen years of marriage. She didn't believe the same was true for him. "I'm not firing Nate," she finally said. "But I'm not going to cheat with him either. Nate's practically like my older brother."

Ted rolled his eyes and sighed. "Okay," he said. "Fine. You

don't have to fire him, but my term is the same as yours. No cheating."

"Fine," Julia said quickly.

Ted held out his hand to shake.

Julia hesitated for only a few seconds before she shook it.

As Julia drove home, alone in her own car, her hands still shook as she gripped the steering wheel. What had happened in there? What had she just agreed to? Maybe she should've insisted on more counseling, a different therapist, instead. How could Julia have failed so miserably that this was how her marriage would end up?

But it hadn't actually failed yet, she reminded herself. Ted's deal bought her a lot of time. She would just figure out how to fix everything in the next four years, that was all. And at least they had agreed to keep it together in the meanwhile for V's sake.

Her phone rang. *Nora.*

Julia picked up quickly, the way she always did when her sisters called her. Nora sniffled a greeting on the other end of the line—she was crying. "Nora, what's wrong? Are you okay?"

"We're closing January second," Nora exclaimed through sobs.

Oh, her show. She was losing her show. *I'm losing my husband,* Julia thought. But what she said out loud was, "Oh, sweetie, I'm sorry. I'm sure you'll get something else. And you get six more months. It's been a great run. You should be so proud."

"What if my career is over?" Nora sobbed.

What if my marriage is really over? Julia thought.

"What if I never get anything else?" Nora cried.

"No way!" Julia insisted, momentarily pushing her own problems to the back of her mind. "You're much too talented. Onward and upward, Nora, that's all this is."

Nora hiccupped on the other end of the line. "Do you really think so?"

"I do," Julia insisted. "Remember what Grandma Vera always used to say about stars?"

Nora didn't say anything for a moment, and then she said, "The darkest night always gives us the brightest stars."

Julia felt so certain that was true for Nora in her career, but not so certain it was true for her in her life. Ted wanted a divorce. Veronica only had four more years left at home before she left for college. What if Julia herself was inherently flawed, unlovable? What if her impending darkness was just really . . . darkness?

"Are you busy this weekend?" Nora asked, interrupting her thought spiral. "I'll take off sick and come see you."

Seeing Nora sounded like exactly what she needed, but Julia suddenly couldn't stomach the idea of being in her own house this weekend, pretending that everything was right and normal. "What if I bring V into the city this weekend instead? She needs a dress for Em's wedding and you can help us find something. And we can see your show again too." This felt like a win-win. A break from Ted to process what she'd just agreed to. Veronica adored Nora and dress shopping would be much less contentious together.

Nora sighed dramatically. "I don't know, Jul. I'm just so damn tired of this city."

"I'll buy you dinner tomorrow," Julia said, suddenly feeling desperate to get out of her house, her life. "And I'll get a nice hotel in the city and you can come stay with us tomorrow night, and we'll do a whole girls' retreat thing Sunday after your show. My treat. Plus, you know Veronica worships you. It'll be great for your ego."

Nora chuckled a little on the other end of the line. "She does worship me, doesn't she?" She let out a tiny, happier-sounding sigh. "Okay, so then tell me more about this girls' retreat you're proposing. Are you buying facials, manicures . . . ?"

"And massages," Julia added.

"Ooh!" Nora said. "I have this great woman in Astoria now. I'll see if we can book her for Sunday evening. Her hands have done more for my body than any man's ever have."

Now it was Julia's turn to laugh. A real genuine laugh that

made her forget, for a moment, about her conversation with Ted in the therapist's office, about the impending doom and darkness of her life, her marriage.

"I'm almost home. I'm gonna go book a hotel, and then I'll text you when we're on the train," Julia said.

"Jul," Nora said softly, just as Julia was about to end the call. "Thanks."

CHAPTER 27

2019

NORA RAN UP NATE'S porch steps and knocked on his screen door. "Mal," she called out. "Are there enough pancakes for me and Em too? We're starving, and it's too hot in our house to cook."

Emily might normally feel embarrassed for Nora's brazenness with Nate, especially after the way she'd been throwing herself at him last year. But now Emily just felt relieved that she wasn't the one having to beg. She walked across the yard and by the time she reached Nate's door, Mallory was already there, opening it, nodding (plenty of pancakes!), and inviting them both in.

Then, as they were sitting around his dining table, Emily thought Nate looked uneasy at the sight of her and Nora across from him. But maybe she was imagining it.

"So what were you doing in LA?" Nora asked Nate in between bites of pancakes, after Mallory had finished gushing about the *Playbill* Nora had given her.

"Teachers' conference," Mallory piped up cheerfully, and it was clear how proud she was of her dad. Emily suspected he was also probably the most loved teacher by all his students.

"Teachers' conference?" Nora said. She raised her eyebrows and gave Emily a look that said: *On a Sunday? Of Memorial Day weekend?* Emily nodded slightly, so Nora knew she understood.

They didn't have to say anything, in that way sisters could just communicate with looks and nods. They both agreed, Nate was definitely hiding something. The question was, what?

"What kind of—" Nora began, but Emily kicked her under the table and shot Nora another look. *Mallory.* Then Nora nodded slightly and said, "What kind of blueberries did you use in these pancakes? They are truly delicious."

"Just regular old blueberries," Mrs. McAllister said.

"California blueberries," Emily rambled. "Better than East Coast blueberries." She heard how silly the words sounded and yet they were masking the ones she wanted to say. Nate was lying. Julia was missing.

What the fuck was really going on?

When the pancakes were all finished, Mallory went upstairs to take a shower, Mrs. McAllister left to go home, and Emily and Nora remained at Nate's dining room table, refusing to budge.

"I should go call Tim about your AC," Nate said, moving to stand.

"What were you really doing in LA?" Nora asked. She heard the noise of water running through the pipes from upstairs and figured Mallory was in the shower. "On a Sunday of a holiday weekend? You were not at a teachers' conference."

Nate frowned and crossed his arms in front of his chest. "It's not any of your business," he finally said. "I'm not trying to be rude, Nora . . . It's just . . . personal."

Nora felt wounded by his words. He wouldn't trust her with something *personal*? He was clearly hiding something from them. "I think you know where Julia is and you're not telling us." Nora blurted out her accusation, the pitch of her voice rising. Nora might be forty now, but she could still use her emotions to elicit a response.

Nate shook his head. "Come on." His voice softened. "I wouldn't do that. You know you three are like . . ." Maybe he was going to say the word *sisters*, but then he reconsidered, as if maybe that didn't feel like the right word anymore. "Family," he finally said.

"So Julia isn't in LA?" Emily sighed, wondering if Nate was a dead end after all. Maybe whatever secret he was keeping, whatever reason he was acting evasive, had nothing to do with Julia.

"I . . ." Nate started. "I didn't say that." He paused and ran his fingers through his messy hair. "I said I didn't see her there. I didn't go to LA for Julia. And I don't know anything about where she is." Then he added, "Not for certain."

"But you have a guess, don't you?" Emily said.

As Nora said, "So wait, you think she might actually be in LA?"

Then Emily and Nate exchanged a strange look that made Nora's head tingle with that awful feeling she'd felt her whole entire life of being left out. Did they both know what was going on and only she was in the dark? Usually, it was Emily and Julia who made her feel this way. Was it possible that Emily could have secrets with Nate too?

"I don't know," Nate finally said. "I honestly don't know where she is for sure. But . . ."

"But?" Nora pressed.

He looked from Emily to Nora. Then back again. "That other time, when Julia *disappeared.* She was here with me for a little while and then . . . she went to Santa Monica. I went with her. I took her there."

"What the hell is in Santa Monica?" Nora asked.

"Not what," Emily said softly. "Who."

CHAPTER 28

2016

EMILY DIDN'T LIKE LA on principle.

When Cecile suggested she attend the National Aquatic Museums conference there, Emily cited all the things she hated: traffic, smog, too many vegetarians, and too many try-hards.

"Well, I could go," Cecile said, "and you can stay with the boys." She squeezed Emily's hand in that gentle way she did when she was trying to be completely reasonable in the face of what she saw as Emily's annoyingly adorable stubbornness. "But Em," she tried again, gentler. "You'll already be out there in California for your sisters' week. It makes more sense for you to just go to the conference on the way there. I know you don't like LA, but it's three days. You don't have to move there!"

Of course Cecile was right: If either of them had to go, it made much more logical sense for her to go, given she was already going to California around then anyway. But she still didn't want to go. She still couldn't stop this surge of anger rising in her chest that Cecile was making her go to the one city, and more specifically the one exact place within this city, she had successfully managed to avoid her whole adult life: Santa Monica.

On the first morning of the conference, Emily skipped out of the ten o'clock session she had signed up for and decided she would just walk by the mailing address that had rattled around in her brain for twenty years, face what she had been afraid of for so long. This place. This person.

Emily walked out of her hotel, pulled up the map app on her phone, and took a deep breath. Then she typed the address in that she had memorized twenty years earlier. Or at least she'd thought she had. When she typed it in the map app, no such exact address seemed to exist.

Had she imagined the whole thing? She'd been in so much pain that stupid morning, maybe she'd hallucinated something in Grandma Vera's armoire that had never even existed.

In Emily's memory, the address on that envelope was *45 Ocean Boulevard*, the street name just like Grandma Vera's. An odd echo that only now seemed too coincidental to have ever been real.

In her map app, she found an Ocean Avenue, an Ocean Park Place, an Ocean Park Boulevard, and an Ocean Lane. But as far as she could tell, there was no Ocean Boulevard in Santa Monica. Also, there seemed to be no number 45 on any of those three streets, perhaps further proof that she had hallucinated the whole thing.

She laughed out loud—relief or nerves or just this momentary inability to control any of her emotions. She could forget all about this, go back to the conference. She *should* go back to the conference, but then for some reason she couldn't quite explain, the Ferris wheel caught her eye in the distance, and she found herself, instead, walking toward the Santa Monica Pier.

The May sisters never went to amusement parks when they were kids. Maybe it was Julia's motion sickness, or Dad just struggling to get by caring for three girls, so it never occurred to him to take them on such a frivolous trip. Nora said the first roller coaster she'd ever ridden was Space Mountain, the day before Emily and

Cecile's wedding when they all did a group family day at Disney World. Emily, in fact, had never actually been on a Ferris wheel, and she wasn't exactly sure what the draw was now except for some wayward silly thought that if she got high enough, she could see the whole city. Like what she was looking for, what she had been avoiding, would suddenly become clear.

She was in this sort of odd daze standing in line, waiting her turn, when she realized the woman right in front of her had turned around and was talking to her.

"We're wearing the same shirt," the woman said. "How embarrassing."

Emily, having almost sleepwalked out of her hotel, realized she was still dressed in the T-shirt she'd slept in, a light gray one with I'M WITH HER boldly emblazoned across her chest. Cecile had approved when Emily had it in the packing pile for California. After their neighbor across the street in Tampa hung up a huge Trump flag, Emily and Cecile had disagreed over whether it was still safe to wear all their Hillary gear out in public. Emily had said fuck the neighbor. Cecile had said it made her nervous. California was the perfect place to wear it.

Emily looked up now and indeed, this woman was wearing the same shirt. Emily chuckled, thinking about how Cecile would get a kick out of this when she told her later. And then the woman gasped. "Shit, Emily? Is that really you?"

She looked up, above the shirt, and then saw the woman's pretty, familiar heart-shaped face. *There's no way.* "Cara?"

"Oh my God," Cara said. "What are the chances? And I never come here. I haven't been here since I was a kid."

What were the chances? Emily felt trapped somewhere between an unbelievable coincidence and some sort of darkly comical kismet.

They suddenly reached the front of the line, and the ticket taker asked if they were together or single riders.

"Single," Emily said.

"Together," Cara insisted.

They were shoved into one cart, and the ticket taker locked the door. What else could Emily do but sit down, stare at Cara across from her, and let out a nervous laugh.

"You know what this is?" Cara said as the Ferris wheel began its slow ascent. Emily shook her head. Suddenly she knew nothing. Her stomach lurched, and she understood how Julia always got motion sickness. "Fate," Cara said.

"I'm married," Emily said, extending her left hand, showing off her pretty lattice rose-gold wedding band.

Cara ignored her. "I mean, this is the second time we've run into each other in some random place unintentionally. Logan Airport. And now the Santa Monica Pier. All these years later, and we're even wearing the same goddamn shirt."

"It's a very popular shirt right now," Emily said. "We're about to have our first woman president."

Cara laughed, that deep, beautiful, familiar laugh, and Emily felt something stir inside of her. It was the feeling of forgotten possibility, of youth, of wanting so much but having nothing. It was simultaneously joy and heartbreak.

She felt completely off-kilter now, and maybe it was this ride, or maybe it was that what Cara said had struck something. Fate. What *were* the chances?

"So, by my estimation," Cara continued. "The universe wants us to be together."

Emily let out another nervous laugh. "I don't think my wife would agree," she said.

Cara nodded. She leaned back against her seat and then turned and stared out the side of the cart.

They were almost at the top now, and in the distance, everything looked miniature, pretend, like none of it was even real. Ocean Boulevard, Park Place, Avenue, Lane, whatever it was—people and houses were too tiny to be anything but fake, props.

"At least let me buy you lunch," Cara said. "So I can apologize and finally explain what happened between us years ago. I tried to do that once before, and you ran away. And it has never sat well with me how I left things."

Emily blushed, embarrassed now, remembering the way she'd left Cara standing on Orange Avenue, unable to hear her out. Her defense mechanism was, and always had been, to run away first, farther.

"What does it even matter now?" Emily finally asked. "It was a million years ago, and I've moved on. I'm sure you have too."

"But if the universe keeps bringing me back to you again and again, there must be a reason, right?" Cara said. "Just lunch. What harm can lunch do?"

Just lunch. She wasn't doing anything wrong.

Still, Emily found herself guiltily checking her phone as she sat across the table from Cara at a seafood restaurant down the pier. Like she was waiting for an angry text from Cecile, who might wonder why she wasn't at the conference, and why she was eating lunch with an ex-girlfriend on the pier instead. Of course, Cecile knew none of this. They had Find My set up on all of their phones, but Cecile likely wasn't bothering to check it. Across the country, it was three hours later, and Cecile had probably just left work to collect the boys from school.

"Do you have something to get to?" Cara pointed to Emily's phone as she checked it yet again.

Emily nodded. "I'm actually here for a conference. I missed the morning so I should probably get back soon . . ."

The waitress walked over, they ordered fish sandwiches, and Cara ordered a glass of Chardonnay. Emily sorely needed a glass of wine, but for once she declined, not wanting to show up back at the conference after this, both late and tipsy.

"My mom got really sick back then." Cara finally said it, like it was bursting to get out of her. Like it had been bubbling inside her for almost fifteen years.

"That's why you ghosted me?" Emily asked, glad there was an actual word in the lexicon she could grab on to now that made sense. *Ghosted.* She hadn't known the term back when Cara had actually done it to her. All she had known was the terrible, shapeless way she'd felt in the aftermath.

Cara nodded. "It's hard to explain, but suddenly I was faced with her death, and I was like twenty-five at the time. I wasn't ready to lose her. I couldn't handle it. I couldn't handle anything."

"You know, my mom died when I was three," Emily said.

"I remember," Cara said. "And this is going to sound awful, but I didn't want to be in your club. I couldn't handle your sympathy, or you telling me I would be fine because it happened to you when you were just a little kid." She paused and took a sip of her wine. "The truth was, I couldn't handle anything back then. I was a fucking mess."

"I'm sorry," Emily said. And she genuinely did feel sorry. It was a lifelong process, being a motherless child, knowing how to exist in the world without the woman who gave birth to you. She was still trying to figure it out.

"But then the craziest part is that she didn't die. I didn't join your club after all. She had like a one percent chance of survival, and she lived. She's seventy-eight now and still doing okay."

"Wow," Emily said. "Well . . . I'm glad to hear that."

"But in those few months when I thought she was dying, I managed to fuck up the best thing that had ever happened to me." Cara said this last part in a rush of breath. Then took another big sip of her wine.

She was the best thing that had ever happened to Cara? A mountain of unspoken what-ifs suddenly sat between them, and Emily twisted her wedding band nervously around her finger. "It was a long time ago," Emily said. "I'm sure many better things have happened to you since then."

Cara offered her a half-smile. "Well, I'm not married, like you." She stared at Emily, like maybe she wanted to know more, about Cecile, about her life now, but Emily bit her lip, not willing to share any of that.

"I understand," Emily said instead. "I forgive you. It's in the past. Let's just forget all about it, okay?"

Cara smiled for real this time. "Maybe we could . . . be friends again. You know, text each other from time to time."

But Emily shook her head, understanding that once she left this table, this city, she was going to have to compartmentalize Cara in the back of her mind, where she had already been for years. She didn't want to think about that mountain of what-ifs. She couldn't handle thinking about them in the middle of the night, when she woke up, sweating, claustrophobic. When she inwardly cringed every time one of the boys called her *Emma* (Cecile's attempt at something cute—a mixture of *Emily* and *Mama*). She couldn't think about another path her life might've taken whenever this one felt too hard.

"I don't think that's a good idea," she said.

For once, Emily was the first May sister to arrive in Coronado, given that she had just rented a car and driven down from LA. She'd been warned by one of the other conference goers that the two-hour trip could take six if she hit traffic, and so she left LA at five on Sunday morning and pulled up onto Ocean Boulevard before seven thirty.

Nate was crossing the street in his wet suit, board under his arm, just as she parked. He saw her, grinned, waved, and jogged up to the convertible she'd rented.

"Fancy way to arrive this year." He patted the hood affectionately.

"I just came from Santa Monica," she said, shrugging.

Nate stared at her for a moment, his eyes searching her face. Then he said, "Who's in Santa Monica?"

She thought guiltily again about her lunch with Cara. Not that she had anything to feel guilty about. But still. Cara had followed it up with a "great to see you again!" text that Emily had yet to respond to. (She was *not* going to respond. She had told Cara point-blank that they couldn't text. Still . . . she hadn't been able to bring herself to block her either.) "Not who," she corrected Nate now. "What. Conference for work."

"Ahh." Nate grinned. "How was it?"

Boring as fuck. Emily loved her job working side by side with Cecile at the museum, but she still had very little true passion for aquatic life. And sometimes she thought those fucking orcas would be the death of her. "It was great," she lied. "Super fun. Oh, I brought Mal some whale pins!"

"She'll love that," he said. Maybe because she was literally a child of the ocean, but Mallory was obsessed with all aquatic life. Last May, she'd regaled them with dolphin facts all week long after they'd spotted some jumping just offshore.

"Did you get to the pier while you were up there?" Nate asked.

Emily shook her head. "No time." She wasn't quite sure why she was lying to Nate, who wouldn't care in the least about her accidental Ferris wheel ride with Cara. But it seemed easier just to reject everything that had happened across the board.

"Ah, well. Maybe next time. I've actually been telling Mal I'd take her to Belmont Park over in Mission Beach. Maybe we could all go together one night this week? Mal's super excited to see her three favorite May aunts."

Emily nodded. "Sounds like fun. I'll run it by the scheduler when she gets here."

Nate laughed. Then he held up his surfboard. "Hey, maybe I can get you back on the board this week too. What do you say?"

"No fucking way." And then Emily thought again about Nate's surfing lesson all those years ago. How she had been in so much pain afterward, it was possible she'd hallucinated something in Grandma Vera's armoire that had never even existed.

On Wednesday night, Mallory, Emily, and Nora rode the Giant Dipper at Belmont Park while Julia and Nate stood below, watching the coaster car rise, their feet planted firmly on the ground. Though the amusement park at Mission Beach was just a short drive over the bridge from Coronado, this was the first time the May sisters had made it here. Julia immediately understood why as she stared at the giant, rickety-looking wooden coaster in front of them. "I want to throw up just looking at that thing," Julia said.

Nate grinned. "I feel like I've seen you do that before."

He said it so easily, like the memory had been rolling around in his head on a loop for years, the way it did for Julia sometimes. Her heart lurched in her chest, or maybe it was her stomach. "That was my only time on a roller coaster, in Santa Monica with you," she said softly. "One and done."

Nate laughed. "Very wise. I've never seen someone vomit that much."

Julia blushed, embarrassed by the memory, even ten years later. "I'm so sorry. That's really horrifying."

But Nate just shrugged like it hadn't even fazed him.

She gestured toward the Giant Dipper. "You didn't have to wait down here with me."

Nate shook his head. "I like waiting with you. Besides, I haven't seen you much this week, and this gives us time to talk. How are you doing?"

She forced a smile. How was she doing? She had the urge to tell Nate that her marriage had been pronounced terminal. Stage four. It wasn't even on life support, it was hopeless. Instead, she said, "I'm good. How about you?"

"Can't complain. Mal's doing great. Work is good, and in three weeks it'll be summer, and I'll have a two-month vacation."

"Teaching is the life," Julia said. Veronica had gotten a job at a local coffee shop for the summer but didn't have her license yet, and Julia was already stressed about how she was going to make all the driving work between Veronica's schedule and her own.

"Money could be better," Nate said. "But we get by."

"Oh God, are we not paying you enough to manage the rental?"

Nate lightly put his hand on her shoulder. "You're paying me too much. I told you a few years ago you could stop. I'd do it for free. It's not that big of a deal. I live next door."

He had told her that. And she had told him absolutely not. He deserved to be compensated for his time. He'd told her then that sounded like *lawyer-speak*, and sometimes family just did favors for each other.

"Well," Julia said. "If you feel you deserve a raise at some point, just tell us. When you agreed to this seventeen years ago, prices were a little different."

"Seventeen years? Has it really been that long since Vera died?"

Julia nodded. "It's crazy because sometimes I still catch myself thinking about her, and I picture her at her house in Coronado, and then . . . it takes me a minute to remember all over again she's gone."

"So . . . I guess that means you've been married for sixteen years, huh?" Nate whistled softly.

"How do you even remember that?" Julia laughed. "I can barely remember myself."

"Well . . . easy. The next year after Vera died . . . you got married. Just like that." He snapped his fingers. Then he opened his mouth, like there was more he wanted to say, but he closed it again without saying anything else.

If she and Ted stuck to their verbal agreement, they would get divorced after nineteen years, not quite making it to the platinum anniversary of twenty. For some reason, that thought filled her with the deepest sense of failure she'd felt since the therapist's office, and she sighed.

"Goddamn," Nate said after a moment. "How did we get so old?"

Julia punched him lightly on the arm. "Speak for yourself, old man. I'm still and always will be a whole year younger than you."

Nate grinned. "That's true. And you still look exactly the way I remember you looking at eighteen too. You haven't changed one bit, Jules."

She laughed again. "You're really full of shit." But she thought about Nora last summer insisting she was still *hot*. Did Nate think that too? Her cheeks burned at the thought.

He met her gaze, and his expression was totally serious. They stared at each other just like that for another moment, eyes locked, unmoving, until Emily and Mal emerged from the exit of the coaster, holding hands and laughing. Nora walked slowly behind them, looking a little green.

"Julia, that was so awesome!" Mal exclaimed. "You should come with us."

Julia put her arm around Mal and gave her squeeze. "Absolutely not. I love you to death, Mal. But there is no way I'm ever getting on that thing."

Five months after she left her sisters and Coronado, Nora went to a party on election night.

It was hosted by Cathay Peters, a big-name old-school Broadway actress who had played her mother, Rhea, in *Hera*. Nora had been thrilled to score an invite, and she texted her sisters a selfie from Cathay's gorgeous Upper East Side brownstone as the returns started coming in: NBD! Just watching the glass ceiling break with a room full of Broadway royalty and fancy champagne!!

Emily quickly texted back a selfie of her and Cecile on the couch in matching red plaid pajama pants and MADAM PRESIDENT T-shirts. Cecile and I just stress-raided the boys' Halloween candy and are watching results in our pjs.

Nora felt this weird pang of jealousy, and it occurred to her that having someone to stress-eat with in PJs for the rest of your life might be the greatest reason of all to get married.

V and I just popped popcorn! Julia texted. She sent a picture of Veronica smiling, holding a huge popcorn bowl.

Nora glanced up from her phone, looked around, and realized the only people she knew at this party were the few other former *Hera* cast members who'd come. Her old coworkers. They were all cordial, certainly, but she didn't quite consider any of them close friends, and they mostly hadn't kept in touch since the show had closed. Who would she hug when they got their first woman president? Who would she squeal with? She suddenly wished she'd taken the train to DC and was sitting with Julia and Veronica on the couch with a bowl of popcorn instead.

But that thought was interrupted by the brush of a hand on her shoulder. She spun around and was face-to-face with Dev.

"Shit," she said under her breath. But she stared at him, and she instantly remembered how gorgeous he was: the perfect lines of his jaw, the kindness of his sea-blue eyes. And she felt her heart thrumming in her chest, like she had just finally come alive again.

"I thought that was you," he said. "I spotted your hair from across the room."

Nora shook her curls gently against her back. She had always believed her long, springy curls to be a blessing and a curse. They set her apart, which in her line of work could be either good or bad. "What are you doing here?" she asked. "How do you know Cathay?"

Dev gave her an incredulous look. "*Wizards*," he said slowly.

"Oh. Right." That had been a stupid question. Nora knew Cathay had played his mother in the entire series. Why hadn't that occurred to her before now? "Well . . ." she said. And so many thoughts sat on the tip of her tongue that she couldn't quite bring herself to say out loud. *It's great to see you after all this time. You still look amazing. I've missed you. I'm sorry about everything. What we had was real. Leo who?* But instead she said, "Small world. She was my mother too. In *Hera*."

"I know," he said. "I saw it. She was great. I mean, so were you."

She suddenly felt self-conscious, thinking that he had been to the show, watched her perform, formed an opinion about her, and that she hadn't even known until now. "You should've come backstage, said hi . . ."

He nodded. "I didn't want to."

So, he was still mad. After all this time. Well, maybe she was a little bit mad too. That he had assumed the worst in her. That he had refused to listen. She put her hands on her hips, and they stared at each other for another moment. Their eyes locked, but neither of them spoke.

"I heard Leo is getting a divorce," Dev finally said, breaking eye contact. "Are you two here together . . . ?" His eyes scanned the crowd of people in the adjoining room behind her.

"Oh God, no. Definitely not," Nora said emphatically. "Is he even here?"

Dev shrugged, like he wasn't sure but had just assumed. Half of Broadway did appear to be here. *Please God, do not let Leo walk into this room right now.*

"I mean, it's cool if you are, obviously," Dev continued.

Nora shook her head. "We're not." Leo had done what he had done. Her career had finally gained some traction. But she'd told him in no uncertain terms, after she'd accepted the role of Hera, that nothing would happen between them ever again. She had not, in fact, heard about his divorce. Nor did she care.

Suddenly they heard a glass shatter in the next room—that broke this stupid conversation, and they both walked over to where a crowd had gathered around a large TV in the living room. Someone appeared to have accidentally dropped their champagne. Broken glass was scattered on the white marble floor. "She's not going to win!" Cathay exclaimed dramatically, holding up her hands.

Nora watched the TV for a few moments, in disbelief at the reddening map. Then she felt a warm hand on hers. *Dev's hand.* "Should we get out of here?" He leaned in and whispered close to her ear.

She felt numb and distant from herself, but Dev's hand was so warm, and she clung to him and followed him through the large brownstone, out the front door. Outside, the night air was cold, and she held tighter on to Dev's warm hand. If the world was going to end, if the world had ended, then maybe she was never going to let go of him.

Dev grabbed his phone and called an Uber with his free hand, which took them to a swanky hotel she'd never been in before near the bottom of Central Park. She held on to him in the elevator, up to his penthouse suite. Amazingly, she hadn't noticed a single photographer on the street, at the hotel. Every one of them was probably at the Javits Center right now for election coverage.

"Nora." Dev said her name in a low voice as he guided her into his suite. She looked up at his beautiful face. How had it not changed one bit in the last few years? She reached her hand up and stroked the smooth-shaven skin of his cheek gently with her thumb.

On the tip of her tongue were the words *Is this okay?* Which quickly alternated with *What are we doing?*

But before she could say anything, he kissed her. Then she was kissing him back. And maybe everything was going to feel terrible tomorrow but Dev felt so good, and she was finally here with him, so she didn't even care.

He unzipped her dress and lowered it slowly.

What are we doing?

She unzipped the fly of his dress pants.

Is this okay?

But he was still kissing her, so she didn't speak, not wanting to break the spell.

She heard her phone buzzing away in her purse—surely, her sisters' chat blowing up—but she ignored it.

She just kept kissing him.

In the middle of the night, Nora woke up naked to the sound of sirens wailing.

It wasn't an unusual sound in the city that never slept, but still the sirens pulsed in the thumping of Nora's heart as she suddenly remembered where she was. Who she was with. Everything that had happened.

A swath of moonlight shone in through the large wall of glass opposite the bed, illuminating Dev's face, the easy motion of his bare chest rising up and down as he slept. Nora stared at him for a moment, deciding whether she should kiss him, wake him. Or whether she should flee.

Fight or flight.

Flee.

She gingerly got up out of bed, pulled on her dress from the floor. She grabbed her purse and took out her phone. She had eighty-three unread texts in her sisters' chat, and she scanned them quickly.

How is this even fucking happening?

V wants to know if we can all move to Canada. Nora are you in?

Where the fuck is Nora? Nora!!

Maybe she fell asleep?

I'm never sleeping again.

I'm here, Nora thought, but she could not respond right then, tell her sisters where *here* was. Or what she had been doing while they were texting. Dev had broken her heart once, and she couldn't withstand the emotional toll of him doing it all over again when he woke up and realized whatever this was . . . it had been a mistake. Her heart thudded so fast. She had to get out of here. Now.

But what if he doesn't break your heart this time? She heard Julia's always wise voice in her head.

Then Emily: *Don't be a bitch and leave like this, Nora.*

She moved away from her sisters' chat and opened up Dev's contact on her phone. Thank you for tonight. Text me.

Then she zipped up her dress, grabbed her shoes in her hand, and snuck out.

CHAPTER 29

2017

"I WANT TO AMEND THE terms," Ted said to Julia, as she was pulling her suitcase out of the closet so she could pack it for Coronado.

His words stopped her, and she stood frozen for a moment, wondering if he'd changed his mind about the divorce. They'd been getting along amazingly well this past year, and most days Julia moved about her life almost forgetting about their deal.

"Amend how?" she said, pushing past him to wheel her suitcase to the foot of the bed, where the clothes she was taking were already sitting in neatly folded squares.

"I think we should amend the term about cheating," Ted said. "I mean, four years is a long time to be celibate."

"What?" She understood what he was saying, but she asked the question to give herself a minute to process how completely she'd misread things. She'd started working full-time at a new job this past year. Veronica had finally gotten her driver's license, and they'd given her Julia's old car to drive, which meant Julia didn't even have to worry about school pickups and drop-offs. Julia had pretty much thrown her entire self into work the last few months. And now, standing awkwardly in front of Ted, asking him to essentially clarify his take on celibacy, she suddenly wondered if she and Ted hadn't actually been getting along at all. Maybe she had just been ignoring him.

"We both agreed that our marriage is practically over. I think we should remove that term from our verbal," Ted finally said.

Julia spun on her heels to face him, put her hands on her hips. "So now you want my permission to go fuck someone else?" Her voice shook, and her heart suddenly pounded in her chest. She didn't even sound like herself with that language. She sounded abrasive, like Emily.

"That's a crass way to put it," Ted said.

"So that's a yes?" she spat.

"Look, it can go both ways. This gives you a hall pass when you see Nate next week."

"A hall pass?" Julia shook her head, suddenly thinking about standing with Nate last May at Belmont Park. "We had a contract."

"A verbal," Ted said. "And I'm saying I want to amend it."

"What if I say no?" Julia asked.

"Why do you even care?" Ted asked. "It's not like we're having sex."

"Is that all you want?" Julia asked. "Sex?" She reached up and unbuttoned her shirt halfway, exposing her white cotton bra. "Fine, we can do it right now. Then you won't have to worry about being celibate."

"Julia." Ted said her name tenderly. He reached up his hands, but instead of grazing his fingertips across her breasts, the way he might've once, years ago, he slowly started to redo the buttons instead.

"Mom!" Veronica's voice suddenly called out from downstairs. "I'm home. Where are you?"

Julia pushed his hands away and quickly did up the buttons herself.

Veronica had been at the mall with her friends, and Julia, who usually compulsively tracked her on Find My when she was out driving, had been busy enough packing and dealing with Ted that she hadn't recently checked. So Veronica's arrival home now felt like a rare surprise. "Upstairs in my bedroom, sweetie," she called back, looping the top button closed, feeling her cheeks flame red and hoping V wouldn't notice.

The bedroom door swung open and Veronica walked in, dressed in denim shorts that Julia found both too short and too tight and a pink crop top that Julia thought revealed way too much skin. But she held her tongue. School had just gotten out for the summer. Veronica had argued just yesterday that there shouldn't be any dress code over summer break. Julia had agreed to that, though now wished she hadn't. In general, she and Veronica had been getting along better the past few months, since they'd walked in the Women's March together in January, wearing the matching pink hats Cecile had knitted and mailed from Florida. They'd felt this glorious solidarity that day and Julia had been trying to cling to that, to keep the rare peace with her daughter. "How was the mall, V?" she said now.

"Jemma invited me to go to Cape May with her family this week, and I already texted Dad earlier and he said it was okay if I bailed on the Hamptons. But he said I had to ask you." Veronica's words tumbled out in a rush. "So can I go? Please, please, please?"

Julia tried to process for a few seconds. Had Ted just essentially asked her if he could cheat, already knowing he would have the next week totally and completely by himself? She was tempted to tell Veronica no, for that reason alone, that she wanted Ted to have a chaperone. But what *real* reason did she have to tell Veronica no that wasn't going to cause a huge mother-daughter blowup? "Her parents are going?" Julia asked cautiously instead.

Veronica nodded.

"And there will be no drinking, drugs, smoking? Or sex without condoms."

"Jesus, Mom." Veronica's cheeks flushed. "Daddy, can't you ask her to be normal, just once?"

Ted grinned and held up his hands, but he and Veronica exchanged a knowing look that suddenly Julia wished she could punch right off Ted's chiseled face.

"What would normal be?" Julia asked. "Telling you to get drunk, ruin your lungs, and get pregnant while you're at it?"

"Daddy!" Veronica protested.

"Mom and I both trust you to make good decisions," Ted said. "Don't we, Julia?"

"So I can go?" Veronica squealed.

Julia felt she had no other choice but to nod. Veronica grabbed her in a brief hug and then ran out of the room, saying she needed to pack.

Julia turned to Ted after Veronica was gone and said quietly, "I should divorce you right now, tell V everything."

"You know better than to do that to V," Ted said, and then he calmly walked out.

After a string of false starts, Nora had finally gotten cast in a new Broadway show. It was a supporting role, not a lead, so it almost felt like a step down after *Hera*. But since it was a comedy, not a drama, Stella swore it would help show her range, help build her into something bigger for the next role. And nearly two years after *Hera* closed, and a half dozen near misses, Nora was just happy to have something booked.

She'd bought herself a new Louis Vuitton bag to celebrate and then carried it with her on the flight to San Diego, stuffing it with all her favorite entertainment magazines purchased at the Hudson's at JFK.

She settled into her seat after the flight took off, pulled *EW* out of her beautiful, beautiful (did she say beautiful?) new bag, stopping for a moment to lovingly stroke the beige leather. Then she reclined in her seat and flipped open the magazine, only to be confronted with the sudden sight of Dev's familiar, attractive face.

Devlin St. Claire and fiancée, Jade, show off their gorgeous new Hollywood Hills home!

It had been six months since Nora had texted Dev and then

snuck out of his hotel room, and she'd never gotten a response. Thank you for tonight. Text me. She'd waited all that day, and then the next, and the next, checking her phone again and again. He never texted her.

A week later, she saw pictures of him and Jade (former Disney star/current rising pop star) together on Instagram, which only reaffirmed for her that sneaking out had been exactly the right way to protect her heart after all. If only she hadn't been stupid enough to go back to his hotel with him in the first place. If only she hadn't felt *so* much that night. If only sex with him wasn't different, better than anything else she'd ever had. Well, clearly it had meant nothing to him. He was on to Jade in no time.

And now they were *engaged*? Ugh. She had up until this very moment missed out on that specific tidbit. And seeing the photographic evidence in print before her, it hit differently: the two of them sitting on a white couch in a gorgeous, wide-open living room surrounded by natural light. A huge renovated farmhouse kitchen, with Jade in an apron (baking a stupid apple pie no less). Dev jumping into a sparkling blue pool in the backyard, a devilish grin on his face.

She examined him closely in the photos now. Dev really had one of those faces that didn't age at all, and he strangely still looked twenty-five even though she knew he was close to forty. Jade had flawless olive skin, straight, shiny, long, jet-black hair, and actually was twenty-five, all of which made Nora feel even more irritated. Also, Nora didn't think her voice was even that good! Her most popular songs relied heavily on auto-tune. When Nora had listened to her live on *Good Morning America* a few weeks ago, she'd been totally off pitch. Dev was both too talented and too old for her.

Not that anyone had asked Nora's opinion on the matter, nor cared what she thought. She closed the magazine and stuffed it in the back of the seat in front of her, feeling annoyed.

And then she asked the flight attendant for a glass of wine.

It might have been fair to say Nora was still a little buzzed when she arrived in her Uber on Ocean Boulevard. Three glasses of in-flight wine had barely smoothed out the edges of Dev. She was last to arrive this year, and Emily, Julia, and Mallory were already sitting out on the front porch.

Mallory had gotten her hair cut, a severe bob that framed her chin in a triangle, like someone had just lopped her long pigtails off with a pair of kitchen scissors at an odd angle. Nora wondered if Nate had actually done this, and she rifled in her purse for the sparkly Kate Spade barrettes she'd brought for Mallory as a gift. Last year, she'd brought cookies from Junior's, but Mallory hadn't been able to stop talking about some ridiculous whale pins Emily had gotten for free at a conference. *You want accessories*, Nora had thought, *I can bring you accessories.* It was a shame Nate had done something terrible to her hair in the meantime, but Nora wasn't quite drunk enough to blurt this out, thankfully.

"Nora!" Mallory exclaimed as Nora wobbled her way up the walkway. "You'll never believe what happened! It rained last week and now we can go see the treasure ship!"

They all knew about the sunken ship that had been discovered just off the shore, down the beach, on the other side of the Del in front of the condos. But it was rarely visible, except in the aftermath of a few storms and strange ensuing tides. They'd never seen it in all the years they'd been coming here.

"I added it to the schedule for before dinner tonight," Julia said. "So Nora, go put your things inside and hurry up so we can walk down there."

Nora wanted to tell them that she had a headache, that she didn't really care about the treasure ship, and that instead she wanted to go inside and take a nap so she could stop thinking about Dev and Jade's stupid perfect house.

"We've been waiting for you!" Mallory exclaimed excitedly.

"Emily and Julia said we could probably go without you, but I said no way, Nora will be super excited to see this."

Nora couldn't help but smile. *Forget about Dev.* She was here for her family, her sisters, Nate, and Mallory, and she wasn't going to let Dev ruin another Coronado week for her. She closed her eyes for a moment, steadied herself, then pulled the barrettes out of her purse and handed them to Mallory. "Okay, but put these in your hair first so you're extra sparkly for the walk down there."

Mallory giggled, and Nora loved the sound of her little-girl laugh. It suddenly sounded like home.

It was the most beautiful of all May days, the sky a stunning blue, the sun a bright yellow ball hurtling across the water toward dusk. They decided to walk down the beach to reach the ship, close to the water's edge. Mallory skipped ahead, dragging Nora and Emily along with her, stopping here and there to pick up and examine interesting-looking shells. Julia and Nate walked slower, lagging behind, talking.

After a year apart, Julia always expected a moment where it would feel strange to suddenly be in each other's company again. But oddly, that moment rarely came. Every first conversation with Nate felt familiar. Again and again and again. May after May after May.

"You know, this is Mal's favorite week of the year," Nate said. "She talks about it constantly for the entire month of May. I mean, mine too, but that goes without saying."

Julia laughed. "Mallory is so great. And not even remotely a teenager yet."

Nate shook his head. "Yeah, I'm not prepared for those years at all."

"You most definitely are not," Julia confirmed with a sigh. Though, she wondered if Mal would be a gentle teen the way she had been a gentle two-year-old. She was easygoing, easy to please, happy-go-lucky. Veronica had always been highly emotional, dramatic like Nora, and a surge of hormones had only seemed to heighten that these last few years.

"You're good though, right, Jules?" Nate stopped walking, looked at her, searched her face with his acorn eyes. It was the question he asked her almost every year. Round and round and round they went. While keeping a safe distance. Never daring to open the vault.

"I'm good." She forced a smile. "Really busy with work. Veronica is driving. Ted is . . ." Suddenly she couldn't stop thinking about the words he'd said to her, *hall pass*. "Ted is the same as always," she finished. Which was not a lie. "What about you?"

Nate nodded. "I have the perfect girl in my life so what else could I possibly need?"

Perfect girl? Was Nate dating someone? The thought struck her with an irritated jolt. Then it quickly occurred to her he must be referring to Mallory, and she smiled. "You know, it's weird," she said. "This time next year, Veronica will have graduated high school. She'll be getting ready to move out and go to college. And then I think, who will I even be if I'm not her mom anymore?"

"You'll always be her mom," Nate said.

But she and Ted would get divorced, and then it seemed inevitable Veronica would take Ted's side. The two of them were always thick as thieves. Julia felt like she was trying so hard to cling to everything she loved, and yet, no matter what she did, how hard she had worked, it was all on the brink of slipping away. "But it won't be the same," she finally said.

"Nothing ever is," Nate said.

She nodded and they walked a little bit farther in silence.

"You know that time when you took me to Santa Monica?" Julia said quietly after a few moments, remembering the way Nate had alluded to it last May, when they were at Belmont Park. Julia often thought about the way she had felt so exhilarated riding the roller coaster (just before she'd felt so nauseous), the way Nate had taken care of her that evening when she'd fallen apart. The way she'd left him in the hotel in the middle of the night and had taken a cab to LAX, suddenly so desperate to get home, back to Veronica.

Nate nodded. "What about it?"

"I've been thinking about it a lot lately."

"That seems like a bad idea," Nate said.

"You're right," she said. "But my brain and my heart don't work together super well these days."

Nate chuckled, stopped walking, and turned to look at her again. Julia suddenly noticed the lines that had cropped up around his eyes, the corners of his smile. The grays that were peppering his messy brown curls on the sides of his head. Like they told a perfect story of everything Nate had become and everything Nate had once been.

"Jules," he said. Then he touched her shoulder gently. "Sometimes I forget my heart even exists. Then you come back here each May, and it starts beating again."

Hall pass, she thought. What if she told Nate right now what Ted had said? Would he laugh, say how ridiculous the whole thing was? Or would he shoot her a sexy half-smile, offer to sneak her in later tonight after Mal fell asleep? And which response would make her happy—joking with him, her oldest and dearest friend, about the complete disaster area of her marriage, or suddenly unlocking twenty years of desire between them from that goddamn vault? The words sat there on the tip of her tongue, but she couldn't bring herself to say them. Her own heart was thumping so wildly in her chest, she could barely hear herself think.

"Dad!" Mallory suddenly cried out. "There it is! Come on!"

Nate dropped his hand quickly, as if Julia's shoulder had turned to flames. He shot her an apologetic smile and then jogged up the beach to see the wreckage Mallory was excited about.

Four months after they left Coronado, when the fall weather had already swept into Maryland and the leaves had just begun to turn,

Emily called Julia in the middle of a workday, sounding panicked. “Have you been watching the weather?” Emily asked.

“What weather?” Julia had been buried in a contentious custody case and had barely come up for air, much less turned on the TV. But there had been one terrible hurricane after another all fall, including Maria, which had devastated Puerto Rico a few weeks earlier.

“You are not going to fucking believe this,” Emily said. “But now there’s a *Hurricane Vera* that formed in the gulf and is forecast to hit Tampa this weekend.”

Julia felt a slight tingling in her head. It was one thing when they half joked about all the *Vera* birds, watching them, following them, helping them, giving them signs. She didn’t really believe in the afterlife. But then again, maybe she kind of did? Now here was a literal hurricane named *Vera* heading straight toward Emily?

“Would it be okay if we drove up and stayed at your house for a few days?” Emily asked.

Emily hadn’t been to her house since before Dad died; she hadn’t seen Veronica since then either. Was this somehow Grandma Vera’s doing? Was she telling them it had been too long? Julia knew that was ridiculous. But the tingling didn’t quite subside. “Of course,” Julia said. “You’re welcome anytime, Em.”

“You sure?” Emily asked. “It was Cee’s idea, and I don’t want to bother you, but honestly I couldn’t think of anywhere else we could all go so last-minute like this.”

“Yes, absolutely,” Julia said quickly, suddenly remembering her house was in complete disarray. The roof had leaked after a vicious August thunderstorm and now, as the repairs were being made, the contents of her closet filled up the guest bathroom, while she and Ted had relocated to the guest bedroom. She wasn’t exactly sure where they were all going to sleep, but she didn’t tell Emily that. She would just . . . figure something out. “It’ll be great to see you,” she said instead. “And V will be happy to see her cousins again.”

When Emily thought about it later, she was able to pinpoint the exact moment her marriage with Cecile started to fracture. They were on I-95, somewhere in North Carolina, as they drove toward Julia's house, escaping Hurricane Vera.

They'd already been in the car twelve hours; Cecile was taking a shift driving. And now it was quiet after the boys got into a blowup fight about who got the last package of peanut butter crackers. Emily had promptly reached into the back seat, snatched the package for herself, and then eaten them, causing Cecile to cast her the worst side-eye. The crackers felt heavy in Emily's stomach now, the weight of always, *always* making the wrong decisions when it came to the boys.

Emily got a text, and she glanced down at her phone. Saw the news about the hurricane, Cara wrote. I hope you're safe!

Cara had been texting her on and off since they'd run into each other in Santa Monica and up until now, Emily had been ignoring her. But she glanced up at the annoyed look frozen on Cecile's face. Then glanced in the sunshade mirror at the boys in the back seat, who were both glaring at her.

And suddenly she had the urge to respond. Safe. Evacuating to my sister's house in MD. Then she added, Thanks for checking.

Keep me posted! Cara wrote.

Will do, Emily responded.

She looked up from her phone, suddenly realizing her face felt hot, feeling like everyone in the car knew what she'd just done, that they could see right through her. But Cecile was still frowning, her eyes trained heavily on the road. And Emily told herself she'd done nothing wrong. There was no harm in a simple, innocent text.

Ted wasn't thrilled to hear about the unexpected company coming to stay in their already messed-up house, so Julia told him he should leave for the weekend. "Go to Long Island and see your parents," she told him.

He nodded, suddenly looking weirdly pleased, and Julia wondered if what he'd actually heard her say was that she was giving him permission to leave for the weekend and cheat on her. "What's that look for? You don't like your parents that much," she snapped.

"Julia," he said. "Don't be like that. Our marriage has been over for a long time."

No, she distinctly remembered he had said four years until their marriage would be over. She still had almost a full year left. Nothing was actually *over* yet.

"We should want each other to be happy," Ted continued. "We said *amicable*, remember?"

"We also said no cheating," she reminded him.

"It's not cheating if we amend our agreement," he countered.

"It takes two people to amend," she spat back.

"Have a nice weekend with your sister," he said. And he shut the door to the guest room hard enough on the way out that it shook the walls.

She had too much to do before Emily and Cecile and the boys arrived to go after him. She stripped and washed all the sheets in the guest room, and then she told Veronica she'd be sharing her room until Emily's family left.

Veronica sighed deeply and asked if she could go sleep at her friend Jemma's for the weekend, pointing out that since her dad left, she should be able to leave too. "Absolutely not," Julia said. "You haven't seen your cousins in years."

"Step-cousins," Veronica corrected.

"The only cousins you have," Julia admonished.

"What am I supposed to do with two ten-year-old boys?" Veronica crossed her arms in front of her chest and shot daggers from her big green eyes. Then she tossed her curls over her shoulders in a way that reminded Julia exactly of Nora when she got irritated.

"I have faith in you," Julia said. "You'll figure something out."

After Emily and her family arrived, Julia made a pot of coffee and she and Cecile sat at the kitchen table, sipping from mugs, leaning in close, chatting and laughing like old friends who were catching up after years apart.

Emily watched them for a moment, feeling this strange itch from deep inside of her that she couldn't quite reach to scratch. It appeared that Cecile and Julia were getting along better than she and Julia usually did. Was she happy that her wife and her older sister were acting like besties or was she feeling weirdly . . . jealous?

In the adjoining family room, Veronica and Mikey and Jim were intensely playing Switch and periodically bursting into laughter. Emily observed them for a few moments too. Veronica seemed to be getting along with the boys with such ease. Why was she the only one who couldn't figure out how to do it?

"I'm going to the bathroom," she said. But no one seemed to hear or notice as she walked off down the hallway.

She didn't really even have to go to the bathroom, but once inside, she locked the door and gave herself a moment to breathe. Something bubbled up inside of her, stress or anxiety or rage. She couldn't distinguish what exactly was making her chest feel so heavy. They had just fled for almost twenty hours in the car from a fucking hurricane that could potentially destroy everything they owned. Maybe that was what was weighing on her now, the realization that in a few days' time there might not be anything left to go back to. *Just stuff,* Cecile had said cheerfully in the car as they'd pulled out of the driveway. *All our people are safe.*

Stuff.

Something peeked out from the edge of the bathtub curtain, and Emily pulled it back. The bathtub was filled with *stuff*—Julia had mentioned some renovation or repair going on in her bedroom and that they would have to excuse the mess, but the house had appeared spotless (of course) upon their arrival.

Emily peered into the tub now, with a morbid curiosity about her perfect sister's hidden mess. Even Julia's mess looked organized though—labeled boxes were piled high: *sweaters, purses, shoes.* But there was one box that seemed weirdly out of place: a medium-sized Priority Mail box resting right on top of everything else.

Emily picked it up now to examine it. It was addressed to Julia, at her old apartment back in DC, before she'd moved into this house. And the return address was Grandma Vera's on Ocean Boulevard. The postmark was from March 1999, a few weeks after Vera had died.

Julia must've sent herself something from the house when she'd gone to clean it out. She had sent Emily a box too, filled with books, but Emily had promptly opened it, discarded the box, and still kept the treasured relics from her grandmother on a special shelf in her house. *Shit.* Now she wished she'd thought to pack those when they'd fled Tampa yesterday.

But why was Julia's box here, like this?

Emily tugged at the edge of the tape and realized it was loose, like it had been pulled off before and then pressed down to reseal. She had no right to be snooping in her sister's things, and yet, she gently eased the tape off across the box and opened it to see what treasure Julia had taken for herself.

Envelopes?

No . . . letters?

A sudden chill came over Emily as she thought about Grandma Vera's armoire. Had Hurricane Vera swept her right here, in this exact moment, to see this proof that she, in fact, hadn't hallucinated what she saw at the age of seventeen? And that maybe there was more to the story than she had ever allowed herself to imagine? There were so many letters. The correspondence dating back for years and years.

She pulled the top letter out, held it in her hands, examined it closely. It was postmarked almost twenty years earlier, *December 1998*, which would've been just a few months before Grandma Vera died, a few years after she'd spotted a letter in the armoire.

445 Ocean Lane, Santa Monica, CA 90401 was scrolled in neat cursive in the top left corner. So, she had misremembered both the street name and number, but what she had seen in the armoire was real.

Her hands shook as she turned the envelope over. It had been opened before. Grandma Vera had read it once, she supposed, and maybe Julia had too. Emily pulled out the yellowing paper, unfolded it. Her heart beat too fast. She didn't want to read this, she shouldn't be reading this. Yet, she couldn't stop herself either.

It began, as if in the middle of conversation, and Emily felt weirdly as if she were eavesdropping.

Well, all hope isn't lost! Voice-over work is finally going well and it turns out profitable too. It's not like I was starving to death before, you know, but I'm building up a nest egg and honing my craft.

Emily dug through the pile, pulling out a letter from much further back: 1985. The year they first went to visit Grandma Vera in May.

I'm glad to hear you and Bob figured everything out. I know you don't agree with us, but please respect our wishes and keep your promise. He's a good dad. The girls are so much better off without me.

In other news, I got an audition for a Jell-O commercial! Wish me luck—

A knock on the door startled her, and she dropped the paper on the tile floor. "Em, are you okay in there?" Cecile must've finally noticed she'd slipped away.

"Uh, yeah. I'm fine. I'll be out in a minute," she called.

"The boys are hungry and Julia suggested we all go out for pizza. Do you want to come, or is your stomach upset?"

Emily sat down on the closed toilet lid and considered what to do. She should put these letters back in the box, pretend she'd never seen them, leave this bathroom, and go eat pizza with her wife and sister. *An audition for a Jell-O commercial?* That echoed in her head, taunting her now. And Grandma Vera and Dad figuring everything out? Grandma Vera keeping a promise, to what? Lie to her granddaughters?

"Yeah, I actually, um, don't feel great," Emily lied. "Too much road food. You go on ahead without me."

"Are you sure?" Cecile asked, concern in her voice. "You'll be okay by yourself? Do you want me to bring back some Tums? Or ask Julia if she has some?"

Emily was certain that her sister had Tums and every other over-the-counter medicine stocked in full supply in this house. "I'll be fine in a bit. Just go enjoy your pizza," she said.

And maybe this was it. Maybe this was the moment her marriage fractured. Her life fractured. She was lying to Cecile about the very thing that had and would define and ruin so many aspects of her life. She was choosing to drown in it now, rather than to get up, leave this bathroom, and be present for her family.

Cecile walked away from the bathroom door and Emily stayed behind, sitting on top of the closed toilet seat, reading through the letters, one by one.

CHAPTER 30

2018

JULIA LOVED THINGS THAT had neat beginnings and endings. Perfect bookends. She enjoyed the finality, the clarity, the completeness.

She had brought Veronica to Coronado the first May after she'd been born, and she decided that it was only fitting to bring her after her high school graduation, the last year that she would still completely be Julia's child.

By next year, Veronica would be eighteen and have already been away at college. Granted, she was only going a half hour away to the University of Maryland, but still, she was moving out. Who knew if, or when, she would ever truly come back to Julia. Maybe she wouldn't come home for the summer, much less want to take a trip with her mother. (Who knew if she'd even be talking to Julia with the divorce still on for next year.)

So Julia booked two plane tickets to San Diego for the last week in May, and then told Veronica the trip was her graduation present.

Veronica frowned a little and said, "But I promised Daddy we'd celebrate my graduation with Grammy and Pop-Pop in the Hamptons that week."

"You can go any week all summer to the Hamptons," Julia said, suddenly thinking she should've coordinated this all in advance with Ted. Which would've been hard, considering they were barely speaking. "We only get this one week in Coronado. Grammy and Pop-Pop stay in the Hamptons all summer long. And they can come down here for your graduation party the weekend before we go to Coronado. Your aunts can't make it." Nora had agreed to sub in for a show she said she couldn't miss, and Emily had something going on at the museum. Besides, Emily had just visited a few months earlier during the hurricane. Julia had, at first, been annoyed that neither of them would make the effort to come back specifically for Veronica's grad party, but then she'd decided it would be better to all celebrate in Coronado the following week anyway.

"Come on, V," Julia implored her. "It'll be a girls' trip and super fun."

"Okay," Veronica said, and she didn't argue any more with Julia. Which was unlike her.

Julia had prepared more counterarguments, and so she kept on talking: "You went there once with me as a baby. But of course you wouldn't remember it. This will be a lasting lifelong memory for both of us."

Veronica nodded in agreement.

"It's my favorite place. My grandma Vera was your namesake. And I want to give you a piece of her world as a gift as you're about to journey off into adulthood yourself." Julia felt tears well in her eyes. Moisture had been permanently poised and ready to spill from her tear ducts Veronica's entire senior year of high school thus far. Every last, every senior night. Julia was one tearful step closer to her own childless future.

"Jesus, Mom." Veronica shook her head. "Are you like going through menopause or something? You've been crying for months."

Julia laughed. "I'm not even forty-five yet, V. Please. Don't make me feel older than I am. I'm emotional because you're my baby, and you're all grown up." She grabbed her daughter in a quick, impulsive hug, and Veronica gave her only thirty seconds before she squirmed to get out of it.

Nora wasn't in the greatest mood when she walked into the house on Ocean Boulevard. It wasn't her sisters' fault. She knew it wasn't. Still, she couldn't help but feel annoyed when she walked in and found Julia, Emily, and Veronica sitting on the couch, laughing together, thick as thieves. Like they were all in on some inside joke without her. (Weren't they always?) Plus, no one had told her Veronica was coming, and for some reason that made her feel worse.

She actually adored her niece, but she was in a terrible mood, and with Veronica here, Nora felt like she was going to have to put on a show all week, and she suddenly felt exhausted. *Happy Nora. Fun Aunt Nora.* When really, she just wanted to grab Emily, at least three bottles of wine, and sit out on the back patio and drink until she forgot why she was so irritated in the first place.

"Aunt Nora is here!" Veronica jumped up from the couch and embraced Nora in a hug, and suddenly Nora's grumpiness lightened.

Veronica looked (and acted) more like Nora than either Julia or Ted. She'd grown her hair out since Nora had seen her last at Christmas, and now her curls hit just below her shoulders, same length, texture, medium brown color, and springiness as Nora's. They had the same little button nose too that Grandma Vera had had, and they were just about the same height and build. Julia was a little taller, a little thinner, a little smaller-chested than Nora. Veronica had gotten the same round hips and boobs as Nora, and it occurred to Nora that they probably could share clothes if they ever were to live together.

"Hey, Ron," Nora said now, feeling just the tiniest bit calmer in the glow of her niece's admiration. "Your mom didn't tell me you were coming."

"Surprise!" Julia said, jumping up from the couch, sounding overly effusive. Nora and Emily exchanged a look. Julia typically hated surprises.

"Sorry I missed your graduation," Nora said to her niece now. "I have your gift back in New York. I would've brought it if I'd known." She'd bought Veronica an expensive and beautiful purse. Maybe it was guilt at missing the graduation and the party, maybe it was wanting to show off to Julia that she could afford it. But she had gotten on the plane this morning on the brink of sabotaging her whole career. It was possible she was going to have to return the purse when she got back to New York.

"You didn't have to get her anything," Julia said, standing up to give Nora a quick hug. "We get to all spend this week together, and that's the best gift of all."

"Ugh, Mom. You are so sappy," Veronica said. "Like who even talks like that?"

Emily laughed, got up, and gave Nora a one-armed hug. "Agreed, Ron. Your mom is literally the worst."

"Great," Julia said. "I love you guys too." Then she checked her watch. "Everyone go get changed. We have a beach walk on the schedule in twenty minutes."

Emily had considered talking to Julia about the box she'd found in her bathroom months earlier. She'd thought about it time and again these last few months and had even called Julia with the idea of broaching the subject. But then they'd ended up talking about mundane stuff instead—the weather, the boys, Veronica's college applications—and she hadn't been able to bring herself to say anything over the phone. They could talk in Coronado, she'd told herself. But when Julia showed up unexpectedly with Veronica in tow, Emily suddenly felt like she wouldn't get the chance. Maybe the best course of action was just to pretend she'd never seen anything. Just like she'd been doing all this time.

Instead, she eagerly checked her phone again as soon as she was upstairs alone in her room. *One new message*, and she felt anticipation building in her chest.

Then she saw it was from Cecile. Hope you're having fun with your sisters. Boys and I miss you. 🖤

She swallowed hard, really feeling like shit. But she texted back quickly. Miss you too.

Then she flipped over to her other chat, with Cara. The last thing in it was a text Emily had sent earlier this morning before she'd boarded her flight, telling Cara how badly she was failing at being a stepmom. Again. How Mikey had actually slammed a door in her face yesterday after dinner when she'd reminded him to do his homework, and how she constantly felt like she was doing everything totally wrong. Cara had responded, You're awesome! What do boys know anyway?

Emily had written back, Truth.

After Emily had broken down and texted Cara while evacuating because of Hurricane Vera—which, as it turned out, much like Vera herself, was a whole lot of drama but very little damage, as it had last-minute shot south and luckily missed Tampa altogether—she and Cara had kept in regular touch. It was as if finding the box of letters in Julia's bathroom had broken something inside of her, and Emily had pushed some internal self-destruct button that caused her to keep on responding to Cara in ways she logically knew she shouldn't.

Cara texted her happy birthday in January and then asked if she was spending the day with her wife. And Emily had told her how the boys had a robotics tournament and Cecile was there while Emily was holding down the fort at the museum. That kind of sucks, Cara had written. You should be celebrated on your day! And Emily had stupidly agreed with her.

Of course, she and Cecile had gone out to dinner to celebrate the following weekend, and she would never tell Cecile not to be there for the boys. But Emily never texted Cara that part.

Cara had become a little bit like the proverbial devil sitting on her shoulder. A devil who could text. And they'd been texting every few days.

"Tell me a secret," Emily said to Nora later that night, gulping down a glass of wine too fast. Julia had gone to bed, and Veronica was sitting out on the patio with them. Nora glanced at her niece and hesitated.

Veronica suddenly realized things were about to get interesting, and she sat up and leaned in close to her aunts. "Can I have some wine?" she asked.

"Your mother would kill us," Nora said.

"Brutally murder us, chop up our bodies, and throw the pieces into the ocean," Emily said. Still, she stood, walked into the kitchen, came back with a third glass, and poured a little for Veronica. "So we will never, ever tell her about this," Emily said, giving her niece a stern look. "Agreed?"

Veronica nodded, took the glass. She took a small sip and made a face.

"It's cheap, grocery store shit," Emily said. "In a few years we'll take you out and buy you something better."

"Or . . . you could take me out now." Veronica took another sip, then laughed. "I look exactly like Aunt Nora. I could borrow your ID."

She had clearly already thought this through and had come up with a solid plan. Nora saw a glimmer of Julia in Veronica. The solid-plan part. The breaking-the-law part, not so much.

"Maybe later in the week," Emily said. "The first night we drink cheap grocery store wine on the back patio and divulge our secrets. It's a ritual. Nora," Emily commanded. "You first."

Nora swallowed a gulp of wine and then sighed. "Fine. I just got offered this amazing show, like a life-changing opportunity I haven't come close to having since *Hera*. But . . ." She paused.

"But?" Emily raised her eyebrow.

"I think I'm gonna turn it down."

"And why would you do that?" Emily said.

"Because Dev is the male lead." She gulped down the rest of her wine too fast and it burned the back of her throat.

"So, you're gonna what? Throw this amazing opportunity away because of some asshole you dated for five minutes? I can't believe no one has MeToo'ed him by now."

Nora shook her head, feeling Emily's words pierce her skin, like tiny little knives. Each one hurting. Dev wasn't actually an *asshole*. At least not completely. But Nora didn't say that. Nora also didn't want to mention the embarrassing night they'd spent together in 2016, or the fact that she'd since then been carefully following the details of his extremely short marriage and subsequent divorce from Jade. "I don't know," she said instead. "I just don't think I can work with him."

"It would be pretty badass if you did, though," Veronica chimed in.

"That's exactly what I'm saying." Emily turned and high-fived her niece.

Nora shook her head. How could she possibly see him every day? Work side by side for hours? Kiss him in the final scene of the first act, eight times a week? "You go," she said to Emily.

"I don't want to," Emily said. Nora was already upset, she didn't want to make it worse. And besides, Veronica was here. She couldn't say anything about the letters. And if she said anything about Cara out loud, well, then suddenly it would be real.

"No fair!" Nora exclaimed. "I went first."

Emily shook her head and gulped her wine. "There's nothing to tell this year," she lied.

"I'll go," Veronica said. "But don't tell my mom."

Nora and Emily exchanged a look that basically said, *Well, shit, Julia is really going to murder us now.* Emily was struggling enough trying to figure out how the hell to be a stepparent to two preteen boys. She definitely could not suddenly take on the responsibility of a teenage-girl secret. Worst-case scenarios flooded her mind: sex, drugs. Oh God, could she be pregnant?

"I just got off the waitlist at Adley," Veronica said.

"I'm confused," Emily said. "Why is that a secret? That sounds like great news!"

"You know my mom," Veronica said. "She's married to her stupid plans. And we have this whole plan already in place. I'm supposed to go to college thirty minutes away from home, to Maryland. Adley is a six-hour drive. And they offered me a spot as a spring start, so I'd have a gap semester in the fall. I wouldn't even start college until next January. Which has never been the plan!"

"Sweetie." Nora put her empty wineglass down and leaned over to rub Veronica's shoulders. "If this is what you want, you have to tell her."

"But I feel like she's gonna be really mad about me not starting until January. And she'll want me to turn it down. She even has this calendar on her desk where she has been marking off 'months until college' ever since I started high school."

Emily laughed into her wine. "That's the most Julia thing I've ever heard."

Nora shook her head. "Just make her a new calendar and she'll readjust her plan. She'll survive it. More than any plan, your mom wants you to be happy."

But Veronica frowned, like maybe she wasn't sure. And then she quickly finished off her glass of wine.

"Nora's right," Emily said. "I've been fucking with your mom's plans for over forty years. She always gets over it."

"It is my dream school," Veronica said. "You really think she'll understand?"

Nora and Emily exchanged a brief sisterly look, wherein they both communicated their tacit understanding as to how much this was going to freak Julia out. But then they both turned to Veronica, smiled, and said, "Yes."

That week, they checked things off Julia's schedule one by one: walks on the beach, breakfast at the Del, dinner at the Brigantine.

A crab roast with Nate and Mallory. The ferry downtown to shop. The zoo. Buying romance novels at Bay Books, and celebrity magazines at Walgreens, and then reading on the beach and gossiping over the glossy pictures of Meghan and Harry's wedding inside the pages.

By the end of the week, Veronica still hadn't told Julia about her change of college plans. Nora still hadn't found the courage to call Stella and tell her what she'd decided about starring opposite Dev. And Emily and Cara had exchanged exactly five texts.

On their last night, after they got back from their dinner at the boathouse, Julia went up to bed, and Emily and Nora decided to walk to the Irish pub for one last drink. Veronica begged her aunts to bring her along.

Nora opened her wallet, pulled out her license, slipped it into Veronica's hand. "One drink," she whispered. "And if you get caught, I say you stole this."

"Because she really looks almost forty." Emily rolled her eyes.

"Well, I don't look almost forty either!" Nora insisted, shaking her curls against her back as all three of them walked outside into the cool night.

Emily choked back a laugh as her phone buzzed in her pocket. She told herself she wouldn't check it. She shouldn't.

And then the three of them headed up Isabella to Orange and took a table on the large outside patio at the Irish pub. The Padres-Dodgers game was playing up on the big TVs in front of them, and as Emily sipped her glass of wine, she pulled her phone out, just to check what the buzz had been: I hate knowing you're so close right now and I can't see you.

Emily shoved her phone in her pocket and quickly ordered another glass of wine, while Nora and Veronica followed suit.

Later, Nora had lost count of how many glasses of wine she (and Veronica and Emily) had had. Later, Nora would barely remember what they talked about while they drank, or how it made her giggle when everyone on the patio cheered after the Padres won, or even the fact that Emily kept checking her phone. Later, Nora would barely remember most of this night, except for how it would end. Nora was finally drunk enough to feel light. Untethered.

When the bar closed down after midnight, Emily ordered them an Uber, because walking all the way back to Ocean Boulevard felt too arduous a task with bodies that light. The three of them tumbled into the back seat, Nora and Veronica both giggling for most of the five-minute ride.

Then, as Emily helped Veronica out of the car on Ocean Boulevard, up the walk to the house, Nora turned toward next door, where Nate was sitting out on his own porch, drinking what looked like an extremely late-night whiskey.

Emily checked her phone again once she was back alone in her bedroom. I took the ferry to Coronado after the game, Cara texted. I'm at the ferry landing right now. Where are you in Coronado exactly?

If she hadn't drunk so much, she never would've done what she did next, which was to text Cara the address of the house on Ocean Boulevard.

She never would've walked back down the stairs, grabbed a bottle of wine from the fridge, walked back outside, crossed the street, and waited for Cara on the beach. She never would've sat in the sand and talked and drank wine with Cara all night, until the sun rose the next morning.

She never would've hugged her goodbye either. Or held on tightly as Cara whispered in her ear: "I hope I see you again soon."

But what she couldn't quite explain, when Cee would read all her texts six months later, was exactly why she'd texted Cara the next evening once she got home to Florida, once she was long sober: It was so great to see you. I hope I see you again soon too.

After she got out of the Uber, instead of walking into the house behind Emily and Veronica, Nora wobbled up the front path to Nate's porch.

"Oooh," Nora exclaimed loudly, pointing to Nate's whiskey. "I want one!"

Nate let out a dry laugh. "Noradora, you look like you've already had enough."

"I haven't, Nate." She held up her hand. "I solemnly swear."

But somehow holding up her whole hand caused her to lose her balance, and next thing she knew, she was tumbling, straight into Nate's lap. He put his arms around her, trying to steady her. Then he patted her thigh gently. "Come on, I'll help you get back next door. Why don't you stand up slowly."

"What if I don't want to," she protested, wrapping her arms around his neck instead. "You know I was in love with you forever," she blurted out. "Until I met Dev. But Emily said he's an *asshole*."

Nate let out an uncomfortable laugh. "Come on, Nora," he said, gently tugging at her arms, but she continued to hold on tight. "You'll thank me in the morning if you let me help you walk home."

"Or," Nora said, still refusing to let go of him, pulling her body in closer to his. "You could let me stay right here with you, like I did when Mal was a baby."

Nate bit his bottom lip, and Nora suddenly remembered all the years in her late teens and early twenties she'd wanted him, she'd loved him. Everything had been perfectly platonic when she'd stayed here years ago, when Mal was a baby, of course. Nate always kept her at arm's length. And Nora hadn't ever been brave enough to push.

But now, all these years later . . . now that she was this light, the only thought she had was how sexy he still looked, even in his forties, a single dad. He was definitely a hot dad. Was there such a thing as a *dilf* or did she just invent it right now? Because that's exactly what Nate was. She lifted her forefinger and traced his bottom lip with it slowly.

"Nora." She felt the warmth of his breath on her finger as he spoke her name. She couldn't tell if his voice was imbued with annoyance or desire.

"Yes, Nate?" she said.

"You're really drunk."

Even in her *really drunk* state, that much registered to her as true. And she nodded.

But then she leaned in closer and put her lips on his, like she had wanted to do so many times in her life. Sixteen-year-old Nora, twenty-six-year-old Nora had never been brave enough to do it. But thirty-nine-year-old Nora? She finally, actually kissed him!

He tasted like whiskey and his lips were just as warm, as soft as she had once imagined they would be. But they didn't feel at all electric, like Dev's. They just felt . . . comfortable. Nate was a warm woolen coat, a cup of hot chocolate on a snowy day. God, she could really use some hot chocolate to sober up right now—

Nora suddenly heard a small, high-pitched noise. A bird sound she didn't quite recognize. *Dammit,* this was the moment Grandma Vera had chosen to come watch over her?

Then Nate pushed her back and she tumbled a little, landing softly on the porch, her hand hitting a flip-flopped foot with a perfect rose-colored pedicure.

Julia?

"How could you, Nora?" Julia was saying. But the words felt as if they were buzzing straight through her head, in one ear, out the other. Julia was close but her voice felt so far away.

Nora wanted to explain about the kiss, that she hadn't really meant it. She had just been light enough to try it after all this time. That she at least owed that much to teenage Nora. But suddenly, she couldn't remember how to string a coherent thought into words.

"She's seventeen!" Julia yelled at her. "I should call the police right now and have you arrested."

Nora shook her head. Nope. Nora was almost forty. She wasn't the baby anymore. She and Nate were both adults now.

Nate stood, lifted Nora by the elbows gently, and was trying to ease her body up to stand. "Come on, no one's calling the police. I'll help you next door. And hopefully you'll forget all this in the morning."

"Well, you know who is never going to forget this?" Julia yelled. "Me!"

And then Nora noticed Julia was waving her license in the air. Nora held out her hand to take it back, but Julia threw it down and then stomped back across the yard.

Unfortunately, that was the first thing Nora remembered when she woke up the next morning with a screaming headache, having both slept through her alarm and missed her flight.

Julia, Veronica, and Emily were gone. The house was empty. All that was left behind was Julia's annual reminder note about running all the bedding through the wash for the next renters.

All that replayed in Nora's head, again and again, was that stupid kiss. And Julia yelling that she was never going to forget it.

CHAPTER 31

2019

SITTING AT NATE'S KITCHEN table, a year after her drunken escapade, it suddenly occurred to Nora that maybe whatever was going on with Julia wasn't actually her fault. Was it possible Julia's absence now had nothing to do with her? She was momentarily flooded with relief before it hit her: Something much more serious than a stupid drunken kiss and giving Veronica her license might be going on.

"Why would Julia be in Santa Monica? What the hell is in Santa Monica?" Nora asked.

"Not what," Emily said under her breath. "Who."

"I don't understand," Nora said. "*Who* is in Santa Monica?"

Emily and Nate exchanged a look. Nate opened his mouth but then Emily cut him off. "I think it might be Mom," Emily finally said.

"What?" Nora said. "But Julia said her ashes were scattered in Lake Michigan. Is she actually buried in Santa Monica?" Emily's eyes and Nate's locked on each other in a way that made Nora want to slap them both. "Oh my God!" Nora was practically yelling. "What are you two keeping from me?"

"Nora," Emily said softly. "I didn't want you to ever find out. This has seriously been fucking with my head for twenty-five years."

"Find out *what*?" Nora exclaimed, exasperated. Because she was still confused about what was going on. Even if Mom was buried in Santa Monica, why was Julia there now? And why had it been a secret? "Emily May-Daniels!" She shouted her sister's full legal married name the way Dad used to yell Nora's full name when she was in trouble as a kid. "Tell me what the hell is going on! Right now!"

"I don't think Mom is actually dead," Emily said quietly. "I think . . . she's living in Santa Monica. Or at least she was . . . twenty years ago."

When Nora got extremely stressed, she sometimes felt like she'd left her body and imagined her life as a scene. It was how she had conquered stage fright, or that moment in her new show when, night after night, she had to kiss the one man she shouldn't ever be kissing again.

But now the set was Nate's kitchen table. The characters were two sisters who probably loved each other deep down, but who on the surface drove each other crazy. There was a man, a friend (*family?*) who somehow knew the greatest secret about their lives. A secret that even the youngest sister never knew. How was this possible?

Nora momentarily hovered up above, like she was watching it unfold. And she wished she had a script, that someone would feed her the next line because she had no idea what to say next, how she was supposed to feel. What she was even supposed to think.

Mom was alive, at least as of twenty years ago? Living in Santa Monica?

But Nora was forty. And her whole life she'd been told their mom had died giving birth to her. Why had they all lied? And forty years later, how did they all know this except for her? Emily? Julia? Even Nate?

Finally, she turned and glared at Emily. She couldn't find words. Her feelings about her sister's betrayal were too complicated to process in the moment—she would deal with her later.

So instead she turned to Nate: "Tell me everything you know," she demanded. "Right now. Leave nothing out."

CHAPTER 32

2006

JULIA WAS CURLED UP on the couch next to Nate, her legs tucked underneath her, as the end credits for *Some Like It Hot* rolled on, sitting in a way that made her look smaller, that made him suddenly remember her as a kid, a teenager. She was sixteen, running on the beach, laughing, calling after him to follow, to keep up.

I would follow you anywhere, he'd thought then.

But, of course, that wasn't how things worked out. Julia went back to Chicago, then to college in New Haven, law school in DC, and he had settled here, in the house he'd grown up in. As teenagers, they'd talked about moving somewhere together after college, but when his mom got sick, he'd suddenly understood he couldn't leave. And Julia? Julia had wings. The truth was, his whole life, he only got to follow her one week a year, one May week. Except for this year, when her terrible loss had inadvertently turned their time together into three weeks.

Julia chewed on her bottom lip, that way she did when she was thinking. "I'm going to tell you something I've never told anyone, but you have to promise me you'll put it in the vault."

The vault. It was the worst goddamn idea Nate had ever had. But he didn't say that to Julia now. He simply nodded.

"I mean it, Nate. You can't tell anyone. Not even Nora or Emily. Especially not Nora or Emily. They can *never* know."

"The vault is sacred," he said. What he really meant was *stupid.* The vault was stupid. But he would never betray Julia's trust.

"I think my mom is in Santa Monica." Julia said the words in such a rush that Nate thought he'd misheard them.

"What?"

"My mom," she repeated. "She's living in Santa Monica."

"I thought your mom died giving birth to Nora?"

Julia nodded. "So did I. But I found some letters Grandma Vera had in her armoire." She paused and chewed on the side of her thumbnail. A nervous habit that Nate had seen her do since she was at least twelve. "They all had a return address with my mother's name, a place in Santa Monica. And postmarks that spanned at least fifteen years after Nora was born."

"What did the letters say?" Nate asked, skeptical that any of this could be right. It felt like a mistake, a giant misunderstanding. Vera herself had told him her daughter was dead when he was just a little boy. Why would Vera have lied?

"I don't know," Julia said. "I never read them. They're in a box in my closet. I haven't opened the box since I cleaned out Grandma Vera's house."

Nate thought about that week seven years earlier: the last time Julia had been in Coronado alone, without her sisters. The last time they'd put something in the goddamn vault. How broken she'd seemed that night. How she had begged him to hold her close, and how much he'd wanted to even though he knew he shouldn't. When she'd left the next morning after they'd spent the night together, he'd even written her an email, asking her to come back, to forget about renting out the house next door and to really consider moving in after she graduated law school. He hadn't worked up the courage to actually send the email though, and next thing he knew, three months later she was engaged to Ted.

"But I memorized the address." He realized Julia was still talking, and he turned back to look at her. "Can you take me there now? Please?"

The problem with Nate was that he could never resist Julia,

not when Julia needed him for something. He knew deep down he should've told her to go home as soon as she got out of the hospital. And he knew that he shouldn't agree to take her to Santa Monica now either. What good could come of this? If her mother was there, it would destroy her. If her mother wasn't there, that might too.

"Please?" Julia pleaded. "I just want to see if she's real. I just want to talk to her. I need to ask her why she did it. Why she left us."

"Okay," Nate said, fighting against all his instincts to say no. "But why don't we sleep on it and see if you still want to go in the morning. If you do, then I'll take you."

Julia woke him at six the next morning, asking if they should get out in time to beat the traffic. He threw on some clothes, grabbed the keys to his truck, and next thing he knew he was driving her up I-5. Traffic was still light and they didn't stop through San Diego or Orange County, not even for coffee, until they hit Santa Monica proper. And only then did it occur to Nate to ask Julia exactly where they were going.

"445 Ocean Lane," she said, "but let's not go right away." She pointed to the Santa Monica Pier in the distance. "Let's go spend the day there instead."

It seemed like a strange request after she had spent most of the last two weeks pale, listless, and inside his house. And Julia didn't seem like she would enjoy the rides. "Are you sure?" he asked her.

"I've never been to an amusement park," she said.

He laughed. "We should've stopped at Disneyland on the way."

"Maybe on the way back," she said, sounding completely serious, though he had been joking. "Will you ride that roller coaster with me now?"

"It's not going to give you motion sickness?" he asked.

"It probably will. Will you hate me if I puke?"

"Jules," he said softly. "You know I could never hate you."

They rode every ride on the pier and Julia threw up twice.

Then they ate cotton candy for lunch and fish stew for dinner. They walked along the beach, and as it started getting dark Nate wondered out loud if they should get a hotel. Julia nodded. "Yes!" she exclaimed, sounding more alive than she had in weeks. "We'll stay the night and then we'll do Disneyland tomorrow."

He knew something wasn't completely right, but he didn't question her. He drove them to a little inn he'd stayed at once with Becca.

"This is adorable!" Julia gushed. "Why haven't I ever been to Santa Monica before? It's so lovely here!"

Nate shrugged. He would take the more low-key vibes of Coronado any day of the week.

"Okay," Julia suddenly said firmly. "Now I'm ready. Can we go to her house?"

"Now?" Nate glanced at his watch. It was after eight, already dark.

Julia nodded.

And so they walked back out into the parking lot, to his truck.

Number 445 was a small house, a Mediterranean-style bungalow with a tiny porch and a tile roof. A residential area, not too far from the water.

They sat in Nate's truck in the dark for a few minutes, and he could hear Julia take a few deep breaths as they both stared at the house across the street from them. He wanted to reach out, hold on to her, but he continued gripping the steering wheel instead.

The blinds were open in the large front windows of the bungalow, the lights were on inside, and everything was illuminated. Suddenly a woman walked into the front room, straight into the lights. She was late middle-aged, with long curls, shockingly like

Nora's. And it hit Nate that this was really her. That Julia hadn't been mistaken.

"Shit," Nate said. He hadn't meant to say it out loud, and Julia offered him a small frown, then shushed him.

The woman inside the house was talking on a cordless phone, Nate noticed now. She had it tucked between her ear and her shoulder as she spun around the room. Suddenly she burst out laughing. Her small frame shook with joy. She seemed giddy. A woman who didn't have a care in the world.

"Drive," Julia said so quietly he almost wasn't sure she'd said anything.

"Don't you want to go talk to her?" Nate asked.

She shook her head. "No," Julia said firmly. "I want to leave."

Nate drove them back to their room at the Ocean Inn, and when they walked inside, it suddenly occurred to him there was only one bed. They hadn't brought an overnight bag. They had nothing but the clothes on their backs and each other. It seemed like a terrible combination. But now it was late, and he was overcome with exhaustion.

"I can . . . sleep on the floor," Nate offered, eyeing the cold hardwood.

Julia shook her head. "Please don't. I just had a miscarriage. It's not like I could do anything, even if I wanted to." She said the words so sharply, he felt physical pain in his gut. "Just . . . sleep in the bed. Like you said before, I'm pretty much your sister."

He bit his bottom lip. He had said that. But he had never once in his life thought about Julia like he would a sister.

It was a king-sized bed at least, and he lay down on one side, all the way near the edge so she could have her space. She did the same and then she flipped off the light. The only sound in the darkness was her breath escaping her chest. Then what sounded like the tiniest of sobs. *Was Julia crying?* Nate wasn't sure. But he felt something expanding in his own chest.

"Nate?" she said quietly after a little while, testing maybe to see if he was still awake.

"Yeah?" he answered.

"Will you really take me to Disneyland tomorrow?"

He hadn't been to Disneyland since he was a kid, with his mom. But he nodded, and then realized she probably couldn't see him in the darkness. "Sure," he said. "If that's what you want."

"Nate?" she said his name again.

"Yeah?" he answered again.

"Why are you always so kind to me?" She choked out the end of the sentence, and now he was sure she was crying.

Dammit.

He rolled closer to her, reached for her, and wrapped his arms around her. Maybe it should've felt strange or awkward. But instead, holding her close to him, he felt like he had finally come home after the longest time away. "Is this okay?" he asked her instead of answering her question. "Can I hold you like this, just until you fall asleep?"

"Put it in the vault," Julia said sleepily, curling her body back into him. So what choice did he have but to pull her even closer, hold on to her tighter? He kissed the top of her head softly. And then she murmured, "Disneyland."

But when he woke up the next morning, Julia was already gone.

CHAPTER 33

2019

After Nate had finished telling them about Julia's miscarriage and how he had eventually taken her to Santa Monica, he pulled his keys from his pocket and held them out, a peace offering. A command? "I'd take you myself," he said. "But I don't want to leave Mal again. You two take my truck and go find her."

"You really think she's in Santa Monica now, at this . . . Ocean Inn?" Emily asked, skeptical. Her mind was still reeling from everything Nate had just told them, mostly that Julia had had a scary miscarriage so many years earlier that she'd never mentioned to her sisters.

Nate nodded. "You know Jules. She likes to finish everything. Perfect circles. No loose ends."

"But back then she must've been struggling so much after just losing a baby." Nora's voice faltered. "It's thirteen years later? Why now?"

Emily nodded, suddenly realizing that Nate was actually making a lot of sense. That maybe Nate had always understood Julia better than she and Nora had. "Veronica just moved out. She and Ted are getting divorced. She's unmoored now. She's probably spiraling. It sounds like she was spiraling back in 2006 too. But now, maybe she's even worse?"

Even though Nora was still steaming mad about being the only one who didn't know about their mother, her stomach suddenly hurt thinking about the fact that she hadn't spoken to Julia in a whole year. If Julia had gone and done something like this, not according to her plan, she must be in really bad shape.

Emily had talked and texted with Julia from time to time over the past year, but it was casual exchanges, random bird pictures. She'd been too wrapped up in the mess she'd made of her own life to realize Julia had been in a mess too. She felt guilt rise in her throat, bitter, acidic. How was it she'd had no idea what was really going on with her older sister? Thirteen years ago, or now.

Nora snatched the keys from Nate's hand and then handed them to Emily. "You drive," she said.

"Why me?" Emily frowned.

"I'm a freaking New Yorker. I haven't driven a car in at least five years."

Even though Emily drove a Prius at home, and the thought of driving Nate's giant truck on the eight-lane California freeways terrified her, she took the keys.

Emily and Nora drove up I-5 toward LA in silence.

Emily gripped the steering wheel tightly, driving too slow in the farthest-right lane up the coast—through and out of San Diego, Carlsbad, past Camp Pendleton, through Orange County and Long Beach—and once they hit the bumper-to-bumper traffic of south LA, Emily felt so nauseous, it took everything she had not to throw up. She suddenly thought about the last time she'd been in Santa Monica, running into Cara at the pier. And now the irony hit her—that she had inadvertently driven to where Cara lived, after promising Cee that she would *never* see her again. What if Cee checked Find My right now and saw where Emily was? What would she think?

Nora interrupted her thoughts as she gave Emily directions to the Ocean Inn from her phone. Siri directed them the last hellish few miles, through the beach traffic of Memorial Day. If Julia was here and safe, Emily thought as she finally awkwardly parked the truck, she might just kill her herself.

CHAPTER 34

2019

IN JANUARY, AFTER THEY moved Veronica into her dorm in Connecticut, Julia and Ted drove back home together to Maryland, taking two-hour shifts each on the six-hour drive, which they passed listening to a murder podcast. Julia found herself thinking the whole ride back, *Why couldn't we just exist like this for the next thirty years?*

But as soon as they got home, Ted started packing up his things. They'd already pushed their divorce plan six months, when Veronica switched to Adley as a spring start. And apparently, Ted's girlfriend, a young paralegal at his firm, had already moved into a bigger apartment in anticipation of Ted's finally joining her. He didn't want to make her wait even another moment.

He told Julia this while he packed up his clothes, and then he told her she could stay in the house for a few months while she figured things out. That he didn't think they should worry about putting it on the market until summer, after Veronica's first semester, when they could tell her about the divorce too.

"God, you're such a cliché," Julia told him as she stood in the doorway to their bedroom, watching him fold his shirts. "You're actually leaving me for some twenty-five-year-old?"

"Julia," Ted said calmly in response. "I'll try to say this in the nicest way possible, but you don't want me, and you don't want this life. You haven't been happy in years." He paused for a moment, and then added, "And you can't say I'm *leaving* you when you checked out of this marriage a long time ago. Do yourself a favor and figure out what you actually want."

"Fuck you," she said in response, her voice shaking.

Then Ted suggested they take a cooldown period where they wouldn't speak at all until summer, so they could hash out the details amicably come June or July once she was *feeling calmer.* Never mind that they had already been in a four-year cooldown period. Julia said nothing in response. Ted took his bags and left.

Suddenly, all alone in her huge, quiet house, Julia didn't know what to do with herself. So she worked, and she worked. And she worked some more. Some nights she fell asleep at her desk after midnight and woke up at four a.m., not even bothering to go home and shower before she started work again later that morning.

And by May, she was so exhausted and burnt out that she made a huge, ridiculous mistake and filed the wrong brief for the wrong case. Her boss pulled her aside, told her she was worried, and that she thought Julia looked terrible and needed a break. *I want you to take all your PTO and come back to us refreshed.*

So, Julia wasn't exactly fired on top of everything else. But she did have a six-week forced vacation starting in the middle of May.

She had all the time in the world, so why not drive to Coronado?

She remembered Emily had done it once, years ago, in the old beater family car. Certainly, she could pack up her fully loaded 2018 Volvo SUV and make the drive in one piece. She'd always wanted to do a cross-country road trip with Ted, when Veronica was younger. But there was never enough time. Never enough vacation days to make all the effort. And now, finally, she had the chance. She convinced herself this was a good thing. An adventure.

Two murder podcasts later—somewhere in Arkansas (or maybe it was Oklahoma?)—Julia stopped at a gas station to fill up, and then she ran into the very dark, disgusting bathroom to pee.

Another hour of highway passed before she realized she'd been driving in silence, that she had put her phone down on the sink in that gas station bathroom to thoroughly wash her hands, and that she must've forgotten to pick it back up again before she left.

She would get off at the next exit, circle back.

But by the time she made it back to the disgusting bathroom, her phone was long gone.

At first, Julia burst out crying when she'd realized she'd lost her phone in a gas station bathroom.

What else? What more could be taken from her? She'd already lost everything. Everyone had left her. Her stupid phone was her lifeline, and now that was gone too?

But then she'd bought a map at the gas station. She'd charted an old-school path to California with a pen, and she followed road signs, the way Emily must've done when she drove a similar route almost twenty years earlier.

Without murder podcasts to listen to, she turned on the radio, and suddenly she was singing along to eighties rock, remembering what it felt like to be young, free. Untethered. To be herself. Here she was, all alone, no connection to her (former) world. And she was just someone, a person, again. Not a wife, not a mother. Just a singular being. Just *Julia May*, driving on the wide-open highway, belting out Springsteen at the top of her goddamn lungs.

No one needed her. No one could find her, even if they wanted to.

Then, without her phone, she lost track of time, of days, of where she was headed or why. She strangely found herself following the signs to LA instead of San Diego. She should go to Disneyland!

She had never made it there. She didn't stop, though. She kept driving straight through Orange County too.

No, there was one thing all this time, all these years, that she had never confronted. A literal Pandora's box. She had opened it up only once, in the summer of 2006, after she'd finally made it home to Maryland, broken, bloodless, and feeling like the worst mother in the world. She hadn't been able to bring herself to confront Meredith May when Nate drove her to her house. But after she'd gotten back home, she had brought herself to open up the box of Meredith's letters from Grandma Vera's armoire. She'd read through enough of them to learn that Meredith, at least as of 1998, had been working in LA with some success as a voice-over actress under a stage name.

But why, Julia had wondered then, couldn't Meredith have done that from Chicago, while staying with her daughters? Her family?

And now, as she drove past the exit for Disneyland, she understood that there had been an anger, a resentment brewing inside of her since she'd opened up that Pandora's box in 2006. It had seeped into her pores, eventually spilling over, out of her, into everything in her life. Her career, where she felt a desperate need to fight for children who couldn't fight for themselves. Her unrelenting need to keep Veronica so very close. She had worked so hard to be the opposite of her mother, and somehow, in the process, had still ended up ruining everything? Her job. Her relationship with her daughter. Her marriage.

And that's when she realized where she was actually driving to, where exactly she needed to go.

It took her three days after arriving in Santa Monica to track Meredith May down.

Her house on Ocean Lane had been sold three years earlier, after Meredith had a stroke. Julia finally found her by visiting the office of the Realtor who'd handled that sale. Meredith was in an assisted-living facility now, near Burbank.

Julia showed up there on the day she was supposed to show up in Coronado, though by then she had completely lost all sense of time without her phone. She suddenly found herself sitting at a table across from a wheelchair-bound stranger, in a lovely, bright, windowed common room, decorated in red, white, and blue for Memorial Day. This looked like a nicely kept up facility. Julia supposed her mother was being well taken care of near the end of her life. And while that thought should've made her happy, weirdly, it only made her feel irritated.

"I'm Julia—" she began as she sat down.

"I know who you are," Meredith said slowly. She had blue-gray eyes that reminded Julia of eroded beach pebbles. And it occurred to her she hadn't remembered the color of her mother's eyes before now. She and Nora had green eyes; Emily had hazel. And she would not have expected their mother's eyes to look at her so stonily, to be so gray. "Why are you here?" Meredith asked.

Julia suddenly had so many questions. And yet she couldn't manage to articulate any of them in real words. Her mother. *Her mother* sat before her, aged. Alive. She hadn't died giving birth to Nora or in the forty years since. She'd run away. She'd written to Grandma Vera, but she'd never once reached out to her daughters. Not in forty years.

"Why visit me now?" Meredith said.

Julia thought about Ted, about Veronica. About her stupid lost phone. But she didn't say any of that. "I guess I just wanted to see if you were real," she finally said.

"And your father couldn't talk you out of it?" Meredith said, an edge to her voice.

Her father. She thought about how he evaded her questions, even when he was going through chemo. In some twisted way, he'd been lying to protect them. Having a dead mother was, in his mind, better than having a mother who'd abandoned them. She suddenly pictured the steep look of disappointment that would overtake his kind face if he could somehow know that she was here right now. "Dad died five years ago," she finally said.

A flicker of something washed across Meredith's face. But Julia wasn't sure what emotion it was.

"Cancer," Julia added.

Meredith sighed. "I wish you hadn't told me that. I liked thinking he was still alive."

"But he's not," Julia said firmly.

"Sometimes it's better not to know the truth," Meredith said.

Julia wasn't clear whether she was referring to Dad's death or Julia having discovered her here now. She looked into Meredith's face, searching for any signs of familiarity or compassion or love. This was her *mother*. Was she really an actress, like Nora? Julia had gathered as much from the letters she'd read, but Nora had the most expressive face Julia had ever seen. Meredith's face was a blank slate on a stranger.

"Maybe I shouldn't have come," Julia said, hoping, looking for any reaction.

But Meredith simply nodded in response.

Julia continued staring at her, realizing what she had been feeling these last few days, months, really, was the deep ache of loneliness in her chest that came from being *left* by her family. And seeing Meredith, here, like this, was only making that ache stronger. What Julia really wanted to know was what was so wrong with her that made everyone who was supposed to love her keep on leaving? Meredith had left her too; Meredith had left her first.

Meredith's hands were rocking the wheels of her chair steadily back and forth, and Julia realized now she was a minute away from wheeling herself off.

"I want to know why." The question burst out of her, the words feeling heavy, an ache that could never subside. "Why did you leave? Why did you let us believe you were dead all this time?" Julia asked.

"I couldn't do it," Meredith said quietly. Her stony exterior crumbled for the first time, and now Julia wondered whether her eyes weren't so much cold as they were terribly sad. "I was never cut out to be a mother. And I was trying to avoid . . . this."

That last part stung. Julia had held on to Veronica so tightly her whole life, perhaps too tightly. How had Meredith just let go . . . walked away from them and never even looked back? "But you had three kids!" Julia exclaimed. "If you weren't cut out to be a mother . . . how did you let that happen?"

"I was only nineteen when I fell in love with Bob," Meredith said. "And you know, I thought being in love with someone meant you were supposed to want everything he wanted."

Nineteen? That was close to Veronica's age now. Julia shook her head, unable to imagine V being mature enough to fall in love with anyone.

"When I got pregnant with you a few years later, Bob was so excited. And then, a few years after that, he really thought you should have a sibling, and that seemed like what I was supposed to want too. And then . . . the third time was an accident, and I just, I couldn't do it anymore. I was suffocating in that life. I felt like if I stayed, I really was going to die." She chewed on her bottom lip, the same way Julia did when she was upset.

"So you were depressed," Julia said matter-of-factly. "You could've gone to therapy. Or . . . taken medication."

Meredith shook her head. "In the seventies no one talked about things like that. I just knew . . . I just knew . . . I couldn't stay there anymore. It was soul-crushing. I didn't want to be a mother, I wanted to be an actress."

"Plenty of moms work at what they love and don't abandon their children," Julia said. But she felt the smallest flutter of understanding in her chest. She knew all too well the precarious balance, between being good at a job you loved and being a good mother. She had spent years feeling like she was failing at everything all at once. Still, she couldn't have ever imagined *leaving* V. Pretending she was dead?

"I had no choice," Meredith said. "I left to save myself. And to save the three of you from me."

"You always have a choice," Julia said firmly. It felt like she was talking to four-year-old Veronica again, trying to teach her about acceptable behavior. Good choices. Bad choices. There were always *choices*. Every mother knew that. Every woman knew that. But then she wondered what it might've been like growing up with Meredith there, miserable. Their childhood had largely been filled with happiness, laughter, and normalcy in spite of being raised by their single dad. Maybe, though, it wasn't in spite of. Maybe it was because of that.

"You sound just like my mother," Meredith said.

"Grandma Vera." Julia said her name softly.

Meredith nodded. "Bob and I made her promise she would never tell you girls the truth. She wasn't happy about it, but she kept her promise." She paused. "I mean, she didn't tell you before she died, right?"

Julia thought about the way Grandma Vera had accidentally led her to the wrong drawer in her armoire once, when Julia was still a teenager. And now she wondered if maybe that hadn't been an accident at all. Technically, Vera had kept her promise and had never *told* Julia anything. But if she'd led Julia to the truth *by accident*, then was that her loophole? Had she actually wanted Julia to find out about Meredith years ago?

Julia looked up at the wall of windows just behind Meredith, hoping to see a bird hovering there now, confirming her instincts. But all she saw was an empty palm tree, the bright blue, cloudless sky above it. "No," Julia finally said. "Grandma Vera never broke her promise."

"I need you to promise the same now. Go home and keep pretending I really am dead."

"What if I don't want to?" Julia hated the way she sounded petulant, even though Meredith was the one in the wrong.

"I can't do this." Meredith's hands rocked on the wheels and this time, she slowly pushed herself back from the table.

"Wait . . . you're leaving?" Julia asked. "Just like that?"

"Take care," Meredith said, the way you might say it in passing, to a stranger.

And then she wheeled herself out of the decorated common room, back down the hallway toward her room.

Julia felt somewhere outside of herself as she stood to leave. Her hands were shaking, and she realized she might not have eaten all day. (Did she eat yesterday?)

"It's nice to see her have a visitor," the nurse said to Julia with a smile as she walked out. "You're her first one in three years."

Julia went back to her room, took a sleeping pill, willing it to calm her, to lull her into an easy sleep, but instead she started to cry and pace the room. Ted left her. Veronica didn't need her. Was she bound to end up in assisted living, with no one to care or notice or visit her for three years? She thought about what her dad said once: *The only thing certain in life is death.* Is that all she would have to look forward to now?

Then the tiredness hit her, swept a calming sort of exhaustion over and through her, and she lay down in the big, empty bed.

For such a long time, she had just wanted to ask her mother one question. *How did you have everything and then walk away from it all? Not one daughter but three?*

But when, all those years ago, she had seen through the window how happy Meredith looked without them, how at ease, Julia hadn't been able to face her.

And then, later that night, when she had woken up in Nate's arms, here, in this very hotel, in the pitch-dark of night, the only thought in her head was: *Veronica, Veronica, Veronica.* Oh God, she'd been in such a daze since the miscarriage, she'd unintentionally done what Meredith had. She'd left her child.

She'd run home, and for so many years after that she'd held on to Veronica tightly, vowing she would never leave her again. Never let her go. She refused to let go of Ted and their marriage, believing that she had to do everything in her power to keep her family together. She had worked so hard to be everything her own mother wasn't: the reliable mother, the reliable wife.

"And now Veronica resents me," she said to no one, into the empty room. "And Ted wants someone else."

She had done the exact opposite as her mother, but still, somehow, had done it all wrong?

And that was the last thought she had as she finally drifted off to sleep.

CHAPTER 35

2019

JULIA AWOKE TO A pounding noise, and she struggled to open her eyes, groping around the night table for her phone to check the time.

Right, she didn't have her phone.

"Julia, we know you're in there. Open this fucking door or I'm breaking it down."

Emily?

Julia blinked and sat up. What was her sister doing here? What time was it? What *day* was it?

"Julia, come on. I know you're still mad at me, but you're really scaring us."

Nora?

Julia rubbed sleep from her eyes, kicked back the covers, and walked quickly to the door.

She flung it open, and there, standing just outside her room, were both of her sisters, hands on their hips, frowning. "How did you . . . get here?" Julia asked. She blinked again, genuinely confused, wondering if she was still dreaming.

Emily and Nora exchanged glances. "You didn't show up in Coronado, so we were super worried," Nora said.

"We thought something terrible had happened!" Emily snapped at her. "What the actual fuck, Julia?"

"Nate let us borrow his truck," Nora said.

Nate. Julia wondered how much he'd told them, and she chewed on her bottom lip.

"No one has been able to get in touch with you," Nora continued in a rush. "You wouldn't even answer your phone!"

"I lost my phone," Julia finally said sheepishly. "And anyway, no one needs me right now. I didn't think it mattered. I'm sorry, I didn't mean to worry you."

The three of them stared at one another for a moment. Emily and Nora exhaled with the relief that Julia seemed vaguely all right; Julia suddenly felt smaller, ashamed. It truly hadn't occurred to her that so many days had passed, that she could be late to Coronado. And then her own relief suddenly flooded through her: She'd been all wrong last night. The only thing certain in her life wasn't death, it was her sisters.

"So . . . did you . . . find her?" Emily finally asked quietly, shifting subjects. Emily's eyes searched Julia's face in some unfamiliar way. Usually Emily was all sharp edges, but now she just looked sad, defeated.

Julia nodded. "How did you know?" she asked. "Did Nate tell you?"

Emily shook her head. "No. I saw a letter, in Grandma Vera's armoire. I thought I was the only one. But then I saw the box of letters at your house during the hurricane . . . so I figured you probably knew too. But I couldn't bring myself to talk to you about it."

The words hit Julia with a jolt. Emily had known, all this time? Had Grandma Vera *accidentally* on purpose pointed them all to the truth? "Nora?" Julia said. "You too?"

Nora folded her arms across her chest. "No, I never saw anything in Grandma Vera's armoire, and no one ever tells me anything." She glared at Emily, who cast her eyes down at her feet. "I literally found out like two hours ago," Nora said. "I am super pissed, at both of you."

"Okay," Julia said softly. She probably deserved every bit of

Nora's wrath even if she had just been trying to protect her all this time.

"So, you know where she is?" Nora said, anger driving her voice to rise.

Julia nodded. "I do."

"Then I want to see her," Nora demanded.

Emily drove the three of them to Burbank in Nate's truck. Nora had her arms folded angrily across her chest in the back seat and Julia sat up front, staring out the window, the edges of everything still feeling softer from the sleeping pill. Or maybe she could just breathe a little easier again, now that she was back with her sisters.

In the parking lot, Nora hopped out, but Emily kept the engine running and made no attempt to leave the truck herself.

"Don't you want to see her too?" Julia asked.

Emily shook her head. She had nothing to say to a woman who'd left her when she was three years old. Cecile always told her that being *Emma*, being a mom in general, just meant showing up. Every time something went wrong between Emily and the boys, which was somewhat often, Emily told Cecile she was missing the crucial component, some secret ingredient other women were just born with that made them natural mothers.

You're overthinking it, Cecile would say. *Just be present! Be there for them!*

And for the first time it hit her that maybe Cecile was actually right.

Nora walked inside the assisted-living facility, a very distinct memory replaying in her mind. That night in the rain, after opening night of *Romeo and Juliet*, that woman who'd called out to her, who Nora had found looked strangely like Julia. Had it been her? Had it really been her mother? Had she tried once? Had she tried, in that one moment, to show up for Nora?

But as soon as she saw her, Nora realized that Meredith May looked nothing like that other woman, nothing at all like Julia. She had Nora's body shape, Nora's heart-shaped face. Grandma Vera's (and Nora's) button nose. And her hair hit her shoulders in long, gray, springy curls.

That woman, that night in New York City, had been an illusion. A woman she had in her imagination turned into the shape of her mother. *This woman* was the one who'd abandoned her from her very first moment of life. *This woman* turned her head, looked up at Nora, and then frowned. Nora felt certain *this woman* had never come to New York City to watch one of her shows or cared to keep up with her girls in any meaningful way.

If Nora were in a play now, if this were a scene, she would probably have done something incredibly dramatic. Like cry, scream, slap this woman's cheek. Or maybe they would embrace, and lost time would rush away like a summer rainstorm.

But all Nora did instead was stand there frozen and stare for a few moments at this complete stranger with an odd echo of her face, her body, her self.

"Emily?" Meredith May finally said.

It was a ridiculous guess, considering Nora and Emily looked nothing at all alike. Considering *this woman* was their mother, who should know her daughters better than anyone.

Nora shook her head. "Nora," she finally said. "I'm your youngest daughter, Nora."

Meredith didn't react. There was no joy or heartbreak or remorse on her face. She simply sighed. "I don't know why you and Julia came here, after all this time."

"Well, Julia found you, and I just wanted to see what you were like," Nora said. "I've never met you. I thought you were dead until about three hours ago."

Meredith nodded. "That's what I wanted you to think. Bob promised me he would give me that much."

Bob. Nora thought about her father, in the cold, cold ground in Chicago, complicit in this, whatever this was, and suddenly her heart hurt. "But why? Why make Daddy say you were dead? Why leave us in the first place?" Nora asked.

"I told Julia everything yesterday," Meredith said, resigned.

Nora stared at her hard, unwilling to let her off the hook. "Then tell me too. Don't I deserve at least that much?"

Meredith stared at her for another moment before she spoke. "My whole life all I ever wanted was to be an actress. I had to follow my dream, or else, who was I?"

Nora sucked in her breath, remembering how Grandma Vera had told her once that her mother had loved to act. She'd always thought it was the one thread that had somehow tied them together, but no, she'd been wrong, it was the very thing that had torn them apart. Is that why her father had always been so against her career? Had he been trying to protect her from whatever this was all along? "Shit," she said softly. "I'm an actress."

Meredith's face turned, and instead of annoyed she looked, for the first time, remotely interested.

"I'm in *The Secret Life* on Broadway right now. You've heard of it?" Nora suddenly had this strange urge to impress her, like if only she understood that Nora had done something worthy, achieved something in her acting career, then maybe Meredith could finally figure out a way to want her, to love her.

Meredith shook her head. "I'm sorry. I don't follow theater much."

"I'm playing opposite Devlin St. Claire," Nora continued. "I'm sure you know of him. *The Wizards of Central Park*."

Meredith nodded, a flicker of recognition crossing her face. "Wow, good for you." She paused for a moment, looked up at the ceiling and then back at Nora. "So then you, more than anyone, should know what it takes. You don't have kids?"

Nora shook her head.

"Married?"

Nora shook her head again.

"Julia was angry with me, but you, Nora, you get it? Perfecting our craft takes everything we have. Everything we are."

"You think we're the same?" Nora spat, anger rising up hot inside of her. She had often thought, over the years, she would've done *anything* to make it as an actress. But now she understood that wasn't true. She never would've done something like this. "You had me think you'd died giving birth to me. My whole life I believed that. I thought I killed you just by being born. How fucked-up is that? I chose not to have kids—I didn't have them and then pretend to die. We are *not* the same."

"When you put it like that, you make it sound so . . . so . . . Dying was the easiest way," Meredith said, conviction in her voice. "It was the best way to protect everyone."

"That's the stupidest thing I've ever heard," Nora said. "Was it worth it? Did you make it big?"

Meredith shook her head. "It wasn't about making it big. It was about me not wanting to suffocate in that life. Or being so miserable that I damaged all of you." She paused. "I couldn't stay, but I never wanted to hurt you girls. I didn't want to be the villain of your lives."

Her words felt like ice, like the coldest air Nora had ever felt on that February day in Chicago when they'd buried their father.

"You are the villain, though," Nora said defiantly.

Meredith paused for a moment before saying, "But as you know, a villain is always a main character. Am I really that important to your story, Nora?"

And then Nora wondered if maybe she was right. Maybe Meredith May was more like an extra whose background presence was barely known, hardly memorable.

In Nate's truck, Julia and Emily sat in silence for a little while.

Then Emily said quietly, "How come you never told us about the miscarriage?"

"Miscarriages," Julia corrected softly. "There were three. The last one in 2006, that Nate knows about, was the worst."

"Jesus," Emily said. "Three? And you never said anything to me and Nora?"

Julia turned and stared out the window for a moment. "You know, we all agreed when we were kids that we were never going to have babies. It felt too dangerous because of Mom and all that."

Emily nodded, remembering. First her fear was physical: dying. Then it became emotional: that she couldn't understand how to stick around because her own mother hadn't.

"I didn't want you guys to worry," Julia said. "There was nothing you could've done anyway."

"So instead you kept it all bottled up until you blew up your life all these years later?" Emily said.

Julia shook her head. "Veronica went away to college. Ted chose to move out. I didn't blow up anything." But for some reason, she thought about what Ted had said as he'd packed his things. That she had checked out first. And maybe that last miscarriage, her ensuing fixation on what their own mother had done, had broken something in her that she hadn't truly realized before now.

"And Jul, did you really, honestly think no one needed you?" Emily continued, gentler.

Julia nodded. "My house was so quiet all spring."

"You should've called me or Nora. We would've come to visit."

Julia waved her away with a flick of her wrist. "You're busy with Cee and the boys. And Nora has a new show. I wasn't going to bother you two."

"Bother us?" Emily laughed dryly. "No, Julia, you don't get it. We need you. Nora is a mess. And so am I. My life is like total shit right now, and I have no idea how to fix it."

Julia thought about the last time she'd seen her sisters in Coronado, a year earlier, and she hadn't noticed anything off, but maybe she'd been too focused on Veronica that week. Julia hadn't spoken to Nora all year after the incident on Nate's porch. And she'd spoken to Emily only a handful of times. But she knew that Nora was cast in a new show and seemed to be killing it in her career. (She'd read the glowing review in the *Times*.) And Emily had seemed good, normal, on their few phone calls. What did Emily mean about her life being *total shit*? She was married to an amazing woman, who Julia was certain would never, ever treat her the way Ted had treated Julia these last few years.

"And I think Nate might need you too," Emily added.

"Nate?" Julia questioned. The last time she'd seen him, his lips had been locked on Nora's.

"Something is up with him," Emily continued. "I thought he was just being evasive because he didn't want to tell us where you were. But that wasn't it."

She and Nate had exchanged only a few brief texts and emails over the last year. After witnessing the kiss on his porch last May, and overhearing Nora talk about staying in Nate's house after Mallory was born, she'd wondered all year if he and Nora were a couple. If they had been together on and off for years and she had been left stupidly in the dark. But every time she'd had that thought, it had made her stomach hurt until she'd pushed it away. It'd felt easier to distance herself from both of them than to consider the reality that they'd fallen in love right next to her. But now? She had no idea what was going on with either of them. And suddenly that made her feel incredibly sad.

"I'm serious, Julia," Emily said. "We all need you. What did Grandma Vera used to call you? The glue?"

"Can't make a s'more without the marshmallows," Julia said. And in her own voice she heard an echo of who she used to be, as a girl, a teenager, a woman. Of who she still was, maybe, somewhere deep down.

"Or the chocolate," Emily added.

"Or the graham crackers," Nora said, suddenly jumping into the back seat, sounding out of breath.

"You're back already? That was quick," Emily said.

Nora nodded. She looked less angry, but she didn't elaborate.

Then she said, "Can we go back to Coronado now, please? I am so ready for sisters' week to start."

"We can stop at Vons for s'mores ingredients on the way," Emily said hopefully.

"And wine," Nora added.

They both looked at Julia. She chewed on the skin around her thumbnail, where her normally perfect manicure was peeling. "I think I need to stop at a Verizon store first," she said. "It's time I got a new phone."

CHAPTER 36

2019

THERE WOULD BE NO printed schedule this week.

Still, as soon as they all got to Coronado they found themselves in an easy, familiar rhythm. S'mores on the back patio by the firepit. Wine poured in glasses, and secrets poured out.

Nora and Emily insisted Julia call Veronica right away, as soon as she had her new phone activated, to let Veronica know she was okay and clear the air between them.

Veronica was relieved and also asked Julia to add her back on Find My. Just in case.

Julia and Nora took Emily's phone and deleted Cara's number altogether. Then insisted she go call Cecile, apologize for leaving in the middle of their fight, explain exactly what had happened this week and why she had gone to LA. And promise to go into therapy for real this time when she went home.

Julia asked Nora if she was still with Nate, and Nora explained how she was never with Nate. All Julia had witnessed was a completely unreciprocated, very drunken kiss. Then Nora admitted the one man she couldn't stop thinking about was Dev.

"If that's how you really feel, you have to tell him!" Emily insisted.

"Didn't you call him an asshole who should be MeToo'ed last year?" Nora asked.

Emily shrugged into her wineglass. "I don't know, I was just trying to be supportive of you."

"If you want my *old lady* advice," Julia said. "It would be that hiding your real feelings is never the right way to live your life. Just tell him the truth, Nora."

Nora shook her head. "It's too late."

"It's never too late," Julia insisted.

"And you'll never know if you don't try," Emily said. "If you want my *old lady* advice." Then she added, "Hey, so speaking of being old ladies, are any of you having hot flashes yet?"

Julia was mid-sip and she suddenly laughed so hard she spit wine across the patio. It took her a full minute to catch her breath, and then she said, "Em, I've been doing a lot of research on the best supplements to help with perimenopause symptoms. I'll email you everything I've gathered so far."

"Oh my God! You both are old, like for real." Nora giggled.

"I'll email it to you too," Julia said. "It's good knowledge to have, Nora."

Nora rolled her eyes. But then she thought about how maybe sometimes it was actually nice to be the youngest. To have two older sisters who experienced everything first, and who shared about their lives, and this house with her each May. No matter what.

They walked along the beach early every morning, traipsing through the low-lying cloud cover in sweats, ate breakfast at the Del and Clayton's. They took Mallory shell seeking when she got home from school, and Nora French braided her hair one evening out back by the firepit, promising Mal that the next year, she would teach her how to do it herself.

On their last night, Julia and Nora shared a bottle of red wine on the deck at the Bluewater Boathouse restaurant on Glorietta Bay, but Emily kept her promise to Cecile and ordered a Shirley Temple.

And then, on Sunday morning, Emily and Nora shared an Uber to the airport, since their flights were at similar times.

Julia had her car, and she supposed that meant she could leave whenever she wanted. She would close up the house, she would throw all the linens in the washer for the next renters. And then she would drive back across the country, having promised her sisters she would absolutely *not* lose her phone in the process and would text nightly to let them know where she was and that she was safe.

After Nora and Emily left, Julia went outside and found Nate sitting on his porch. Emily's words about something being off with him had been floating around in her head all week. At first, she'd thought maybe it was some feelings he might have for Nora. But Nora had said that absolutely wasn't true. Then she'd thought maybe it was just something personal that was none of her business. But now she had to admit, he looked pretty forlorn sitting on his porch rocker, slowly rocking back and forth, staring off toward the water.

Julia went and sat down in the rocker next to him. "You gonna tell me what's going on?" she said. Then she added, "I'll put it in the vault."

"I hate the goddamn vault," Nate said quietly. "Let's blow the thing to smithereens."

Julia laughed. "That seems overly violent. But okay." She was about to be a middle-aged divorcée, and now anything they'd put in the vault over the years felt like it was verging on ridiculous. "Are you still mad at me?" Julia asked softly. "For disappearing? For not telling you about my divorce?"

She had already apologized to him, explained to him what had been happening in her life and that she hadn't meant to worry him. He had already apologized for telling her sisters about what happened to her all those years ago. *Desperate times*, she'd said, feeling weirdly grateful he'd broken his promise, that her sisters had shown up exactly when she'd needed them most. And they'd left it at that.

"I'm not mad," he said, and he turned and flashed her a half-smile. "But hey, you should get ready to leave, if you want to make it through the mountains before dark."

"Nate," Julia insisted. "I'm not going anywhere until you tell me what's going on with you."

He stared at her for a moment, but he had known her long enough to know when she was serious. "Heidi wants full custody," he said. "I went to LA to try and talk her out of it last weekend. Unsuccessfully."

The words felt so unexpected that it took her a few moments to process what he was saying. Heidi, Mallory's mom who'd run out on her twelve years earlier to follow some guy from the base, suddenly wanted full custody? "Oh, hell no," Julia finally said.

Nate stood up. "The mountains get treacherous at night. You should go. I don't want to have to worry about you on the road."

She knew Nate was right. The switchbacks would be more dangerous in the dark, but still, she didn't move out of the rocker. What exactly was she driving toward? What was waiting for her in Maryland? Not Veronica, who would spend the summer semester at school since she'd started in the spring. Certainly not Ted. Not even a job, at least not until after July Fourth. She remembered something Nate had said to her twenty years ago, just after Vera had died. *They have lawyers in San Diego too.*

"What if I don't go today?" Julia said. "What if I stay in Coronado for a little while?"

Nate shook his head. "The house is completely rented out. Come on," he said, walking across his yard. "I'll help you load the car."

Julia finally got up and ran after him. She caught his arm and he stopped walking, right on the line between both their houses. "So what if I rent something else?" she said, breathless from chasing after him.

"Why would you do that?" Nate asked.

"Well, I could help you with custody, for one."

"You don't have to." Nate waved her offer away. "One of the

English teachers at school is married to a lawyer, and she said he might be able to give me some advice, pro bono."

"Nate," Julia said firmly. "Absolutely not. I'm going to be your pro bono attorney, and we are not going to budge an inch. Mallory is staying right here, in your custody. I'm honestly really very good at this kind of thing. This is what I do for a living."

"Jules." He said her name quietly, sweetly, but he shook his head.

"I want to help you," she insisted. "You're like my . . ."

"Your brother?" he finished her sentence.

"No," she said. "I was deciding between first love, family, or best friend. But I've never once thought of you as my brother."

He grinned, almost in spite of himself. "I guess you could stay with us for a few days while I help you find a short-term rental to move into. God, Mal would be thrilled if you stayed in Coronado for the summer. And I would really appreciate your help. She doesn't even know about this yet . . . and I can't lose her."

Julia felt a little thrill ripple through her, feeling needed, feeling wanted, feeling like she might actually be able to stay for a while in the one place that had always felt to her the most like home.

"I think if I learned anything these last few months, it's that I need to figure out what *I* really want now. What's going to make *me* happy going forward," Julia said. Though it pained her slightly to admit it, Ted's parting words to her hadn't exactly been wrong.

"And Coronado is a part of that?" Nate asked.

Julia thought about the advice she'd given Nora earlier in the week. *Hiding your real feelings is never the right way to live your life.* "Actually, I think you're a part of that," she said. "Maybe what makes this my favorite place is that my favorite person lives here?"

Nate smiled again, a real, wide smile now. "Me?"

She nodded and returned his smile. "Like you said, let's blow the vault to smithereens?"

"Now who's being overly violent?"

"Ever since I was twenty, Nate, and you told me on that beach right over there that you couldn't love me . . . I've been trying so hard not to love you," Julia said. "But what if I do love you? What if I've always loved you? And what if now you just let me? Would that be so terrible?" As she spoke, her chest suddenly felt lighter, like she had finally, finally let out something that had been hiding in her heart for twenty-five years. And now it was there, before them, in the open. Not locked away in a vault, not hidden at all.

Nate reached for her hands, clasping them in between his own. "I've regretted saying that to you since the moment you left that summer."

Julia gasped. "How come you never told me that, in all these years?"

"I almost did, a whole bunch of times. But then you had college and law school. You got married and you had Veronica. And then I had Mal to take care of. And I figured at least I got to see you one week a year and that, I don't know, maybe that would have to be enough."

Julia nodded. "Well, I don't think that's gonna be enough for me anymore."

Nate squeezed her hands gently in between his own, and then he smiled that gorgeous lopsided smile again. "Jules, it was never enough for me."

EPILOGUE

2025

ON SUNDAY OF THE last week in May, Emily arrived on Ocean Boulevard first.

Well, technically, she wasn't truly first, since Julia lived here now. She'd moved into Nate's house during the pandemic, telling her sisters at the time that she was forming a *quarantine pod* with Nate and Mal. But five years later, she still lived in Nate's house and had started her own small law firm with a rented walk-up office space on Orange Avenue. She seemed happier than she'd ever been. Emily hoped she'd never leave.

"It's beautiful here!" Cecile gushed from the passenger seat as Emily pulled up in front of the house. "Right, guys?"

She turned around to glance at the boys in the back seat, who had somehow in the last few years managed to make it through high school and take on the appearance of full-grown, six-foot-tall men. They would both be moving out, off to different colleges in August, and when Julia had suggested they make their May sisters' week this year a full-family affair, Emily and Cee had jumped at the chance to turn this into a family vacation. They'd even rented a car so they could drive up to Disneyland later in the week.

"This house looks super chill," Mikey said, and Jim nodded to agree.

"I'm so excited, we finally get to spend some time in your

Emma's favorite place in the world." Cecile sighed happily as she stepped out of the car.

After a few years of therapy, Emily and Cee were in a good place, and now instead of worrying about how to be a mother, Emily worried more about how much she was going to miss the boys when they moved out in August. Who was going to eat her grilled cheese and strawberry jelly sandwiches on Sunday afternoons? Who was going to catch her up nightly at dinner on all the high school tea? Who was going to ask her for help with a history essay? What were she and Cee even going to do on weekends without soccer and basketball games, band concerts, and high school theater productions to attend?

Life is just seasons, Cee had told her when she'd worried about all this out loud after the twins' high school graduation ceremony, at which Emily might have cried more than Cee and Rick combined. *You and I are just going to walk into summer together, hand in hand.*

But for now, they walked up the front path and into the house on Ocean Boulevard together, hand in hand.

Emily gave Cee and the boys a tour of the house, and she was just showing them the backyard firepit, and explaining about how Nora had learned to sing out here with Grandma Vera, when she heard Julia's voice echoing from the front of the house: "Em? Cecile? Is that your rental car in the street?"

They walked back into the living room, where Julia was fiddling with her roller bag. She might live next door now, but one week a year, Julia still packed her suitcase and came to stay in this house with her sisters.

Just then, Mallory and Nate walked in the front door, Mallory clutching a manila folder. "Julia, you left this on the dining room table," Mallory said, handing the folder to Julia. "Dad and I thought you wouldn't survive the week without it."

Emily glanced at Nate, who winked at her, and she swallowed back a chuckle.

"Thanks, Mal, and here"—Julia pulled out a copy of the schedule and handed it to Mallory—"this is your copy." Then she pulled out another one and handed it to Nate. "And this one's for you," she said cheerfully.

"Thanks, Jules." He grinned and took it. "Guess I'd better go get my wave time in now before I'm all scheduled up." He gave Julia a quick kiss on the forehead before he walked out.

"Ooh, do I get one too?" Cee asked, gently squeezing Emily's hand with one hand, reaching out with her other for a schedule.

"Of course!" Julia said. "I printed a copy for each family member and two extras in case anyone loses one."

Emily squeezed Cee's hand back, keeping her snarky comment in her head. For now. It would land better once Nora showed up anyway.

Three hours later, Nora rolled up to the curb in a rented BMW SUV. Dev was driving, and Veronica was in the back.

Julia hadn't thought Veronica would be able to get off work to come—Nora must've made this arrangement in secret? And when she saw, from her spot on the porch, her daughter step out of the back seat of the car, she yelped with joy and ran toward her.

"Oh my God," Mallory was saying behind her. "I will never get over Nora being married to Will the Wizard."

Nora had seemed so happy since the two of them had moved in together right after Broadway went dark during the pandemic. They'd all traveled to Nora and Dev's wedding in New York City two summers ago, and Mallory was still talking about it.

Though Julia knew V was twenty-four, an adult, with a terrific job as an environmental advocate, sometimes when she hugged her daughter after many months apart, she could briefly remember hugging her at four, at fourteen too.

"Mom, you're squishing me!" Veronica protested, but she pulled Julia tighter.

Julia leaned back just a little and brushed a wayward curl off V's forehead. "Honey, I'm so glad you're here," she said. "But I thought you couldn't make it because of work?"

"Aunt Nora said something about Disneyland and the whole family coming being a big deal, and I talked to my boss." Veronica shrugged. "I worked it out."

"And what about me?" Nora said, marching around dramatically to the back of the car. "Don't I get a hug? I drove into the goddamn wilds of Connecticut a few weeks ago to talk this one into coming." She tapped Veronica affectionately on the shoulder.

Julia freed up an arm to give Nora a quick hug too. "Thank you," she said. "What a lovely surprise this is."

"*You* drove into the wilds of Connecticut?" Dev said as he walked around from the driver's seat to the sidewalk. He wrapped his arms around Nora, rested his chin on the top of her head, and sighed. "She means her chauffeur drove her."

"Nora, you have a chauffeur now?" Mallory gasped.

Nora laughed. "No, Mal. He means him. Dev is my chauffeur." She turned and playfully swatted him on the shoulder. "Also, he's my chef. And my favorite costar."

"Guilty as charged." Dev held up his hands, then swooped in and gave Nora a kiss.

"Oh my God, the two of you!" Emily exclaimed, walking down the front path to the sidewalk.

Julia chuckled, but she actually thought Nora and Dev were adorable. They were in a new show together starting previews in August, and she and Nate already had their tickets for September, the week after they would drop Mal off at college. She was staying close to home, going to UCSD, but still moving out of the house and into a dorm. And Julia thought that a trip to New York City, some time with Nora and Dev, would be the perfect distraction for all those empty-nest feelings she knew were about to hit them both.

"Seriously, get a room!" Emily was saying to Nora and Dev now, as Nora gave him another quick kiss.

"Oh, I'm excited to show you my room here!" Nora squealed to Dev in response, ignoring Emily's teasing. "I have the best view of any of us."

"Nope," Emily said. "Julia would definitely disagree."

"I would?" Julia asked.

"You're right, Em." Nora nodded vigorously. "I only see the ocean from my room. But Julia? Julia can gaze out her window longingly at Nate next door all night long."

"Eww, you guys," Mallory said. "I'm standing right here."

"So am I!" Veronica protested.

"Wow, I'm so glad you're both here," Julia said to Nora and Emily. But she was smiling. Her sisters' teasing warmed her, even in the gray chill of a particularly gray May day. She was truly glad they were here.

Nora and Emily looked at each other and they both giggled.

"Where else would we possibly be the last week in May?" Nora said.

"Damn right," Emily added. "It's May day."

Later that night, after the sun became an orange ball of fire and sunk behind the Pacific Ocean, all ten of them retreated to the backyard, crowding around the outside firepit, roasting marshmallows on sticks, assembling their s'mores.

Once upon a time . . . Julia thought, looking at Emily, then Nora, suddenly remembering the sweet song of Grandma Vera's voice. *There were three sisters* . . .

She saw the three of them sitting right here at ten, at twenty, at thirty, at forty. At fifty. Their minds and bodies changed and shifted, their hair started turning gray, they wore readers now, and their skin had new wrinkles. They fought, but then they laughed. They held their secrets, and then they shared them. Their hearts broke and then, together, each May, they became whole again.

And now, twenty-five years after they'd started their May sisters' week as the owners of this house, Julia, Emily, and Nora had transformed themselves into a ten-person family. All the people they loved most, together in the one place they all had loved most their entire lives.

They sat in front of the fire, they ate their s'mores, and the sound of laughter rose up over the backyard. It floated out across Ocean Boulevard, the beach, and then hovered there above the cool blue water of the Pacific, where, just offshore, a lone seagull sat lolling on a wave, listening.

AUTHOR'S NOTE

CORONADO, LIKE JULIA SAYS in the book, has never been my home, but it has long been my happy place. A beloved yearly family vacation spot since my kids were small, we return summer after summer. I always feel a sense of calm driving over the bridge, just like the May sisters do.

In June 2021, all newly vaccinated, my family left our city for the first time since Covid hit, and where did we go? Coronado, of course. We rented the second story of a historic house instead of staying at a hotel, which I learned, at the time, was only available as a weekly rental because the house was zoned as a hotel. (There is an ordinance in Coronado that house rentals can't be for fewer than twenty-six days, so I took a little bit of fictional liberty with this in the book. Luckily, Nate knows someone on the zoning board!) Although the house I stayed in in 2021 was not on Ocean Boulevard like Grandma Vera's, it was what first gave me the idea for creating *The May House*.

The places the May sisters visit in Coronado are mostly real and favorites of my family. Every summer we have dinner at the Brigantine and Miguel's and on the deck of the Bluewater Boathouse, ice cream at MooTime and pizza at Village Pizzeria, pie and breakfast and coffee at Clayton's. We go to Vons and Walgreens for wine and snacks, take long walks down Ocean Boulevard and on the beach, and down Orange Avenue to the ferry landing. We sit on the beach and marvel at the low-landing military planes. One of my first stops is always Bay Books on Orange Avenue to buy books to read on the beach. There really are two community theaters on the island, though I have never been able to fit in a show while we've been there. The sunken treasure ship, the SS *Monte Carlo*, is also real, but I do not believe it would've been visible in May 2017 when the May sisters and Mallory and Nate go to see it.

Over the forty years this book takes place, the majority of the referenced historical events in the background are real and accurate for the times. One notable exception is that there was no Hurricane Vera in 2017. There was, however, a Hurricane Milton in the fall of 2024 when I was finishing up the first draft of this book, which almost inexplicably and accidentally brought my sister and I to the same city for a few days for the first time in several years. We both felt strangely certain that our dead grandfather, Milton, somehow had something to do with it. My sister and I did not discover a box of family secrets in the bathroom during Hurricane Milton, but we did get some rare and special time to reconnect in person, and when I got home, I knew I had to give the May sisters their own fictional hurricane.

ACKNOWLEDGMENTS

THANK YOU TO MY wonderful editor at Atria, Laura Brown, who believed in this story before I was even completely sure I believed in it myself. Your amazing editorial insights and ideas always make my work shine brighter, and I'm so grateful for all the stories we've gotten to work on together. Thank you for believing in me when I said I wanted to try something different with this one, and for helping me organize my thoughts on all the stops along the way. Thank you also to Natalie Argentina, Gena Lanzi, Dayna Johnson, and the entire Atria team for their enthusiasm and support and for giving me, and this book, the best publishing home!

Thank you to my extraordinary agent, Jess Regel, at Helm Literary. I am so lucky to have you in all my corners, from the business side to the editorial—I truly could not do this without you. Thank you also for telling me an early draft of this book was fifty pages too short. You were, as always, right! Thank you to Jenny Meyer and her amazing team for bringing my books around the world.

Thank you to my sister for filling my childhood with so much memorable sisterly conflict and for growing into an amazing friend as an adult. I love writing stories about sisters because you made me understand how truly special that relationship is. (If a bird happens to be watching as you read this, it's definitely Grandpa.)

Thank you to Gregg, who dazzled me in 1993 and still dazzles me today. B and O, writing and editing this book spanned both of you leaving for college, and Julia's story came to me as a result, but I promise you, I will never leave my phone in a gas station bathroom or disappear. Thank you for all the Coronado weeks and memories that inspired so many pieces of this story, and for all the musicals you went to with me that inspired Nora's career.

Thank you to my parents who always encouraged my love of reading and writing and never once told me not to go into a creative career like Nora's dad did.

Thank you to all my friends who lift me up, make me laugh, and inspire me. Maureen Kilmer and Tammy Greenwood—I am so grateful for your enduring friendship and writing/publishing support and advice.

Thank you to the readers, booksellers, and librarians who continue to read and support my work. I am so grateful I get to keep telling more stories!

ABOUT THE AUTHOR

JILLIAN CANTOR has a BA from Penn State University and an MFA from the University of Arizona. She is the *USA TODAY* and internationally best-selling author of fifteen novels for teens and adults that have been translated into fifteen languages. Cantor currently lives in Arizona with her husband and two sons. Find out more at JillianCantor.com.

ATRIA BOOKS, an imprint of Simon & Schuster, fosters an open environment where ideas flourish, best-selling authors soar to new heights, and tomorrow's finest voices are discovered and nurtured. Since its launch in 2002, Atria has published hundreds of bestsellers and extraordinary books, which would not have been possible without the invaluable support and expertise of its team and publishing partners. Thank you to the Atria Books colleagues who collaborated on *The May House* as well as to the hundreds of professionals in the Simon & Schuster advertising, audio, communications, design, ebook, finance, human resources, legal, marketing, operations, production, sales, supply chain, subsidiary rights, and warehouse departments who help Atria bring great books to light.

EDITORIAL
Laura Brown
Natalie Argentina

JACKET DESIGN
Min Choi
James Iacobelli

MARKETING
Dayna Johnson
Morgan Pager

MANAGING EDITORIAL
Paige Lytle
Shelby Pumphrey
Abby Borchers
Sofia Echeverry

PRODUCTION
Sonja Singleton
Alicia Brancato
Jane Elias
Davina Mock-Maniscalco

PUBLICITY
Gena Lanzi
Kayla Slusser

PUBLISHING OFFICE
Dana Trocker
Suzanne Donahue
Abby Velasco

SUBSIDIARY RIGHTS
Nicole Bond
Sara Bowne
Rebecca Justiniano